LESLEY CREWE

BEHOLDEN

Vagrant
PRESS

Vagrant Press is an imprint of
Nimbus Publishing Limited
PO Box 9166
Halifax, NS   B3K 5M8
(902) 455-4286

Printed and bound in Canada
NB1693
Cover design: Heather Bryan
Author photo: Nicola Davison

This novel is a work of fiction. Names, characters, places, and incidents are either the product of the author's imagination or are used fictitiously. Any resemblance to actual persons, living or dead, events or locales is entirely coincidental.

Library and Archives Canada Cataloguing in Publication
Title: Beholden / Lesley Crewe.
Names: Crewe, Lesley, 1955- author.
Description: Series statement: Lesley Crewe classics | Previously published: Halifax, NS: Vagrant Press, 2018.
Identifiers: Canadiana 20220455252 | ISBN 9781774711897 (softcover)
Classification: LCC PS8605.R48 B44 2023 | DDC C813/.6—dc23

Nimbus Publishing acknowledges the financial support for its publishing activities from the Government of Canada, the Canada Council for the Arts, and from the Province of Nova Scotia. We are pleased to work in partnership with the Province of Nova Scotia to develop and promote our creative industries for the benefit of all Nova Scotians

For the grandmother I never knew, Bridget O'Gorman.

PROLOGUE

1950

It was habit now, that George switched off his car's headlights when he turned from the main highway and travelled along the dirt laneway to Nell's house at the top of the hill.

"No one needs to know our business," she'd say. "The town gossips seek fuel for their fire every morning, and I won't give them the satisfaction."

It was nearly nine o'clock, and the stars were beginning to peek out from behind the clouds on this warm night in mid-September. George had spent the day fishing in one of his favourite spots just outside St. Peter's, Cape Breton. Whenever his busy medical practice allowed it, he'd leave his family in Sydney and travel back to his hometown to spend a day or two by the river.

River water was the finest water there was, as far as George was concerned. Always moving, breathing life and carrying momentum along its journey to the ocean. Sometimes it would slow and calmly gather in soft pools, where tranquil fish would hide under the rocks away from prying eyes. At other times, the gush and force created by strong winds and rain would create white foam as it gurgled and roared past.

A river was the only place George found peace.

A river, and Nell.

He knew the laneway by heart and drove the car around the house and parked in the back. Usually Nell had the outdoor light on, but tonight it was dark. She knew he was coming, so that was odd. He was a little later than he'd intended, but she always waited up for him.

George got out of the car and walked up to the back door, giving a quiet tap as he opened it. He eased his way through the screen door into the kitchen and turned on the light.

"Hello?"

She didn't answer him.

Her supper dishes were still on the table and her beast of a cat, Cat, was licking his chops in the middle of the mess.

"Do you ever stay off the table, Cat?"

Cat gave him a grim look and continued to lick his paw and rub his face with it.

Nell was not a good housekeeper. She said that was for drudges. But there was a fascinating beauty to her parlour, which wasn't a parlour at all.

"Why would I keep a room for company, when I have none?"

It was her dressmaking studio, with rolls of fabric standing in groups at every corner and against the furniture and her wide work table. There were two dressmaker's dummies at opposite ends of the room, which always made George uncomfortable. They looked like they were staring at him. Condemning him. And always, her fragile paper patterns were blown about in a chaotic order that only Nell understood. Her large black sewing machine was in the middle of the mayhem.

George quickly looked around, then started up the stairs. "Nell. Where are you?"

No answer.

And then his eyes rested on the gin bottle by the open front door. He slowly pushed the screen door wide and stood on the covered front porch. Nell was sound asleep in her big rocking chair, a wrap around her shoulders and an empty glass on the floor beside her.

She always denied she drank and would cut him off if he pursued it. "It is none of your concern. You don't live here."

He looked down at her face, so hard and soft at the same time. She wore her auburn hair as she'd always worn it, in a messy bun to keep it out of her eyes. She had no time for combs and toiletries. "A lot of vain nonsense. I can think of better ways to spend my time than prancing about trying to impress a man."

George knew if she was in her rocking chair, she was worried about something. She said that chair was her friend. George understood what she meant. What was troubling her? It bothered him that she was always alone with her demons, but drinking gin wasn't going to solve anything.

He picked her up in his arms and carried her upstairs to her room, shutting the door behind him with his hip. He placed her on the unmade bed, took off her shoes, and loosened the top buttons on her blouse. Undressing in the dark, he covered them both with a sheet and snuggled into her back, with his arm draped over her breasts, his face buried in her soft curls. She always smelled of sunshine and ironed linen.

He was asleep in minutes.

☜☞

HIS EYES OPENED TO THE FAR-OFF RUMBLE OF THUNDER. THE bedroom looked dim and gloomy even though it was sunrise. He'd be driving home in the rain. George turned over, expecting Nell by his side, but she was already up. A tinge of disappointment fell over him. He got up on his elbow and called out, "Nell?"

"Yes?" She sounded like she was in the kitchen.

"Are you coming back upstairs?"

"No. Get dressed."

George flopped back on the bed. She didn't sound like herself. He wondered what was going on. So much for being together this weekend.

His shoes sounded loud on the wooden steps. He ducked going through the kitchen doorway. Nell was sitting at the head of the table, presiding over the mess.

LESLEY CREWE

"No breakfast? Would you like me to rustle something up?"

"No, George. Sit down. I have to talk to you."

Before he pulled up a chair, he leaned over and kissed her full lips. "I've missed you."

She didn't respond.

George's brow furrowed. He reached in his jacket pocket and took out his pipe and pouch of pipe tobacco. "Okay. Let me light up first. I think more clearly through a cloud of smoke." He gave her a saucy grin and lit his pipe with a stainless-steel lighter, taking long drags to make sure it caught. When he snapped the lighter shut and returned it to his pocket, he said, "Shoot."

Nell reached up and tucked a tendril of hair behind her ear. "You are going to do something for me, George. Whether you like it or not."

"Okay."

"You may find this request outrageous, but I have my reasons for it. I think you'll agree that I've never asked you for anything in my life. True?"

"True."

"I'm asking now. Look out the kitchen window."

George took a few puffs of his pipe before he got up and went over to the sink. "What am I supposed to be looking at?"

"There's a girl in your car."

George's head leaned forward. She was right. There was a young girl sitting in the front passenger seat of his station wagon. His head whipped around. "What's going on? Who is she?"

"Her name is Jane and she's fourteen years old. I want you to use your resources to find her a good home, make sure she continues her education, and then find her a job so she can support herself and she never has to come back here again."

George put his hand to his head. A wicked migraine was peeking around the corner of his inner eye. He sat on the nearest

4

chair and took a deep breath. "You want me to kidnap a child and take her from her family?"

"She has no family."

"Why don't you take her in?"

"She deserves more than I can give her. I don't want her in this town."

"Nell, do you know what you're asking?"

"Yes."

"How am I supposed to explain this to Mavis?"

Nell jumped up impatiently. "Do I have to do all your thinking for you? Tell her she's a cousin who lost her family and you feel an obligation to protect her."

"And this child is going to go along with that?"

"What choice does she have?"

George shook his head. "This isn't right, Nell. You're playing with people's lives here."

Nell pounded her fist on the kitchen table. "You will do this for me, George. You owe me. Or are you just a man who gets his thrills by cheating on his wife?"

A visual aura exploded inside George's brain. He knew what was coming next so he lurched to his feet, slammed open the screen door, and headed around the back of the house to vomit in the long grass. It didn't make him feel better. For a moment he thought he was dreaming, but almost instantly he was in the middle of a downpour, and that was real enough. He ran back into the kitchen, shaking the rain off his clothes, and went to the sink to rinse his mouth out. Nell was where he left her, standing defiantly, although it appeared she was shaking. With outrage? Fear? He wasn't lucid enough to figure it out.

"There's got to be another way. This is ridiculous."

"If I could think of another way, I would, but I can't."

"Call the authorities."

"They won't listen to me."

"I find that hard to believe."

Her eyes narrowed. "Oh, do you? Well, I've tried, and it's no use. This girl has been neglected for almost her whole life. George, you may never understand why, but I'm asking for your help. I've never asked anyone for anything in my entire life. I want you to trust me when I say that this child needs a second chance."

What could he do? There was no use standing here arguing with her. He knew her well enough to know that she wasn't going to change her mind.

"If I do this," he said, "I don't want you to contact me. I'll ring you."

"I never have contacted you. Why would I start?"

"Because now I'll have someone you care about. Do you need to say goodbye to her?"

"No. We did that earlier."

"I better go then."

"Yes."

The worst part was not kissing Nell goodbye.

He ran to the car and got in the front seat, slamming the door behind him. A very young-looking girl stared at him with big blue eyes. He held out his hand. "I'm George."

She kept her hands firmly on the carpetbag in her lap. She nodded. "I know."

"Did Nell tell you what's happening?"

"She said you were going to make everything better."

George winced and gripped the steering wheel as he started the car and headed down the driveway. The windshield wipers whipped back and forth, trying to get rid of the torrent of rain. As they turned onto the highway, George put the headlights on. A voice in his head said to turn back, but he couldn't. He was stuck.

As the miles rolled by, his head pounded to the rhythm of the wipers. The girl didn't talk. He wondered if she was slow.

Every so often she'd squirm in her seat, but she spent most of the time looking out the rain-streaked side window.

George wondered if this was the worst day of his life.

And then, suddenly, it was.

He didn't see the buck until the last second. He swerved violently and instinctively threw his arm across the girl's chest as the car skidded across the waterlogged road and careened off the edge, disappearing.

CHAPTER ONE

NELL
1915

The worst day of my life was when I was five years old and my parents told me we were moving into town to live above the store my father bought.

"But there's no grass."

"What do you need grass for?" my mother said. "You're not a cow."

I ran out the door and disappeared into the woods behind our house, down to the brook that bubbled through our property. All my imaginary friends lived there. There was LouLou the good fairy, and old Hank, who lived under the mushrooms by the juniper tree. A family of moles liked to come by and nibble at my toes if I was very still. The wind would rustle the leaves above my head and the sun would play hide-and-seek with me through the birch trees.

I'd made a kitchen with flat rocks as plates and twigs as cutlery. There was a piece of bark hanging off one of the trees, and that was my stove. I would mix up grass and mud and acorns and put it on a rock and bake it in my oven. The Forgetful Sisters would eat all my cakes and tell me stories about how they forgot their way home and had to live in my woods.

I cried for a long time, and in the end I didn't tell my friends I was leaving. At some point, I must have fallen asleep because it was quite dark when I heard my mother yelling for me. When I eventually emerged from the trees, I saw her march towards me with a switch in her hand. She grabbed my arm and hit the back of my legs with it, over and over again.

"You ungrateful child! Scaring me half to death. You come when I call you. Do you understand me? Now get in that house and stop causing trouble."

LIVING OVER THE STORE WAS EVERYTHING I'D THOUGHT IT would be: miserable. My parents worked every moment of the day and I was left alone to play in my room. I wasn't allowed to play with other kids, for no reason I could figure out. It just made life easier for my mother not to have to look for me. I spent years with friends I made out of rags and buttons and old socks. I'd line them up on my bed and we'd play school, or princess, or witches. I liked the witch stories the best. Princesses were a lot of trouble, but being a witch was powerful.

By the time I was fifteen, in 1925, I spent my weekends washing down the store windows inside and out while the rest of the kids at school came by and bought candy bars or pop, or picked up a can of corned beef or a chop for their moms. The girls usually travelled in groups of two or three. One girl, Myrtle, always gave me a bright smile.

"Not going out today, Nell? Too bad, you're going to miss my dance party." She'd snicker and the other girls would follow suit. I'd daydream about lassoing her with rope and tying her to a railroad track.

The boys were just as awful. It was like they could sense I was different and had to come sniffing around to see for themselves. Three of them surrounded me in the schoolyard one morning.

"How come you don't talk, Nell? Ain't you got nothin' to say?"

"I won't waste my breath on the likes of you." I tried to push pass them, but they blocked me. Angus reached out and tugged my hair. "Bet you never been kissed, Miss Nell. Why don't I show you?"

George Mackenzie pushed his way between us. "W-w-why don't you leave her alone?"

The other boys started laughing. "W-w-w-w-why here's the mighty stutterer, George, comin' to the rescue. Looks like you got an admirer, Nell."

I reached out and slapped Angus across on the face. He pushed me and then George and the other boys went at it. The teacher came out then and we all stayed after school. George got the worst of it, with a black eye and bloody nose. I swore I was going to get Angus back someday by putting a personal hex on him.

My arms ached washing those darn windows every weekend, and standing on a stepladder that high up wasn't easy, but it gave me a perfect view of George flying down the hill on his bike one morning. His brown hair was every which way and his shirt was untucked. He looked like an unmade bed, and he was going much too fast by the time he reached me. The bike slid from under him and he jumped off just in the nick of time, creating a great cloud of dust. As it cleared, I saw he'd managed to keep his fishing rod in hand.

I waved my arms around and coughed. "Thanks, George. Now I have to do this window over."

"S-sorry," he panted. His eye was now deep purple and a sickly shade of yellow.

I pointed at it. "That hurt?"

"Nah, I'm good."

Climbing down the ladder, I put my cloth back in the soapy water and twisted it to wring it out. George watched me. I finally looked at him. "You've got nothing else to do?"

"Gotta get some shoe polish for my dad."

"You're not going to get it out here."

"D-do you want to go fishing with me?"

At this point I would've done anything to get away from that window.

"I'll have to ask my mother."

We went into the store and my mother was behind the long wooden counter, gossiping with a lady. That's all she did. Never stopped talking long enough to catch a breath. The only time I ever saw her smile was at someone else.

I didn't dare interrupt her, so George and I stood there like statues until she finally looked up and scowled. "What is it? Can't you see I'm busy?"

"May I go fishing with George? I'm almost done the windows."

"Certainly not. You have work to do."

Knowing the answer ahead of time doesn't make it any easier. I turned on my heel and left George standing there, then went back to my ladder and soapy bucket. He stayed behind, presumably to buy his shoe polish. When he came out, I couldn't look at him. He picked up his bike and straddled it.

"I'll see ya, then."

Just go, I screamed in my head.

Off he went.

For the next year, we'd chat during lunch break at school, but that was about it. It would be a long time before he'd ask me to go fishing again.

☙❧

ON JUNE 27, 1927, MY SEVENTEENTH BIRTHDAY, I HAD TO MAKE supper early for my parents because they were going out that evening, so I was responsible for closing the store. They never told me where they were going and never said goodbye when they left. All I know is that we had a lot of customers that night, and I never did get a chance to eat my own birthday supper.

It was a hot evening, and I lay on my bed with the window wide open, listening to people walk down the street laughing and a couple of dogs barking in the distance. There was even an owl hooting quite close by; I couldn't imagine why it decided to leave the comfort of the woods to sing its song for me, but I was grateful.

The next thing I knew, there was a loud banging on the back door that led to our apartment. I didn't know what time it was. I waited for my father to go down and see who was there, but no sound came from my parents' room.

The knocking continued. I lit a lamp, went downstairs, and opened the door. It was the chief of police and Dr. Mackenzie. George stood behind them. Something wasn't right.

"Hello, Nell. May we come in?"

"What do you want?"

"We need to speak to you."

Still groggy from sleep, I wasn't connecting the dots—but by the time we walked up to the kitchen, it was dawning on me that my parents weren't home.

The three men filled the small kitchen. I was aware I had on only my nightdress. I clutched the front of it, holding it up to my neck. "What's the matter?"

Chief Graham took off his cap. "I'm sorry to have to tell you this, Nell, but your parents died in a car accident tonight."

They waited for me to respond.

"Where?" was the only thing I could think of to say.

"Just five miles from here. If it's any comfort, I don't think they suffered."

"Father always drove too fast, but he never listened to me."

Dr. Mackenzie reached over and guided me to a kitchen chair. "This is a terrible shock, Nell. I want you to know that we will help you in any way we can in the days ahead."

"I'm all right."

"There are a lot of details that need sorting," Chief Graham said. "I'll be back in the morning to give you a better idea of where we go from here."

"Would you like a cup of tea?" George asked.

I'd forgotten he was there. "Okay."

George set about putting the kettle on and his father gave him a grateful look. "I brought George because he said you two were friends. I thought it might be easier."

"I'm fine."

Dr. Mackenzie gave Chief Graham a knowing look. Was I not doing this correctly? What did they want me to say? "I'd like to be by myself now."

"I don't like to leave you," Dr. Mackenzie said. "You've had a nasty shock."

"I'll stay with her," George volunteered.

I found myself saying, "Yes, George can stay with me."

Eventually they left, saying they'd be back in the morning. The doctor gave me a shot of something to help me sleep. George said he'd sit in the parlour, but if I needed him, all I had to do was shout.

I lay on the bed and waited but I couldn't close my eyes. Eventually, I called out and George poked his head in my bedroom door.

"I can't sleep. Would you lie with me?"

George looked around as if to ask someone permission before he entered the room. "Are you sure?"

"I wouldn't ask if I wasn't sure."

I turned my back to him and faced the wall. He lay down beside me, as stiff as a board.

"Put your arm over me, George."

He complied, and though it felt very odd, at least I wasn't alone. We didn't say anything, just breathed in the dark. My owl was still hooting.

My eyes got heavy, but before darkness overcame me, I know I said, "I'm glad they're dead."

༄

PEOPLE WHO HAD NEVER BEFORE GIVEN ME THE TIME OF DAY were all over me at the funeral. It was quite an event for the town. Two well-known people who had owned the best store around were suddenly gone in the prime of life, leaving an only child behind. I was a big deal for a change.

But I could see right through them. They didn't impress me with their promises of help. I'd seen enough of their behaviour all my life. Pious types who were all smiles when they chatted together at the store, but the minute one of them left, the other would turn to my mother and regale her with the latest gossip. I didn't believe a word they said.

Dr. Mackenzie's wife, Jean, came up to me after the service. "I insist you come to dinner with us, dear. It's been a long day and you looked peaked."

I said yes because George would be there.

We sat down to a ham and scalloped potato supper, with lemon meringue pie for dessert. I'd never had such good food. We'd only ever eaten out of a can. So, this was something else I could blame my mother for. Never caring enough to put on a good meal.

George's house was very cozy. It looked lived in. The only word I could think of was *full*. It was filled with things that mattered, like family pictures and china ornaments. Items that meant something to those who lived there. As soon as I went in I saw George's fishing rods and baskets in the corner of the back porch.

I marvelled at the rugs on the floor and the doilies on the backs of the chairs and settee. There was flowered wallpaper in every room and embroidered curtains on the windows. Everything gleamed. I wanted to live in this house.

The only damper on the evening was George's brother, Donald. I didn't know him well, as he was younger, but I knew he had a reputation for being a handful. I'd heard that one day while I was scrubbing the store floor.

"Jean Mackenzie better watch that youngest boy of hers," a neighbour had said. "He thinks he's the cock of the walk."

The way he smirked at me across the dinner table was all the evidence I needed.

"So, what are you going to do now, Nell? The world's your oyster."

His mother put down her fork and knife. "What a ridiculous thing to say, Donny. And on the day she buried her parents."

"Sorry. I didn't mean it that way. I was just wondering what she's going to do."

Dr. Mackenzie put a piece of pie in his mouth. "That's her business," he mumbled.

"You must have some plans."

George leaned forward and glared at his brother. "It's not your concern."

"That's all right, George," I said. "I know exactly what I'm going to do. I'm selling the store and moving back to my father's old house."

"That's probably the best idea," Dr. Mackenzie said. "You're too young to handle the store by yourself."

"I could run it as well as my parents, Dr. Mackenzie. But I hate it with a passion. I never want to step inside that store again."

Jean looked concerned. "Will you cope in that big house by yourself? It's farther from town."

"That's why I love it. I'll be fine. I've been taking care of myself my whole life. It won't be anything new."

When they exchanged glances, I noticed. "The rumours are true. My parents never wanted me. They only ever had time for each other. They didn't love me, and I didn't love them. I'm happy they're gone. If that makes me a terrible person, then I guess I'll be burned in hell, but since I've already been living in hell, I doubt I'll even notice."

Jean put a napkin to her eyes. "Oh, dear child."

Donny was actually shocked into silence. Dr. Mackenzie stared at his plate. Only George gave me a sympathetic smile.

At that point, I knew dinner was over. "Thank you, Mrs. Mackenzie. I better go."

George jumped out of his seat. "I'll walk you home."

His father looked up. "Nell, I'd like to help you with the sale of the store. I have a lawyer who can deal with the business side of things. I want to make sure everything is done properly. I don't want to see you taken advantage of."

I hesitated at first, but George's father seemed to be a nice man. And he was a doctor, so being trustworthy was his job. He'd probably come in handy in the days ahead. "I appreciate that. Thank you."

George and I didn't talk much on that walk home. I was comfortable with him; he never judged me. He never judged anyone, come to think of it. He was an old soul. I'd heard that somewhere and knew instantly George fell into that category.

We were halfway home when a car honked as it zoomed by with a chubby girl hanging out of the back window. She yelled, "Georgie Porgie, pudding and pie, kissed the girls and made them cry!"

The car had disappeared by the time she got to the end, but we saw her waving frantically before they rounded a turn.

I looked at him. "Was that Eileen?"

George smirked. "Yeah, my crazy cousin. She's a rig."

"I didn't know she was your cousin. That must be nice. I don't have any."

When we got back to my kitchen, I was ashamed of it, after all the cozy fullness of George's house. It looked like we'd just moved in. Tears started to fall down my cheeks and they wouldn't stop. George put his arms around me and let it happen. Later, we sat at the table and drank cocoa, even though the weather was warm and humid.

"I suppose I shouldn't have said all that to your parents."

"Don't worry about it."

"I really didn't hate my parents, you know."

"I know."

"I'm not glad they're dead."

"I know."

"I'm just sorry I'll never get the chance to ask them why they didn't like me."

"I'm sure they loved you. Some people just don't know how to express it."

That was the moment I fell in love with George. Not that I told him that. But it was a nugget of warmth that I held close to my chest after he left. I wasn't quite so alone after that.

∽∾

I'M NOT SURE WHAT I WOULD HAVE DONE WITHOUT GEORGE'S dad. He set up meetings with interested buyers and negotiated a good price for the store and apartment above it. Then he took me to the bank and had them explain the best option for me, as far as the income from the property.

"This is your nest egg, Nell. This is what we call your capital," the banker said. "We don't have to touch that. You can draw on the interest this money will make for your everyday expenses. And once you're married, you won't have to worry. Your husband will look after you."

"I'm never getting married," I told the banker, who looked at Dr. Mackenzie with amusement. Why did men always do that?

"Now, I'm sure a pretty little girl like you won't be on the market for long."

Dr. Mackenzie stood up and held out his hand across the desk. "Thank you for your time."

I think he was afraid I was about to say something rude.

He was right.

George and his mom, Jean, came with me to open up my father's house. It was a good mile from the centre of town and about half a mile from George's house. It was back off the road and up a steep hill. There was a small cottage near the highway on the left-hand side. It didn't seem occupied.

Trees enclosed most of the house, but it was the alders that made the house look like it was being swallowed. It was larger than I remembered it. An almost perfect gingerbread house, with elaborate finishing on the eaves, its dormer windows and wraparound porch. The shingles were peeling and the front steps looked crooked, but on the whole, it seemed sturdy enough.

All I wanted to do was run into the woods to see my brook, but I had to save that for when I was alone. I put the key in the lock and walked into my childhood. But it wasn't the way I remembered it. Everything was covered in dust and cobwebs, with dead flies and mice and stale air rushing out to greet us.

"Oh dear," Jean said. "This is a huge job."

"I don't mind. I'll do a little at a time."

"I'll help you," George volunteered.

Jean continued to rummage around and walk through the rooms. "We're going to have to make sure the chimney is still in good working order and that the roof is sound. I just don't know how you're going to manage here in the winter. You'll never get shovelled out."

"Don't worry so much, Mrs. Mackenzie. I like a challenge."

Jean turned around and put her hand on my shoulder. "You're still very young, Nell. You have no idea what awaits you. I just don't know if this is a good idea."

"I love this place. This is my home. Just wait until I fix it up. You'll love it then."

It was nice of Mrs. Mackenzie to want to help me, but for a moment I balked at being told what to do. I'd had enough of that in my lifetime, with my parents controlling every move I made. And it didn't stop there. Jean and a few of her friends came to help me set the place to rights, even though George and I said we were fine on our own. I noticed that the ladies did their best to make sure we were never alone in the same room.

"I think they don't trust us," I said. "Are they afraid of what people will say?"

"Most likely. They're just being mothers."

"I wouldn't know. I didn't have a normal mother."

George didn't like it when I talked like that, but he never told me to stop. He'd just frown or make a face. As much as he thought he understood, he'd never know.

The woods were grown in and I had a hard time finding my old hideaway, but once I located the brook, it all came flooding back. I belonged to this place. It was happy to see me again. My friends were still here, although I'd never tell a soul about them.

When I ran into Myrtle and her gang one day over the summer, they wanted to come over and see the place. There was something mystifying about a girl living by herself.

"Sorry. I don't invite people home."

Myrtle laughed. "Why ever not? What's so special about it?"

"I get to do what I want now, and that includes keeping awful people away from my door."

"You've always been a stuck-up snippet, Nell Sampson!" She flounced away with her lackeys behind her.

The summer was going to fly by, and regrettably I'd have to go back to school with Myrtle and her ilk. Thank the Lord it was my last year. The only reason I stayed in school was because George thought it was important. I'd always hated it and could never figure out why I needed to know about long-dead British kings.

The only class that helped me was math. Learning how to do fractions made sewing easier. My one big purchase was a Singer sewing machine. I'd asked my parents for one and they'd ignored my request, so I bought the most expensive one in the Eaton's catalogue.

It was the best day of my life when George and his father picked it up for me at the post office. When his dad went back out to his car, I grabbed George and gave him a big kiss. The poor boy turned bright red, but he kissed me back. Soon that's all we did when we had a few moments alone, but I was very careful not to let anyone see us. All I needed was for someone to object to our friendship and my life would be ruined.

By that Christmas, I had the house the way I wanted it. During the summer, Dr. Mackenzie arranged for a handyman to scrape and paint the peeling white shingles on the outside of the house. I chose a dark grey, with cream for the trim and shutters. It looked much more substantial in the darker colour. A large haul of firewood had been delivered in October to see me though the winter, and a ton of coal was poured through the chute into the cellar. Dr. Mackenzie had arranged that as well. The Mackenzies also invited me for Christmas dinner. Sometimes I wondered why they were so nice to me. They weren't getting anything out of it, as far as I could see, so I asked George.

"That's what people do," he said, smiling. "How does anyone get on in this world without other people? And don't cut me off and say that you got along all your life without them. You're turning into a terrible cynic, Nell."

"Hush now. You have no idea how some people live."

"I've heard lots of stories from my father. Which is why I'm going to be a doctor, just like him."

From that point on, that's all I could think about. George going away to become a doctor. I brought it up at the dinner table as Dr. Mackenzie passed me a plate of carved turkey.

"So, you're going to have two Dr. Mackenzies in the family."

His parents looked surprised. "Oh?" they said together and turned to look at George.

George gave me a look, and I realized he'd told me something in confidence, something I shouldn't have blabbed.

"That makes me very happy, George," Dr. Mackenzie said. "I'm sure you'll make a fine doctor. But shouldn't you be applying for university if that's what you want?"

"I already have," George said.

"You're a dark horse, son," Dr. Mackenzie said. "If it weren't for Nell, we'd never know what was going on."

Donny looked annoyed. "I told you years ago I was going to be a surgeon. You never told me it would make you happy."

"As long as you're only dealing with people under sedation, Donny, you'll be fine. A bedside manner, however, is something else."

All of us laughed at that. Even Donny.

George walked me home, as it was a calm, starry night that evening. I poked at the fire inside the coal stove in the kitchen to get it going again and added another shovel. When I turned around, George was standing with his arms out, holding a small box.

"Happy Christmas."

"Oh, George. I don't have a gift for you."

"That doesn't matter."

It was a gold, heart-shaped locket inset with a small pearl. I immediately put it on and looked in the small mirror above the kitchen sink. "It's beautiful."

"It has your birthstone on it."

"I love it." I kissed him for a long time, so long that we lost track of time and were breathless by the time we parted.

"I don't want to go," he whispered in my ear.

"Come back tonight when they think you're asleep. I'll keep the outside light on."

"Do you want to do this?"

"More than anything."

And that was the start of it. We didn't get a lot of nights together that first winter because of the snow, but once spring came, it was easier. Although after a while, George became more and more upset with the lies he was telling.

We sat together on my settee, my hands in his thick brown hair. I traced the freckles on his face and marvelled at his straight, white teeth. He was filling out now, and he wasn't so much like a crane fly, the name his mother would tease him with, telling him he was all knees and elbows. It made me happy to know that George was going to be taller and better-looking than Donny, since Donny still thought he was the cat's whiskers.

"We're graduating high school next month," George said. "Why can't we tell people we're stepping out?"

"I don't want people to know."

"Why?"

"You're all mine. It's private."

"My mother knows I like you a lot."

"Your mother knowing is different. I don't want the Myrtles and Anguses of the world knowing."

George smiled. "Are you aware that they're a couple?"

"They deserve each other."

I celebrated the end of my school career by buying a horse and cart, which would make things easier when I wanted to buy things in town. There was already a small sleigh in the barn that I could use in the winter. I also invested in a cow for milk, some chickens for eggs, and a goat to keep me and the horse company and the grass short. Respectively, I called the animals Cow, Chicken, and Goat. Why complicate matters?

Having breathing animals in my life lessened the loneliness of living by myself. Soon I had some barn cats and even a dog who followed me home one day. Dog instantly made me feel better, because he barked when he heard a noise. It was reassuring to have him on patrol, although I forgot to tell George, and Dog ripped his trousers one night when he came in the back door.

That summer, I spent all my time tending to my garden. It kept me from thinking about George going away. He didn't talk about it, but he was going whether he said so or not. Eventually I said it for him.

I was on my knees weeding one morning in August when he showed up on his bike with two fishing poles in his hands, a wicker basket around his shoulder.

"Wanna go fishing?"

"No, thank you."

"Why not?"

Once I got off my knees, I brushed the dirt off my hands. "Because I don't want to spend one more minute with you not telling me when you're going."

His face fell and he looked at his feet. "I don't like thinking about it."

"That makes no sense. Just spill the beans."

"I'm going to Dalhousie in September."

"Halifax?"

He nodded.

"Next month."

He nodded again.

"So, you'll be home for Christmas and the summer?"

"That's about it, I guess. I don't have a lot of money for travelling back and forth."

"Did it ever occur to you to not go? To do something else with your life, so you could stay here? With me?"

He gave me a sad look and shook his head.

My stomach was a little sick, though his news was inevitable. "I'll miss you."

He dropped his bike and fishing rods and took me in his arms. "When I finish this, I'm coming back for you. We'll be together then. Please believe that."

"We can't plan that far ahead. I could be killed in a goat accident."

He burst out laughing. "Stop it."

I kissed his nose. "Go fishing. I have to finish this."

For the next month, our visits were bittersweet. When he

came to me the night before he left, we didn't talk at all, just spent the hours holding each other as close as we could. I had no doubt that this boy loved me.

But when he finally left before dawn, the emptiness I felt was unlike anything I'd experienced before. I knew that my life had changed in some way, and for the first time I was frightened.

CHAPTER TWO

1935

The first time George asked me to marry him was after his first year of medical school. He repeated his request every year after that and I always said the same thing.

"No."

My life had a comforting routine, and I was afraid to break it. I had everything I needed and was content. People in town thought I was odd because I never socialized, but it was such a relief to not have to deal with them. The only time I did was when I sewed for them.

George had been away for a couple of years when the girls in town started to take notice of my handmade dresses. Surprisingly, it was Myrtle who started the ball rolling.

We bumped into each other at the post office. She looked me up and down.

"Did you buy that from the catalogue?"

"No. I made it."

"You sewed that yourself?"

"Don't you believe me?"

She stared at my dress so long that it became unnerving. I turned to go.

"Would you make a dress for me?"

My first thought was to tell her to go jump in the lake, but something told me to hold off. If I made something for her, she'd have to pay me. I could use the money.

I turned around. "What kind of dress?"

"Angus and I are getting married. I need a going-away outfit."

Very quickly, I had more customers than I needed. That's because I didn't charge a fortune. I'd learned a few lessons on marketing at the store. Always give people a bargain and they'll be back. And because rural people don't have a lot of distractions, the one thing they loved to do more than anything else was gossip. While I fitted and measured women in my sewing room, they talked my ear off about what was going on in town. None of them needed any encouragement, and maybe because I was so quiet, they often told me more than they should have.

More often than not, the women asked me about my love life.

"What's a pretty girl like you doing alone?" my mother's customers would say.

"I have no intention of getting married."

"You'll change your mind when the right fellow comes along. I hear George came home last night."

They'd wait to see if I had any reaction, but I never gave myself away. It annoyed me, however, that despite our best efforts, mine and George's names were often linked.

He would show up about three nights after he got home. I knew he did it on purpose, but I never let on. He wanted desperately for me to miss him, and I did, but there was a part of me that didn't want to give in. He left *me*. It wasn't the other way around.

He knocked on the kitchen door around nine that night.

"Come in, George."

At the age of twenty-five, George was such a nice-looking fellow. Tall, with broad shoulders, but still a little on the slim side, with long legs and hands. His brother always envied George's hands, since he was studying to be a surgeon. George was soon to be a gastroenterologist. I made him spell it for me the first time he told me.

He came up behind me at the kitchen sink, and put his arms around my waist, kissing my neck. "You smell so good."

"I smell like goats and hens."

"That's the way I like it."

I shook the water off my hands and wiped them with a dish-towel. Then I turned around and looked into those big brown eyes. "How long are you here for?"

He kissed me rather than answering, so I knew something was up. Never mind. I'd find out all in good time.

We went upstairs and the world disappeared, as it always did when we were together.

After breakfast the next morning, we sat on the front porch with our coffee, both of us in heavy sweaters. It was spring, but in our part of the world, snow could still be peeking around the corner. I was in my rocking chair and he was on the swing, smoking his pipe. It looked like he was thinking deep thoughts, but I knew different.

"So, how goes the dressmaking?" He took a sip of his coffee.

"I have more than I can handle."

"Look at you, Miss Nell. Actually mixing with the public. That's the part I find hard to believe."

"As long as they pay me, I can put up with them for a couple of hours."

"Who'd have thought that you'd have a business of your own?"

"It's hardly a business."

"Don't sell yourself short. You're making a living. Be proud of yourself."

When George said things like that, I believed him. I never thought of it on my own. He was the mirror I could finally see myself in.

"And what is happening in your world?" I asked him.

He put his head back and sucked on his pipe before he answered me. "I've been offered a job in Sydney."

"Are you going to take it?"

He took the pipe out of his mouth. "I'd like to...."

"But?"

"I want you to come with me. It's not that far away, Nell."

"You just said I should be proud of myself for having my own business. Why would I leave that?"

George leaned forward and put his arms on his knees. "You can do the same thing in Sydney, Nell."

"And leave my home? Leave my animals? Don't tell me I can have a farm in downtown Sydney. I'm not that naive."

He leaned back against the swing and put his hand through his hair. I knew he was exasperated. "I've asked you to marry me at least eight times, and you keep putting me off. What the devil am I supposed to do? Neither one of us is getting any younger. Don't you want a family, Nell?"

That was the first time he'd asked me that, and my answer slipped out before I had a chance to consider it.

"No."

He looked at me in confusion. "No? Seriously?"

I shrugged.

Now he got up off the swing and paced along the porch. "I'm starting to lose patience. I thought maybe you were being coy and wanted to see if I actually made something of myself. It never occurred to me that all this time, the thought of living with me and having children together wasn't what you dream of. I dream of it every day! It's what's kept me going all these years. Don't you love me, Nell?"

"I do. You're the only person I've ever loved. But I don't want to be a mother. I wouldn't be any good at it."

"Nonsense! You'd have me with you."

"You have to believe me, George. Even if I did marry you, you'd resent me after a while. I have only lonely and desperate memories of being a child. I can't relive that time. It would haunt me."

George stopped pacing and gave me a stony look. "You are being deliberately melodramatic. You've been yanking my chain for years and I've been too stupid to see it."

I rose from my chair. "I am telling you the truth and you're getting angry about it. Do you see why we can't have a future together? You refuse to see me as I am—a person who needs to be on her own. How many more times are you going to ask me to marry you, and how many more times am I going to say no?"

He shook his head and I could see the tears in his eyes. "No more. Never again. I need to move on. I will always love you, Nell. And for what it's worth, I think you're making a huge mistake. We could've walked through life together. And you know we were meant for each other. That is never going to change."

"I'm sorry, George."

"No, you're not."

He walked back into the house and a few moments later his car came from behind the house and slowly drove away. Truthfully, I was in a daze. It happened so fast that I had to shake my head to know it wasn't a dream. I'd just told a man I loved to live without me. George had been my rock, and I'd thrown him away.

I shut down. The only thing that kept me from staying in bed was having to get up to feed the critters. That's how the days passed, one after the other.

෨෬

TWO MONTHS LATER, GEORGE'S MOTHER, JEAN, PAID ME A VISIT, pretending she needed me to make her a dress. She was as kind as ever and brought me a lemon meringue pie. She remembered how much I enjoyed it.

Once the measurements were done, I asked her if she'd like a cup of tea and a slice of the pie. She accepted. We had our tea at the kitchen table, with my newest housecat, Cat, sitting on one of the empty chairs.

"He's a handsome fellow." Jean smiled at him and he meowed back at her.

"It's funny how one cat decides he doesn't want to live in the barn anymore and just moves in. I had no say in the matter."

"It happens with people too. Like George."

I knew it. I sipped at my tea and said nothing.

Jean took a deep breath. "None of this is my business, Nell. But I've known for a very long time how much George loves you. He told me he asked you to marry him and you refused. And that is within your right. I just want you to be aware that he's mentioned a girl named Mavis a few times when he's been home. I don't think it's serious yet, but it could be. I want you to be sure that this is the right decision, because I know he'd come back to you in a heartbeat if you gave him the slightest encouragement."

She deserved the truth. "Mrs. Mackenzie, I'm not a good person. George needs someone who will give him a family, and I seriously doubt I'd be able to. I will always love him, but he's better off without me."

She patted my hand. "My dear child. You are too hard on yourself. How do you know you can't have a family?"

"I'm sure I can, but...I just don't want to be a mother. I don't want to become my mother. I'm not a happy person. I'm hard to be around. George only sees me occasionally. He'd be fed up with me after a couple of weeks together in a row."

When she laughed, I laughed.

She took a big gulp of tea. "You know what? You're probably right. You know yourself better than anyone, and if that's how you see it, then that's how it is. And please don't say you're not a good person, because only a good person puts others before themselves. You just demonstrated to me that you do love my son very much. For what it's worth, I think you're wrong, but I promise I will stay out of your business from now on."

"Speaking of business, do you really want this dress?"

"Of course! I'm about the only woman in town who doesn't have a Nell Sampson original."

❧

THE FIRST TIME I HEARD MYSELF REFERRED TO AS A SPINSTER was about a week after my talk with Jean. I was at the back of my parents' old store. As much as I hated going in, it was sometimes necessary, and after ten years, it at least looked quite different.

A salesman was asking the proprietor if there was anyone around who might be interested in a set of encyclopaedias.

"Probably not around here," he replied.

His wife spoke up. "What about the spinster on the hill? She's got nothing else to do in the evenings."

They laughed together. The man left and I came forward with my dish soap, tins of sardines, and Epsom salts from the back of the store. The couple gave each other a guilty look as the owner rang up my purchases.

"I didn't mean anything by it," the wife finally said.

"No. Your sort never does."

Two days later there was a knock on the front door, which was odd, since everyone knew to come to the back door. Dog lay like a lump and didn't move a muscle. He was seriously flawed in the watchdog department. I missed my old Dog.

I opened the front door. A man holding a leather case under his arm tipped his hat. "Good day, madam. I'm Cyril Brooks and I was wondering if you'd be interested in a set of encyclopaedias. Let me tell you why they are worth your time and money."

He delivered this last sentence in a big hurry, as if he was afraid I'd shut him down before he had a chance to say his spiel.

"Why don't you come in?"

He looked so surprised, it was almost funny.

"Let's go into the kitchen and you can tell me about it."

Ever since that day at the store, I'd been thinking of the ency-clopaedias and how they might be just what I needed on a cold winter's night. I wasn't much for borrowing books from the library because I couldn't always get them back in time, but the thought of books of knowledge at my fingertips intrigued me. I had a few dollars stashed away and never spent them on anything. I was interested to hear more.

He was indeed a good salesman. A bit pushy, but informative. It was only after ten minutes that I realized his attention was not entirely on the subject matter.

Out of the blue, he said, "Do you live here alone?"

My skin prickled. "No. My husband will be home any minute."

He smiled at me. "But you're the spinster on the hill, aren't you? I was picturing an old lady. Imagine my surprise when you opened the door."

I stood up. "That's enough. Please leave."

He stood up as well, and for the first time it registered that he was a big man. Just as I was thinking I never should have let him in, he grabbed my wrist and pulled me to him. He pressed his mouth against my ear. "You must get lonely up here all by yourself. I bet you'd like to have a man teach you a thing or two."

I wrenched my wrist from his grasp and ran across the kitchen to the sink. I picked up a knife. "Get away from me this instant. If you think I'm afraid of you, you're wrong. You don't scare me in the least. You're a bully, which means you're a coward."

He got red in the face and charged me. I held up my knife, but he batted it out of my hand as if it were a fly. Now I knew that I was in deep, deep trouble.

Fighting as hard as I could, I scratched and bit him and screamed for all I was worth. Dog ran in but the man kicked him and he slunk away. The salesman punched me in the face and I fell to the floor. He was on top of me in an instant, so heavy I couldn't breathe.

"I'm going to teach you a lesson you'll never forget."

Somewhere in the back of my mind, I knew if I wanted to live, I needed to stop fighting. He liked the power it gave him. I went limp and stayed that way, even after he was done. I kept my eyes closed.

I heard him get up, still breathing heavily. "You shouldn't have tempted me like that. It's your fault this happened. Do you hear me?"

Time had stopped. I wasn't sure how long he was gone before I opened my eyes. Dog was in the doorway, whimpering. I held out my hand and he came over and licked my cheek. I held on to him for a long time, because I didn't want to get up. If I did that, then I'd have to acknowledge that this had happened. All these years, thinking I was in charge of myself, thinking I could handle my life, and in one moment, my security was shattered.

When I finally got to my feet, I ached all over. I boiled water to add to the warm bathtub water. I scrubbed myself clean over and over again. When I looked in the bathroom mirror and saw that I had two black eyes, I burst into tears and cried all night long. I know I called out for George, but because of my own foolishness, he wasn't there to comfort me.

For a long time after that, I panicked when anyone knocked on my door. I had locks put on both doors and I bought myself a rifle. I had the man who sold it to me show me how to use it. I'd practise shooting at tin cans out back. The animals didn't like it; neither did I. But it was a necessary evil. I'd never be without a way to defend myself again.

Just before Christmas, something unexpected happened, but I found myself glad of it. A young couple moved into the small cottage at the bottom of the laneway. It was a comfort to see the smoke from their chimney and lights burning through the trees at night. I didn't feel so alone anymore.

Two days after Christmas, a woman carrying a wicker basket trudged through the snow up to my back door. She held out her hand to shake mine.

"I'm Maggie Landry. My husband, Gervais, and I are your new neighbours. I thought I'd introduce myself."

Because I was so pleased to not be alone on the laneway anymore, I was more pleasant than usual. "Please, come in. I'll put the kettle on."

"I made some cookies. I thought you might like some."

"Thank you. Sit down."

At first glance Maggie looked a bit roly-poly, short and squat, but when she took off her cloak I could see she was very pregnant.

"Goodness. When is your baby due?"

"New Year's Eve."

I put on the kettle and settled back at the table. "Is this your first?"

She nodded happily. "I'm more nervous than I thought I'd be. Do you have children?"

"No. Not unless you count critters."

"If you have to feed them, it counts."

I liked Maggie. She had an innocence about her. "Is this your first home?"

She nodded. "We're from New Brunswick originally, but Gervais wanted to help a friend of his so we came here and, with the little bit of money we saved, we were able to buy the cottage. Gervais works in the woods. He's gone a lot. I'm so happy to know I have a neighbour close by."

We finished our tea and cookies and she asked me if I knew a Dr. Mackenzie. Someone had recommended him to her. I gave her his phone number and reassured her that he was a wonderful doctor. She was pleased.

Her baby held off until a week after New Year's Eve, so George's parents were able to go to the New Year's Eve dance at the legion. The only reason I knew they were going was because I made Jean's dress. She loved my first one so much, she had commissioned a few more.

Maggie brought the baby up to see me a couple of weeks after she was born. I felt like a heel that I hadn't gone down to see them. I hadn't been sure what to do, to be honest. I wasn't in the habit of visiting people.

Maggie unwrapped her baby bundle. "You can hold her if you like."

"I've never held a baby before. I might drop her."

"Nonsense. Sit on the chair if it makes you feel better." So that's what I did. She placed the child in my arms and I was so surprised to see the baby's eyes open and look straight at me.

"Hello," I whispered.

"Her name is Jane. After my grandmother."

"Hello, Jane. You have a beautiful name."

"She's such a good baby. She never cries. It's almost worrying that she hardly makes a peep, but Gervais says I'm looking for trouble where there is none."

"I imagine mothers do worry more than fathers." Then I realized what I said. Sometimes mothers didn't worry at all. Had my mother loved me when I was this small? Had she been happy holding me? I couldn't remember her ever kissing or hugging me. The longer I held Jane, the sadder I got.

"You best take her," I said.

Maggie gave me a funny look, but took Jane in her arms and smiled happily down at her daughter. "I always wanted a girl. Gervais was hoping for a boy. You know men. He wants me to have another baby right away. I told him to hold his horses! He didn't like that very much."

Maggie came up to see me often. More than I would've chosen, as I did have a lot of work to do, but I realized she was lonely and so anxious to show off her baby. By the time spring rolled around, I'd made Jane a few outfits to surprise her mother and decided to take them down to their cottage. I'd never been in it before.

Maggie had made the space as homey as she could. But when she'd said they didn't have a lot, she'd meant it. When I gave her the pinafores and dressing gowns for Jane, her eyes welled up. "Thank you so much! This is the nicest gift I've ever received. Oh, I can't wait to try them on my Jane. She will look adorable."

She made me a cup of tea and we shared a few oatcakes while Jane sat quietly on her mother's lap. We all jumped when the back door opened with a bang. I assumed it was Gervais standing there looking put-out. I hated him instantly.

Jane started to cry, and I didn't blame her.

"Gervais, what are you doing home so early?"

"Never mind." He looked at me. "Who are you?"

"Gervais, this is our neighbour from the top of the hill. You remember. I told you about her. Nell Sampson. Look at what she made for Jane. Aren't they beautiful?"

He completely ignored her as he slammed the door shut and sat in a chair by the wood stove. "Where's supper?"

I stood up. "I think I'll go, Maggie. I'm glad you like the clothes. I'll see you again."

As soon as I got outside, I took deep gulps of air. Gervais and the salesman had exactly the same kind of stink. Their disrespect for women. They were the total opposite of George.

Now I had something else to worry about: Maggie and Jane living in that cottage with the big bad wolf.

CHAPTER THREE

1940

I spent a lot of my time listening to the wireless, following the news about the war. It still seemed impossible that young Canadians were being sent overseas to fight. I ran into Jean one day at the gas station and had to ask about George. I'd heard rumours that he was already overseas and was possibly married. It was better to know than not know.

"He hasn't enlisted, has he?"

"No. Part of him would like to go. You know men. But he's valuable to the hospital and he has a family to think about now."

Having known it would eventually happen didn't make it any easier. "So, he did marry Mavis?"

"Yes."

"Do you like her?"

I caught Jean's slight hesitation, but she covered it well. "She's a pleasant girl. Likes her creature comforts."

She was spoiled. Poor George.

"Do they have children?"

"Not yet. Soon, I hope. Donny's married too, but no sign of babies. If they don't get on with it, Joe and I will be too old to chase our grandchildren around."

I lay in bed that night thinking of George. I wondered if he ever thought of me. Probably not. He'd been so angry and disappointed the day he left. He'd moved on with his life and I was a memory. Just as well.

At daybreak, I went to the barn to milk my two cows. It was my favourite thing, to lean against their warm, soft bulk and swish the streams of milk into the bucket. There were times I actually dozed off in the middle, that's how relaxed I'd get, but this morning I had company. I heard Jane before I saw her.

"Nelly! Nelly!"

"I'm in the barn!"

Four-year-old Jane appeared with her nightgown and housecoat still on, her blond curls a tousled mess. She often wanted to see me first thing, and I told Maggie that she wasn't in my way. It gave Maggie a break. Anything I could do to make her life easier. She was less chatty now and often had a sad look around her eyes. I knew who'd put it there.

"Nelly, my dolly broke."

She held out an old rag doll she carried around with her. I took it from her and wrinkled my nose. "This doll has had the biscuit."

"Biskit?"

"You need a new dolly. You and I are going to make one, how's that?"

She smiled.

I finished my milking and Jane followed me into the house. I fed her a bowl of porridge with lots of cream and brown sugar. She was such a spindly little thing. I was afraid she wasn't eating enough, so I stuffed her full every chance I got.

We ventured into the workroom and I gathered the material I'd need to make a doll. The first thing I did was have Jane go through my button collection. "You look for the prettiest buttons for the dolly's coat."

"Can she have a red coat?"

"Of course."

We were so caught up in making the doll, we didn't hear Maggie at the back door.

"I hope you two are in here, or I'm a very bad mother! It's almost noon!" She appeared in the workroom and Jane jumped off the chair and hugged her mother's knees.

"Wait 'til you see!"

Maggie came over to the table. "Oh, my goodness! What's this?"

"My new dolly! She has a red coat."

"A red velvet coat! Goodness, Nell. You shouldn't have wasted velvet on a doll."

"Nonsense. She's almost done." I sewed a ribbon onto the top of the doll's head, with soft yellow yarn used as the hair. I painted a Kewpie-doll face, and by the time I was finished, the doll actually looked like Jane.

I held her up. "What do you think, Jane?"

"I love her."

"You thank Nelly for this wonderful gift," Maggie said.

Jane hugged my knees.

"What shall we call her?" I asked.

"Bridie," said Jane.

Both her mother and I laughed.

"That was quick," Maggie said. "Why Bridie?"

"I like it."

"Do you know anyone named Bridie?"

"No."

We never did find out where she heard the name, but it didn't matter. Her doll was the best thing ever.

While Jane played with her new friend, I made Maggie a sandwich. She looked pale and out of sorts. I urged her to eat.

"Are you okay?"

She shook her head. "Gervais has been drinking more often. He says he can't find a steady job, but I think it's because he's late for work. The foreman, his friend, can't rely on him, so he doesn't ask for him anymore. I try and tell Gervais that, but he doesn't listen to me."

"Is there anyone you can talk to? Family?"

"I only had my parents, and they died within six months of each other, before I married Gervais. Sometimes I think I married him just so I wouldn't be alone."

I reached over and held her hand. She gave me a grateful smile.

❦

THE WHOLE WORLD THINKS OF DECEMBER 7, 1941, AS THE DAY Japan bombed Pearl Harbor. I remember if for a different reason. I was sewing the hem of a dress when I heard something not quite right. I listened, waiting to hear it again, a shout or a cry. There it was. I leapt up from my chair and looked out the living room window. Jane was running up the laneway as fast as her little legs could carry her. I dropped everything and ran out the door, not caring about the dusting of snow on the ground.

"What's wrong?" I shouted at Jane.

She was breathless when she got to me. "Nelly..."

I grabbed her arms and bent down to look her in the face. "Tell me."

"Mama won't get up."

I picked her up and ran down the laneway as fast as I could. The thought of what I might find scared me, but I kept going. The cries were coming from the house. I shoved open the door and saw Gervais kneeling over Maggie. He had her in his arms and his sobs were genuine.

"No! No! Maggie, don't go!"

I put Jane down and ran over to him. "What's happened?"

He didn't hear me, so I shoved at his shoulder and made him look at me. "Gervais. What's happened to Maggie?"

"She fell down the stairs. She tripped and fell down the stairs."

It looked like he was telling the truth. She was at the bottom of the stairs with a clothes basket on end beside her and clothes strewn all over the floor.

"Let me see her. I need to see if she's breathing."

I elbowed my way between them and could tell by the way Maggie's head was hanging to one side that her neck was broken. She had no pulse. She looked like a dead animal.

"I'm going to the house to call the doctor. I'll take Jane with me."

Gervais was holding his head in his hands, wailing. I picked Jane up and ran back to the house.

"What's the matter with Mama?"

"Everything will be all right, Jane. I'll make sure you're all right."

Dr. Mackenzie arrived and pronounced Maggie dead. Gervais was next to useless. I smelled alcohol on his breath. A fine way to cope. It's like he forgot he had a daughter. I told him I would keep Jane for the night and it barely registered with him.

It turned out I kept Jane for three nights. I stayed with her during the funeral. I knew that Maggie would want me there for her daughter, instead of standing by a graveside. We rocked in the rocking chair by the wood stove, Jane with Bridie in her arms.

"When can I see Mama?"

"Your mama died, Jane. That means she's gone to heaven. You won't see her for a long time, but you can always see her in your mind. You have many happy memories of your mama that you can remember whenever you want to."

"Doesn't she want to be with me?"

I squeezed her. "Oh yes. She wants to be with you more than anything. But when people die, that's not possible."

"Why did she die?"

"She had an accident. She fell down the stairs."

Jane looked up at me. "No, she didn't. Daddy pushed her."

The rocking chair stopped, as I held my breath. No. Please no.

"He was sorry. He said he didn't mean it. You can't tell anyone. He didn't mean it."

After I put her to bed, I tossed and turned all night. My fury lit up the room. That bastard.

He showed up at my door at six the next morning.

"I want my daughter."

"She's still asleep."

"Get her."

I put my finger in his face. "I know you pushed Maggie. I'm telling the police."

He grabbed my hand and squeezed it. "It was an accident, pure and simple. Just leave us alone." He dropped my hand and looked behind me. "Jane, let's go."

Jane was in her nightie with Bridie in her arms. She immediately obeyed her father and out the door they went.

At nine, I went down to the police station. Angus Turnbull was on duty. He smirked when he saw me.

"Miss Nell Sampson. To what do I owe the pleasure?"

"I want to report a murder."

He laughed out loud. "Well, now, I didn't expect that. Who did you murder?"

"Gervais Landry pushed his wife down the stairs."

"Were you there?"

"No. Jane told me."

"Jane?"

"Their daughter."

"How old is she?"

"She's five, almost six. Old enough to know what she saw. What are you going to do about it?"

"There's no evidence. There's nothing I can do about it. It's purely hearsay."

"I know what that man is like. He drinks and he's moody. There's no way that child should be under his care."

Angus gave me a big sigh and for the first time looked resigned. "If I had to take children away from their fathers for drinking and being moody, there's be no kids left in town. Drop it, Nell."

"You're not going to do anything? Maggie is dead. A child is without her mother because of that goon."

"I'll talk to him."

"I'm coming with you."

"Suit yourself."

He followed behind me in his police car. When we arrived at the cottage, Gervais was standing in his doorway.

"I can't believe she's dragged you here on a wild goose chase. She needs to mind her own business."

"We need to talk, Gervais. Let's go inside."

It was the first time I'd been inside the cottage since the accident. The place was a tip. Dirty dishes on the table and clothes everywhere. Even the fire was almost out. I wanted to punch him.

"Nell tells me your daughter said you pushed her mother down the stairs. Is that correct?"

"No, I didn't push her down the stairs. I'm not a monster. She tripped while she had the laundry basket in her arms. She lost her footing because she couldn't see the stairs. Why is Nell causing trouble? This is harassment. I'm a grieving widower. I shouldn't have to listen to this."

"I'd like to talk to Jane."

"This is ridiculous!" her father shouted.

"Never mind that. Let me speak to the child."

For the first time, I felt a flutter of hesitation. "Do you have to question her? She told me about it. I'm not lying."

Angus turned and faced me. "You started this. I need to hear it for myself."

Gervais gave me a look filled with hatred. Even with Angus beside me, I felt frightened.

"Jane! Come down here," he shouted.

Jane appeared at the top of the stairs. She looked nervous, but then she spotted me and raced down the steps. She held onto my legs.

Angus knelt down and spoke to her directly. "Jane, I'm a police officer. I need to know if what you said to Nell is true. Did your father push your mother down the stairs?"

She looked up at me. I'd betrayed her. She'd told me not to tell anyone.

"Jane? I need an answer."

Jane looked at him and shook her head. "No."

"Are you sure?"

She nodded.

"You see?!" Gervais shouted. "This meddling bitch has had it in for me since we moved here. You tell her to leave us alone."

I pleaded with Angus. "She's not going to say anything in front of her father, is she?"

Angus straightened up and turned to Gervais. "Make sure you give this child the care she needs. You owe her mother that. Nell, let's go."

Gervais put his hand on Jane's head and steered her away from me. I had no choice but to follow Angus outside.

"You've opened up a huge can of worms, Nell."

"What would you have me do? Jane said he pushed her. I couldn't just ignore that."

"No, but now you've made an enemy for life. You obviously care about this little girl, and now you may not be able to see her. You have to pick your battles."

"He's getting away with murder!"

"Life is unfair. If I could do more, I would, but there's no evidence and I sure don't want to put that child through any more upset. Do you?"

When I didn't say anything, he got in his car and drove away. The minute the car disappeared, Gervais came outside and rushed to my side, his face mottled with hate. "That's enough, lady. You mind your business and stay away from my daughter or so help me, you'll regret it."

"And if you touch one hair on that child's head, I'll kill you. Have you got that, Gervais? I will kill you stone dead."

༄༅

FOR TWO YEARS I HARDLY SAW JANE. I'D CATCH GLIMPSES OF HER going to school, but she didn't play outside anymore, which broke my heart—I knew what that was like. I stayed away for her sake, but I often wondered if she thought I didn't care anymore. It was a pitiful situation and I often regretted confronting Gervais. It might have been the right thing to do, but was it the smartest? Nothing in life is easy.

And then it got very complicated.

Dr. Mackenzie died. He had a heart attack while out on a call, and the whole town was devastated at his passing. I knew I had to show up for the funeral, because Jean had been so good to me over the years. There was no excuse I could think of to not attend.

And it annoyed me that I primped in front of the mirror and wore a black dress that showed every curve for the wake. It wasn't so much for George as it was for Mavis. I didn't want to be found lacking when we set eyes on each other for the first time.

The minute I stepped into the funeral parlour and saw the lineup of people waiting to give their respects to the family, my heart started to race. It had been eight years since I last saw George. I knew I would recognize him, but had he changed from the boy I loved?

I spied him first, standing so tall beside his mother. His handsome face had filled out and he had a confidence about him that I'd never seen before, but also a sadness, which was only natural. He loved his father very much. I envied him that.

Mavis stood beside him. The first word that came to mind was *prissy*. She was overdressed for the occasion and wore too much makeup. She was actually tittering as people spoke to her, like she was a queen bee. I disliked her on sight. She knew people were looking at her and she was lapping it up. I noticed she turned to Donny a lot and simpered. Donny was as I remembered him, but his wife wasn't what I expected. She looked like wallflower. How odd that the two of them were together. It didn't make sense. But then, I didn't know a whole lot about how the world worked.

George suddenly caught my eye and he gave me a genuine smile before he remembered where he was and focused on the person in front of him. I was relieved. He didn't hate my guts.

I reached Donny and his wife first.

"Nell Sampson," said Donny. "Thank you for coming. You look great. This is my wife, Loretta."

I shook their hands. "How do you do? I'm very sorry about your father, Donny. He was the kindest man."

"He was that. He's pretty hard to live up to, although George and I are giving it the old college try. I'm sure George can't wait to see you again."

Then he winked at me. What an ass. I felt sorry for Loretta.

Mavis was next. She held out her hand. "I'm George's wife, Mavis. And you are?"

"A family friend."

George reached over with both hands and held mine. "It's so good to see you, Nell. Thank you for coming."

"Your father was a wonderful man. Everyone will miss him terribly."

"How do you and George know each other?" Mavis asked.

"We went to school together," I replied.

She looked me over. "Who made your dress?"

I was stunned. Now was not the time to be chatting about clothes.

George answered for me. "Nell made it herself."

Mavis looked at him strangely. "How would you know?"

I wanted to curl up right there. He'd put his foot in it.

"My mother told me. She often buys Nell's dresses."

"First I heard of it." Mavis frowned.

Fortunately, the person in front of me moved on from Jean, so I quickly went up to her. "I'm so sorry, Jean. Dr. Mackenzie was very good to me."

Jean hugged me and nodded. "He thought you were a lovely girl. Thank you for coming, dear."

She smiled at me and then quickly looked at George. I believe I saw regret in her eyes, but I might have imagined it. It was time to go.

The funeral was the next day, the church so full that people had to stand outside. I joined them and heard the hymns through the doorway. I watched the family come outside and depart in cars for the graveyard. George saw me and tipped his hat as he drove by. I left and went back home.

At ten o'clock that night, I heard a soft knock at the back door. I was half expecting it but hadn't thought about what I'd do if it came. When George walked into the kitchen, it was a flashback to old times.

"Hi, George."

He nodded and stood there. I went up and put my arms around him. He cried for a very long time. Eventually, I let him go and made him a cup of cocoa. He sat at the kitchen table, looking done in. Cat came over and sniffed his shoes.

"Another cat called Cat, I presume?"

"Why interfere with a good system?"

We looked at each other across the table. Nothing had changed. Nothing. The only thing I felt when I gazed at George was love. It wasn't hard to see that it was the same for him. To stop things from getting too awkward, I quickly asked, "Do you like being a doctor?"

"Yes, I do. It's hard work, but very rewarding."

"You should've become a GP like your dad. Then you could've come back here and taken over your father's practice."

"No."

"Because of me?"

He smiled. "Yes. Besides, Mavis wouldn't want to move here. She's a city girl."

"Do you always do what Mavis wants?"

"I find it's easier."

I shook my head. "I'm sorry. I shouldn't have asked you that. I don't want to know about your life with Mavis. She doesn't matter to you and me."

"How have you been? You've not met anyone who's tempted you to marry?"

"I told you years ago that I would never marry. I meant it."

He looked around the kitchen. "You don't get lonely?"

"Sometimes. But it's not a terminal disease."

George laughed. "Do you mind if I smoke?"

"Help yourself. Why are you asking me permission?"

"Mavis hates my pipe."

"Sounds like Mavis hates everything you love."

He nodded. "She hates fishing too."

"Never mind. We're not spending our time talking about Mavis."

We spent an hour just chit-chatting. He looked so much more relaxed by the time he left. He gave me a hug, but I didn't let him hold me for too long. Before he stepped out the door, he turned. "Do you mind if I come to visit you from time to time? I come home occasionally to go fishing."

"Do you think that's wise, George?"

"Maybe not, but the thought of not seeing you again makes me crazy."

He showed up out of the blue one fall day. We didn't speak a word. He came through the door and took me in his arms. He carried me upstairs, and there we stayed for the entire night. I didn't give Mavis a thought. We weren't cheating on her. We'd been cheating ourselves of the bliss we created when we became one.

I wasn't sorry in the least.

CHAPTER FOUR

1946

The months after the war were a happy time for everyone. It was memorable for me because Jane suddenly appeared in my life again. At ten, she was still thin and pale, but she looked more like her mother and that pleased me. I wondered if it bothered Gervais.

When I saw her meander up the laneway, picking daisies as she went, I rushed outside.

"Jane! It's so good to see you."

She gave me a shy smile, but didn't come too close. "Hi."

"I think of you every day. How are you?"

"Okay."

"I don't want you to get in trouble by coming to see me, but I'm delighted you're here."

She looked behind her, as if to make sure no one followed her. "Dad isn't home. He hasn't been home for a couple of days."

My fists clenched at the thought of that miserable man. "Does he do this often?"

"Only one night before, but I'm okay. I know how to cook."

"Why don't we go inside and I'll make you breakfast, like I used to. Porridge, your favourite."

She smiled again and nodded her head.

We had a fine morning. We took a picnic down to the brook and she told me that she still had Bridie, and that she wasn't doing very well in school because she wasn't there often.

"Why not?"

"I get colds and things."

"Do you have friends?"

She shook her head. "Dad wants me home."

"Is he good to you, Jane?"

She shrugged. "He doesn't talk a lot. He mostly drinks and falls asleep."

"If ever you're afraid or feeling unsafe, I want you to come to me, no matter what time of day or night. I'm always here for you, even if you don't see me often. Your father doesn't want you to spend time with me, but if he's gone for long periods, I don't see why you can't come here. You don't have to tell him where you are."

"All right."

So that's how we left things. She would come to me at odd hours and we'd read together or make cookies. I made sure she wasn't around when I had fittings to do, not wanting anyone to know that she was in my house in case it got back to her father.

It occurred to me one night, while I rocked in my rocking chair on the porch, that I had only two meaningful relationships in my life, and both were a secret. I didn't tell George about Jane; it was too complicated, and I didn't want him to tell me I was doing the wrong thing. It was between Jane and me.

I didn't feel too badly about it, because George and I had this unspoken pact. He didn't tell me anything about his life in Sydney. When he was with me, it didn't exist. It worked both ways.

❧

THE YEAR JANE TURNED TWELVE, I FOUND HER SOBBING IN MY back porch.

"Jane, what's wrong?"

"I'm dying. I've got blood everywhere."

"Oh, Jane." I took her in my arms. "You're not dying. I should've told you long ago. You've got your period, that's all. All women do when they get to be a certain age."

"Even you?"

"Even me. Come in and I'll show you how to deal with it."

I was annoyed with myself that I hadn't prepared her properly. I sent her home with everything she'd need. She asked me if she had to tell her father. I told her no. It was not likely he'd care. She lived in the same space, but he didn't pay any attention to her. From what she said, his drinking was getting worse. I had no idea how he put any food on the table, or if he even worked full-time.

The extent of his neglect showed itself when he actually caught Jane and I walking together down the laneway. He got out of his old truck and looked at us for a moment, and then he walked right into the cottage and slammed the door.

He had to have known that Jane was coming to me when she was lonely. It was like he didn't care anymore if she did. That seemed worse to me, but it did make our lives easier. We all pretended nothing was going on. It was like being part of a dysfunctional family.

Sometimes, after George would leave me in the early morning, I'd think back to the day I told him I'd never have children. What was Jane, if not my child? I had been so wrong on that score. Of course, I'd never admit it to George. There was nothing either of us could do about the situation now. My stubbornness was the root cause of this situation. It didn't feel good to know that. Sometimes I fixated on it and couldn't shut my brain off. One day I found myself in front of the liquor commission and went in and bought a bottle of gin. I hurried out the door and ran into Myrtle Turnbull. She looked at the brown bag in my hand and smirked.

"Why, goodness me, Nell. I didn't know you imbibed. I can't believe you've stooped so low. How does it feel to be like the rest of us?"

I wasn't in the mood. "Do you ever have anything nice to say,

Myrtle? Do you stay up at night thinking of mean things to say to other people, or does it just roll off your tongue with ease?"

Her smirk turned to a frown. "Why do you think you're better than everyone else, Nell Sampson? You always have your nose in the air when you grace us with your presence here in the village. That's why you don't have any friends."

"I have all the friends I need."

She leaned forward and said in a loud whisper, "Sleeping with another woman's husband doesn't count."

An electric shock ran up and down my spine. Myrtle saw that she'd scored her point and sashayed away. My hands trembled as I drove home. How on earth did she know? Did everyone know?

I'm ashamed to say the gin didn't last long, and I paid for it the next day. But it didn't stop me from getting another bottle a few weeks later. Gradually, I came to understand the appeal of alcohol, but I didn't get carried away.

That's what I told myself, anyway.

Jane and I celebrated the New Year together: 1950. The year she'd turn fourteen. It excited both of us. Everyone was happy to see the forties over with. Happy to say goodbye to the war years. The papers were filled with good-news stories about how the economy was booming and good times awaited all Canadians. I fervently believed that the future was bright for a young person like Jane. I'd been putting away money for her for many years, and when she was old enough, I wanted to surprise her with it. At first it was intended for university, but I soon realized Jane wasn't the sort who would thrive in academia. She was a little too shy, and somewhat backward, if I was truthful. It wasn't her fault. She'd grown up with next to no stimulus whatsoever, after her mother died, and I believe it dulled her senses. As much as I tried to read to her and get her to engage with worldly matters, she seemed content to just pass the days in her normal routine.

In mid-January, I was coming out of the barn from milking the cows. It was a bitterly cold day and I was in a hurry to get inside. I slipped on a patch of ice and went down heavily on my right ankle. The pain was excruciating. I managed to haul myself into the house using my hands and good foot. I examined my ankle and didn't think it was broken, but I knew I'd twisted it badly.

Jane found me later that day, with my leg up on the couch under a few pillows. She made me some scrambled eggs and toast and spent the evening trying to cheer me up.

"It's ridiculous that I'm in this predicament. I have chores to do."

"I'll milk the cows and feed the goats and hens."

"I can't ask you to do that."

"I'm doing it."

I reached over and held her hand. "Thank you. I don't know what I'd do without you."

George looked at it when he arrived the next night. "Are you keeping off this foot?"

"I try. But it's not always possible."

"A bad sprain can be just as bad or worse than a broken bone."

He fried up a couple of steaks and baked potatoes for supper. He wouldn't let me do a thing. When we were almost finished our meal, I brought it up.

"I saw Myrtle Turnbull recently in the village."

"I'm sure she had something pleasant to say."

"She said that she knew I was sleeping with another woman's husband."

His head shot up. "What? Did she mention me by name?"

"No. She didn't have to."

George reached automatically for his pipe from his pocket. He didn't say anything as he puffed away.

"Maybe you shouldn't come here anymore."

He dismissed me with his hand. "She has absolutely no proof. It was a lucky guess on her part. She's always stirring the pot."

"But what if—"

"Mavis is never going to find out. She hates St. Peter's and she's never coming here again. Myrtle doesn't know where I live and I doubt she's ever even been outside the village."

"But her husband is a police officer. He can find things out."

"Angus Turnbull could care less about my love life. He has a pretty checkered one of his own."

I sighed. "Okay. If you're not worried about it, then I won't be."

☙❧

It was the first of February, and I was hunched over my sewing machine. At the age of forty, I found my neck was bothering me a lot. I'd sometimes have to put hot or cold compresses on it to keep it from aching. A hazard of my job.

When I went upstairs to get a warm facecloth, I happened to look out the bathroom window. It had a great view of the field behind my barn. Normally, no one walked that way, as there were only deep woods beyond that point, but I was sure I saw two figures walking towards the edge of the trees.

I pressed my nose closer to the glass. It looked like Jane, and walking beside her was a young man. They disappeared quickly from view. My heart constricted. I knew she was in danger. I don't know how I knew, but I did. In my rush to get downstairs, I went over slightly on my ankle again and cried out, but I grabbed my boots and put on my coat and started to run as fast as I could past the barn, over the fence, and into the field.

There was a light coating of snow and because of the terrain, I fell a few times in my rush to get to Jane.

Finally, I spied footprints and followed the path they made for me. Calling her name, I was out of breath when I got to the woods. I was able to pinpoint where they were from the sound of twigs breaking. I thought I saw something, so I rushed headlong through the dead fir branches and came to a bit of a clearing.

A young man I'd seen before in the village was rushing away from me.

"Stop!" I yelled. "What are you doing? Stop this instant!"

He ignored me and disappeared.

"Jane! Jane, where are you?"

I heard her call to me. Brittle twigs hit my face as I hurried towards her voice. I finally found her lying on her back, her dress up around her waist. She was crying.

"Oh God, no! NO!" I dropped down beside her and took her in my arms. "It's okay, Jane. I've got you."

"I don't know what happened," she cried. "He got on top of me. I thought he liked me."

At that moment I wanted to kill him. I didn't even know I was crying until I saw my tears fall on Jane's hair.

"We have to go," I said. "It's too cold to be out here. Let's go home."

As I was helping her up, I noticed something shiny underneath her. It was a pocketknife with initials on it. Perfect. I've got you, you bastard.

Somehow, we managed to lurch home. I stoked the fire and ran a warm bath for Jane. She was still crying and did everything I told her, as if she were a toddler. I dressed her in a flannel gown and fed her warm soup. Then I rubbed her forehead and sang to her. Eventually, her breathing quieted and I knew she was asleep.

The pain in my ankle registered at some level, but I was too furious to care. My inability to protect Jane from the same heartache I'd experienced all those years ago made my blood boil. Why did men think they had a right to our bodies? I wasn't going to let this go.

Jane stayed with me for a few days before she said she really had to go home. I didn't want her to, but the minute I drove her home, I continued on my way. I knew where I would find this guy. I'd seen him working at his father's garage.

I pulled up to the garage. I wanted to spit on the sign. A man came towards me, wiping his hands on a rag.

"What can I do for you?" he said.

"You are the owner, are you not?"

"Yes, ma'am."

"We need to talk in your office."

"My office? I don't really have an office."

"You don't want your employees to hear this."

He was instantly on guard and looked around. "We can talk in here." He pointed at a small room off to the side mostly filled with tires. I followed him into the small space, which reeked of rubber.

"What's this all about?" he said as he closed the door behind us.

"Your son works here. He's a tall boy with long, blond hair."

He made a face. "So what?"

"Rather stupid looking."

"Hey! What's the matter with you, lady? You have no business insulting my boy."

"Your son raped a young girl. I caught him at it and I have proof!"

The man seized my arm. "What proof?"

"Let me go unless you want me to call the police."

He let go. "So, show me."

In that instant, I knew it was the wrong thing to do, that he would just snatch the pocketknife and say I never had it, so I kept it hidden in my coat pocket.

"I saw him do it. And the coward ran away when he saw me coming. An all-around champion of a son you have there."

His face turned a lovely shade of red. He stepped towards me. "Now I know who you are. You're the nut who lives on the hill. You've got quite an overactive imagination there. Must be from spending too much time alone with dirty romance novels. Now I'm warning you. You mention this to anyone, and you'll find that one night your old house will go up in flames. Do you understand what I'm telling you? I don't have time for gossips. And no one will ever say anything about my boy. Now get out of here before I do something drastic."

As I walked back to the car, still seething, I knew I was help-less against this man. It made me sick to my stomach.

The unfairness of it all.

But one thing I did do was go straight to the bank and open a safety-deposit box. I put the knife in there. If my house did suddenly catch on fire, at least I wouldn't lose that crucial piece of evidence.

❧

GEORGE CAME FOR A QUICK VISIT THAT JULY AND SAID HE wouldn't be back until the fall. I didn't ask him why and he didn't offer an explanation. I loved being with him, but the burden of not telling him anything about my life was starting to affect me. He should've been the one person I could tell my troubles to. I was becoming dissatisfied with our arrangement. I was always here and available whenever he wanted. Didn't that diminish me somehow?

But the minute he held me, my loneliness would overtake me and I only wanted his body close to mine. To think I could have lain with him every night of my life. My own stupidity often crushed my spirit. But I didn't let on. Or at least I thought I didn't. Sometimes George looked at me as if trying to figure out what was wrong with me.

We had two nights together before he left. I almost told him about Jane as we sat together at supper, but I felt I was being disloyal to her if I talked behind her back with someone she didn't know. What was the right thing to do?

I was rocking in my chair on the porch, thinking about our last hours, when I saw Jane walk towards me. I waved, then paused. I looked again at her with her blouse blowing open in the wind.

The thought, once planted, stayed. I beckoned her to come up onto the porch.

"How are you feeling today, Jane?"

"Good."

"Anything new?"

"No. There's never anything new."

"Jane, I want to ask you something. I don't mean to pry but it's important."

She looked away, the wind blowing her hair straight back. "Okay."

"Have you had your period lately?"

 She fiddled with the stalk of grass between her fingers. She still wouldn't look at me.

"Jane?"

"How did you know?"

Merciful God. What was I going to do? I immediately put my thumbnail in my mouth and started to chew. What was I going to do? What was I going to do?

"Have I done something wrong?" Jane asked quietly.

I immediately got out of the rocking chair and joined her on the steps. I put my arms around her. "No, of course not."

"What does it mean when you don't have your period?"

I couldn't face it just then. "That sometimes happens. It doesn't mean anything. Want a cookie?"

Later that night I got down on my knees by my bed and said a prayer to a god I wasn't sure I believed in. "Please help me.

I don't know what to do. I don't want to scare her and tell her she's having a baby. She's just a child. And her father will kill her. What's going to happen to her? Please tell me what to do."

I prayed all summer but got no further ahead. Fortunately, Jane was a small girl and her little bump wasn't noticeable to anyone but me. No one else cared enough about her to bother looking.

And then after one sleepless night in the overwhelming heat of late August, it occurred to me. George would help. I'd get George to take her away. He'd look after her somehow; he loved me and he'd do anything for me. He was a doctor; he could find her a good home and watch over her. He'd be able to find a good home for the baby. I'd send him the money I had saved when the time came, and Jane could find her own way in the world. I didn't want her in this town with her rapist lurking around and her miserable, murderous father so full of anger. If he found out about the baby, God knew what he'd do to Jane. It was the only solution.

It was now mid-September. I knew George was coming that night. He'd sent me a letter a week before, so I waited until the very last moment to talk to Jane. That afternoon Gervais's truck wasn't around when I knocked on the door. Jane opened it, surprised to see me.

"Sorry, I didn't mean to startle you."

"That's okay."

"I guess your father's not home."

"He hasn't been for a few days."

"Let's go inside. I need to talk to you."

The cottage was so neglected. No child should be living here. I was doing the right thing.

We sat at the table and I held her hands. "Jane, I want you to trust me. I have a very dear friend named George who is going to make things all better for you."

"What do you mean?"

"I want you to go away with him. He's going to find you a better place to live. You can't continue to live here. It's not right."

"Why can't I live with you?"

"Because your father would never let that happen."

She started to get upset. "But I'll miss you."

"One day, you and I will be together again. Once you've grown and have an education and a nice life, you can come back to me and we can be best friends again. I just need to get you away from here. It's not safe right now."

"I don't know—"

"Jane, I didn't want to tell you this before, but you have to leave. You're going to have a baby."

Bless her heart, she looked at me in confusion. "What do you mean?"

"Remember the time in the woods with that young man? He made you pregnant, and that's why you haven't had your period. I didn't want to tell you before, because I didn't want you to be frightened. But now that George is going to help us, everything will be all right. He can find a home for the baby and take care of you at the same time."

"He's going to take my baby away from me?"

"He'll find a good home for the baby, because you are too young to have a child. It wouldn't be fair to the baby and certainly not fair to you. I want you to grow up to be a young lady who can take care of herself."

"I'm not sure...."

"Jane, if your father knew you were having a baby, he'd throw you out, or worse. Do you understand?"

"But—"

"Dearest, do you trust me?"

She looked at me with her big blue eyes. "Yes."

LESLEY CREWE

"Then trust me that this is the right thing. I want you to gather a few clothes and things you might need and put them in a suitcase and come up to my house at six tomorrow morning."

"Should I take Bridie? She might miss her home. And my father would be alone."

"Bridie can stay here for now, if you like. If you need her later, I'll send her to you."

She nodded. I kissed her cheek and left before her father came back.

❦

WHEN I WOKE THAT MORNING, NEXT TO GEORGE, I WANTED nothing more than to curl up in his arms. It bothered me that I had drunk so much I didn't wake up when he brought me to bed. He didn't like the idea of me drinking and I hated being exposed like that.

But as much as I wanted to be with him, I knew I had much more important things to do. I hurried down to the kitchen and, on the dot, Jane was there, holding an old carpetbag in her hands.

"Good girl. Is your father home?"

She shook her head.

"I want you to wait in the car until George comes out. Then you will drive home with him."

She nodded. I think she was afraid to speak in case she cried, which just about killed me. I reached into my housecoat pocket.

"I want to give you something, Jane." I held up the heart necklace George had given me so many years ago. "I want you to wear this and know that I am always close to your heart. I'll think of you every day while you're away. Please know I love you very much."

I put the necklace on her and saw tears in her eyes. I held her against me. "You are a brave and beautiful girl. I believe in you."

62

She nodded and I opened the car door and she sat down, gripping her luggage in her lap.

"Take care, little one."

I shut the door.

I can't remember what I said to George. I think I was in shock. When I saw him drive away with my precious child in the car, I broke down and cried all day. And the next.

Had I done the right thing? Had I even told George she was pregnant? I couldn't remember. It was all one great big blur. And knowing she wasn't close by made me lonelier than I've ever been.

Her father finally showed up five days later. He knocked on the back door.

"Is Jane here?"

"No, she isn't. Have you lost her?"

"She's not home."

"How would you even know? You're never home to check. Normal parents care about what happens to their children. But not you. You're a disgrace, Gervais. I wouldn't blame her if she ran away."

"You should shut your mouth."

"Gladly." I slammed the door in his face.

❧

I'D TOLD GEORGE I WOULDN'T CONTACT HIM, BUT FOR SOME reason I thought he'd be in touch with me much sooner. It had been almost two months since they'd left. Surely he'd have things arranged by now. The baby had been due in October. Maybe he was waiting until the baby had a permanent home.

On November 19 I finally saw his car come up the laneway. I was so excited I bolted out of the house in my slippers, through the snow. He took his time getting out of the car. I was so impatient, I threw myself into his arms and kissed his warm neck.

"I've missed you so! Why didn't you call me? I've been on pins and needles for weeks."

"Let's go inside," he said.

I pulled him along by the hand. "Tell me everything!"

He stood in the kitchen and looked ten years older than when I'd seen him last. He kept looking at the floor. A feeling of dread washed over me.

"What's wrong? What's happened?"

"I don't want to tell you."

Fear prickled my scalp. "Just say it. Is she all right? Is the baby all right?"

"Why didn't you tell me she was pregnant?"

"I didn't tell you?"

"No!"

"I'm sorry! I truly am. I meant to. What's wrong, George? For the love of God, tell me!"

He choked up and I had a hard time hearing him. "There was an accident. A buck was standing in the middle of the road and I didn't see it until it was too late. The road was slick with rain and we went right over the side."

"Was she hurt? Tell me she wasn't hurt?"

"She died, Nell. She died in my arms."

I started to scream. I screamed and screamed and screamed. I went over to him and pounded his chest. "I asked you to do one thing! One thing! It's all your fault! It's all your fault! You killed her! You killed her!"

George took my arms and shook me. "I didn't kill her. You did. You sent her away—you had no right to do that. I knew I should've turned around and come back, but I was so afraid of you that I didn't. What does that say about me? What kind of a person am I, that I override my own instincts because of you?"

"Oh my God. Oh my God. My baby is gone! She's gone!" I wrenched myself from his arms and tore into the sewing room.

I grabbed a pair of scissors, raced back into the kitchen, and lunged at him. He took my wrists once more and yanked the scissors from my hand, throwing them on the floor.

"Stop it, Nell!"

But I was beyond help. I saw myself out of my own body, struggling, crying and kicking at him. I wanted to make him hurt.

I wanted to make *me* hurt.

Finally, I had nothing left. I lay crumpled on the floor. George sat in a kitchen chair, his head in his hands.

"Why?" I cried, my voice hoarse. "Why? All this time, I've been thinking of her getting comfortable in her new home. You would've found a family for the baby. She'd be happy. And now she's in the ground. Why didn't you tell me? Why did you wait this long?"

George didn't lift his face; his voice was muffled by his hands and his breath sounded ragged. "Because I'm a coward. I didn't want to tell you. Here I thought we could tell each other everything, but we never actually talk about anything important. We've been living a lie this whole time."

My grief and my anger fed each other and I could feel myself beginning to spin again. "And whose fault is that? I'm not married, am I? You're the one cheating on your wife. Mr. Holier-Than-Thou. Such a good man. Such a saint in his mother's eyes. And all you've been doing is screwing the spinster on the hill. You men are all the same. You take what you want when you want it, and to hell with the women in your lives. I hate men. I hate you. I hate Gervais. I hate that goddamn man who raped her. I hate the bastard who raped me!"

Even amidst the rest of my tirade, this hit him, and he finally lifted his pale face, almost unrecognizable in his anguish. But I wasn't about to let him interrupt me. I was done. "You can all go to hell! I never want to see your face again, George Mackenzie! You come anywhere near me and I'll shoot you dead with my rifle."

"Nell—"

"Get out! Get out and never come back. I hate you. I hate you so much!"

He stood, shaking. I'd done it. "At this moment in time, Nell, I hate you too."

He went through the door and banged it shut. I lay on the floor and howled my despair throughout the night.

I was the one who had killed her. I was the one who had hatched the grand plan. It was all my doing.

But I wasn't done yet. I remembered I had one of Jane's sweaters in my spare room. I held it and cried and cried. Then I took it down to the nearest beach and let it lie in the water and sand. When it was thoroughly soaked, I dragged it back to the laneway and stopped at the cottage. Gervais's truck was outside. I threw open the door and there he was, asleep at his kitchen table. I grabbed his hair and pulled his head back. His eyes fluttered open.

"Wha—What's goin' on?"

I pushed the sweater into his face. "Do you see this? Do you know what this is? It's Jane's sweater. Guess where I found it? It was washed up on the beach. Her favourite sweater. She hated you so much, she drowned herself rather than stay here with you! She's gone, you son of a bitch, and it's all your fault! She's dead because of you!"

He kept blinking and shaking his head, trying to understand what I was saying.

"You can't leave a child for days at a time and expect her to feel loved. You killed her mother and now you've killed her. She's gone and she's never coming back! I hope you die too."

And then I remembered: Bridie was here in the cottage. So I ran upstairs and grabbed the doll that was still on Jane's bed. Why hadn't I made her take it? That's when I groaned with the realization that my girl was never coming back and she'd died alone.

I tore back downstairs, Bridie in my arms, and ran out the door to shut myself up in my house.

My lonely, lonely house.

CHAPTER FIVE

EILEEN
1945

The worst day of my life was when I was ten. I told my mother that I loved my cousin George and I was going to marry him some-day. She was peeling carrots at the time.

"Sorry, sweetie. First cousins can't marry each other."

"What's a first cousin?"

"Your aunt Jean and I are sisters. Our children can't marry each other. You'll have to fall in love with someone else."

I dramatically fell on the daybed by the stove. "NO! That's not fair! I wouldn't give a hoot if it was Donny, but George? He's the only boy who's nice to me."

"I'm sure you'll find another boy someday."

Not likely. I'd heard my sister Betty say that I was as homely as a hedge fence. I told her that she looked like a skunk. She laughed and said that didn't even make any sense. It made sense to me. She stank.

The best day of my life was when I was twelve and broke my leg very badly. Our families were all at the beach and George dared me to jump off Dead Man's Cliff. So I did. But I should have known better; I was always hurting myself. I was a big, awkward girl, even though I pretended otherwise.

When I hit the water, I was in mid-scream at a very odd angle. I probably would have drowned if George hadn't gotten to me first. He held my head out of the water and tried to carry me to shore. I didn't even feel the pain. I was too enraptured by the feel of George's hands on my body. He was my knight in shining armour and I was the Lady of Shalott.

"Eileen! A-A-Are you okay? It's all my fault. I shouldn't have told you to jump. I'm-m-m sorry!"

I waved my arms around as he struggled to keep me upright. "I can't breathe! My leg! Hold me." It was wonderful. Everything I'd imagined.

I saw my father and Uncle Joe run into the water. I wanted them to stay away for a few more minutes at least...but then the initial adrenalin wore off and the pain in my leg grew so big, I fainted dead away. The "best" part of the best day of my life ended rather abruptly.

And that's why I walk with a limp. And that's why I've never had a boyfriend. Who wants a wife who limps? At least that's what I tell myself. Of course, Betty married when she was eighteen. She didn't want me as a bridesmaid because of my gait, but our mother, Jessie, put an end to that nonsense. She made me the maid of honour. I did my best to hobble horribly. Betty pretended to stab me in the heart when no one was looking.

George always felt awful about it. He'd look at me with big sad eyes until finally one day I told him to knock it off. "I didn't have to jump, you know. You didn't push me."

But that's the kind of guy he is. You can't help loving him.

I'd prepared myself for a long and boring life, since I was still living with my parents at the end of the war. I was thirty-five and a bit on the large side. A classic old maid. George had married Mavis five years before. Her only relative was a stepfather who lived out west and didn't bother showing up for the ceremony. Who doesn't have a family? They must have all run away; she was vile. I hated her instantly and spent their entire wedding crying into a hanky. I told Aunt Jean it was hay fever, but the way she smiled at my mother, I suspect she knew the real reason. Sisters never do keep secrets. Fortunately, Betty and I don't have that problem, as we never tell each other any.

The only thing I was good at was cooking. That's because I like to eat. There's not much else to do in River Bourgeois in the winter.

I was having a bit of a mid-life crisis for a time. My parents were worried about me. Even Betty would come by and try to get me to go shopping. But I wasn't interested.

And then one day out of the blue, George showed up, handsome as ever. I tried not to focus on his wedding ring, but it sure did irk me. He asked if he could talk to me privately. I lived in hope it was to tell me that Mavis was lost at sea and he'd realized his tragic mistake in not marrying me.

That wasn't quite it.

He leaned forward in his chair and clasped his hands together. "I have a proposal if you're interested."

Did he say proposal?

"As you know, Mavis and I have a baby now."

Darn. I'd forgotten that. Or I tried not to think about it. "Yes, little Patricia."

"We call her Patty. She's a bit of a handful. Suffers from colic. On top of that, Mavis isn't doing well. Sometimes new mothers have something called postpartum depression, and I'm afraid Mavis has it in spades."

"I'm sorry to hear that, but how can I help?"

"I was hoping you'd come and live with us for a time. Our house is large enough. Off the kitchen there's a bedroom, bathroom, and sitting room that were once a maid's quarters. Obviously, I don't want you to be our maid, but for the time being, I need someone in the house to help Mavis with the meals and taking care of the baby. I'd rather have someone I love and trust in the house than hire someone I don't know, and I thought you'd be perfect. I'll pay you well."

Did he say love?

"Now, I know it's asking a lot, Eileen, to uproot you from your life—"

"What life? I'm yours."

He gave me a huge smile. "That's such a relief! Thank you so much, Eileen. You're a doll."

I pointed at him. "My mother didn't suggest this, did she? As a way of cheering me up?"

He genuinely looked confused. "No, not at all. It was my idea."

That sealed it.

So that's how I came to live in my cousin George's house. All my dreams had come true.

Well, not quite. Mavis was still on the scene.

It took a while to figure that one out. She was so grateful to see me when I first showed up that I thought maybe I'd gotten the wrong end of the stick about her, but she soon shot that down.

Little Patty was a cute enough baby, but she did cry a lot. No wonder, with Mavis as her mother.

"I love Patty," Mavis sniffed one day as I brought her breakfast in bed, a custom that lasted for years, long after her baby blues had disappeared. If they ever really did.

Another day, another moan. "I can never have another baby, Eileen," she snivelled as she held up her feet so I could vacuum the rug under her chair. "I never want to go through that again. Men just don't know what it's like to suffer like we do."

I had a hard time trying to work out how exactly Mavis was suffering. She spent most of the day in bed while I bathed, clothed, and fed the baby. She usually went out with friends while the baby had a nap, and I did the housework and made preparations for supper.

She'd spend most of dinner whining to George about one thing and another while he nodded his head and smiled vaguely. He'd disappear into his study to smoke his pipe in peace and Mavis would moan to me about how men were so ungrateful.

This went on for years. Despite Mavis, I grew to love my life in George's house. I loved my kitchen, and the garden I planted out back. As Patty grew and became easier to deal with, her mother paid more attention to her. Mavis would dress her up in pretty party dresses and never let her get dirty. George would say he'd like to take Patty fishing, but Mavis would give him a horrified look.

"Have her around those stinky old fish? Have you lost your mind?"

I knew that George loved his little girl, but he never really saw her much. Mavis would send her to bed early so she could invite people over. I knew George hated the cocktail parties that Mavis insisted on throwing.

"They're good for your career, George. Don't you want to be a big shot at the hospital?"

"Not really."

"Men! I have no idea why we women have to do all the heavy lifting. Someone has to think about our future."

"What's wrong with our present? We live in a great house and have everything we need."

"There's nothing wrong with making more money."

"Why bother?" George would grumble. "You'd only spend it."

Mavis would walk up to him and peck him on the cheek. "Exactly."

George would often find solace in my kitchen. I'd make him a cup of tea and a warm biscuit with homemade strawberry jam.

"You are the best cook around, Eileen. Don't tell my mother I said that."

"Hey, no one can beat your mother's lemon meringue pie."

"True."

"I wanted to show Patty how to make cookies the other day, but Mavis didn't want her to get her dress dirty."

George shook his head. "You can't tell that woman anything."

"You can say that again."

He looked at me seriously. "Eileen, I am well aware that after five years, my wife's medical condition has vanished. I feel like I'm keeping you here under false pretenses. If you ever want to go home, I don't blame you. But I have to tell you that I would sorely miss you."

"I feel like I'm taking advantage of you. You really don't need me anymore, and yet you're still paying me."

"Oh, we need you. More than ever. If you're happy staying here, I'm delighted. You can stay forever."

"Then I will." We clinked our teacups together.

I just love that man.

☜☞

It was mid-September in 1950 and George was off on one of his fishing excursions. And while the cat was away, the mouse did play. Mavis had a wild party at the house one night with the hospital gang, including her brother-in-law, Donny, who kept coming into the kitchen for more shot glasses.

"Hey, cuz! How's life treating you? Ya got a good gig goin' here. Still playing on George's guilty heartstrings?"

"You're an ass, Donny Mackenzie."

"So true. And that's Dr. Donny Mackenzie to you."

"You'll always be Donny the Jerk to me."

"Priceless!"

I caught him and Mavis kissing in the pantry a few hours later. She at least had the decency to look flustered as she rushed out. Donny winked at me. "Loose lips sink ships."

As if I'd tell George about those two. They'd get what was coming to them. They didn't need any help from me.

The next day, while Mavis nursed her hangover, the phone rang. I picked it up. "Mackenzie residence."

"It's me."

It was the way he said it. "What's wrong?"

"Meet me at the hospital. I'll be there shortly." He hung up.

I rushed about getting my coat, hat, and purse. I charged up the stairs and knocked on Mavis's bedroom door, opening it slightly. "Sorry Mavis, I have to go out. I don't know when I'll be back."

She lifted her head off the pillow. "That's very inconvenient. Who's going to look after Patty?"

"I'll take her over next door and ask the maid to watch her for a couple of hours."

"I should think so. Oh, my head."

Despite the fact that Patty didn't want go next door, I took her. Doris owed me a favour, as I sometimes watched her charges for an afternoon.

I called a taxi and told him to hurry to the hospital. After I paid the man, I jumped out and stood there, unsure what to do. George said he'd be arriving shortly, so that meant he wasn't in the building. After waiting by the emergency entrance for twenty minutes, I was shivering. It was a rainy and windy day, and at that point, I was getting frantic. Just then, an ambulance pulled up and George appeared, looking bloodied and bruised, holding his coat in front of him like a shield. But worse than all that was the colour of his skin. He was as pale as I'd ever seen him. Just a whisper away from passing out.

My first reaction was to hug him. Instead, I hurried over and took him by the arm. "My God, what happened? Are you all right? How can I help?"

"Eileen. Eileen. I've done a terrible thing. I killed someone today."

My mouth instantly went dry. "What...what are you talking about?"

"I killed a girl. She was in my car and it went off the road. I shouldn't have taken her. I should never have let her in the car. It's my fault."

He rushed into the hospital, me at his heels.

"If it was a car accident, you're not to blame. The weather's awful this morning. Anyone could've had an accident."

"But you don't understand." He opened up his coat slightly and I gasped. There was a very small newborn baby clinging to his chest, its tiny fingers entangled in his chest hair.

"Is it alive?"

"Just."

It was a blur after that. George ran into the emergency room and two doctors and a nurse gathered around. George dropped the coat and tried to pass the baby to the doctor, but the baby wouldn't let go. He had to pull her tiny fingers from his skin and he let out a sob as he did. One of the doctors took her and George tried to participate, but he was unsteady on his feet, so another nurse took him away and handed him to me. I made him sit down and asked someone for a glass of water. He drank it quickly.

"I can't believe this has happened," he whispered. "It's a bad dream."

"Where's the girl?"

"She's in another ambulance behind us. Just a young girl, and her life is over. I'll never forgive myself."

I took his hands in mine. "You must have done something right, George. Her baby is still alive, thanks to you."

Another nurse came towards us. "Some police officers are here. They want to talk to you. You can go in the next room."

"Don't leave me," George whispered.

"Never."

We went into a small office. The policemen took up most of the space. I made George sit down on the only chair.

They took out their notepads. "Okay, Dr. Mackenzie, let's go through the timeline of events."

George nodded. "I picked up a girl hitchhiking—"

"Where were you coming from?"

"St. Peter's. I was on a fishing trip and I was driving home to Sydney."

"So, you picked her up where?"

"I'm not sure. Maybe around Middle Cape. She was soaked through."

"Did she tell you who she was?"

"No. It was shortly after that, just before Big Pond...the buck was right in the middle of the road. I didn't have time to think. We slid across the highway and down into a ditch."

"What happened then?"

"The girl was hurt, and when I put my hands on her to see if she broke anything, I realized she was pregnant. Her contractions started almost immediately, but I was terrified because I could see she was bleeding. It was terrible. I did the best I could. I couldn't stop the bleeding. I'll never forget it as long as I live. I couldn't save her. I couldn't save her."

"So basically we have no idea who this girl was or where she came from?"

"It seems to me she was running away," I told the police. "Who else would be hitchhiking in a storm, but a girl half-crazy with fear? I bet her people threw her out. That happens, you know."

The police officers looked at me. "And you are?" said one of them.

"I'm Dr. Mackenzie's cousin. He called me."

The police closed their notebooks. "We'll be back if we need to ask any more questions. We'll see if we have any missing persons in the area. If we don't find her people, I'm afraid we'll have to bury her in an unmarked grave."

"I'll pay for her burial," George said.

"And what about the infant?"

"Don't worry," said George. "I'll contact social services here at the hospital. There are always people willing to take in a newborn, once she's recovered her health."

The officers left and George held his hands over his face and cried. I rubbed his back and made soothing noises. I didn't know what else to do. If I'm being truthful, something about the story didn't seem quite right to me. I know it was a terrible thing, but the depth of George's despair was deep. There was something personal about it.

That's when it hit me. I wondered if this was George's baby. But how could that be? He'd never be involved with a child, surely. Nothing made much sense. My head hurt just thinking about it.

He looked up at me. "Eileen. You have to help me."

"Of course, George. Anything you ask."

"I can't let this little girl down. I couldn't save her mother, but I can save her. I want to bring her home and raise her. But I need you. Would you be willing to look after another child? To raise it as your own?"

I was stunned. A baby of my own? It was something I had always wanted but had tucked away with the rest of the disappointments in my life, and now this amazing opportunity was being handed to me. Was it God's will? How could I say no, if this was preordained? My brain felt like it was on fire. I could only nod at first, but then I remembered. "What will Mavis say?"

"I don't care. Do you think we can make this happen? I need you, Eileen. That baby held on to me as soon as she came out, so trusting, so helpless. I love her. I can't explain it, but I love her so dearly. I can't be parted from her."

"We'll make it happen, George. You and me."

He grabbed me and held on for dear life. "Thank you, Eileen. I love you."

The feeling was mutual.

We waited to hear about the baby. It was a good hour before the doctor who'd taken her came to fetch us.

"I think she'll live. We have to wait and see, but you must have done something right, George. She's holding her own."

We went up to see the baby. She was being closely monitored in an incubator. Her hair, now that her mother's blood had been washed from it, was a soft fuzz of blond. She was so incredibly tiny, with her wrinkled skin and small fists. George put his hand in the opening and let her grab his finger. "Hush, little one. You're safe now."

"She's beautiful," I whispered. "Even as small as she is."

"Her name is Bridie. Her mother lasted long enough to tell me that. Bridie."

George wanted to be informed when the young girl's body arrived. I asked him if he was sure and he nodded. We went down to the mortuary together. It was as if he needed to see her again to make sure that it had happened.

When he pulled back the sheet, he cried. I cried with him, because she looked so young. Too young to be a mother. Too young to be dead. It was such a waste. I vowed then and there that I would love this baby for her with all my heart. I would be the mother I never thought I'd be. God was granting me this gift. I didn't deserve it, but now that it was happening, I would move heaven and earth to do my duty by them both. This would be my mission in life.

And so help me, if Mavis raised a stink about it, I'd kill her and bury her in my strawberry patch in the backyard.

I pointed to the locket around the young girl's neck. "You should take that and give it to Bridie someday. She'd want a memento of her mother."

George wiped his eyes with the back of his hand. "Yes, you're right." He took the necklace off her slender neck and looked at it with a mixture of horror and amazement, it seemed to me.

"What's wrong?"

"N-n-nothing. Nothing at all."

CHAPTER SIX

Mavis did raise a stink. An almighty one.

She was horrified when she saw me help George out of a cab later that afternoon. She threw open the front door and ran down the front walk.

"Where were you, Eileen? I was frantic with worry! And what happened to you, George? Where's the car?"

"Just let me get him in the house, Mavis." I marched past her with George leaning against me, with only enough energy left to make it to the living room. George sat heavily in his armchair, his head hanging down, arms at his sides, looking at nothing.

"Someone better tell me what's going on!" Mavis shouted. "Why does George look like he's been in a fight?"

"George had a car accident this morning."

"What? Is the car wrecked? It's almost brand new."

"Your husband is alive, Mavis. Perhaps you should be thanking God for that."

I'd never spoken to Mavis that way before, and I could tell by the expression on her face that she didn't appreciate it.

"I can see he's alive, Eileen. I just want to know what happened. Is there something wrong with that?"

"No, of course not. I'm sorry. It's been a long day."

Mavis looked puzzled. "Why did George call you and not me?"

"You didn't answer the phone," George said quietly.

"Well, someone should've called me long before this. Why am I the last to know everything?" Mavis reached for her cigarettes and lit one before sitting on the couch, crossing her legs, and looking put-out.

I took off my coat and sank into the nearest chair. "Where's Patty?"

"She's still next door."

"You didn't go get her?"

"Why should I? You took her over there. You can bring her back."

I was afraid I was going to hit Mavis, so I got up and left the living room. Now I'd have to apologize to poor Doris. When I went next door, both Doris and Patty looked at me with a certain amount of hate.

"I'm so sorry, Doris. I just got back. I thought Mavis would've come for Patty long before this."

"You owe me."

"I know."

Patty wouldn't take my hand as we walked out the back door. "Don't leave me there again. She's mean."

"How is she mean?"

"She makes me eat egg sandwiches."

"Oh dear. You'll have to have two cookies for dessert instead of one."

Patty smiled. "Okay."

I was hoping George would've told Mavis what was going on without me, but he kindly waited for me to come back to the house first.

"Eileen, I need you," he called out from the living room.

I took off Patty's sweater and held out the cookie jar. "Take two cookies now and go up to your room and play tea, while Mommy and Daddy and I talk."

Her eyes lit up. She took the cookies and skipped upstairs. I would've happily skipped off in the other direction, but I knew that George needed me, so I slowly made my way back to the front of the house. What seemed like a rational thing to do at the hospital, with the baby in our sights, suddenly became a far-fetched idea now that Mavis was about to hear about it. I prayed for strength.

George gestured for me to sit on the chesterfield. He looked at Mavis. "I'm going to tell you what happened, and I don't want you to say anything until I'm finished."

Mavis looked at me. "What's going on?"

"Mavis! Listen to me. Please."

"Okay! There's no need to shout."

George told her what happened, but he had a hard time getting it out without breaking down. I could tell Mavis was very uncomfortable, but she wasn't completely heartless. Her hands covered her mouth when he told her about the girl dying in his arms.

"That's terrible," she cried. "That poor young girl. How awful."

Then he told her the rest and what he wanted to do. Her mouth opened and stayed open. She looked at me and then back at him.

"Are you insane? A baby? You want to raise a stranger's child as your own?"

"It will be my baby, Mavis. If only you could see her. She's so little and has no one, and I've always wanted a child. I think this was meant to be. We need each other."

Mavis stood up and didn't know who to glare at first. She turned her back on us and stared out the living room window for a good two minutes. It gave George a chance to catch his breath. He looked at me and I could tell he needed me to stay strong. All I wanted to do was run into the kitchen and eat the leftover apple pie in the pantry.

When she turned around again, she had composed herself. "So, you're telling me that Eileen, who is supposed to be working for us, is suddenly going to have her own family, under our roof, while we pay her for the privilege. I'd say that's a very cozy arrangement for her. We provide a roof over her head and a wage that is not inconsequential, and she gets to play happy family with a baby that was literally picked up off the streets."

"I will look after this child, but that doesn't mean I'm going to abandon you," I reassured her. "I love Patty as my own, and I will continue to love her and I will always be here for you. A baby doesn't stay a baby for long. She won't be in the way. She'll stay in my quarters off the kitchen."

"That's a lot of nonsense. This is an outrageous request and I'm putting a stop to it, right this minute. Do you hear me, George?"

George got up off his armchair and walked over to her. "For once in your life, Mavis, you have no choice in the matter. I need to make amends for—for...killing a young girl. She's dead...dead... my fault. I—I have to...I couldn't live with myself if I abandoned this infant. I owe her...Eileen and I will make sure this little girl has a good life. And I know that you're a good woman, Mavis. You can't—you can't possibly be jealous of a baby who has nothing or no one."

Good for George.

Mavis turned bright red. What could she say to that? She marched out of the living room, stomped up the stairs, and slammed her bedroom door. George's shoulders slumped and he looked like he was going to pass out, so I led him back to the chair.

"The worst part is over," I whispered.

He slowly raised his eyes to look at me. "I don't think so, Eileen. She's going to make things difficult for both of us. Worse for you, because you're with her all day."

"I'm a strong person. I've put up with Betty my whole life. I can handle Mavis. We're doing the right thing."

He took my hand and kissed it. "What would I do without you?"

"You'd be screwed."

I saw a peek of a smile.

☙☙

IN A WAY, IT WAS A GODSEND THAT BRIDIE WAS IN THE HOSPITAL for three weeks before she came home. It gave Mavis a chance to get some of the anger out of her system. Not just anger but also suspicion.

Even though I was the villain who was going to raise the child, after five years of bending my ear, the habit was hard to break, and so Mavis would still come to me with her theories.

She sat at her makeup table while I changed the sheets. "The whole hospital is talking about it, you know. Even Donny thinks it's odd. I mean, why is he so stuck on this child?" She looked at me over her shoulder. "You don't think George had an affair, do you? Maybe the baby is his, and that's why he's so adamant about it."

"Do you honestly think George could have an affair, Mavis? Think about it. Is Mr. Straight-and-Narrow capable of such a thing? Donny, yes, but George?"

Mavis flinched a little when I said Donny's name. Good. She sighed. "I suppose you're right. He's too boring."

That irked me. "George isn't boring."

She waved her hand at me. "George can do no wrong as far as you're concerned, Eileen. You're always sticking up for him."

"I suppose that's what cousins do."

Now she completely turned around and faced me. "You're sure you'll be able to look after this baby? It's not yours. And you've been an old maid for years. Do you even have a maternal instinct?"

In my mind, I threw a pillow in her face. In reality, I put a pillowcase on it. "I've been looking after Patty for years. She's like a daughter to me."

"I'm afraid it's not the same thing. Only a mother can love her child completely."

"All I can do is my best."

"Don't come crying to me if it gets to be too much. And don't ever expect me to look after this baby. And don't you dare take time away from Patty. I don't want her to suffer."

"I promise that won't happen."

She faced the mirror again. "It's ridiculous that I have to worry about this. Life was just fine, and now George has gone and mucked it all up. I'm probably a laughingstock among my peers. Whose husband comes home with an infant and says 'We're keeping it'? No one's!"

I let her prattle on. It seemed to help her.

The nameless girl was buried at the Hardwood Hill Cemetery. Only George and I were there. The police got in touch and said that so far, they hadn't had any luck finding anything out, but her file wasn't closed. They'd keep trying.

George would come home and tell me how Bridie was doing. He checked on her every day. I found it harder to leave the house, because Mavis always wanted to know where I was going and concocted ways to keep me at home with her and Patty. I was desperate to see Bridie again, and one day, while I was out getting groceries, I took a cab to the hospital and met George there. He took me up to the neonatal unit and we both took a peek at our girl, who was now two weeks old.

She was still very small, but less wrinkly, and her big, bright eyes were open and taking in everything around her. Whenever George put his finger near her, she held on for dear life and settled right down. The first time I did it, she fussed a bit, but soon drifted off to sleep. I loved her so much. The thought of actually holding her in my arms kept me up at night. It seemed as though it would never happen.

Technically, I couldn't adopt Bridie because I was single, so George went to court to become Bridie's legal guardian. When I called home to tell my mother what was happening, she was alarmed.

"Are you sure this is the right thing to do, Eileen? It's not like getting a puppy. This child will be your responsibility for the rest of your life."

"What a glorious thing," I answered. "I've always wanted to be a mother, and now I will be."

I forgot that my mother would tell George's mother, and George hadn't said anything to his mother. That caused quite a stir.

"Thanks a lot, Eileen," he said. "She wanted to know why I didn't say anything to her, and I really didn't have an answer. Now she's cross."

"Why didn't you tell her?"

"I don't want people at home knowing my business."

A pretty dopey excuse. No wonder Aunt Jean was annoyed.

Over the last five years, I'd saved a bit of money, and I used some of it to buy a few things for Bridie. I didn't want Mavis getting her drawers in a knot, so I bought the crib and high chair. That way she couldn't accuse George of spending his hard-earned money on the "waif," as she called her.

Finally, the day arrived when Bridie came home. It was early October when George brought her in through the back door, cuddled in a blanket against the chill. He handed her over to me and I sat right down in my rocking chair by the stove. A nurse at the hospital had knitted her a pink cap, mitts, and booties. Her perfect little face looked about, so trusting and innocent. She had the longest eyelashes, and her mouth was as pink as a little rosebud. She was exquisite. All mothers think their child is the most beautiful, but Bridie really was. Obviously, she took after me.

"Can you believe it?" I said to George. "We did it. She's here. You must be so happy."

George did look relieved, but he always had this haunted look about him when he gazed at her. I knew he was thinking of the young girl who'd lost her life. That was something he would never get over.

Not two minutes later, Mavis and Patty came into the kitchen.

"She's here, then," Mavis said to no one in particular.

"Let me see the baby!" Patty shouted. "Can I play with her?"

I opened the blanket a little, so Patty could see. "Be very careful. She's tiny."

Patty tried to touch her, and I put out my hand to hold hers. "Not yet, dearest. We don't want any germs on a newborn baby. Pretty soon, she'll be big and strong enough for you to hold."

"That's not fair. I want to hold her now."

"Patty, do as you're told," her father said. "You can't touch her just yet."

"That's no fair." Patty crossed her arms and gave everyone a big pout.

"No, nothing's going to change," Mavis said. "Patty will always be number one in this household. Isn't that right, Eileen?"

George sighed. "Just give everyone a chance to settle in, please. You haven't even looked at the baby."

Mavis leaned over and looked down at her. "She's a baby. Nothing special." She reached for Patty's hand. "Come with Mommy. We're not wanted here."

"Mavis!" George pleaded.

"Never mind. We'll toddle along." She pushed the kitchen door open and she and Patty disappeared. The swinging door went back and forth after they left. Both George and I watched it.

"Oh boy," he said.

"It'll get better."

BOY, WAS I WRONG. MAVIS MADE IT HER MISSION TO MAKE MY life a living hell those first weeks. I was so tired, I could barely see straight. Bridie was a good baby, but she was up a lot through the night because she was so small. Often, George would sneak down the back stairs into the kitchen and hold her for me while I mixed formula and boiled bottles.

The minute I put Bridie down for a nap, Mavis would come up with some obscure housekeeping task, or tell Patty that I would play tea party with her. If I wasn't changing diapers, I was sewing hems, peeling carrots, waxing the floor, reading stories, cooking a ham, or making finger sandwiches for Mavis's bridge club. All these foolish things, when all I wanted to do was sit and hold my baby.

But I was aware that if I folded, if I broke down in front of Mavis, she would declare the situation a mess and demand George reconsider his plans. One day she actually said at the dinner table, "Has it occurred to either of you that this child could be put up for adoption with a young childless couple? Wouldn't that be a better solution for all concerned?"

George got up from the table and left the room.

So, while I made damn sure that I always had a smile on my face and a spring in my step, George did his best to make my life easier when he got home. He'd play with Patty instead of reading in his study, which made a big difference in her behaviour. He should've been doing that all along. The child was crazy about him.

One morning, I was in the kitchen making a cheesecake for Mavis's hospital auxiliary meeting when Bridie gave a terrible cry. I hurried into my room and there was Patty with her hand inside the crib, pinching the baby.

"Stop that at once!" I shouted. When I reached Patty, I grabbed her arm and hit her hand. "Bad girl! Don't you ever hurt Bridie like that. She's only little."

Patty started to cry. "I only wanted her to wake up."

"You're a big girl now. You know that pinching someone hurts, so don't lie to me."

"I'm not lying!" she cried. "I want Mommy!"

I realized I had to nip this in the bud, so I sat on my bed and pulled Patty into my lap. "That's all right, Patty. Eileen isn't cross any more. I know you didn't mean to hurt the baby, and you'll never do it again."

She sniffed and wiped at her nose with her fist. "I just wanted her to wake up and play with me."

"How about I play with you? You go up and get the tea set ready and I'll bring up some sugar cookies. That's your favourite game."

"Okay!" She bounced off my lap and ran out of the room. I picked up Bridie, who had a big red mark on her upper thigh. "Oh, sweetheart. I'm so sorry." How was I going to protect her if I had to be everywhere at once? She settled against my chest and closed her eyes. She sucked on her tiny fist.

Determined not to leave her alone, I took a shawl and wrapped her up against me and tied the ends together. That's how I ended up surviving those first six weeks, with Bridie against my heart and Patty by the hand. I was determined to outwit Mavis at her own game.

And then in late November, George came home one day and said he wasn't feeling well. He told Mavis he'd sleep in his study because he didn't want to give her the bug that was going around. Naturally, I was up through the night, and when I went to get Bridie's bottle, I heard something coming from his study. I tiptoed over to the closed door. George was crying like I've never heard anyone cry before. He sounded totally despondent. I wanted to go in and tell him everything would be all right, but I knew better. This was a man in despair and he needed to be alone.

That night confirmed to me that there was much more to this story than just a helpless girl by the side of the road. I'd probably never know the whole truth, but I knew it had broken George's heart.

And that broke mine.

CHAPTER SEVEN

1955

My little missy was the most adorable child on the planet. She made me laugh every single day. She called me Mama and George was Pops. Mavis didn't like that, but it wasn't short for Papa. He'd given her a balloon once when she was two and it popped in her face. She laughed and laughed and that's how George got his name.

Bridie called Mavis by her first name. I was surprised Mavis didn't insist on being called Mrs. Mackenzie. Patty was Patty-Cake. Patty liked it but had to pretend otherwise. Patty really did love Bridie, but only when her mother wasn't around, which was very confusing for a ten-year-old. I was certain that Mavis would have Patty turning on Bridie before too long.

Mavis was beyond jealous of Bridie. Not just because Bridie was a gorgeous child, but because she was always happy and energetic and ready for anything. Patty was moodier, and unfortunately, she looked more like her mother than her father.

And it bothered Mavis terribly that George adored Bridie. He loved his own child too, of course, but there was no denying the sparkle in his eye when he looked at our girl.

"What shall we do today?" he'd say to the girls at the dining room table on Saturday mornings.

Five-year-old Bridie always put her hand in the air, just like the teacher taught her in primary school. "Let's go fishing, Pops!"

"I hate fishing." Patty would frown. "Let's go for ice cream!"

"Why don't we do both?" he'd say.

"Yay!" Bridie would clap her hands and shake her head back and forth with glee, her golden curls bouncing around her chubby cheeks. I wanted to squeeze her all day, every day.

Mavis always said no to fishing, so George and the girls would end up just going for ice cream, but that was okay with Bridie. As long as she had her Pops by the hand, she was happy.

George was still the only one who could get Bridie to sleep if she wasn't feeling well. He'd hold her close to his chest and she'd be out like a light. He'd sit with her on his chest all night rather than disturb her. Mavis thought it was a lot of nonsense, but George would just ignore her.

He became very good at ignoring Mavis. At times, I almost felt sorry for her. Theirs was not a happy marriage, as much as Mavis pretended it was at her soirees. She'd twitter about and sit on George's lap from time to time. She'd cozy up to him when he was talking to other women, just to let them know that they could look but not touch.

I knew the real story. They didn't often sleep in the same bed. George had a settee in his study that was his favourite place to nap, and I'd frequently hear him come downstairs after midnight to spend the rest of the night alone.

There were a lot of things I saw about marriage that didn't quite fit the fantasy. I became relieved I'd never bothered. Not that I had ever had an opportunity, but I liked the story that I'd been wooed by many but was just too darn choosy.

And it turned out I was intimate with a man. George and I shared a lot over the years. Things he really should've been sharing with his wife. But we were such close friends, George knew he could tell me anything.

Well, not everything. I figured if he wanted me to know Bridie's story he would've told me by now, so I never pushed.

The only thing I missed out on was sex, which never interested me. Too messy and awkward, from what I understood. And you can't tell me that a double chocolate cake doesn't give you as much pleasure as rolling around in sweaty sheets. No, there was nothing missing from my crazy life.

I had more than enough love.

IT WAS ABOUT CHRISTMASTIME THAT YEAR WHEN PATTY SHOWED up after school without Bridie. She was responsible for walking Bridie home. When she came through the back door without her, I was instantly fearful.

"Where's your sister?"

"She's not my sister. Stop calling her that. All my friends think I'm weird because I have to look after a servant's kid."

I stopped breathing for several reasons. For now, I was concerned only with Bridie. I walked over to Patty as she took off her boots and shook my wooden spoon at her. "You tell me where she is, or so help me, I'll give you a smack."

"You do and I'll tell Mother!" Patty stuck her tongue out at me. I'm not sure who was more surprised, me or her.

I wasn't getting anywhere with the obstinate child, so I put my own boots on and got my coat, hurrying up the street, trying to find Bridie. I kept calling her name until my throat closed over with fear. For the first time in a long time, I realized I was in really bad shape; I was completely winded by the time I got to the school. It occurred to me that I should get George involved, but that would mean running back to the house. Luckily, I didn't have to decide what to do, because there was Bridie, swinging on a swing in the school playground.

I waved at her and she waved back. My relief was overwhelming. This mothering business was a giant can of worms. Fabulous on one hand, but thoroughly terrifying on the other.

"Hi, princess," I panted. "You were supposed to come home with Patty. You had me worried."

"Sorry."

She kept swinging.

"Are you all right? You look a little upset." I forced my own large bum into the swing next to her. It was very uncomfortable. I'd be lucky if I got out of it.

"I don't like Patty-Cake anymore."

"And why's that?"

"She said I didn't belong to anyone. She said everyone has a family, but I don't. That you're not my mother and Pops is not my father. That I came out of a cabbage patch."

Why hadn't I addressed this sooner? I'd known I would have to at some point, and suddenly here it was, with no warning.

"Well, I can tell you one thing, Bridie. You didn't come out of a cabbage patch."

"Oh, I figured that out myself. I'm not round *or* green."

I looked away so I wouldn't laugh.

"Patty is wrong. You do have a family. I am your mother, in that I take care of you and love you just like any mother, and Pops is your father, because he looks after you and loves you just like any father. Your real mother died a long time ago, so Pops took you home. And I'm so glad he did, or I'd have no one to look after. We chose to have you with us, and that makes you a very special girl. Not everyone gets chosen."

"Does Patty-Cake like me?"

"Of course she does. She was being silly today. Sometimes people say things they don't mean."

"Does my real mother live in heaven?"

"Yes. And she watches over you every day. You have your very own angel looking after you."

Bridie put her feet in the sand to stop the swing. "I wish she were here. Why did she go?"

"She didn't want to. She had an accident and Pops tried to save her, but he couldn't. It was a terrible time for him, and the only thing that made him feel better was you."

"Poor Pops. We should make him fish for supper."

"As a matter of fact, we're having salmon. Want to come

home and help me poach it? I have to make a white onion sauce too. You can stir it."

She gave me a small smile.

Walking home holding hands with my sweetie, I debated whether to tell George about what happened. I didn't like to get Patty in trouble, but I knew that her words must have come from Mavis, and they had to be stopped. Unfortunately, when I did tell him, he didn't wait to talk to Patty quietly.

It was just after supper, and Bridie was excused from the table. George signalled for Patty to stay. She looked at me as if she knew what was coming.

"Why didn't you make sure that Bridie came home with you after school today?"

Mavis spoke up. "The child wouldn't leave with her. What's Patty supposed to do? Drag her home?"

"I'm asking Patty."

Patty looked fearful. "She wouldn't come."

"And why wouldn't she come?"

"I don't know."

"Did you tell her that she doesn't belong to this family? That Eileen isn't her mother and I'm not her father? That you don't like having to take care of a servant's kid?"

Patty's head hung down.

Mavis was all set to say something, but George put up his hand and stopped her. "There are no excuses, Mavis. She had no business saying those things to a five-year-old. And I have to wonder where she heard that sort of talk. Eileen is not our servant, for one thing. We were going to tell Bridie the circumstances of her birth when she was a little older, but it seems it's been handled now. I would just like you to remember, Patty, that being a member of a family doesn't always mean you have to be a blood relative. People come into our lives who have no connection to us at all and end up being closer to us than anyone. We are all God's children. We are all members of the same family, and in this family, we love and take care of each other. You are Bridie's big sister, and it's your job to always make sure she feels safe and loved. You protect her the way that we protect you. I know you're a good girl with a big heart, and you'll never make Bridie feel badly about herself again. Isn't that right?"

Patty's tears fell down her cheeks. "Okay, Papa. I'm sorry."

"I know you are. Now come here." George held out his arms and Patty ran into them. He kissed the top of her head. "That's my girl. Now you're excused."

She quickly left the room without a backward glance. Mavis sat stony-faced at the end of the table. "That was quite a performance. Everything the child said was true. You're not her father and Eileen is not her mother. And what is Eileen if not our maid? She cooks and cleans and we pay her. Is that not the definition of a maid? Stop finding fault with your own kin. If Patty grows up thinking you love Bridie more than her, what kind of a father are you? Put that in your pipe and smoke it!"

Mavis got up and left the table too. George and I sat there looking at each other. He did light his pipe and smoke it, just to settle his nerves.

"I shouldn't have said anything," I said.

"You were right to tell me." George blew a smoke ring. "Although it's times like this that I wonder if I did the right thing. It's as if there are battle lines drawn in this family. No one is able to relax and just enjoy each other. It was probably too much to ask of Mavis, and she's right about Patty. I don't want her feeling like I have a favourite. I'll have to be more careful."

I nodded my head. "Me too. I threatened to hit Patty with a spoon if she didn't tell me where Bridie was. Not exactly an adult thing to do."

George took a long draw on his pipe. "You know something else? I'm thinking that Mavis always feels like the two of us gang up on her."

"We do."

"I should take her away for a few days. Just her and me. Would you be okay with looking after the girls?"

"Of course. What are servants for?"

"I love you, Eileen."

"I know."

෯

HE ENDED UP TAKING MAVIS TO HALIFAX FOR A WEEK OF SHOP-ping in the new year. While they were away, I was able to cement the relationship between the girls by letting them both sleep in my bed with me. We shared late-night snacks and read stories and they stayed up later than they should have, but sometimes breaking the rules is a potent tool.

Without George and Mavis around, the girls relaxed, and we spent a lot of time baking cookies. Patty didn't have to worry about getting her clothes dirty, and she was in her glory. Sometimes we just had cake for supper. I made a big deal about how they had to keep it a secret and they giggled in excitement about pulling one over on the adults.

When George and Mavis came home, I could tell instantly that the trip had done both of them a lot of good. They were more pleasant to each other, and Mavis had let down her guard. I hoped it would last, but I was realistic. We were in a honeymoon stage, and I'd go along for the ride as long as I could.

෯

BY THE TIME PATTY WAS FIFTEEN AND BRIDIE WAS TEN, THEY were as different as chalk and cheese. Patty loved movie maga-zines about her favourite stars: Rock Hudson, Paul Newman, Elizabeth Taylor, and Doris Day. She spent most of her week-ends with a transistor radio stuck to her ear, dancing to "The Twist" or crooning to "Let It Be Me" by the Everly Brothers.

Bridie would stomp into the kitchen in her dirty T-shirt and cut-offs, her hair in messy braids.

"Mama! How come Cake won't help me build the treehouse? I've been out there for two hours and all she does is lie there on the chaise lounge. Why does she want a tan? What's so great about that?"

My hands were full of biscuit dough, so I ran them under the tap and wiped them on a dishtowel. "Want a drink?"

Bridie wiped her nose on her arm. "Kool-Aid, please."

I went to the fridge and took out a pitcher of her favourite liquid, even though George said it wasn't good for her. "When something stains a countertop, what's it doing to her stomach?" he'd gripe.

Pouring a glass, I brought it over to the table where she sat. "First of all, stop calling her Cake. You know she hates it."

"That's why I do it. She's so easy to annoy."

Takes after her mother, I thought. I sat opposite her. "When some girls get to be a certain age, they like to be pretty, and getting a tan makes you pretty, I guess. That's what my sister Betty always said, though I never saw the sense in it."

"I can't figure it out either. It's so boring. You'd think she'd want a treehouse. That way she could spy on Ray across the street. She likes him. Did you know that?"

"I didn't."

"Oh yeah. She waits around until he comes out of his house to go to school. Then she just happens to come out and they walk together. It's sickening."

"There's nothing wrong with liking a boy."

"Ugh. Cake wants to be his main squeeze."

"Main squeeze? Where did you hear that?"

"Kids at school. I keep my ears open, ya know."

Bridie also kept her mouth open at school. There wasn't a parent-teacher conference I went to that one of the teachers didn't comment on Bridie's talkative nature. I got annoyed with her grade-five teacher.

"It seems to me you'd want a child to be inquisitive. It shows she's thinking."

"She's thinking about everything under the sun but her schoolwork. It's hard to teach a chatterbox."

George never met Bridie's teachers because he knew Mavis would have a fit, so I'd report back to him and he agreed with me. "How's a child to learn if she doesn't ask questions? That's the trouble with school. They want to make every kid fit the mold, and not the other way around."

But I did understand how difficult it would be to keep Bridie from being bored. She was like a firefly, flitting from one thing to another, always searching for the meaning of things. As much as she seemed like a confident child, I know she felt insecure, especially if her father wasn't around. Sometimes George would have to go to a medical conference, and while she never cried in front of him when he left, I'd hear her in her bed at night, sniffling, before she would crawl in with me. I never asked her what was wrong. I knew the feeling. When George was gone, we both felt a bit lonely.

I'm afraid as hard as we tried over the years, the chasm between the two factions in our house became well established. It was Mavis and Patty versus George, Bridie, and me. Mavis worked in secret over the years to get Patty to prey on George's guilty conscience about Bridie. Whatever she wanted, Patty got. George didn't really notice anymore; he was a very busy man, and the less grief he got from Mavis and Patty, the better.

I could hardly say anything. I wasn't George's wife, as much as I fantasized I was. I lived in my own little world and was fine with that. The only time it ever got awkward was when I was with family.

In 1961 my father died, and George and I went up to River Bourgeois for his funeral. Mavis said she refused to take Patty because Patty didn't know him from a hole in the ground. As ever, her sensitivity knew no bounds. George didn't want to take Bridie, as much as Bridie begged, because he thought she was too young to attend a funeral. There was no way on God's green earth that I was going to let Mavis look after Bridie alone, so I rang up the mother of Bridie's best friend, Judith, and asked if Bridie could stay with them for the weekend. She was happy to help and Bridie was over the moon that she was going to have her first sleepover.

There was a good crowd at the church, the cemetery, and the church hall afterward. Betty made an ass of herself boo-hooing. A fifty-three-year-old woman with three hulking sons in their twenties, none of them married, going on like she was six, about how her life was over now that "Daddy" was dead.

Betty didn't even like our dad. He always told her to take the muck off her face and stop being so boy crazy.

At the end of the day, we went back to the house. As the male relatives gathered in the living room, we women sat at the kitchen table, drinking yet more tea and hoeing into the crustless sandwiches the church ladies had packed up, all of us with our shoes and girdles off.

My mother looked done in, with big circles under her eyes. I patted her hand and she gave me a grateful look.

My aunt Jean took a sip of her tea. "How are things in Sydney, Eileen? It's not like I can call Mavis and chat, or, God forbid, drop in for a visit to see Patty. She barely knows who I am. What a cold fish her mother is. I can't for the life of me understand why George puts up with it."

"He doesn't notice."

"Of course he doesn't," Betty sneered. "You're there to make things all better. If you left, maybe he'd take a look around and give her the boot. It's like he's not a member of the family anymore. We never see him. Did you know that people talk about your 'arrangement'? Not that anyone seriously believes that George loves you in that way. I mean, look at you. You're as big as a house."

My mother banged down her teacup. "Honestly, Betty. Do you ever have anything nice to say? And while we're on the subject, you should talk!"

Betty looked horrified. "Mother! Daddy just died."

"You haven't seen him in eight months!" Mom said. "Just keep your trap shut. You're wearing me out."

I'd never heard my mother say anything critical to Betty, so she really was distraught. Betty turned a lovely shade of puce.

My mother turned to me. "How's Bridie? You never bring her to visit. You know I can't be traipsing down to the city, with my heart condition."

"I'm sorry. I wish I had a car."

"George could take you up here when he comes on his fishing trips," Aunt Jean said. "There's no reason we can't see that child more often. It's like she's a secret or something."

Betty folded her arms across her chest. "The whole story smacks of deceit. I can't figure it out. Suddenly a child just falls into your lap and everyone is okay with you looking after it? I think Mavis needs her head examined, putting up with you two."

"You're just jealous, Betty. I have a beautiful daughter and you don't."

Our mother put her hands over her face. "Please. Stop it."

Aunt Jean jumped up and put her arms around her sister's shoulders. "You two should be ashamed of yourselves. Your poor mother has just had the worst day of her life and you're squabbling like children. Pull yourselves together."

"I'm sorry, Mom." I left the table and went out on the porch swing. I knew Betty wouldn't come outside. The woman never took a breath of fresh air if she could help it. It was a good thing her sons spent their leisure time with their dad growing up, hunting and fishing, or they'd never have seen the light of day.

When someone else called attention to my life and asked nosy questions, my unease grew. It probably did look fishy to others, all of us living under the same roof. But really, did anyone give it much thought, other than Mom and Aunt Jean? They certainly didn't have the kind of relationship a grandmother would like with her grandchildren, but I'd always assumed it was Mavis they blamed for the distance between the generations. Not George or me.

But something under my skin always made itself felt when I thought about George. He was the one who never wanted Bridie to come to St. Peter's or River Bourgeois. He always had a hundred excuses to not take us with him, when he did come. Bridie would beg to go fishing in his old childhood river and streams, but he stuck close to Sydney or Mira when he took her with him.

I watched the sun go down across the field of my childhood home. I'd never again see my dad walk out of the barn and come across the yard for supper. Tears sprang to my eyes. I'd spent too many years in Sydney and not enough time coming home to visit my parents like a good daughter should have. The time I wasted only thinking of myself and George and Bridie.

Bridie was my child, but she wasn't. As much as I pushed the thought away, I knew that George was Bridie's father. He had to be. He loved her with a passion that defied all logic.

But if that was true, then George wasn't who I thought he was. I just loved him too much to accuse him of such a beastly thing. So I kept my mouth shut.

My father would have been ashamed of me.

CHAPTER EIGHT

Two years later, when Bridie turned thirteen, the real fireworks between the girls started. With four women in the house, two on the upside of puberty and two on the downhill slide, the atmosphere crackled with angst and hostility.

Patty shouted down the stairs, "Eileen! Tell that brat of yours that if she goes in my underwear drawer one more time, I'm going to knock her block off!"

Before I even had a chance to answer her, Bridie yelled from the dining room, where she was setting up her science project. Naturally, it was a volcano. Why not have everything erupt?

"I wasn't in your stinkin' drawers!"

Mavis was on the phone in the living room, smoking her cigarettes and having her second martini of the afternoon. "Why can't I have some peace and quiet in this house!"

When one of these episodes happened, I was the one who would station myself in the hallway, where I had a good view of all the warring factions. Patty raced down the stairs and held a bra in my face. "I know she had her grubby little hands on this! There's sawdust on it!"

"Maybe from you rolling in the hay with Sting Ray!" Bridie chirped.

"Eileen, will you shut these girls up?"

I whispered to Patty, "I'll talk to her." Then I reached into my apron pocket and took out a ten-dollar bill. I'd learned years ago to defuse hostility with money. "Go buy yourself another one. My treat."

Patty took the money—without a thank you, I might add—and stormed back up the stairs. I shut the French doors to the living room so Mavis could have some privacy and went into the dining room. My hands were on my hips and I scowled. It didn't bother Bridie in the least.

"Will you please stay out of her room? What do you want to go in there for, anyway?"

"It's my mission in life to find her diary."

I kept a straight face. "A person's diary is special, and it's none of your business. I forbid you to go into Patty's room. Do you hear me?"

"Yes, ma'am."

"I'm not fooling around. I'll tell your father, and he'll be very disappointed."

That's all I ever had to say. For Bridie, that was the worst thing that could happen, having her father disappointed in her. But she was getting braver as she grew older, and two months later on a hot June day, Patty found Bridie coming into her room through the upstairs window.

Patty let out such a screech that her mother and father and I came running up the stairs and hurried into her room, just in time to see her push Bridie back out the window. I thought George was going to faint.

Bridie stuck her tongue out at Patty before the trellis she was hanging off of broke and Bridie went crashing into the cedar hedge below. We were all screaming, as we raced down the stairs and rushed outside.

"Oh, great!" Patty wailed. "Now she's dead and Daddy will blame me!"

George got to her first. I could tell right away her arm was broken. She had blood running out of her nose and mouth. Even Mavis looked horrified.

"Mavis! Call an ambulance," George shouted. Mavis took off like a shot. I was ever so grateful. I knelt by Bridie's side and tried to comfort her. "Sweetheart, you're going to be all right."

"It's important to keep still," George told her. "We have to be careful of your neck."

"Am I a pain in the neck, Pops?" Bridie whispered.

"You sure are," Patty snivelled. "But don't you dare die. Prom's coming up."

"I won't die. But just in case, can I have your Shirley Temple doll?"

"Why do you want her? You hate dolls."

"Her eyes close."

George touched Bridie's cheeks and forehead. "Stop talking, little one. Patty, run inside and get me a blanket."

Bridie spent the next week in the hospital. They operated on her arm, which was badly broken, and as I sat with her, I told her of my adventure with my broken leg, minus some details I'd never tell anyone.

"And that's why I limp."

"Will my arm work when I get the cast off?"

"It will be fine. Your uncle Donny did the surgery and he's very good."

"I don't like him."

"No one likes him," I confided, "but that doesn't mean he's not a good surgeon."

"I don't think Patty hates me anymore."

"Why's that?"

"She gave me her movie magazines to read. They're boring, but it was a nice gesture."

I agreed. It was a nice gesture.

Patty almost didn't make it to the prom. Her father was so angry at her for shoving her sister out the window, he said she was grounded for twelve years. Even I thought that was a bit much. Mavis went on the rampage and told George he was being an ass. It wasn't Patty's fault the trellis broke, and she hadn't forced Bridie to climb the thing.

In the end, Patty did go to the prom. Ray arrived at the door with a corsage in a box. Bridie sat on the stairs watching the proceedings, weighed down by her heavy cast. George and Mavis took pictures, and Patty even asked to have a picture taken with me. She waved Bridie over too.

"Nah," Bridie said. "I look a fright."

George and I grinned at each other. Mavis said that at least ten times a day, and our little parrot had picked it up.

It was a long and hot summer for a girl who loved to climb trees, play baseball, and build forts. She could do none of those things well with the cast on her arm, and slowly, I saw some of Bridie's spunk leave her. I was worried about her and said as much to George one night in his study.

"She didn't even want Kool-Aid today."

"That's a good thing."

"You know what I mean. I've never seen her sad, and it breaks my heart."

"What do you suggest we do?"

"Take her on a fishing trip to Grand River. Show her the places you loved as a kid. My mom would love to see Bridie, and so would your mother. There's no reason to keep her cooped up here for the summer. Even if you only come for a day or two, I could stay up there with her until the end of August, and then her cast comes off and she'll be ready for school."

George instantly got that vaguely worried expression he wore whenever I mentioned home. "Do you really think that's necessary?"

I finally blew my top. "What is wrong with you? Why do you keep Bridie from her family, the people who would love her the most? She lives with constant stress. She knows Mavis and Patty think of her as an outsider. Is that fair? You asked me to help you raise this child. Well, I'm telling you, it's time to stop being so selfish and let me do what I think is right. I'm her mother, goddammit."

George stared at me for a few moments while my heart pounded in my chest.

"I'm sorry, Eileen. You're right. You've done everything I've asked of you and more. I'll arrange for a few days off and we'll have a jolly adventure."

When I told Bridie we were going to stay with her grandmother Jessie, she hopped around like a bunny rabbit, even with her enormous cast. She couldn't wait to tell Mavis and Patty at dinner.

"And we're going fishing and everything! Oh, this is so great! Do you have a dog at your farm, Mama?"

"I think there's a couple," I said. "And best of all, there are chickens at my house. You can collect the eggs for your grandmother."

"I've died and gone to heaven," Bridie sighed, before stuffing her face with mashed potatoes.

"Don't drown with that cast on," Patty said.

"Really, Patty?" her father said. "That's the best you can do?"

"Have a great time, squirt. Go bug other people for a change."

Bridie grinned.

Mavis was playing with her food. "How long will you be gone, George?"

"Three days. I can't afford to take off any more than that right now."

"So, going to Halifax for a few days will have to wait until September, is that right?"

I glanced over at George, who looked confused and then sheepish.

"Oh, right. I forgot about that."

"Apparently."

Don't do it, I thought to myself. Don't let her bully you into reneging on your promise.

George hesitated and my heart sank. Then he said, "I'll take you to Halifax for a week, Mavis, to make it up to you."

Mavis sat there, all butter wouldn't melt, now that she'd secured a victory over her thirteen-year-old nemesis. God. How I refrained from choking Mavis was a mystery.

☙☞

BRIDIE HAD HER NOSE PRESSED TO THE BACK WINDOW OF THE car the entire time it took to drive to St. Peter's. She never stopped talking and asking her Pops what it was like as a kid growing up in the country.

"We were pretty close to town," he said. "Your mama was further out. They lived on a real farm. My dad was a doctor, like me, so he needed to be closer to folks."

"Did your dad teach you to fish?"

"Yes, but he didn't go as often as he would've liked. Kind of like me, I guess."

"Did Uncle Donny like fishing?"

"Yep. Fishing for girls."

Bridie laughed and laughed.

I put the window down and didn't care if the wind whipped my hair around. Looking out at the blue Bras d'Or Lakes, with green hills rolling down to the water and the smell of the ocean filling my lungs, made me feel giddy. This scenery lived in my heart, and just the sight of it made me feel like a young girl again. How I wished I were Bridie's age and had the chance to start over. Why had I been so worried about everything back then? Life had been simple and heavenly, if only we'd known it. This was what I wanted for Bridie. The simple enjoyment of a summer's day in the country, with wildflowers and the scent of strawberries in the air.

I turned to say something to George as we were going around a curve and saw he was pale and perspiring.

"Are you okay?"

He nodded. "Just indigestion. It'll pass."

We stopped at George's house first so Aunt Jean could have a visit before we drove to River Bourgeois. She was at the clothesline when we pulled into the yard. Bridie was out the door before we'd come to a full stop. She ran up to Aunt Jean and put her arms around her as best she could with her cast.

"Remember me?" Bridie grinned.

"Who could forget you?" Aunt Jean laughed. She bent down and gave my girl a big hug. It made my heart glad.

"You see, this was a great idea," I said before I got out of the car. George was a little slower getting out. Indigestion, my eye. He was getting funny again about being home. I felt like choking him too.

Aunt Jean had a great lunch prepared, with seafood chowder, tea biscuits, tea, and lemon meringue pie. Bridie had two pieces.

"This is delicious, Pops's mom. You're a great cook."

"Why, thank you, honey. I baked it in your honour. And please call me Gran. That's what Patty calls me."

"I'm a really good cook too, aren't I, Mama? I'll have to add this recipe to my repertoire."

Aunt Jean covered her mouth with a napkin, not quite hiding her delighted smile. She winked at me and I looked over at George. He was looking down at his soup bowl.

It was such a pleasure to sit at a table and be able to focus on my girl. Aunt Jean wanted to know all about Bridie's life, and Bridie happily filled her in on what was going on in her world. How she and Judith were best friends, and they liked to go up in the treehouse and spy on Patty and Ray kissing in his backyard.

"How is that possible?" her father asked.

"We use binoculars."

"Bridie, it's not nice to spy on people. How would you like it?"

"I'd love it!" she said. "I'd pretend I didn't know anyone was watching and pick my nose."

Aunt Jean couldn't stop laughing. After a while, George finally cheered up and relaxed, happy to show off this delightful creature to his mother. It was just the best afternoon.

When we finally pulled into my mother's yard, she too was sitting out waiting for us on the porch swing. Once again, Bridie made a beeline for her grandmother and nearly knocked her over with the weight of the cast. To add to the melee, our two border collies ran around in circles and jumped all over Bridie, who then took off across the yard with them yapping at her heels.

"This is the best place in the whole world!"

George stayed for a bit but then went back to his mother's. He said he'd be along in the morning to take Bridie fishing. She jumped into his arms and hugged him tight before saying goodbye.

Mom, Bridie, and I had a light supper of tomato soup and grilled cheese sandwiches, with molasses cookies for dessert. I was the happiest I'd ever been. To see the look of love on my mother's face for this exquisite child filled me with gladness. But how I wished my dad could have spent time with her.

At bedtime, Bridie insisted on going outside to kiss the dogs good night first. When she was ready for bed, I popped into her bedroom and sat by her side.

"I've had the best day of my life. Can I live here forever?"

"Would you like that?"

"Oh yes. As long as Pops came with us."

I brushed her hair away from her forehead. "And what are the chances of that happening?"

"Not good."

"You'd miss Judith."

"You're right." She gave a big yawn. "Maybe I could come here for the whole summer next year?"

"That sounds like a grand idea."

She was asleep before I reached the door. When I went downstairs and joined my mom in the living room, I collapsed on Dad's old reading chair. "What a day."

Mom put down her knitting. "She is the sweetest child I have ever met. And that includes you and your sister."

"Gee, thanks, Mom. But I know, she is, isn't she?"

"And she's so beautiful, with that golden mane of hair. How sad that her people will never know about her. I wonder who her parents were? Did you ever find out any more information on that score?"

"Nothing. As far as I know, the missing person case is still open, but no one ever did report anyone missing at the time of the accident. And who doesn't call the police if their child is missing?"

"It's a mystery, all right. Let's just be happy she came into your life, because it's been a blessing for you. I always knew you would make a wonderful mother. Better than your sister."

"How is the royal pain?"

"She's convinced her husband is having an affair."

I rolled my eyes. "Fraser? Fat chance! Unless he's dating a moose."

"Betty's on a campaign to spruce herself up. She dyed her hair blond."

"This I gotta see!"

"It looks terrible, but I kept my mouth shut. You know what happens when you cross Betty."

"Are you sure we're sisters, Mom? Did you have an affair of your own with the milkman?"

"I wish. Luther was a good-looking fellow."

I was up at dawn, thinking I'd be shaking my sleepyhead awake, but she was already sitting at the kitchen table, impatiently shaking her foot. "When's he coming?"

"Soon. I'll make your breakfast and pack you both a lunch."

"I can't eat. I'm too excited."

"And here I thought you'd like to gather eggs from the hens this morning."

She bolted out of her chair. "I forgot! Can I? Can I?"

We went out to the henhouse with a wicker basket. I showed her how to put her hand gently under the hen, but that didn't go so well. Mother hen was not impressed and flew at Bridie, feathers flapping. We ended up gathering the eggs of the hens already eating their feed outside. Some had brown shells and the others white.

"I want only the brown eggs!"

I let Bridie crack the eggs in a bowl and she scrambled them up, declaring they were the most delicious eggs in the universe.

"You'll have to tell the hens that," I laughed.

George was at the door on the dot of seven. I passed him a wicker hamper with their lunch inside. "There's a bottle of milk in there for Bridie, but you can use some of it for your tea. I put it in a Thermos."

"Sounds great. Come on, chicken little. Let's go find some fish!"

Bridie ran out to the car and sat in the front seat. As George pulled away, she rolled down her window. "I forgot to kiss you goodbye!" She blew kisses in the air until she was out of sight.

Mom wasn't up yet, so I poured a cup of tea and sat on the porch swing, my favourite place to sit and think. I resolved that Bridie would spend all her summers here from now on. My mother wasn't getting any younger, and I needed to be here for longer than a day or two. Come to think of it, I wasn't getting any younger either. It was hard to believe, but George and I were fifty-three.

I felt my age by the end of the day and knew I should try and lose a few pounds, because I was wheezing when I went up the stairs, and a few times I'd get pain in my shoulder or arm. Mom had a heart condition. Maybe I did too, but it was too upsetting to think about. What would Bridie do without me? Who would look after her if something happened to me? And what if something happened to George? Who would my darling girl live with? Mavis would leave town and not tell Bridie where she was going. The thought of Betty coming to the rescue made me shudder; she'd have that free spirit hogtied in a matter of days.

Sitting there in the early morning sun was supposed to be relaxing. Instead, I'd worked myself into a lather, and when Mom joined me on the swing, tears were falling down my cheeks.

"Good gracious, child. What's wrong?"

"Who's going to look after Bridie when I'm dead?"

"Well, hopefully you'll live until she's a grown woman and she'll take care of herself. I have no doubt that she'll make it in the world with or without you. There's just something about her."

That made me feel better. "I never thought about it before, but I should make a will."

"I thought you only made a will if you had property. Do you even own a pot to piss in?"

I was instantly indignant but quickly fell to laughing. "You're right. I have nothing that's mine except Bridie's old crib and high chair in the garage. And the clothes on my back. But I do have a small savings account if I need it, so I'm not a complete failure."

Mom reached over and slapped my knee. "You are not a failure at all, child. Stop being silly."

We sat and watched the dogs have a great game of hide-and-go-seek with the barn cats. Then my mother turned to look at me.

"I plan on leaving the house and property to you. I just have to make the arrangements."

A shiver went through me, like someone had walked over my grave. "Betty will never let it happen. She'll haunt me for the rest of my life and say you're being unfair."

"I won't be here to listen to her."

"That's too generous. I don't deserve it."

"I think you do. Betty has a house. She doesn't need another one."

Taking my mom's hand, I rested my head on her shoulder.

"You don't know your own worth, Eileen. Why do you think Bridie is as special as she is? It's because of you."

☙☙

I WASN'T USED TO DOING NOTHING ALL DAY, SO I BUZZED AROUND my mother's house and gave it a good mucking out. It needed it. As I dusted and mopped, I thought about all of it being mine. What a lovely surprise. Maybe I could persuade George to let me live here while my mother was alive. He could come up and visit Bridie. Surely that would make Mavis and Patty happy.

By the time Bridie and George got home, I had it all mapped out in my own head. It was a great plan. But right now, there was a little girl who was bursting to tell me about her wondrous day along the river, catching fish.

"It was amazing, Mama! My next project is to make my own flies! Did you know there are as many flies as there are fish? Each fish loves a different kind. And it takes a lot of practise to get your line in the water. I got the hook caught in my sweater a couple of times, and once in Pops's hat!"

George called to Bridie from the screen door. "There's another part of fishing you need to learn. We have to clean them next. Get Mama to give you some knives and come out to the well."

Bridie's sun-kissed cheeks shone. "Oh goodie, fish guts!"

I handed over the knives. "Point them at the ground, please."

Needless to say, we had a mess of trout for dinner, with new potatoes and green beans. Bridie fell asleep in my dad's chair while she listened to the adults talk about nothing in particular. George got up to go.

"I have to run some errands for my mother tomorrow morning, so I'll be over after lunch to pick up Bridie. I'm not sure I could do another full day of fishing with her. She scared off more fish than we caught with her constant chattering."

"She needed this." I smiled at him.

He smiled back. "You're right."

In the morning, Bridie collected the eggs by herself, and again she insisted on eating only the brown ones. She made a couple of banana loaves with my mother and rolled out the pastry for a blueberry pie, telling her grandmother that she didn't think it was necessary to drench the blueberries with nutmeg. "Nana, cinnamon is all you need. Cinnamon, sugar, and flour."

"Is that so?" Mom nodded.

"Nutmeg has a bitter aftertaste, don't you find?"

"Can't say I do."

At ten-thirty, Betty showed up. I almost didn't recognize her with her blond hair. It looked ghastly, but Betty was obviously proud of it. She put her purse on the table and her hands on her hips. "Well, now. Here's a surprise! How are you, Eileen? Hello, Bridie. Let me take a look at you."

Bridie turned around at the kitchen counter as instructed and I could see Betty was dazzled by Bridie's untamed tomboy beauty.

"Look at that hair!" Betty cried. "It's almost the same colour as mine!"

In your dreams, I thought.

"I think your hair would be described as brassy," Bridie told her. "I read that in a magazine once."

I could see my mother's shoulders shake up and down as she tried to keep her laughter to herself. She pretended to shine the toaster with a dishtowel.

The wind went out of Betty's sails. She sat at the table and crossed her legs, picking at the edge of the plastic tablecloth. I joined her.

"How are the boys? Any future daughters-in-law in the picture?"

"That will be the day. They're perfectly content to let me do everything. It's like having a herd of elephants for dinner every night. I might as well run a boarding house, with the amount of food I make."

Bridie sat at the table and stuck a knife down her cast to relieve the itching. I'd given up telling her to stop. "An itch needs to be scratched," she kept telling me.

She looked at Betty. "What's a boarding house?"

"You can rent rooms in your house and people stay there. You have to feed them too, and they pay you for it. A lot of widows do it for the money. There you go, Ma, something to think about."

Mom put the kettle on. "The last thing I need is a bunch of strangers in my house. I'm quite happy living alone."

Betty made a face. "I'd hate to live alone. I don't know how the spinster on the hill does it, living by herself since she was young girl."

"What's a spinster?" Bridie asked. "Do they always live on hills?"

"A woman who never married," I answered, "and no, they don't always live on hills."

"So you're a spinster?" Bridie deduced.

"I guess I am." I turned to Betty. "Who's the spinster on the hill?"

"Nell Sampson. You remember. Her parents used to own the store but they died when she was a teenager. Uncle Joe helped her get on her feet when it first happened."

I did remember her, of course; everyone knew when her parents died. But we'd never spoken at school that I could recall. She always kept to herself.

"She sews beautifully," Mom said. "Jean has several of her dresses. Don't know why I never bothered."

"The kids in town call her a witch. I have to go there in a few minutes to pick up a dress I ordered a while back," Betty said.

"Can I go with you?!" Bridie shouted. "I've never seen a spinster witch. Wait until I tell Judith!"

"No," I said. "She's just an ordinary woman."

"She can come for the drive," Betty said.

"Please, Mama! Please."

"I never see the child. What's wrong with that? We'll be a half hour at most."

I didn't trust Betty's driving. "I'll go too then."

"Well, since we're all going, would you like to come, Mom?" Betty asked.

"I'll stay home and watch the pie."

So off we went in Betty's Rambler, Bridie with her face between ours, leaning over the back seat. We actually had a pleasant conversation as we travelled down the road, remembering this and that from when we were youngsters, who lived where and wondering what happened to childhood friends. Being sisters as adults was a lot easier. I found I was comfortable with my child beside me. Bridie always gave me the confidence to stick up for myself. For the first time in my life, I liked my sister. Who knew?

When we pulled off the highway about a half a mile from Aunt Jean's, we passed an old cottage first.

"Why is that place boarded up?" Bridie asked.

"No one lives there now. The mother fell down the stairs and died years ago. The way the story goes, the daughter then drowned herself, but they never found her body. Her sweater washed up on the shore. A few weeks after that, the husband was found hanging from the rafters. No one wants to buy the place, and now the kids say it's haunted."

Bridie gave me a shocked look.

"Thanks a lot, Betty," I hissed. "You couldn't have kept that to yourself?"

"She asked me! It's the truth. Sometimes tragic things happen, Bridie, but that doesn't mean anything is going to happen to you. It was all a very long time ago."

I'd never seen Bridie quite so shaken. She slipped into the back seat and stared out the window. Betty had the sense of a goose. Honestly.

We pulled in behind a large house. It almost looked like a gingerbread house, the way it was perched up on the hill. There was something magical about it. There was a long clothesline of beautiful, colourful fabric hanging out to dry.

A black cat crossed in front of the car and sat on the back porch looking at us.

"She *is* a witch," Bridie whispered.

"Nonsense!" Betty laughed. "Do you want to come in?"

"No thanks," I said.

"Just as well. She's a bit cranky. You have to know how to handle her. Creative types are such a pain."

We watched Betty knock at the back door and barge right in. She was gone for a good fifteen minutes. I kept looking at my watch, hoping that George wasn't waiting back at Mom's.

"How long do you think it takes for a person to die when they hang themselves?"

I was so mad, I whipped around in my seat. "Betty had no right to tell you that. It's not something you should worry about. It's a sad, sad thing, that's all. And I don't want it ruining your trip. Do you hear me? Now stop thinking about it."

"How do you stop thinking about something?"

I wanted to hit Betty.

She finally came out with a dress wrapped in plastic draped over her arm. The spinster stood on the porch and watched her walk to the car. Betty opened the back door and asked Bridie to hold the dress in her lap. Then she got in and started the motor. The woman on the porch gave us a quick wave goodbye. Bridie was hiding, her head hardly above the car window, but she put her fingers against the glass in farewell.

When we passed the cottage, she covered her face with her hands.

CHAPTER NINE

It was around four-thirty when George and Bridie returned from their afternoon of fishing. I could tell something was wrong the minute they got out of the car. Bridie walked straight into the kitchen and glared at me.

"You better give him a talking to, because he's as grouchy as a bear. I didn't do a thing wrong. And I caught more fish than he did. He looks just like Patty when he sulks too!"

She stormed passed me and met her grandmother in the hallway.

"Did you have a nice afternoon, dear?"

"No, Nana, I didn't. I'm sorry, I'm not in the mood to discuss it. If you'll excuse me." And up the stairs she went, slamming the bedroom door for good measure.

Mom and I looked at each other. Then I went out on the back porch and stood there until George noticed me.

"We need to talk," he said.

"Come inside."

"No. Out in the barn." He stormed off.

Mom whispered behind me, "What's going on?"

"Damned if I know."

I crossed the yard and entered the dark, earthy gloom of the cow barn. Normally, I loved this quiet place, with its shafts of light peeking between the dried wood, but now I was on edge. I'd been on edge all afternoon, hoping that horrible story Betty blabbed wouldn't give Bridie nightmares.

"I knew this was a mistake!" he said. "Coming back here to this sad little town, with its miserable gossips and its backwater attitudes!"

"What are you on about?"

"That ridiculous sister of yours, telling Bridie all kinds of horrible tales about falling down stairs and drownings and hangings. Calling people witches and spinsters on the hill. That poor woman! What right does anyone have to say such things about an innocent soul. And who is she to fill that child's head with such monstrous stories? I'm sure her own dumb lugs don't care about stuff like that, but Bridie is a sensitive child, and filling her head with ridiculous notions will cause her imagination to run wild!"

"I was just as annoyed when she blurted it out, but that's not what Bridie seems to be upset about. It's you she's furious with. She says you've been as grouchy as a bear all afternoon and she didn't do a thing to deserve it. Why are you taking it out on her?"

"I think you and Bridie should come back with me tomorrow. I don't want her here."

I took a step towards him. "What are you talking about? She loves it here and I promised her. I want to spend time with my mother. We have two more weeks before her cast comes off. I'm staying put. I'm her mother and that's that."

"And I'm her father and I say she's coming home with me!"

Before I knew what I was doing, I reached over and poked his shoulder with my index finger. "Are you, George? Are you *really*? Because if you are, you have a lot of explaining to do. How old was her mother? Fourteen? A few months older than Bridie? Are you *quite* sure you want to admit to fathering that child?"

He looked horrified. "Is that what you think of me?"

I threw my hands in the air. "What else am I supposed to think? You love Bridie more than your own child, and don't say you don't, because you do, and we all know it. Patty knows it. Mavis knows it. Bridie knows it. What is it about her that makes you love her so much, George? She's not just any child to you. What is it you're not telling us?"

He broke down and covered his face, the same way Bridie had only hours earlier. He fell to his knees in the hay and sobbed. I was dumbfounded and unsure what to do, so I just stood there, watching him.

Gradually, the shuddering stopped and he wiped his eyes with the sleeve of his shirt. He reached out and I took his hand to help him off the dried, muddy floor. We held each other for a long time.

"I'm sorry, Eileen. I'm sorry for involving you in this."

"Thank God you did, George. You know Bridie's my world, but there's a piece missing. Are you sure you want to keep it a secret?"

"I swear on Bridie's life that I am not her biological father. You see, there's someone else I'm protecting."

"I thought as much."

He reached in his pocket and pulled out a hanky, wiping his eyes and nose once more.

"You're reluctant to have Bridie come to this place, because the person you're protecting lives here?"

He nodded.

"And you don't want this person to see Bridie?"

He nodded again.

"Okay. Will you let us stay here, if I don't take Bridie off the property? She'll be quite happy running with the chickens and dogs. There's no need for her to go to town. Your mother can come here and visit with her. And I certainly won't let Betty take her anywhere again."

"Okay," he said softly. "Promise me?"

"Pinkie swear."

We eventually went back to the house, after George's face finally looked like he hadn't just cried his heart out. He went upstairs and knocked quietly on Bridie's door and I heard her say, "Enter at your own risk."

They were upstairs for over an hour. Mom kept fretting that the meatloaf she'd made would be dried out if they didn't appear soon.

"Throw some gravy over it. They'll never know."

Eventually the pair appeared, George saying he better go because his mother had planned a nice roast dinner for his last night home.

"You better get going, or that will be dried out too," Mom said.

He kissed us all goodbye, saying he'd be back in two weeks. Bridie went outside and ran beside the car with the dogs as far as the gate, then came charging back in the kitchen.

"I'm starved."

We sat together and said grace. Mom handed Bridie a napkin, and she tucked it into her T-shirt.

"So, is everything okay between you and Pops?" I asked her as I ladled a spoonful of fresh peas on her plate.

"Yes, we settled our differences. He promised to stop treating me like a baby, and I promised to not believe everything I hear."

"Interesting."

She took a big gulp of her milk. "And for some reason, he said I wasn't to go in Aunt Betty's car again. I thought that was odd. What did that car ever do to me?"

"Adults are weird," said my mother. "The sooner you learn that, the better."

By the time I locked up for the night, I was beat. I heard my mom snoring in her room, and when I went by Bridie's room I could see her reading under the covers with a flashlight. When I finally crawled into bed I let out a big sigh.

So, George was upset about the drowning and hanging story, as was I, but then he went on about the miserable gossips in town and specifically mentioned the spinster on the hill. Why would he care about all that, unless she was important to him? This spinster was a missing piece in the puzzle. I was almost sure of it.

WE HAD A GRAND TIME THOSE LAST TWO WEEKS OF AUGUST. We picked wild blueberries and walked along the shore gathering shells and driftwood. I'd take a lawn chair and sit near the rocks, reading, while Bridie and the dogs swam and dove in the icy water. We had picnics and small bonfires, where we cooked hot dogs and marshmallows and sang campfire songs. Mom would sit on the swing and tell Bridie stories of when she was a young girl.

One day I panicked because I couldn't find Bridie, but it turned out she was asleep in the hayloft, with three of Mom's recipe books beside her. She had developed a real love of cooking with my mother by her side and it made me stupidly happy to watch them together.

All the wasted summers I didn't spend here. What was I thinking? For years I'd done George's bidding and hadn't considered what I wanted. Well, that was going to change. Perhaps I could buy a second-hand car and learn to drive so I could take Bridie places, instead of waiting for her father to come home.

With all the extra hours I had, I found myself brooding about the spinster on the hill. Just what was her connection to Bridie? George and the spinster had known each other in school, but they never dated as far as I knew. Not that I had listened to any gossip concerning George. I knew best and he was forever mine. To think otherwise usually ruined my day. So what if they were lovers before he met Mavis? Had he been having an affair with this woman all this time?

She obviously wasn't Bridie's mother. I'd seen Bridie's mother lying lifeless on a metal cart. Had Bridie's mother been the spinster's daughter? If so, why was George raising Bridie? If he loved this woman, why would he deny her the chance to raise a beloved granddaughter after losing her own child?

Was the young girl on the slab George's daughter, and Bridie really his granddaughter? Was that why he was so distraught?

But again, why would he keep Bridie a secret from the spinster? He'd made his life a thousand times more complicated by keeping the baby. And I'd helped him do it. I was as much an accomplice as he was, only he didn't tell me about it. I just trusted him implicitly and was at his beck and call.

That didn't sit well with me. The more I thought about it, the angrier I got. Now that I knew what it was like to have a daughter, how could I deny that love to another woman? The rightful woman. And who was George to decide her fate? And mine!

One day, near the end of our stay, Aunt Jean was over and Betty dropped in for lunch. Bridie was in her element; she had a captive audience for her antics. It was obvious my mom and Aunt Jean were in love with her. She made them laugh like I hadn't heard in years.

"Why did the chicken cross the road?"

"Why?"

"Why not? It's a free country."

We groaned.

"I made that up."

"I could tell," I laughed.

"Two students walked to school. One of them was carrying a ladder."

"Why?" said my mother.

"He wanted to go to high school."

We groaned again.

"Pops told me that one. Blame him."

At the end of lunch, Betty said she had some errands to do. I walked out to her car with her. "Where do you have to go?"

"The drugstore, the bank. Wanna come? You must be bored by now. Oh yes, and I also have to go to Nell's to drop off a couple of pairs of pants I need taken out."

Now was my chance. "Okay, I wouldn't mind coming. I'll tell Mom and grab my purse."

I told the others I was going with Betty and I'd bring Bridie back a treat. She was just as happy doing a puzzle with her two doting grandmothers.

Betty and I chatted as she drove. Even though she'd barely ever spent time with me, she was happy to spill the beans about her marriage.

"Men are devious. My friend Mabel told me what to watch out for, and dang, didn't Fraser check off everything on the list."

"Like what?"

"Like coming home late every night."

"Doesn't Fraser have three jobs?"

"You can't tell me that fishing, logging, and farming take up that much time."

I looked out the window. "I guess not."

"He always forgets my birthday and our anniversary."

"That's not good."

"I know, right? And he had lipstick on his collar one night, and he blamed it on his mother. Granted, it was her shade, but that means nothing. Lots of women wear Avon Persimmon."

"Still, I think you should give him the benefit of the doubt."

Betty honked at the car in front of her as she pulled into the drugstore. "Spoken like a true old maid."

We separated as we entered the store. I headed right for the indigestion tablets and the Archie comic books and grabbed a bottle of Pepsi, a bag of chips, and a chocolate bar for my girl. I picked up a couple of bars for myself too, to eat in my room while I was alone. I'd been feeling the need for a bit of comfort.

While Betty went to the bank I waited in the car, watching people go in and out, trying to figure out if I knew them or not.

Too much time had passed. Eventually, Betty emerged and I was glad of it; I was getting more and more nervous as the minutes ticked by. What was I doing, spying on a woman I didn't know? Maybe I had the wrong end of the stick. Maybe it was another woman he was talking about.

Before I knew it, we were once again driving past the boarded-up cottage and pulling in behind the house on the hill. Betty gathered her pants from the back seat. "Wanna come in? She's a character."

"Might as well," I said.

We slammed our doors at the same time, which alerted a big dog who came charging from behind the house, barking. He looked friendly enough, but you never know.

Nell came out from the kitchen door. "Dog! Get over here."

Dog trotted up to her obediently and went in the house.

"Sorry about that. He's usually inside when I know people are coming."

"No worries," said Betty. "Nell, this is my sister, Eileen. She's home for a few weeks visiting."

"I saw you in the car last time."

I nodded at her. "Yes, that's right. We went to school together, once upon a time."

"I remember. Come in."

When we walked into her kitchen, the first thing I thought was that Bridie would love it. It was completely unorthodox and brilliantly messy. Nell probably knew where everything was, but it was a system known only to herself. That must come from living alone. You put things where you want them and don't worry about other people. She had herbs and garlic hanging from rafters and flowerpots crowded on windowsills. Her dishes were stacked on open cupboards and none of them matched. Neither did the chairs around her pine kitchen table. Hooked rugs were thrown everywhere and she had a huge iron pot on the wood stove.

She saw me staring at it. "That's where I dye my fabric."

I smiled and nodded.

Nell walked out of the kitchen, so we followed her. What would have been her living room was a dressmaker's studio. I didn't know where to look first. I'd never seen anything like it. Didn't everyone live with a kitchen, dining room, and living room? The entire house was suited to what Nell liked and how Nell worked. It was amazing.

She immediately got down to business, asking Betty what she wanted. While Betty showed her the three pairs of slacks, I had a chance to observe Nell up close. She hadn't changed much from what I remembered as a kid. She was slight but seemed strong, as if she could hike the hill out back and not be out of breath. That I admired. Her faded, coppery hair was held up in a loose bun, and she wore no colour on her lips or cheeks, and yet she was what I would call very attractive. The simple skirt and blouse she wore suggested style, but they were obviously her work clothes. She draped a tape measure around her neck like a doctor does a stethoscope and used it as she talked to Betty.

There was something about her that I liked very much, despite the fact that this could very well be someone George loved. They looked like they belonged together. In a parallel world, they would walk hand in hand and no one would question it. It made sense to me, but why had he married Mavis when this creature was in his life? Hell, I'd marry her.

And why was I not jealous of this woman, when I'd loved George all my life? It was the strangest thing. But when I thought about Bridie, my heart lurched. She would love this woman. Nell outshone me in every way. And that made me sad.

I kept waiting for the spinster to behave badly or be short with us, but she was perfectly pleasant. Not overly friendly, but efficient and to the point.

Before I knew it, we were out the door and going back down the laneway.

"Why do people call her a witch?" I asked.

"The kids do, that's all, because she overlooks the old cottage. They say she caused all the tragedy with that family, which is ridiculous. People don't like her because she keeps to herself. They figure she's got her nose in the air just because she doesn't suffer fools gladly and she says what she thinks, whether you like it or not."

I sighed. "I wish I were like that."

✷

GEORGE WAS QUIET ON THE DRIVE HOME, BUT STILL PERFECTLY pleasant, listening to Bridie's chatter about her marvellous stay in the country.

"I'm going to live there when I grow up," she declared. "I'm going to be a baker, a fisherman, have chickens and a barn and dogs and maybe even run a boarding house, because I plan on being a spinster."

I glanced at George and he looked grim.

"Do you know what a spinster is, Pops?"

"Yes."

"Well, since Mama is a spinster, I plan to be a spinster too, because they're the best women in the world."

"You're right about that, baby girl."

The minute we crossed the threshold of the house, I could sense trouble. Mavis and Patty were at the kitchen table having a sandwich. Peanut butter, I noticed—the only thing Mavis knew how to make. George carried in our suitcases and then quickly disappeared.

Bridie threw her arms in the air. "Hello, fellow family members! Did you miss me?"

Patty chewed with her mouth open. "Oh my God, look at the dirt on that cast! It's disgusting!"

"My cast and I had a perfectly wonderful time, thank you

for asking. I hope you passed your summer pleasantly as well. Did you and Ray do it yet?"

"Bridie!" I choked on my own spittle. "Where did you pick up that awful phrase?"

"It was in Patty's diary."

Patty screamed and jumped up from her chair. "She's not in the house five minutes and she's already driving me crazy! Why don't you go away and never come back, you little brat?!"

"Ah, it's so good to be home." And with that, Bridie ran out of the kitchen and up the stairs. Patty stormed out of the house. Which left Mavis and I to look at each other.

"Did you enjoy your endless vacation?" Mavis asked.

"It was two weeks. You must have missed me."

"I didn't. I missed what you do for me."

Something had changed in me. How on earth had I allowed Mavis to talk to me like that? And why was George okay with it?

I put the food hamper on the kitchen counter. "Well, you better get used to it, because I'm going next summer as well, for two months."

"You won't be paid."

"I'll survive."

Mavis watched me as I unpacked the hamper and opened the fridge to put items away. I pretended not to notice her, and then I said, "By the way, what would you like for dinner?"

The relief on her face said it all. "Roast beef with Yorkshire pudding."

You miserable bitch. It'll be the best roast beef you ever tasted.

Over dinner, we learned that Patty wasn't going to university after all.

"I thought you were going to St. FX," I said.

"I changed my mind."

"You mean, Ray changed it for you," George grumbled.

"He did no such thing, Daddy. I don't want to go to university. I'm going to secretarial school. I'm sorry you don't like it, but it's my life and I can do what I want."

"I hope that applies to me when I graduate from high school." Bridie grinned.

George pointed at her plate. "Don't be smart. Eat up."

We were back one night, and I could already see Bridie losing some of her shine.

It was a big day when her cast came off. Her arm looked shrivelled and weak. "It's as light as a feather," she told me, waving her arm through the air. "Wait 'til I show Judith."

☙

MAVIS CONTINUED TO RUB ME THE WRONG WAY, BUT I REALIZED she wasn't getting worse—I was getting better. Those two weeks away with my mom and Aunt Jean had reminded me that I was a good person, not just a punching bag for Mavis. I'd lay in bed at night and dream about having my own home like Nell. A place where everything I touched was mine and I didn't have to ask permission of anyone.

I realized that I'd made a huge mistake agreeing to come and live with George—or, more to the point, overstaying my welcome.

Three days before Thanksgiving, I was at the kitchen table making a grocery list for the weekend. George was pouring himself a coffee before he left for work. To our surprise, Mavis showed up in her bathrobe, yawning and stretching her arms over her head.

"To what do we owe the pleasure?" George said. "You usually sleep until noon."

"I forgot to tell you yesterday that we're having a dinner party on Saturday night, so don't take anyone's shift in the ER. I invited ten couples."

George made a face. "What can there possibly be to talk about anymore? You invite the same gang over every two weeks. Why doesn't one of them have a party instead? I'm tired of feeding the five thousand."

I looked up. "But Sunday is Thanksgiving."

"So?"

It was the way she said it. My head started to pound and my darn indigestion didn't help.

"I have so much to do. I'll just get the dinner party mess cleared up and I have to put the turkey in the oven at six in the morning, if you want Thanksgiving dinner at noon."

"Oh, boo-hoo. That's what we pay you for."

I stood up and threw my notepad at her, hitting her square in the face. It startled her more than hurt her. I shouted, "Don't you ever talk to me like that again!"

Then I ran into my room and slammed the door. I couldn't stay still, just kept pacing as I heard Mavis raging in the kitchen, yelling at George, saying she was owed an apology and that I was in the wrong and he'd better not stick up for me or there'd be hell to pay.

Finally silence and then a soft knocking at my door.

"Go away, George."

"Open up, Eileen. I can't go to work and leave you like this."

I did open the door. I flung it open in anger. "You leave me like this every morning! What's so different about today? Because I finally said what I was thinking? Why do you let her treat me like dirt? You keep saying I'm not a maid. Well, what am I, then? You're certainly not my husband, and this isn't our marriage and this isn't my house. So what am I in the grand scheme of things? I cook for you, clean for you, and bring up your children. I have all of the responsibilities of a wife and none of the perks. I feel like a servant, and I'm being treated like one by your wife, who never appreciates a thing I do for her. It's ridiculous that I even stay here. Mavis doesn't want me here and she certainly doesn't want Bridie!"

I ran over to my wardrobe and threw it open, grabbing my suitcase off the top shelf. "I'm leaving. I'm taking Bridie and I'm going home to my mother. I'll take a taxi; I'm painfully aware you hate going to your hometown because of your precious secret."

"Eileen—"

The top of my head felt like it was going to explode. I sat on the bed and held up my forehead with my hand. "I've been such a fool. I loved you my whole life. I thought it was enough to be near you. It's been a ridiculous fantasy. I don't own my own life. I've lived yours. How did I let that happen?"

He sat beside me on the bed and put his arm around me. I cried into his armpit. I had no shame left. He knew everything now and I didn't care anymore. He was my best friend, goddammit. Who knew me as well as he did? I needed him as much as I wanted to leave him. Life was frightening without his steady presence. What was I going to do?

"Here's what we'll do," he said softly. "Let me handle Mavis. As of right this minute, you are not responsible for anything in this house except Bridie's well-being. You take care of Bridie. You make her meals and your own. You're not to worry about me or Mavis or Patty. It's high time Mavis started behaving like my wife, and my daughter will be responsible for her own meals, her own laundry, and her own room. She can help her mother clean the house."

"But—"

"I won't pay you anymore, except for child care. I'll tell Mavis that. But only you and I will know that I have an account for you both, from which you can withdraw funds when you need them. You don't have to worry about this anymore, Eileen. I've been as much a fool as you. I intend to remedy that today. Do you believe me?"

"Yes," I whispered into his jacket. "Thank you."

"I can never repay you, Eileen. I love you. So very dearly."

He gave me a squeeze and kissed the top of my head, then got off the bed and closed my bedroom door. I fell back into my pillows and just stared at the ceiling.

∽⊙〽

IT GOT TO THE POINT THAT I WAS ALMOST SORRY I OPENED MY big mouth. Mavis was livid and let me know at every opportunity. At least George got away from her during the day, as did Bridie and Patty, but Mavis was like a cornered alley cat and she hissed at me every chance she got.

"Because of you, I've had to cancel my dinner party."

"I'd be happy to show you how to make the canapes. Dinner would be a rack of lamb with roast potatoes, and your guests love my chocolate mousse. It's simple to make."

"If it's so goddamn easy, why won't you do it for me?"

"Because George said—"

She threw her hands in the air. "George said, George said... I don't give a rat's ass what George said! He can't just suddenly announce that our routine is changing and that's that! Goddamn men! They think they run the world!"

"They do, unfortunately."

She saw an opening and stepped towards me, grabbing my shoulders. "Why are we listening to him? We can do what we want. If you agree to make the meal, I'll pretend I made it and he'd never know the difference!"

I stared at her. "How is that fair?"

She pushed me away. "It's fair to me. I don't care about you."

"And there's the rub, Mavis. There's the whole problem in a nutshell. I wouldn't mind doing exactly what I did before, but I need to feel appreciated every so often. Not treated like the gum under your shoe."

"Okay. Please make our Thanksgiving dinner, and I want an apple and pumpkin pie this year. Thank you very much, Eileen."

"Go suck an egg."

I thought she was going to hit me. I wish she had.

So much for making a stand. I wanted Thanksgiving dinner. It was my favourite meal of the year. I ended up doing everything because I didn't want Bridie to suffer. I noticed George, Patty, and Mavis took seconds.

"Why can't you cook like this, Mom?" Patty said.

"One good thing," said George, "is that I lost five pounds this week."

Mavis turned and glared at her husband. "Keep it up, and you'll lose ten more when I cut off your head."

Bridie laughed so hard she spilled gravy down her shirt.

❧

BRIDIE MADE A FORTUNE. PATTY PAID HER TO DO HER CHORES, and then Mavis started paying her as well. The genius got Judith involved too. They were in their usual place at the kitchen table, supposedly doing homework. Judith was staying for supper.

"If you help me, I'll give you half, and then we'll both have enough money to go the movies or buy milkshakes whenever we want. And the work will take half the time."

"I don't even clean at my house," Judith said. "What if my mom finds out?"

Bridie turned to me. "You won't breathe a word, will you, Mama?"

I zipped my lips with my fingertips.

"You see! Mama's the greatest."

❧

MOM CALLED ONE DAY AND SOUNDED A BIT DOWN.

"How are you feeling?" I asked her.

"So-so. My arthritis is acting up. I just hate the thought of winter coming. Christmas isn't fun anymore without your dad."

"At least the boys will be there with Betty and Fraser."

"No, Fraser's mother isn't well, so he wants to spend Christmas with his people. Can't say I blame him."

I got a big, fat, juicy idea. "Why don't Bridie and I come up for Christmas?"

Her voice rose. "Really? Oh, that would be marvellous! What a wonderful idea! Now I have to put up a tree. I wasn't going to bother."

"As soon as school is over, I'll get George to drive us up, and the three of us can do all our Christmas baking together. How does that sound?"

"Like heaven! You darling girl."

When I told George, he looked a little down in the mouth, but he quickly agreed when he saw my face. And when I told Bridie, she just about flew around the room.

"How fantastic! And we're doing all our baking together?! And we'll have the dogs and the chickens? I have to go clean Patty's toilet! I need some moola to buy Christmas gifts!"

When I went to bed that night, I knelt by the side of my bed and thanked God for giving me Bridie, the sweetest child in the world; George, the best friend in the world; and my wonderful mother. For too long I had taken her for granted. It's only when you get older that you realize what a gift it is to spend time with your parents.

And then I remembered something else: "And give Mavis the strength she needs to cook a Christmas goose all by herself. Amen."

ॐ

TWO WEEKS BEFORE CHRISTMAS, I GOT A PHONE CALL FROM Aunt Jean. I could hardly understand her between sobs.

"What's wrong?"

"Oh, Eileen. It's your mother. She died today. I simply can't believe it. She just fell off her chair as we were having tea. I'm so sorry, Eileen. I told Betty I'd call you and George. I can't believe this has happened!"

I dropped the phone and the room spun around me. I backed into a kitchen chair and fell onto it. My mother? My mother was dead? I never even got a chance to say goodbye. The last time I saw her, she was standing on the porch, waving until we were out of sight. I promised her I'd bring Bridie back for Christmas, and now it didn't matter.

My mother had always loved me. And now that unconditional love was gone. How do you live without it? Who do you call when you're afraid? When you can't remember your great-grandmother's maiden name? When you need her recipe for Christmas pudding?

I'm not sure how long I sat there. I only remember Bridie coming in the door with Judith after school. I burst into tears and heard Bridie say that perhaps Judith could come back at a more convenient time. Then she put her arms around me.

"What's wrong, Mama?"

"My mother is gone! She's gone, and I'll never see her again."

She didn't say a word, just held onto me for dear life, and oh, how I needed that. I needed that so badly.

At one point, Mavis came into the kitchen and I heard Bridie tell her to call her father. He was needed at home immediately.

I really don't remember a whole lot after that. I think George gave me a pill. I hung onto his hand. "Bridie. Take care of Bridie."

"Don't worry, Eileen. I've got her. She'll be safe with me."

CHAPTER TEN

GEORGE

Eileen was so distressed, I ended up giving her a mild sedative to try and get her to settle. Bridie was nestled against her, with Eileen's arms wrapped around her. Finally, at ten o'clock, both of them were asleep. I took Bridie back to her own bed and looked in on Eileen before I called my mother. It was late, but I knew she wouldn't be sleeping.

"Mom."

She immediately started to cry. "I'm so sad. I can't believe she's gone. I've already tried to call her to tell her the terrible news, but *she's* the terrible news. Who am I going to call from now on? I feel like I'm disappearing. Everyone I love is so far away. It's terrible to get old. I wish I were dead too."

Hearing my mother so distraught filled me with anguish. I'd abandoned her. Donny had abandoned her. It had been easy to let her live alone with her sister just up the road, but now there was no one.

"I'm sorry, Mom. I know how awful this must be for you."

"I'm not sure you do. You've never lost a sibling. How's poor Eileen? And Bridie?"

"Eileen is in shock. It's hit her hard. Bridie is frightened. She's never seen her mother so helpless. It's tough. How's Betty?"

"Betty screamed so loud over the phone, my ear is still ringing."

"I guess it's too soon to know the arrangements?"

"Fraser said he'd take care of it. Betty's lucky to have that man. He might be a bore, but he's reliable."

"I'll call you in the morning. Eileen might be focused enough by then to talk to you."

"Kiss the poor girl for me."

"Will you be all right tonight? Is a friend staying with you?"

"I thought about calling Alice up the road, but I'm too tired. I'll drink some hot milk and go to bed."

"Good night, Mom."

"Goodbye, dear."

As I sat in my study, I heard Mavis walking upstairs, doing her nightly routine. Patty was out with Ray and said she'd be in by midnight. At least she said she was sorry to hear about my aunt. Mavis hadn't said anything. She was too spooked by Eileen's behaviour.

"Is that normal?" she whispered, when we finally got Eileen in her room. "She's behaving like a zombie. Who sits on a chair for hours and doesn't want to be moved?"

"It's shock, Mavis. It affects people differently."

"Eileen's always been an odd duck."

I didn't have the energy to engage her.

The mantle clock bonged three times. It startled me. I'd fallen asleep in my chair at my desk. Now I had a bad kink in my neck. It took me a few minutes to remember why I felt out of sorts. Oh, right. Aunt Jessie was gone. She was such a nice person. I never gave her a lot of thought over the years. It was just comforting to know she was there. In the background, but someone who was always glad to see me.

My throat was parched. I went out into the kitchen and got a glass of water. I decided to take some aspirin to try and ease my neck. As I went by Eileen's bedroom door, I opened it wider to check on her. The light from the kitchen shone on her face. She was finally in a deep sleep; her arm had fallen off the side of the bed and was hanging there. I moved towards her to tuck it in under the blanket.

The minute I touched her, I knew.

The doctor in me put my fingers on her neck to check for a pulse and started cardiopulmonary resuscitation. But even as I frantically worked on her, I knew it was a lost cause. Eventually, despair won and I laid my head on her chest and began to weep. Quietly, so as not to wake the rest of the household. This was the last time Eileen and I would be alone together, and as I knelt by the bed, I played the record of our lives.

She was always so much fun, driving her big sister crazy. Who did that remind me of? She did her best to keep up with me and Donny. I always knew she liked me, in a cousin sort of way, but hadn't realized her feelings ran so deep. Eileen was one of those women who quietly went about their day making others feel better, whether it was through her cooking, or cleaning, or just being there with a cup of tea and a listening ear.

I had been wrong to ask so much of her. I'd taken her for granted. I'd found the best mother in the world for Bridie, but at what cost to Eileen?

"I don't want you to go, my dearest friend. Who will save me now? Who's going to tell me what to do?"

"I will," said a small voice.

I whipped my head around. There was Bridie in the doorway, the light shining behind her. I fell apart. "Oh Bridie. I'm so sorry. I'm so, so sorry."

She ran to me and I held her in my arms, close to my chest, just like I had the day she was born. She shuddered and cried for what seemed like forever. At one point, she had a hard time breathing, so I wiped her nose and mouth on my shirt. Then she crawled away from me and lay beside her mother.

"Mama. Mama. Can you hear me? Please, come back. Please don't go. Pops and I need you. I love you, Mama. I'll be good. I won't bother Patty any more, and I'll stay out of Mavis's way. You need to come home."

There was nothing I could do. I let her lie there. Even after Mavis and Patty showed up at the door, I let Bridie be with her mother. Patty started to cry and even Mavis got teary. I was touched by that.

ॐ

EILEEN AND HER MOTHER WERE CREMATED AND THEIR ASHES buried together. That was the only thing that gave Bridie some comfort. She insisted on writing out her mother's and Nana's favourite recipes and burying them with the remains.

Even though I knew it was risky, I didn't even try to shield Bridie from the funeral in St. Peter's. That would be too unkind, and she'd never have forgiven me if I'd kept her away. Besides, all my secrets seemed silly now that our world had fallen apart.

I was so proud of Bridie that day. Betty put on a ridiculous show, sobbing for all to hear that she was now an orphan, that she didn't have any family left—which must have made Fraser and the boys feel odd, but I knew what she meant. Who was I to judge? It was terrible for her.

Bridie stayed by my side throughout the funeral, people shaking her hand or shaking their heads at the unfairness of it all. All the old biddies in town showed up to see the circus and eat their fill of the inevitable funeral spread.

One of them came creaking over and patted Bridie on the head. "Don't worry, dearie. Your mother is now singing in a choir of angels."

"They'll kick her out. Uncle Donny says she sings like a foghorn."

Somehow, we muddled through until the last person shuffled off. Donny and his crowd left to go back to Sydney because his youngest was in a Christmas pageant. Then we headed back to my mother's. Betty didn't want any company, and I didn't blame her. It was very odd to have Mavis, Patty, and Bridie all together at my mother's dining room table. I could tell my mother was nervous, as if she were entertaining royalty instead of relaxing on this trying day.

None of us said much, as it turned out. And not much was eaten either. When we were having tea and lemon loaf, Patty spoke up.

"I hope you don't mind, Dad, but I asked Ray to pick me up tonight instead of staying over. He has a company Christmas lunch tomorrow and he asked me to go. I'd hate to disappoint him."

I looked at my mother and wondered what she was thinking. She made it easy. "That's a good idea, honey. You don't want to be rushing tomorrow."

Patty gave her grandmother a grateful look. At this point, I didn't really care.

Mavis piped up. "Well, if that's the case, I might as well get a drive back with you two. Why have Jean make up an extra bed?"

It was hardly an extra bed. She'd be sleeping with me.

Patty gave her mother an annoyed glance. "You don't need to come. Ray and I never have any time alone."

"Nonsense. It's all settled."

I could have stepped in and demand that Mavis stay with me, but in all honesty, I couldn't wait for her to leave. She made my mother nervous, and the thought of just being with Bridie and my mom was appealing.

Ray showed up at four, and I could tell he was disappointed to see Mavis and her carryall bag waiting as well.

I bent down to kiss Mavis. "I'll be another few days."

"Take your time," Mavis said. "It's not like it's going to be a cheery Christmas anyway." And then she bent down and kissed Bridie on the cheek. "I know you're going to miss your mama. Be a brave girl."

She even kissed Mom goodbye. "Thanks for everything, Jean. Always a pleasure."

She and Patty waved from the car as it drove through the snow and back out onto the highway.

We three were left wondering if we'd just witnessed to a Christmas miracle.

"Now that Mama is gone, Mavis is nice to me?" Bridie scowled. "Who does she think she's fooling? Not me, that's for sure. What a jerk."

I should have said something, but I didn't have the heart. Bridie's face was wet with tears as she stared into the fire. She was exhausted and soon fell asleep on the couch. Mom and I were in the two easy chairs on either side of the fireplace.

"Should I let her sleep here?"

Mom nodded, so I tucked a couple of wool throws around her and banked the fire. We sat and watched the flames as they crackled and popped in front of us. Finally, a moment of quiet to try and take in our new reality.

"Suddenly, it feels like a very small family," I mused. "Dad, Uncle Roger, Aunt Jessie, Eileen. Half of us are gone."

"The one I feel sorry for is Bridie. How on earth do you survive when you lose your mother at thirteen? You're going to have a hard time, son. Especially..." Her voice faded away.

"I know. Especially with Mavis."

"Despite her display today, she's not a demonstrative woman, even with her own child. How will you manage?"

I grunted. "Badly."

My mother looked at me with almost pity. "Would you say your marriage is a happy one, George?"

I shook my head.

"Why? Why did you marry her?"

The flames leapt before my eyes. "You know why."

"Did you purposely set out to find someone who didn't measure up?"

My temples throbbed. "Mom, I can't deal with this right now."

She gave a big sigh. "Someday you better figure yourself out. Before it's too late. I'll say good night."

"Good night, Mom."

She got up slowly and shuffled over to give me a kiss on the head before disappearing upstairs. I sat and watched the fire, looking over at Bridie and taking in that perfect face. The idea of raising her alone filled me with dread. I couldn't depend on Mavis for help. Patty was almost out the door. She and Ray were probably going to be married someday. Who would Bridie turn to? The thought crossed my mind that I should quit my job, but that didn't seem sensible. Bridie would have go to university. Being a secretary was the last thing she would aspire to.

Why wasn't Eileen here? Why did she have to die? I should've pushed her to take better care of herself, especially with the history of heart disease in the family. I missed her so much. The thought of spending the rest of my life without her haunted me. Another woman I loved gone forever.

I'd never felt so alone as I did that night. I was only a half a mile away. So near. And yet it might as well have been across an ocean.

☙

THE NEXT DAY, BRIDIE ASKED IF WE COULD GO AND VISIT HER grandmother's farm. I called Betty and she said she'd meet us there. Mom wondered if it would be too much for Bridie, but I reasoned that if she asked to go, then she must be ready.

I should have asked if *I* was ready, because the sight of it reminded me of our fishing trip and how happy Eileen had been to be home. This was going to be bad.

Betty got out of her car and walked towards the farmhouse with her keys. Bridie followed behind her. "Where are the dogs?"

"They're at our house."

"And the chickens?"

"The farmer next door took them for me."

Bridie frowned. "They'll be sad. What about the barn cats?"

"He took them too."

Was she telling the truth? You never knew with Betty. But surely she wouldn't leave the cats to fend for themselves.

"Maybe we could go over and get the cats, Pops?"

Goddammit. "Sorry, sweetie. Mavis is allergic to cats." It wasn't Mavis's fault, but at that moment it seemed vindictive and mean that Bridie couldn't take something from the farm home with her. I saw her face fall.

We walked in the kitchen and it was as if Aunt Jessie and Eileen were just in another room. There were even dishes in the sink. Bridie wandered through all the rooms by herself. Betty and I sat at the table feeling miserable.

"I hate this," Betty said. "It doesn't seem real. I can't believe my mother isn't here to make me a cup of tea. Why is it always the little things that kill you?"

"I know. All I can think of is what we're going to have for Christmas dinner. Mavis can't boil water. I'll have to learn how to cook."

"Why can't she learn how to cook? She doesn't do anything else around the house, from what I understand."

"Look Betty, I know that's true, but I really don't like people constantly saying negative things about Mavis. She is my wife, remember."

Betty looked put-out. "Too bad she doesn't remember that fact herself."

"Okay, let's drop it."

"Fine."

And that's why Eileen was always my favourite cousin.

Bridie eventually wandered back into the kitchen and sat down with us. She put her elbows on the plastic red-checkered tablecloth. "I'm going to miss this room the most."

We nodded.

"Would it be possible to have Nana's recipe box, Aunt Betty? Will you be using it anytime soon?"

Betty looked around and got up to retrieve the little tin box from the windowsill above the sink. "I have most of these anyway. And it's not like the boys are interested. You're welcome to them."

That was the first nice thing I'd seen Betty do. I could've kissed her.

"What about her recipe books?"

"Okay. I guess so." Betty fiddled with the keys in her hand. "Actually, I meant to tell you that I'm selling the farm."

"Really?" I said.

Bridie looked at her with big eyes.

"Fraser has enough property to look after, and none of the boys are interested in farming. It just seemed like the thing to do. I hate to see it go, but now that Eileen is gone, I'm the only one left. Mom didn't leave a will, so it passes to me anyway. You have to move on, and we could use the money, to give us a little nest egg."

"Will this be the last time I'm ever in this house?" Bridie whispered.

Betty looked uncomfortable. "I'm afraid so."

Bridie jumped up from her chair. "That's the meanest thing I've ever heard! Mama just died! What if her soul wants to come back here for a little while? How dare you sell her things? You're supposed to be her sister!" Bridie pounded her fist on the kitchen table. It made Betty and me jump.

"I'm sorry—"

"Since you're so eager to get rid of everything, I'm sure you won't mind me going into Mama's room and taking what's hers."

What could Betty say? "Okay, I guess."

Bridie got up from the table. "Pops, get some boxes."

She had Eileen's childhood room stripped of everything inside an hour. We took the bed frame in pieces, the bureau with its round mirror, a trunk, a couple of lamps, everything in the closet, the hooked rugs, her photo albums, and miscellaneous junk that had accumulated in her desk. By the time we were finished, my station wagon looked like a covered wagon ready to head for California in the Wild, Wild West.

I don't think Betty quite knew what hit her. By that time, Bridie was really brave. "I'd also like Nana's pots and pans. And her cooking utensils."

"But they're such old pots. Most of them are banged up."

"They're perfect. I'd also like her favourite teacup and my mother's favourite teacup."

Now Betty got exasperated. "Maybe I want my mother's favourite teacup. Have you thought of that?"

We both looked at her and the sentence hung in the air.

"Oh, all right."

Before we got in the car, Bridie and I went into the barn to smell the air and soak up the last memories of the place.

"Someday I'm going to have a barn, Pops."

"I don't doubt it."

"And I'm going to fill it with critters, so I don't have to be alone."

She fell to her knees in the hay and I gathered her up and held her close.

"Why am I alone? Why did both my mothers leave me? God must hate me."

"I'm so sorry, darling. Life isn't fair, but God doesn't hate you. He wanted you to live, and that's why you're here, in spite of the terrible circumstances of your birth."

"'My mother is gone! She's gone, and I'll never see her again.' That's what Mama said when she found out about Nana. This is how she felt. I think I'll die of a broken heart too. Am I going to die, Pops?"

"No, sweetheart. Mama had a weak heart. You're not going to die."

Eventually, I dried her tears and put her down.

She looked at me with solemn eyes. "Thank you for helping me take Mama home."

"My pleasure."

I said farewell, to a still visibly dismayed Betty, and Bridie refused to look at her as we took our leave. When we got back to Mom's, I showed her the car through the kitchen window.

"Bridie thought of that herself. It never would've occurred to me."

Mom shook her head. "That's not how it was supposed to be. Jessie wanted Eileen to have the house, but she never got around to seeing a lawyer. You always think you have more time. And now it wouldn't have mattered anyway, but still, it's indecent. The funeral was yesterday, for crying out loud. What's Betty's hurry? Didn't she think that perhaps I'd like a look around too? It's my sister's house. I've been in that place at least four times a week for almost fifty years. I loved my sister, but she was way too soft with that girl. Betty thinks of herself first. Good for Bridie. It never would have occurred to Betty to give something of Eileen's to the child, so she took it for herself. I really don't think you're going to have to worry about her, George. Bridie is a clever girl."

"As clever as she is, she's still a child who needs a mother."

Mom turned to me. "I'll do what I can, if you'll let me."

I took my mother in my arms. "We'll be back more often. I promise."

⚬⚬

MAVIS WAS GOBSMACKED WHEN WE GOT HOME. "WHERE IS ALL this stuff going? Your bedroom is already full."

"I'm moving out of my bedroom, Mavis. I'm moving into Mama's room. I'll have my own suite."

"Is that reasonable, George? A child on her own on the bottom floor of the house? Why, she could leave through the back door and we'd never know it."

"Patty used to leave through her bedroom window until the trellis broke," Bridie informed her.

There were times when I wished Bridie would be a little more circumspect.

We spent the rest of the morning bringing in Eileen's belongings from the car and rearranging the bedroom and sitting room off the kitchen. Bridie worked into the night, making sure she had everything the way she wanted it. She brought down some things from her old room and took other things back up there because they didn't fit.

I noticed she didn't take the pots and pans, the tin recipe box, or the recipe books out to the kitchen. She put them on her windowsill as decorations. She placed her mother's quilt over the bed and wanted her mother's lamp on the bedside table. It was obvious that she was working constantly so she didn't have to sit still and reflect on what had happened. I waited for more tears to come, but she remained stoic. It concerned me, because I was on the brink of tears all day, but she was like an adult, putting her head down and soldiering on. I wondered how long she could keep it up.

When I tucked her in that night, she had dark circles under her big blue eyes.

"Your mama would be very proud of what you've done here."

"I feel her around me. Do you think she can see what I've done?"

"I'm sure she can."

Bridie sat up, reached over, and opened the bedside table drawer. "I found this today, while I was moving things." She opened a lace hanky and inside was a gold necklace. "Is this Mama's? I never saw her wear it."

It was the necklace I'd given Nell all those years ago, the one I'd taken off Bridie's mother's neck. Eileen had kept it all this time.

"This belongs to you, sweetheart. Mama and I were going to give it to you on your sixteenth birthday, but I think you should wear it now. Your mother was wearing it the day she died. Mama and I thought you might like to have it someday, and I think that day has come."

She looked at it in awe. "This is my angel mother's necklace?"

I nodded.

"Golly. It's so pretty. Was she pretty, Pops?"

"Very pretty."

"Will you put it on for me?"

She turned her back to me and I took the necklace and draped it around her neck. I had a hard time with the tiny clasp, but finally it held and Bridie jumped up from beneath the covers and ran over to her Mama's round mirror to look at herself.

"This is very beautiful. Can I wear it all the time? Even in the tub?"

"I don't see why not."

She held it between her fingers as she got back into bed. "This makes me happy, and I'm sure my two Mamas would want that."

I tucked her back in.

"I know I was rude to Aunt Betty today, but I couldn't help it, Pops."

"You're allowed to be angry, and I think Aunt Betty will forgive you. It's okay to express your feelings. Don't keep things hidden away."

"I have to keep some things hidden away, Pops. Inside my head, I'm a lonely wolf baying at the moon."

CHAPTER ELEVEN

1964

*By the time the next Christmas rolled around, we were in a work-*able rhythm. The household was calm enough, though only because Bridie took over where Eileen had left off. I tried to tell her that it wasn't necessary for her to be cooking and looking after the house, but she said it calmed her. And since fourteen-year-olds were usually volatile creatures, I had to take her at her word.

"I feel Mama next to me when I'm in the kitchen."

"But Mavis—"

"Cooking is not Mavis's forte, Pops."

Where did she come up with this stuff?

She and Patty got along well enough, possibly because Patty was never home. She was nineteen and had no interest in being with her family.

I'd spent the year since Eileen's death trying to lessen a bit of my workload so I'd be home at night for Bridie. Mavis noticed.

"Must be nice for some."

As ever, my guilt about everything nearly ate me alive. I developed ulcers and my hair started to recede at a rapid pace. It was turning grey, too, which was a bit much. I asked Mavis about it one night before bed.

"I'm starting to look like my dad."

"Men look distinguished with grey hair. Women just look old, which is why I will be dyeing my hair until I'm ninety."

I crawled into bed. "You look great, Mavis. I don't know why you worry so much."

She put her book down, took off her glasses, and shut off her bedside lamp. That was the cue that she was coming in for a snuggle, so I switched off my light as well. We held each other in the dark.

We'd never had a passionate romance, which was my fault. She seemed content with my arms around her and a once-a-month Saturday-night date that was as regular as clockwork.

When you've had a love affair that has devoured you body and soul, everything else is like a watercolour without the colour.

That's why I put up with Mavis's dissatisfaction with most things in life. She knew in her heart that I wasn't in love with her, and I felt badly about it. I had no business marrying anyone, knowing how I felt about Nell. Life would have been simpler if I'd stayed a bachelor. I would have been lonely, but I was already lonely.

Still, we had Patty, and I couldn't imagine my life without her.

But I was doing the same thing with Patty that I did with Mavis. Whereas Mavis was overshadowed by Nell, Patty was eclipsed by Bridie. And I didn't know how to undo it, so I lived with a deep shame that took its toll on me.

Was my life happy? Not really.

I never should have let that child in my car, never mind that Bridie was my greatest gift.

❧

TWO DAYS BEFORE CHRISTMAS, MAVIS AND PATTY WERE OUT shopping. Bridie was making a gumdrop cake in the kitchen. I worried about her because Judith and her family had moved to England a couple of months before, so Bridie spent a lot of time alone. Whenever I asked her if she was okay, she'd nod.

"Don't worry, Pops. Judith and I are pen pals, and that takes our relationship to a whole new level. We seal our letters with wax. It's like getting important state secrets from King Henry VIII."

She had a bad habit of telling me not to worry, which always made me fret. Sometimes it felt as though Bridie was the adult and I was the child. She kept a stiff upper lip for me but I knew she still cried at night for her mother, and that killed me.

The doorbell rang, so I got up from my desk and opened the door.

Ray was standing on the front step. "Hi, Dr. Mackenzie."

I reached out and shook his hand. "Season's greetings, young man. I'm afraid Patty isn't home."

"I know. I saw her leave. It's you I wanted to speak to."

That was odd. The kid had never said a whole lot to me. He was a nice enough chap...oh. It hit me. He was going to ask me for Patty's hand. My stomach churned. I hoped he didn't hear it.

"Well, come in. We'll go into my study."

"Who's at the door, Pops?" Bridie yelled from the kitchen— another bad habit I couldn't get her to stop.

"Ray."

"Hi, Sting Ray!"

"Hey, Squirt."

That's when I remembered that I liked Ray. He was always nice to Bridie. That said something about his character, even if Bridie was hard not to like.

"Have a seat." I gestured to the chair in front of my desk as I went around it and sat on my leather wing chair. "How's the family? I saw your dad bring home a pretty big tree last week."

Ray squirmed in his seat. "Yeah, he gets a bigger one every year. My mother gets mad at him."

"A fairly common thing when you have a wife."

Ray turned bright red. "Speaking of wives, I was wondering... I mean...I thought...if you didn't mind...what I want to say is..."

"Spit it out. I have a fairly good idea what this is about."

"I'd like to ask Patty to marry me and I want your blessing."

"YAHOO!" Bridie yelled from the behind the closed door.

"Bridie! Stop listening to private conversations!"

"Sorry, Pops."

Ray laughed nervously. "She's a crazy kid."

"She is. Well, Ray, I suppose this day was going to come sometime. You and Patty have been faithful to each other for quite some time now. But you're both so young."

"I know, sir, but I have a steady job with my father, and I'll take over my family's lumber yards one day, and as you know, Patty has been accepted for a position in a law firm. Between the two of us, we'll be able to rent an apartment together. I know Patty would like to have a nice wedding. I'm not sure when, but I do know she's looking forward to wearing an engagement ring. I'd like to give it to her for Christmas."

I nodded. Was it possible that Patty was old enough to marry? Where had the years gone? Was I really old enough to have a son-in-law? Patty had never really gone out with another boy. Was that smart? Did she know what love was at this early age?

What was I thinking? She was just like her father.

Ray looked like he was about to faint. Better put him out of his misery. "You have my blessing. I hope you'll be very happy together. It means a lot that you came over and asked me. It shows me what kind of man you are."

The man, who still had a few acne scars on his face, reached out to give my hand a shake. "Thank you, sir. You won't regret this."

Let's hope Patty doesn't, I almost said out loud, but I took pity on him and kept my big mouth shut.

After he left, I wandered into the kitchen. Bridie was looking through the glass on the oven door. There were two dozen peanut butter cookies cooling on racks on the counter beside her. I chose one and took a bite. "So, what do you think? Did I make a mistake telling him he could marry Patty?"

"No. This way you look like a good guy and Patty doesn't have to elope."

"She wanted to elope?"

"She was musing about it."

"To you?"

Bridie looked guilty. "Not exactly."

"What have I told you about reading her diary?"

"Not to do it."

"And yet, you persist."

"It's like a drug, Pops. My life is so boring. I need to be entertained."

"Then watch Ed Sullivan. I mean it. No more snooping, or I'll be very disappointed." She opened the oven door and took out the gumdrop cake with Eileen's pot holders. "You're right. I'm sorry. I won't do it again."

I didn't believe her.

Despite my fears that this Christmas would be sombre, it turned out to be a nice time. Donny had picked up Mom a few days before, and we were all going over to his place for dinner. Patty was over the moon with her engagement ring, and she couldn't wait to show it to the whole family. Mavis beamed with pride, and I have to say, so did I. It felt wonderful to see Mavis and Patty so happy for a change.

We didn't often go over to Donny's place. His wife, Loretta, didn't like to socialize or leave the house. Donny said she had agoraphobia, but I think she was just a shy woman who felt more comfortable in her own home. It couldn't be easy to watch Donny flirt with anyone wearing a skirt. How odd that he'd ended up with her. Maybe he knew he needed someone holding down the fort while he schmoozed his way through life. Mom always said he'd be lost without Loretta, and she was probably right.

There would be eleven of us around the dining room table, including my nieces and nephews, Bill, Dave, Cheryl, and Ellen. We weren't close to them. Loretta spent a lot of time with her family, and since Donny and I never socialized if we could help it—except for at Mavis's miserable cocktail parties—it was only natural they were closer to their maternal cousins.

Patty had always ignored her cousins because she was the eldest, but I never understood why Bridie hadn't charmed her way into their circle. She was always quiet around Donny's bunch, for whatever reason. I thought it was because Loretta was a bit straight-laced. She never approved of our unorthodox arrangement raising Bridie. Someone told me at the hospital that she referred to her as "the foundling."

The three of us were by the back door, ready to go. Patty kept holding up her hand to look at her ring.

"Hurry up, Bridie!" Mavis called out. "We're going to be late."

"Just a minute!"

Bridie came through the door and we stared at her. For the first time in her life, she had her mess of blond curls pinned up, and she was wearing a soft shade of pink on her lips. "Do I look okay?"

Mavis and Patty didn't say a word, so I jumped in. "Very nice, sweetheart. Are you sure you're not too young for lipstick?"

"I don't think so. What do you think, Patty? Does this make me look too old?"

"You look great," Patty said. "Really great."

I wanted to put my hands around Mavis's neck. Say something to her.

"Let's go before they start dinner without us" was her contribution to the conversation.

Everyone was very excited to see Patty's engagement ring. I was happy for her. All Mavis and Patty and Loretta talked about was wedding ideas. Normally Bridie would have added her two cents, but once again she didn't say much. I was glad she was seated next to her Gran. They looked like they were having a nice chat.

Donny was doing his impression of an ass, as usual, and naturally made a big fuss about Bridie's appearance.

"Where's Bridie? All I see is a princess in the making. I'll miss our lumberjack."

She looked up at him. "I'll never be a princess, Uncle Donny."

"Well, now, don't be so sure about that. You clean up pretty good."

Loretta and Mom shot him a look and he simmered down a little. It was hard to believe he saved lives every day, because he behaved like an idiot most of the time. Even his kids didn't seem too impressed with him.

By the end of dinner, I was ready to leave. Family gatherings are okay up to a point. We were taking Mom back with us for a couple of days, so she went upstairs to gather her things and I corralled my crowd. I told Mavis to wait for Mom while I went out to the car to get it warmed up. Bridie quickly followed me and crawled into the back seat.

"I don't like Uncle Donny," she said.

"He's harmless," I told her. "Ignore him."

Mom stayed until New Year's with us, and we fell into the same routine we had with Eileen, only it was Mom, Bridie, and I at the kitchen table, drinking tea and eating scones in the late afternoon. Mavis had her own car, so she never stuck around, not with wedding fever driving her every waking moment.

"Be prepared to pay a pretty penny for this wedding," Mom laughed. "It's a good thing Bridie is a lot younger. You'll need those years to fill up your bank account."

Bridie ate a spoonful of jam right out of the jar. "I'm never getting married, so Pops won't have to worry about it. I'm going to be a spinster."

Mom gave me a quick glance. I hated it when Bridie used that word. It brought me back to that awful day in the barn with Eileen.

She patted Bridie's hand. "I'm afraid that's going to be impossible, honey. You'll have young men lined up at the door with that face of yours, not to mention your Goldilocks hair."

Bridie folded her arms across her chest. "That's ridiculous. People only liking you for your looks. How do they know what I'm like? I plan on being a prickly pear. Now, if I could marry a horse, I'd consider it."

"Oh, Bridie. I do love you," Mom said to her. "I so wish I'd had a daughter."

A thought hit me. "Mom, would you like to come and live with us? I worry about you all alone in the winter. We have plenty of room."

"That would be supercalifragilisticexpialidocious!" Bridie shouted.

Mom squeezed my hand. "That's very sweet of you, George, but I'm afraid I'm a creature of habit, and I don't think I'd survive long without my own things around me. I hope you understand."

"I do," Bridie said. "It's like they're your friends."

The day I planned on driving Mom home Bridie came down with a bad throat, so I ordered her to bed and told her to stay there. Mavis said she'd ply her with salt water to gargle, but I think that was only to impress Mom. I knew Bridie would take care of herself.

The roads were a bit slick on the drive to St. Peter's, and by the time we got to Mom's it felt like I had a pinched nerve in my neck from gripping the wheel so tightly. That set off a huge migraine. Mom thought I should stay the night and I felt crummy enough to realize she was right, so I phoned Mavis.

"I'll leave in the morning and hopefully this misery will have passed by then."

"Okay."

"How's Bridie feeling?"

"Okay."

"Have you checked on her?"

"I'm not her evil stepmother! Of course I checked on her. She was asleep for most of the day."

"Sorry. I was just asking."

"Call when you leave tomorrow, so I'll know when to expect you."

"Righto. Good night."

She hung up on me without saying goodbye. She always did that. It bugged me.

It was strange to be back in my childhood room, lying on my bed, listening to my mother putter downstairs. At one point, I thought I heard my father's voice, but I must have been dreaming. When I got up it was late in the afternoon. I felt drained and done in, but my migraine had mostly disappeared. All that was left was that heavy sensation across my brow.

Mom had a pot of homemade soup on the stove. "You look like you've been dragged through a knothole. Come and take a few sips of this. It might help."

I sat at the table. "Do you have any painkillers?"

She looked in the cupboard over the sink. "I should." She took down a bottle and shook it, then looked inside. "One left. Darn."

"Never mind. I need some air. I'll go to the drugstore after. Anything else you want?"

"No, I'm good."

The chicken soup was delicious, but I didn't have much of an appetite. Mom said I better get going before the store closed so I put on my coat, boots, and gloves and headed out. It was almost dark and the air was crisp and cold. It felt good just breathing it in.

The roads were still slippery. It was the right thing not to try to get back to Sydney today; that stretch was long and lonely at this time of year.

I made it to the drugstore just before they closed and picked up what I needed, as well as a paper and a package of gum. At the last moment I saw a package of Chicken Bones, Mom's favourite candy, so I bought that too.

On the way home, I'm not sure what came over me, but I drove past our driveway and headed up the road a little farther to see if the lights were on at Nell's. It was a ridiculous notion that I instantly regretted. Swearing under my breath, I knew I needed to turn around and go back home where I belonged, but as I rounded the familiar corner my headlights picked up a car that had one wheel in the ditch of Nell's driveway. Oh God, please don't let it be her.

A figure got out of the car and flagged me down.

There she was. Looking as beautiful as ever. How was that possible?

I pulled the car over and she approached me as I got out.

"Sorry about this," she said. "I just need a..."

She realized it was me.

"H-hi, Nell."

"George. What are you doing here?"

"I drove my mother home today. She spent the holidays with us."

"Of course. What a stupid question. How are you?"

"Fine. You?"

"Fine. Well, not fine at the moment. I need a push to get the car back up the driveway."

"You need some reflective lights, so you know where the ditch is in the winter."

"You always were clever. Can you help me?"

"Of course. Get in and hopefully I can have you on your way."

She got back in her car and I placed myself behind the left fender. "When I say go, you step on the gas!" I shouted.

"Okay!"

"Go!"

The car moved forward only a few inches as I pushed against it.

"It's really stuck," she yelled out the window.

"I'm going to rock it. You press the gas when you feel me push forward, and then let up until I push it again!"

My pride got the better of me and I pushed with more strength than I had, but finally the wheel found the road again and she drove it out of the rut. I was panting by this time. I walked up to her car window.

"That wasn't so bad," I said.

"Thank you very much."

"You're welcome."

We looked at each other.

"Why don't you come up to the house for some cocoa? Your reward for a job well done."

"You still drink the stuff?" I laughed.

"Who doesn't like chocolate?"

"Okay," I said, thinking what a bad idea this was.

She drove away up the hill and I got in my car and followed her. What was I doing? The last time I was here was the start of the whole thing. She'd said she hated me and never wanted to see me again. That was fourteen years ago. Did time heal all wounds?

When Nell opened the back door, a dog I assumed was named Dog came bounding out, wagging his tail. He sniffed me thoroughly and kindly let me in ahead of him.

Her kitchen was exactly the same, only fuller somehow. She clearly never threw anything out.

"Sit," she said, as she removed her coat and left her boots in the porch. I followed suit and sat in the one chair that didn't have anything on it. As if time stood still, a cat was on the kitchen table, washing his face.

"That can't possibly be the same cat," I blurted.

"No. That's a newer version. Say hello, Cat."

Cat blinked and went on with his business.

I watched her as she busied herself pouring milk into a pot on the stove and taking the can of cocoa and a bowl of sugar from a shelf. She didn't look at me, so I knew she was nervous and probably regretting the invitation.

She hadn't aged at all. Well, a little bit, a few wrinkles around her eyes, but she looked younger than I did. She wore her hair the same way, and her figure was still as fabulous as ever. I felt flushed, a sheen of perspiration covering my body, which made me shudder. My clothes were damp from the exertion outside.

"Are you cold?" she said.

"Not really."

"The cocoa will warm you up."

She stirred the pot endlessly, it seemed. I wanted her to sit down. No, I wanted her to kiss me. No, I wanted to leave. No, I wanted to wrap myself in her arms. No, I wanted to stop thinking about Bridie. I was going to blow it. Why didn't I tell her about Bridie? She was going to hate me all over again and I deserved to be hated.

"George?"

I realized I blanked out for a moment. My cup of cocoa was in front of me.

"Sorry. Thank you."

She finally sat opposite me with her own mug and took a sip.

"So here we are," she said. "Together again."

Nodding was the only thing I could do. I didn't dare open my lips, for fear of it all tumbling out.

She took a deep breath. "I regret the things I said the last time you were in this kitchen. Grief overtook me. I've wanted to get in touch with you over the years, but the more time that passed, the more I was sure you hated me and there was no point."

"I don't hate you."

"It was my fault. It wasn't your fault. It was all mine. I should have asked someone for help in finding a solution for Jane instead of taking it upon myself to remove her from her home, which was the cabin on this road. It belonged to a Gervais and Maggie Landry. Maggie died years before and Gervais was a terrible drunk who neglected Jane to the point of abandonment. She was their only daughter. I put you in a horrible position and I had no right to do that. Jane's death falls squarely on my shoulders. I will never forgive myself."

"You had no way of knowing we were going to have an accident. And perhaps I was in a position to have helped her, if things had gone differently." I picked up the mug of cocoa and downed it. Stop talking.

She took a tendril of her hair and wrapped it behind her ear, the way she always did when she was tentative. "While we're talking, and who knows if we will again, I want you to know that I was wrong about something else."

I sat there and waited.

"I should've married you, George. I didn't think I could love a child, but I did. I did so profoundly, and Jane wasn't even mine. My actions set us on a course to live apart forever, and I don't think that was fair to either of us. You've been married a long time, so I have no right to presume your marriage has been a mistake, but I know in my heart that I never would have loved another man as much as I loved you...love you."

I put my arms on the table and lay my head on top of them and cried bitterly. She didn't try and stop me. Years of misery seeped out of me, but it wasn't enough. There was still more I was hiding from her. I was trapped like a rabbit in a snare.

There was no way to do this. There was no way out.

Eventually I looked up and she had placed a box of tissues on the table. I grabbed a handful and wiped up the mess on my face. My heart was racing. What must she think of me?

"I'm sorry, Nell. I'm just sorry about everything. And I want you to know that I do love you still, with all my heart."

She smiled at me and reached for my hand. "Why can't we be together, then? Why can't we undo the mistakes we've made and start over? Our lives are almost done. Don't we deserve to be happy? If you don't love your wife, let her go. She must know how you feel. Is it fair to her to keep her in a loveless marriage?"

My head started to throb again. I needed air. I got out of the chair and reached for my coat. She ran over to my side and put her arms around me.

"Say you love me, George. Let me hear you say it again."

I took her face in my hands. "I love you, Nell. You are my one true love. I will love you until the day I die."

We kissed each other then, and it was as easy as breathing. We were home. This was where we both belonged. How effortless it would have been to take her upstairs and feel the body I loved beneath me.

"Be with me," she whispered into my neck. "I need you. I want you. Please, George. Say you forgive me."

"There's nothing to forgive, Nell."

I kissed her again, knowing it would be the last time I ever would. I needed it to last me a lifetime. She sensed the urgency and pressed against me. We were one in that moment.

Then I gently pushed her away. "I have to go, Nell. I can never see you again. I'm sorry. I'm so sorry."

"But you love me, George." She looked panicked and confused. I wasn't making any sense to her. "You're telling me you love me. You're kissing me like you love me. I don't understand."

"Trust me. It has to be this way. It's nothing you've done. It's my fault. The whole goddamn mess is my fault."

I fled the house and took off in the car as quickly as I could. It was like a dream. Had that happened? Had I kissed Nell?

Mom's house came too quickly. I should have wandered the roads to get my bearings and then gone home, but as I pulled into the driveway I saw her peek out the kitchen window so I had to go inside.

"I was starting to get worried," she said.

"I ran into a friend and we got to chatting." I held out her candy. "Here's your treat."

"Thank you. Are you okay?"

"My headache is back. I think I'll just go to bed. Good night, Mom."

"Good night, honey."

Her eyes were on me as I left the kitchen. Mothers. How come they can always see right through you?

❧

SOMETHING BROKE IN ME THAT NIGHT. I LOVED NELL, AND she loved me, but we could never be together because then she'd know about Bridie and hate me once more. I was still the coward who took months to tell her about Jane and I couldn't face her inevitable wrath over Bridie. Knowing she loved me made it worse, and I knew I would never be the same. As hard as I tried to hide it from my family they knew, without ever knowing why.

I constantly felt I was letting them down. But the fatigue that overwhelmed me couldn't be hidden. It was all I could do to make it through the workday, and I relied on Bridie to keep the conversation going at the dinner table.

"Did you cure a bunch of sick people today, Pops?"

"No."

"You're supposed to say yes!"

"Yes."

"That's better. And how do you like the chicken? I fried it myself."

"Good."

"You're supposed to say *fantastic!*"

"Fantastic."

Patty tried as well. "Dad, what do you think of having a reception at the Keltic Lodge in Ingonish?"

"Umm..."

"You don't like the idea?"

Mavis answered for me. "Don't ask your father. He's not interested, and it doesn't matter what he thinks. He's not planning the wedding."

Patty tried again. "Do you think it's too far away?"

"A bit."

"Where should we go, then?"

I couldn't think, but I was aware that their faces were turned in my direction. Why didn't they leave me alone?

"What about the back garden? You and Ray were brought up on this street. It's where you fell in love."

"That's so romantic!" Bridie shouted.

"Don't be ridiculous," Mavis said. "We can't fit over two hundred and fifty guests in the back!"

"How many?"

"I told you long ago it was going to be a big wedding," Mavis sighed. "You never listen."

"You don't mind, do you, Daddy?" Patty looked uneasy.

It was easiest to say, "No, dear."

❦

ONE SATURDAY IN THE SPRING, BRIDIE ASKED IF WE COULD GO fishing and I flat out said no. I didn't even bother giving her an excuse. The disappointment on her face barely registered with me. The next weekend, Patty sat down next to me in the living room. She held my hand.

"Whatcha doin', Dad?"

"Watching television."

She looked at the set. "It's not on."

"Oh."

She put her head on my shoulder. That was nice of her.

Being a doctor, I was well aware of the symptoms of clinical depression, and I knew I ticked all the boxes, but to admit it would destroy my reputation. Not that I cared about my career, but I needed a job to finance this impressive wedding. I needed to know I could keep Mavis the way she liked to be kept, and I needed to keep saving money for Bridie's future.

Suddenly it was July and the wedding was upon us. For some reason, I thought it would be a longer process, but it was just as well. Living in the house with a heightened state of wedding mania was getting to me. With all the frenzied activity, even Bridie got fired up.

"I'm rethinking the spinster route, Pops."

I poured a bowl of cereal. "Don't do it."

"Patty wants me to wear a long blue empire-waist dress. I have no idea what an empire waist is, but it sounds impressive, don't you think? And apparently, I get to wear a short veil with a flat bow on the top of my head. It's not every day you get to do that. Who knew weddings were so outside the world of reality?"

All I knew was the cost was out of this world. Mavis insisted I buy a tuxedo. When was I ever going to wear that again?

"Can't I just rent one?"

"You can always tell a rented tuxedo. You have a pivotal role in the ceremony. All eyes will be on you and Patty walking down the aisle. You can't screw it up, George. I'm doing everything else, and this is the only thing I'm asking you to do. For God's sake, oblige me."

So I hauled my body into Spinner's Men's Wear and had myself fitted for a black tuxedo. The girls made me give them a show when I brought it home. When I walked into the living room with it on, they clapped and hooted. Mavis ran over and kissed me.

"What a handsome man!" she burbled.

"Daddy, you look fantastic!"

Bridie giggled. "The old dolls at the wedding will swoon at the sight of you."

It's really too bad I felt nothing at all.

Fortunately, you'd have to be dead not to have an emotional response when you see your first-born daughter in her wedding gown. My eyes filled up as Patty twirled for me in her bedroom on that beautiful summer afternoon.

"What do you think, Dad?"

"I think Ray is one very lucky young man. You look beautiful, sweetheart."

"Thanks, Daddy." She kissed my cheek and I held her close. Until she shouted in my ear: "Bridie! Your bow is upside down! You can't possibly think it goes like that!"

"How was I supposed to know?"

Patty rushed off to tear the bow off Bridie's head and put it back the way she wanted it. It looked exactly the same to me. Then Mavis shouted something from our room and Patty disappeared. Bridie looked at herself in the mirror and shook her head.

"For one silly moment, I thought this was going to be fun, but I feel like a fool in this blue veil. It looks like the toilet-paper doll in Mavis's bathroom."

"For pity's sake, please don't say that to Patty."

When you think of what you do at a wedding, it's amazing that it's so bloody tiring. You get in a car, walk down an aisle, sit down, walk back up an aisle, greet friends, eat food, dance, say a few words, kiss people goodbye, and get back in the car to go home. The tiring part must come from the fact that it takes eighteen hours for all this to unfold.

Mavis, Bridie, and I walked into the house silently. We looked at each other.

"That was fun," Mavis said.

We nodded wearily.

"Let's hit the hay," I said.

"I'm definitely never getting married," said guess who.

I COULDN'T BELIEVE MY APPEARANCE WHEN I LOOKED AT THE wedding album a month later. Anyone within a mile radius could see I looked miserable, and here I'd thought I was putting up a good front. It was shocking, and I berated myself for not making more of an effort to look happy on the most important day of my daughter's life.

Once Patty moved out, the house was like a tomb. Mavis was making me pay for being uninterested in everyone and everything, including her, so to punish me she shopped just about every day. It was getting to the point where we had no more closet space in any of our bedrooms. Bridie's old room upstairs was basically a storage facility.

Bridie, bless her heart, carried on as if everything was normal, which must have taken an awful toll on her. As much as I wanted to help her, it was as if my hands were tied behind my back. She was the buffer between Mavis and myself—a terrible burden to put on anyone, let alone an almost sixteen-year-old.

I remember Eileen admiring the light in Bridie's eyes, and I missed seeing it. It was my fault it was gone. The state I was in, I was convinced everything in the world was my fault.

Donny showed up at my office one morning before my first patients arrived.

"To what do I owe the pleasure?" I said.

With his usual tact, he plunked himself down on the chair in front of me. "Mom wants to know what's wrong with you. I told her you've always been a prick. Is she just noticing this now?"

"You're a funny guy, Donny."

His faced turned serious. "What's up, George? You're obviously not yourself. That's all I hear at the water cooler. 'What's wrong with George?' It's getting tiring."

"I'm fine."

"Bullshit."

I got up and looked out the window through the dusty blinds.

"Why don't you get a divorce? Mavis would drive anyone around the bend."

"This has nothing to do with Mavis."

"Look, George, you and I have never been close, but I do care about you. I think you need help, so do yourself a favour and get some. If not here, then somewhere else. Go to Halifax. See a therapist. Talk therapy is becoming more accepted now. Get yourself on an antidepressant. I'm tired of seeing your long face haunting these halls. If nothing else, go on a two-week fishing trip. Surely that would help."

"That sounds nice."

He got up from the chair. "I'm no good at this sort of thing, but think about what Dad would say to you if he were here. I wish he were."

"Yeah, me too."

"Gotta run. Have a bowel re-section first thing this morning. What a shitty way to start the day!"

"Thanks for dropping by."

He closed the door behind him.

How bad must I have been if Donny was trying to help?

The words *fishing trip* kept replaying themselves over and over in my mind. The more I thought about it, the better I liked it. And then suddenly I had a plan. Maybe there was a way out after all.

CHAPTER TWELVE

"This meeting will come to order."

My family stared at me from around the dining room table. I'd even asked Patty and Ray to come over, and Mom was visiting.

"I'm not sure if any of you know this, but I happen to be a crackerjack at reading the stock market, and I've made a little money over the years that I've squirrelled away."

Mavis's mouth dropped open. "Why all the griping about the cost of the wedding, then?"

"I was trying to manage expectations, Mavis. That's all."

"Let him talk, Mom."

"I've decided that since life is short, I want to do something for all of you. A little token of my appreciation. I want you to think of something that you'd like to do or have, and I'll do my best to make it happen."

"I want to go fishing with you," Bridie said.

"Think harder, Bridie. That's hardly enough."

"It's more than enough. We could go for a week."

I smiled at her. "Okay. Done."

"I want to go to Paris," Mavis said.

"Done."

Mavis nearly fell off her chair. "Really?! Are you serious?"

"Why not take my beautiful wife to the city of love?"

Everyone looked at me as if I'd lost my marbles, but I meant it. Mavis jumped up and kissed my cheek over and over. "I can't wait!"

Patty and Ray exchanged glances. "Would you have enough for a down payment on a house we saw last week? It's not extravagant, but it's really nice. We were wowed by the price."

"Done."

Patty jumped up and kissed me as well. "Oh, Daddy, thank you, thank you!"

Ray reached across the table to shake my hand. "That's very generous, George." I'd told him to call me that. I was afraid he'd call me Dad otherwise.

I looked at my mother. "And you? What do you want, you sweet woman?"

"I want you to take care of yourself."

"Spoken like a true mother," I smiled.

Mavis pointed at her. "At least ask for a fur coat, Jean. Remember how cold you were last Christmas?"

"And a fur coat."

We laughed. I looked at Bridie again. "Are you sure you don't want to change your mind?"

"I got the best gift of all."

I went with Patty and Ray to see the house they'd chosen. It was just off Cottage Road. It impressed me. Solid, not huge, but not too small either. They would grow into it. Then off we went to the bank to make the arrangements. They shook the banker's hand and we stood outside on Charlotte Street, on a lovely August afternoon, smiling at each other. They both hugged me before they walked hand in hand down the street. At that moment, I was elated. Patty would be safe and sound in her new house with the man she loved. She was a good kid, and Mavis and I had done as good a job as we could bringing her up. Correction—Eileen had done a great job making her feel loved and secure, with a normal routine and good food on the table. A friend Patty could rely on.

My next stop was to Vogue Furriers with my mother. She was reluctant at first.

"This seems too extravagant, George. Why don't we buy a nice wool coat?"

I put my arm around her shoulder as we walked towards the store. "Mom, it gives me great pleasure to see you in something you deserve. You've sacrificed all your life for Dad, Donny, and me. A warm coat is not foolhardy in the face of a lifetime of thrift."

"Oh, well, when you put it that way," she laughed.

In the end, she chose a mid-calf caramel-coloured mink coat with a high collar and a matching hat. It looked amazing on her.

"It makes you look twenty years younger." I smiled.

She looked at herself this way and that in front of the tri-mirror. "You know, you're right. Oh my, I'll be kicked out of church for being so brazen!"

I could tell she was tickled pink with her purchase and that gave me a warm feeling all over.

It was time to take Mavis to Paris, before she started bellyaching for a fur coat too.

We left the third week of September after two colleagues agreed to look after my patients while I was gone. Mom stayed with Bridie and Patty said she'd be sure to check in on them, and I knew she would. The travel agent made all the arrangements. The first surprise for Mavis was that we flew first-class across the Atlantic, and as we toasted ourselves with champagne in our seats, the look on Mavis's face was exactly what I wanted to see. I knew with this flight alone she'd have enough fodder to entertain her girlfriends for years.

But I didn't expect to fall in love with Paris just as much as Mavis did.

It was complete culture shock just driving into the city. The traffic was mesmerizing, with scooters and motorcycles whizzing past our taxi on either side. We both laughed at the number of women driving scooters with high heels on.

The neoclassical architecture took my breath away—long, tree-lined boulevards of warm, cream-grey limestone buildings with symmetrical windows and wrought-iron balconies. There were shops and cafés on every corner, with the Seine River flowing through the city and bridges everywhere we looked. Parisians gathered by the Seine in the evening, drinking wine and having impromptu picnics with their baguettes and cheese. It was a lifestyle so foreign to us that we really did feel like country mice.

We spent two weeks walking around the city, seeing the sights. The enormous Notre-Dame Cathedral made us quake just walking into it. Striding through the grounds as the Eiffel Tower loomed before us felt unreal. You see it on postcards, but to look up into the tower itself made us feel very small. We drove up to the Arc de Triomphe in a taxi and our driver kindly agreed to take us around it a few times, before letting us out to wander down the Champs-Élysées on our own. To think that Nazi troops had walked up this same route made me shiver. Suddenly the war seemed very close again.

When Mavis stood in front of Versailles, she threw her arms in the air. "Finally! My dream house!" We laughed together and that felt nice.

There was a crowd of people standing in front of the Mona Lisa at the Louvre, so we didn't get a chance to get too close, but it was so much smaller than we imagined it. While we loved the Louvre, I think my favourite museum was the Musée d'Orsay, originally built as a train station for the 1900 World Fair. The openness of it left a great impression on me. It let me breathe, as if I were in the middle of a river back home.

Every night we wandered to a different café for dinner. All our meals were exquisite. Sitting outside on the sidewalk, our chairs facing the street, we pretended we were world travellers used to eating side-by-side with strangers who gestured with their cigarettes and drank wine endlessly. Parisian French is a beautiful language to listen to, even if we didn't have a clue what they were saying. Fortunately, our white-aproned waiters knew English so we didn't have to struggle too badly making ourselves understood.

Our hotel was very comfortable, but the room was small. It had a creaky elevator that only held about two people and took forever to arrive, so after a day we trekked up three flights of stairs because it was faster. Our breakfast consisted of buttery croissants, brie, strawberries, and café au lait.

Mavis wanted me to try the hot chocolate. "This is divine!" I couldn't do it.

At night, we would open our immense rectangular windows that skirted the floor and look out on our still courtyard before crawling into bed. We'd hold each other as we listened to the rain and the sounds of the city. It was the best part of our day.

"We should've done this years ago," Mavis whispered, as she traced her fingers along my chest. "The world is so big, and not everyone lives as we do. I wonder what our lives would've been like if we were born here."

"We'd have gone through a hellish and frightening war up close and personal."

"True." She turned towards me. "Do you love me, George?"

"Yes, Mavis. I do."

"Are you glad we got married?"

"Sure. It's a good thing we did, or poor old Ray would be single. Can you imagine life without Patty?"

"No." There was a long pause and I knew she was going to say it before she did. "But I can imagine life without Bridie."

All the goodwill that had built up the last few weeks melted away in that instant.

"Mavis—"

"I'm sorry, George. That's not exactly what I meant. I guess what I want you to know is that life might have been easier if it had been just you, me, and Patty. Having Eileen become a second wife in the house made me feel expendable. I know I took advantage of Eileen, but it's almost as if I did it to punish her because I knew you loved having her around, and I felt invisible half the time. I know you think I'm jealous of Bridie, and I guess I am. I always felt you loved her more than our child. It sounds ridiculous when I say it out loud, but this trip has made me realize that if we'd had time to be on our own, maybe we would've been happier together over the years."

It was the first time she'd explained herself without rancour and I knew it was from her heart. I squeezed her tight.

She was right: it would've been easier. But the trouble was, I knew Nell before I ever met Mavis. Poor Mavis was doomed to failure from the start. How unfair.

"I understand what you're saying. It's true. But I hope this trip will go a long way in letting you know that I do love you, and I've loved our life together, and Patty wouldn't be here if it weren't for you. I'm grateful for everything and I don't want you to forget that."

We made love that night, without obligation or guilt. It was a genuine expression of gratitude for the years we'd travelled together through life. Just because our marriage wasn't always happy didn't mean we weren't fond of each other. There's power in being beside the same person for most of your life. If they aren't there, there's just a big hole.

One of our last stops was Les Puces, a massive antique market. We went on the Metro. The market was like an outdoor maze of tiny shops, tents, and cubbyholes filled with antique jewellery, rugs, linens, picture frames, machinery, housewares, fabrics, clothing, and purses. We arrived at lunchtime, which we soon found out was not the best time. The vendors sat together on makeshift chairs in front of their stalls and had their hot meal together, heedless of us standing there waiting to buy something.

"Revenez dans une heure," we were told. Clearly, their meal was more important than our money. Now that was something I admired.

We picked up gifts, an antique jewellery box for Patty and a lace handkerchief for Mom.

"You're going to have to pick up something for Bridie and Ray. I have no idea what they'd like."

Rummaging through what looked like a tool shop, I found the perfect gift for Bridie. It was a vintage green metal tackle box that had three trays inside. There was a bit of rust, and it was obviously used, but it was sturdy and reminded me of the one Dad used to have. I wondered what ever happened to his. Bridie could use this one on our trip together.

I picked up Ray a couple of vintage model cars, a 1926 Arcade Model T Coupe and a cast iron 1930s motorcycle with sidecar. Apparently, he liked to collect them.

Our last night in Paris we went to a nightclub and behaved outrageously.

"No one knows us!" I shouted in Mavis's ear. "We can do what we want!"

We drank too much and danced with the best of them on the crowded dance floor. I'll never forget singing and swaying together as we walked the streets of Paris at two in the morning. It was a full moon that night, and the sound of Mavis's high heels clicking on the sidewalk stayed with me as we climbed the stairs of our hotel and collapsed, laughing, in a heap on our bed.

Mavis held her hands to my face. "Thank you, George. Thank you, thank you, thank you."

"Thank you, Mavis."

We fell asleep in our coats and almost missed our plane the next morning. We toasted each other again, this time with a non-alcoholic ginger ale, while flying first class back to the real world.

"That was the best two weeks of my life," Mavis said, beaming.

That's exactly what I wanted to hear.

When we got home, Mom had made a roast chicken dinner with her lemon meringue pie for dessert. She'd invited Patty and Ray over, so everyone was there when we walked in the door.

I could tell the family was amazed at how happy and relaxed Mavis was. She fairly bubbled with joy as she recalled what we had seen and done. My mother and girls were clearly enthralled with the stories, and all of them loved their gifts.

"What was your favourite thing, Pops?"

"Seeing the curtains blow and listening to the rain when the windows were open at night. Knowing I was in Europe. It felt like the movies."

❧

I CALLED SYDNEY ACADEMY AND TOLD THE PRINCIPAL I WAS taking my daughter out of school for a week. He asked why and I said it was a personal matter. He said since Bridie was an exceptional student, it wasn't likely her studies would suffer. I agreed.

Bridie and I hit the road after Thanksgiving, again taking advantage of my colleagues' generous offer to keep my office ticking. One of them said before I left, "I hope this helps you, George." I told him it would.

We packed the car with our fishing gear, warm clothes, and boxes of food. I took her up to the Margaree Valley, where we stayed in a small cabin used by fishermen on holiday.

In the morning, we got up with the sun and had our fill of eggs, bacon, and toast. I put on a pot of coffee for myself and poured orange juice for Bridie.

"May I have a cup of coffee?" she asked.

"How old are you?"

"Pops, you know how old I am."

"Six?"

"Sixteen. My birthday was only last month."

"You're right. It's high time you took up caffeine." I took down an old mug in the cupboard and poured her a coffee. "You'll probably want some cream and sugar in it."

"Let me taste it without."

"If you say so."

She blew on the coffee to cool it a little and took the smallest sip. "Okay, that tastes like a blackboard. Pass me the cream and sugar."

We drank our coffee on rocking chairs on the front porch while I smoked my pipe.

"We look like we belong on the *Beverly Hillbillies*," she said.

"I learned something while I was away. The French make sure they take time for relaxation. They don't feel guilty lingering over a meal. There's more to life than rushing somewhere. Always remember that."

"Which is why you've always enjoyed fishing, Pops."

"I feel more at peace with the world when I'm standing in the middle of a river with hip waders on than I do in church."

Bridie looked at me seriously. "I believe God is Mother Nature. I don't believe in an old bearded man dressed in robes. Animals, trees, people, the sky, water. They are godly. I pray to the moon, myself."

"Well, I suggest we go catch a few godly salmon."

The Margaree River is about as holy a place as I've ever found for fishing. It meanders along the curve of the land, creating deep pools with long stretches of shallow waters cascading above the rocks, interrupted only by islands of loose gravel that poke through the surface and make a great foothold from which to cast your fly.

The banks of the river can be marshy, with long grasses that bend in the direction of the wind, but there are also stretches of sandy shore, perfect for a rest. At this time of year, with the autumn leaves shimmering gold, red, and orange, you can't quite believe the beauty.

We picked a spot I knew of, a little off the beaten track, and set up our equipment on the shore. We even had a small propane stove to make tea, and camping chairs to ease our legs later in the day. Bridie opened her tackle box and showed me how she had organized her flies.

"There's no real system to it. It's more colour-coordinated, which sounds very girly, but I like it like that, so call me crazy."

"Everyone has their own system. Let's go."

We waded out into a section of river that came up to our knees. It made things a bit easier. I went over the technique of fly fishing and made Bridie cast her line several times before I went downstream to give her space. At first, she made the classic mistake of overreaching with the rod.

"Remember," I shouted, "it's more of a flick! Like taking a whip to a horse."

"Don't ever whip a horse, Pops!" she shouted back.

She kept asking me questions for the first hour, but eventually she realized that it didn't matter if she cast it perfectly. It was just fun to see the line sail away in the air and land in the water so you could slowly reel it in, hopefully thinking of nothing at all.

We didn't catch anything until late afternoon. Then Bridie gave a yelp. "I think I have something! I definitely have something! Pops! Help! It's too strong!"

I hurried back, as much as you can hurry in water, and stood beside her, giving her pointers as she pulled and reeled, pulled and reeled. "My arms are going to come off! Take it!"

She passed me the rod and she was right. This salmon felt like a twenty-pounder. Talk about beginner's luck. It took a good amount of effort to bring the salmon in.

"Hold the net steady!"

She held it out, but it took the two of us to handle it. Meanwhile the salmon was thrashing about giving us a mighty fight. Bridie started shouting, "Let it go!"

"What?!"

"It's my fish. Let it go! It's too big!"

Every drop of my fisherman blood rose up in protest, but I could see she was distressed. I pulled the fly out of the salmon's mouth and dropped it in the water. That very lucky critter disappeared in a flash.

She looked at me with big eyes. "Sorry, Pops, but it was big enough to be someone's pet. I don't mind catching normal-looking trout, but I could've given that guy a name. It's wrong to kill something that has a personality. Did you see the look of hate in his eyes?"

"I missed that."

"I'm not sure I'm cut out for salmon fishing."

"Never mind. Looks like we'll have corned beef hash for supper."

We packed up as the sun cast long shadows over the mountains circling the valley. The air had cooled considerably by then, and we were happy to head back to the warm cabin. We sat with our feet up next to the fireplace and ate our hash.

"Do you think fishermen would fish even if they didn't catch anything for years?"

I put my empty plate down on the floor and lit my pipe before I answered. "Maybe. Fortunately, most of us catch just enough to make us hopeful for the next time."

She licked her plate clean and I pointed at her. "What happened to your manners?"

"When you're on a fishing trip, manners go out the window."

I puffed away. "Sounds sensible."

The two of us were asleep by eight.

There were a few days we didn't catch anything, but most of the time we had enough for our supper. The drizzly days seemed to give us our best results. One day was a complete downpour, with thunder and lightning. We stayed close to the fire, playing cards and cribbage. Bridie always beat me. At home she always won at chess too. I tried to show Patty how to play once and she ended up throwing the pieces to the floor in frustration.

Towards the end of the week, we went for a hike instead of fishing. "I'm not spending enough time with you just talking," Bridie complained. So we made a picnic and hiked our way over a marked trail sitting on the edge of a bluff that overlooked the choppy, grey ocean.

"Pops, what do you think I should do with my life?"

"Live it."

"What am I good at?"

I gave it a great deal of thought before answering.

"Survival. You've survived everything that's ever come your way. From the very moment you were born, you've hung on when the circumstances were dire. A lot has happened to you in the last sixteen years, and you've met every challenge with determination and bravery. Come what may, I have no doubt you will succeed and that your life will be a good one. That's because you believe in yourself—a rare quality. A precious possession. Never lose it."

She seemed pleased with my answer.

"Now this question is a tricky one," she said. "You might not want to answer it."

"Shoot."

"Who's your favourite person in the whole world?"

"You are."

She took a big bite of her apple. "How convenient. You're mine."

∞

ON HALLOWEEN, A MAN CAME INTO MY OFFICE WITH HIS WIFE. She had a fatal condition and there wasn't anything I could do for her. Her husband was furious with the world and took it out on me.

"Are you just going to sit there and tell us that nothing else can be done? What kind of doctor are you, not to offer some kind of hope?"

"I understand how you feel—"

"No, I don't think you do. You're like a goddamn robot when we come here. Every appointment we watch you look at your notes instead of at us. Your eyes are dead, man! Maybe you should quit being a doctor if you hate it so much. You don't have an ounce of empathy for anyone! I'm going to report you to whoever is in charge of this hospital. We want another doctor, someone who gives a damn!"

He took his wife's hand and rushed out of my office. I turned my chair to look out the window but there was nothing to see. Just the same brick wall I'd spent years gazing at.

Eventually, I heard a soft rapping at the door. My secretary poked her head in.

"Sorry. Are you ready for your next appointment?"

"Just give me a minute."

She closed the door.

After ten minutes of thinking about nothing at all, I decided the best thing to do was to walk away. I had six patients in the waiting room, and my secretary looked at me with panic as I sauntered out of my office. My first stop was to a downtown store and then to the post office. After that I went home. Mavis wasn't in, and Bridie was at school. I left them a note.

Gone fishing.

182

CHAPTER THIRTEEN

BRIDIE
1965

Eric Wells persisted with his dumb request. He followed me out the front doors as I was heading home from school.

"Who doesn't want to go to a Halloween party?" he pleaded. "Everyone will be there. Come with me. We'll have a blast."

"No thanks. Halloween is for suckers."

"It's a great excuse to dress up, have a few drinks, and terrorize the neighbourhood."

"Tempting, but no."

He threw his hands in the air and grinned. "Why are you such a pain in the ass?"

"I come from a long line of painful asses."

He laughed. "Did you know the guys have a pool going to see who'll be your date for the prom next year?"

"And that's why guys are lunatics, Eric. See ya later."

"Farewell, my one true love!"

I walked home, kicking fallen leaves in my path. It was a bitterly cold day, with a biting wind. Little kids trick-or-treating tonight would surely perish. Time to gather up some of my winter clothes, which made me realize it would soon be two years since Mama died. The world just kept on spinning, and even though you didn't want it to, it insisted on dragging you with it.

Mavis's car wasn't there, as per usual. I let myself in the back door and put my school bag on the kitchen table. Propped up against the sugar bowl was a note in Pops's handwriting: *Gone fishing.*

"Without me? The rat," was my first thought. "On a Monday?" was my second thought. That didn't make sense. He always had his clinic on Monday afternoons. The phone rang then and I picked up the receiver from the kitchen wall.

"Hello?"

"Hi, Bridie, it's Marilyn. Is your dad there?"

"No. There's a note here that says he's gone fishing, but that's odd."

"He left the office this morning with patients sitting in the waiting room, and now there are a slew of them downstairs at the clinic and he still hasn't shown up."

"I don't know what to tell you."

"It's not like him to keep me in the dark. You know your dad. He's always punctual."

"Usually."

"Please ask him to call me. Thanks, Bridie." And she hung up.

I put down the phone, sat at the kitchen table, and looked at the note again. Then I got up and took my book bag into my bedroom and dropped it on the floor. Next stop was the bathroom, where I washed the day's school germs off my face and hands. Back to the kitchen for a glass of milk and a handful of molasses cookies I'd made the day before. Then to my room, where I picked up my copy of *To Kill a Mockingbird*. I'd read it twice before, but this was a book that deserved to be read multiple times. It was that good.

As I lay back against the pillows on my bed, I tried to concentrate on Harper Lee's words, but I munched on my cookies and stared out the window instead. Not that I was thinking of anything in particular, but I just couldn't seem to focus.

Then the doorbell rang.

I hurried to the front door. We weren't expecting anyone. I opened it.

"Trick or treat!"

A witch, a dog, and a peanut stared at me. Damn. I knew there was something I was supposed to do.

"You guys are early."

"Our mom has night school," said the dog. "We're collecting for UNICEF too."

"Just a sec." I left them on the step and hurried out to the back porch, where I had boxes of chips and bags of small chocolate bars and Molasses Kisses. I opened the packages and dumped everything in a couple of big bowls, and took them to the front door. "Take what you want. I've got to get some money."

There was a container of pennies under the stairs for some reason, so I took that and put the pennies in their boxes. It didn't seem like a lot, so I ran back for my wallet and added a few nickels and dimes as well.

Eventually, I just wrapped myself in a coat and mitts and sat on the front step and handed out stuff until I ran out. How many kids lived in this neighbourhood anyway? They had quite a racket going, if you asked me.

I turned out the front light, supposedly a universal symbol for "We're not home," but that didn't stop the doorbell from ringing.

Mavis eventually showed up at eight. She came through the back door and was fit to be tied. "Those goddamn kids threw eggs at my car! I completely forgot it was Halloween tonight, or I never would've gone to Francine's for supper. Where's your father? He's going to have to clean that off."

"Dad isn't home."

She made a face. "Surely the clinic didn't last this long. I always tell him he needs to cut back. Patients take advantage of him."

"Marilyn called earlier. She said he walked out of the office this morning and didn't show up for clinic. She was wondering where he was."

"That's strange."

"He left a note on the table." I handed it to her.

She looked at it. "Gone fishing. On a Monday?"

"That's what I thought."

"And he hasn't called?"

I shook my head.

Mavis went over to the phone. "I'm calling Patty. Maybe she's heard from him."

She hadn't.

Mavis looked at me. "What should we do?"

"Call Uncle Donny."

So she did. Then Gran. Then Betty. No one had heard from him.

Mavis began to get agitated and paced the kitchen floor. "That silly man! What's he playing at? You can't just leave a note like that and disappear for hours. He must know we'll be worried."

The phone rang and Mavis ran to get it. "Hello?"

It was Gran. "Yes, Jean. I'll call you the instant he gets in. Doesn't matter what time it is. I'm sure he's just delayed, or he's had a flat tire in the middle of nowhere. I shouldn't have called you. Please don't worry. There's probably a good explanation."

At eleven, Mavis was frantic and very cross.

"Why does he insist on dragging himself to these godforsaken places that don't have telephones—or people, for that matter? What if he's fallen and hurt himself? There's no one around to help him. What is the lure of fishing? Can you answer me that?"

Patty had arrived by then. "That's what I'd like to know."

I sipped the tea I'd made for us. "To get away from people."

"Oh, spare me!" Mavis shouted. "I could just wring his neck. This is very inconsiderate. His mother is elderly and I know she's pacing the floor at this very moment. Maybe I shouldn't have called her."

Surprisingly thoughtful of Mavis to think of that.

The more Mavis and Patty fretted, the quieter I got. They were sucking the air out of the room. It wasn't their fault, I just couldn't breathe around them.

"I'm calling the police!" Mavis announced. "I should've done it hours ago."

"I'll be in my room," I said.

They didn't hear me.

I shut the door so I wouldn't have to hear Mavis on the phone. With Mama's quilt wrapped around me, I knelt by my window and looked out at the moon shining down between the inky-black tree branches overlooking our yard.

"You're not here, are you, Pops? You're on the other side of that moon."

Even though I knew the truth—that Pops had planned this—I didn't say a word to Mavis or Patty. They'd be furious that I would even think such a thing. They would have to wait for the official verdict, whenever that came.

All I could do was lie low and let it unfold. I certainly couldn't think right now. A black dread numbed me. Mama had sat for hours on a kitchen chair when she heard her mother died. It was like being frozen with fear. But I knew I couldn't handle my anger either. He left me. He left me.

I put Pops in my heart's pocket, knowing I'd take him out one day when I was alone, probably standing in a river, watching the glint of the sun catch the silver scales of a salmon flashing by.

TWO VERY LONG DAYS PASSED BEFORE THE AUTHORITIES FOUND A rowboat drifting out to sea. It had gone much farther than they had calculated it might, probably due to the stiff winds on Halloween night. Although there was no body, the boat had been rented by a Dr. George Mackenzie, and his fishing gear was still on board.

When the police came to the door to tell us, Mavis collapsed on the living room rug. Patty fell to her knees as well, and the two of them clutched each other, wailing. I stood there and looked at the police officers.

"I'd like his fishing gear, please."

They made a note of it.

I called Uncle Donny to tell him. "You're going to have to tell your mother. I can't do it."

"Of course," he said quietly. "I feel so terrible. I told him he should take a fishing trip to cheer himself up. Why did I open my big mouth?"

Mavis and Patty were inconsolable. It fell to me to answer the door and the phone and to deal with people who came crawling out of the woodwork. A doctor's patients are a pretty loyal bunch, and several times a day I'd have to go to the door to receive a pan of squares, a loaf, or a ham and listen to people tell me that Pops saved their life, or that he was the best doctor in the world and how tragic that he'd died so young in a terrible accident.

Did they really believe that?

Mavis and Patty kept waiting to hear that Pops had been found, but as the days went by, their hopes faded.

The phone calls were fast and furious between relatives. No one could agree on the funeral.

Mavis took to drinking wine right after breakfast. "His mother wants him buried in St. Peter's with his dad and to have his memorial in their church. Well, that's fine and dandy for her, but what about me? I'm his wife, and my wishes are what matter. I want him buried in Sydney, where I can visit him. Is that too much to ask? I'll buy a plot for the two of us. And the memorial has to be here, for his friends and neighbours and colleagues and patients. He lived his life here. Doesn't that make sense?" She waved her wine glass about and downed the last drop.

"It does make sense, Mavis."

She looked at me. "You agree with me?"

"But it's kind of a moot point, because we have no body, do we?"

She threw her empty wine glass in the sink. "Goddammit, you know what I mean! If I have to bury an empty coffin, I will!"

"Then let Gran bury an empty coffin too, if it makes her happy. What difference does it make?"

Mavis rubbed her eyes like a little kid, and then pulled her face down with her fingers as she whined, "That just seems so stupid."

"Why not have a memorial service in Sydney and one in St. Peter's? If we find Pops, we'll bury him here. Gran can put a plaque by his father's headstone, with Pops's name on it. How does that sound?"

She slapped her arms against her sides. "I guess. I don't know what I'm doing anymore. Why isn't Patty here? Why am I all alone?"

I sent her to bed.

This whole argument was ridiculous. Pops was where he wanted to be. Out on the water, out of reach of everyone. I just never thought that would include me.

As I sat in school, I was aware of the eyes on me. Most people stayed away, for which I was grateful. Too bad school administrators weren't as considerate. The guidance counsellor called me to his office two minutes into math class. Already feeling like a freak, I had to get up and walk past my classmates to get to the door. My teacher looked pained. Everyone felt so bad. They needed to get a hold of themselves.

I knocked on Mr. Pruitt's door.

"Come in, Bridie."

He was a large man with two wiry hairs emerging from the end of his nose. Why didn't his wife pluck those? No wedding ring. Ah.

"Sit down."

I sat.

"First of all, I'm very sorry to hear about your father. I know what a painful time this must be."

I stared at his nose.

"Is there anything we can do for you?"

"No."

"We can arrange for you to speak to a grief counsellor." He opened what I presumed was my file in front of him on his desk. "It says here you lost your mother two years ago. Is this correct?"

I nodded.

He folded his hands in front of him. "Losing both parents at such an early age can often send a child down the wrong road in life. We'd like to circumvent that by helping you with whatever you feel you need."

"I need to get back to math class. We're having a test."

He smiled and waved that off. "I can talk to your teacher. There's no reason for you to worry about that."

"I'm looking forward to writing it. I've studied for it."

He stopped smiling. "Have you cried yet, Bridie?"

"That's personal, and none of your business."

"Anger is one of the first emotions that we feel—"

I stood up. "Mr. Pruitt. I am neither angry nor sad. I am what you would call incredulous. I am processing this monumental event as best I can, and if I don't seem to be doing it correctly, that's just too damn bad. If I feel the need to lean on someone, I'll decide that for myself. You will not be involved."

I left him with his mouth open. The man really did remind me of a fat gopher.

The math test was easy. As I put my books away, I noticed a note under my scribbler. It said, "Feel better, my one true love."

Smiling, I looked back at Eric. He blew me a kiss. I blew him one back.

❧

Two weeks went by before Mavis felt strong enough to face the public. She also kept hoping that Pops would be found, but we couldn't wait any longer. We had a memorial service at United Heritage Church on Charlotte Street. We never went there except for Christmas Eve service; we were heathens in this space.

The church was packed to the rafters, almost literally. Poor Gran just about fainted when she saw the crowd. I held onto her, and Mavis and Patty had their arms around each other. Uncle Donny, Aunt Loretta, Aunt Betty, and Uncle Fraser, along with their seven offspring, walked behind us up to the first pew. Mavis told Loretta and Betty to get their broods to sit in the pew behind us. It was like she was directing a Sunday school play. What difference did it make where they sat?

The only way I was going to get through this charade was to tune everyone out. I linked arms with Gran, and while she trembled in her mink coat and sniffed into the lace handkerchief Pops brought back for her from Paris, I had my head down, with my gloved hands on my lap.

Mavis, Patty, and Aunt Betty cried enough for all of us.

There was endless pontification from the clergy, who really didn't know Pops, and then two of his doctor pals got up to regale us with hospital adventures, which made the crowd laugh. Unfortunately, Uncle Donny decided he should speak for the family, and he made it his mission to be funnier than the two doctors. He failed miserably. It was painfully awkward, and he peaked with: "I finally figured out why George went into gastroenterology. He was so good at giving people indigestion! Isn't that right, Mavis?!" He realized he'd gone too far when he looked at Mavis's face. Her lips had disappeared thanks to his performance. Just as I thought. Uncle Donny was dead meat.

He hurried from the pulpit.

Mercifully, the minister wrapped things up and then announced a tea would be served by the unflappable church ladies in the hall. I'd totally forgotten about that.

"Do you want me to take you home, Gran?"

"I could do with a cup of tea. I'd like to meet some of his friends."

I was trapped.

One cup of tea led to a whole pot. Gran was seated at the family table, and there was a lineup a mile long to get to her. This was important. She needed people to tell her how her wonderful son had changed their lives for the better.

There was a similar lineup to get to Mavis and Patty as well. I ended up carrying dishes back to the kitchen and filling teacups. Basically, my plan was to hang out with the lunch bunch and hide myself from the mob. But there's always someone who doesn't leave you alone.

Uncle Donny was talking with his mouth full when he saw me behind the counter. He waved me over and I ignored him, but no, he couldn't take the hint. He walked into the kitchen, stuffing another sandwich in his mouth, and put his hands on my shoulders.

"I want to introduce you to some people. You can't be in here. People want to see you."

"I don't want to be seen."

"Nonsense." He dragged me over to a group of three men and their wives. "Here she is! Our little beauty. This is Bridie. She's special, all right. Look at this hair." He squeezed me tightly against him.

"Take your hands off me."

He laughed like he hadn't heard me.

"Take your hands off me this second, before I slap you in front of these fine people."

One of the ladies reached across and took my elbow. "I could use a little air. You?" She led me outside, just in time for me to puke my guts out over the church railing. She opened her purse and passed me some tissues. I gratefully took them and wiped up my mouth and chin as best I could.

"I'm sorry," I said.

"You have nothing to be sorry for. It's your uncle who needs to apologize. Does he always do that?"

I nodded. "He kissed me once on the mouth when I was nine. I didn't know what it was."

"Unfortunately, funny uncles litter the world. Next time, kick him where it hurts and threaten to call the police. That should stop him—he's nothing if not a coward. He tried to corner me once at the hospital fundraiser. He has a horrible reputation among the women he works with. He's a great surgeon but a lousy human being. I could never figure out how he and your dad were brothers."

"I've always wondered that myself."

"I'll tell you a little story. I'm a nurse, and I was working the day your father came in with you in his arms."

I felt my bottom lip quiver.

"I watched him come and visit you every day while you were in the incubator. When he was able, he'd take you out and lay you on his chest, cover you up, and rock you to sleep. All the nurses were in love with your dad because he was so darn cute, and the fact that he loved you to pieces made us drool. He'd sing and rub your tiny head and look so blissfully happy. We all thought you were the luckiest little girl in the world."

It hit me then. My face crumpled and I reached out. She took me in her arms and let me cry into her nice dress. I'm not sure how long I was there, but she held me tight the whole time. I think Pops must have sent her to me.

After a while, people started to leave the church, so we moved to the side of the steps. She opened her purse again and took out more tissues, wiping my tears and her own.

"You sure carry a lot of Kleenex."

"Old nursing habit. You never know when you'll need it."

"Thank you. I don't even know your name."

"It's Laurel Beth."

"I'll never forget you."

"Nor I you. Do you feel like going back inside?"

"No, thank you. I'm going to walk home. See ya."

"See ya."

CHAPTER FOURTEEN

Mavis gave me heck when she got back from the service. Peggy and Ray had dropped her off and not come in.

"Your Gran was wondering where you were. It was your job to look after her. Loretta ended up taking her back with them, because I was in no fit state."

"Sorry. I didn't realize."

"You really should be more considerate, Bridie."

"I'll try."

She took off her hat and threw it on the kitchen table. Then she shrugged out of her coat and let it fall to the floor. I picked it up and placed it over a chair.

"And that goddamned Donny made an ass of himself up there. What was he thinking? No boyhood stories or fun times with the family. I gave him all sorts of ideas to talk about and he used none of them. I would've done it myself, except I'm the grieving widow."

She reached into the fridge and took out a bottle of wine, pouring herself a large glass, which she proceeded to drain and fill up again. "Where are my cigarettes?"

I left her to find them herself. It was only six o'clock, but I was done. A hot bath was in order, to ease the tension in my body. I wanted to float and not think. Which is exactly what I was doing when Mavis barged right in my bathroom. I quickly covered myself under the water.

"What are you doing?"

She had the bottle of wine with her this time. Apparently, a glass wasn't cutting it.

"I have no one to talk to."

"Mavis, I'm taking a bath."

She completely ignored me and sat on the toilet, a cigarette hanging from her lips. "I wanna ask you something," she slurred. "I'm trying to figure it out, but I know nothing about fishing. Would it be a dumb idea to take a rowboat out on the water on a windy day?"

"Yes."

"Even if you're used to the water and boats and shit?"

"Yes."

"So why would your dad take a boat out on a windy day?"

"Your guess is as good as mine."

She nodded and took a drag of her cigarette, then put the bottle to her mouth and chugged until the wine was gone. She hiccupped. "That's what I thought."

She slammed the door on her way out.

❧

THREE DAYS LATER, WE HEADED TO ST. PETER'S FOR THE SECOND memorial for Pops. Mavis and Patty didn't want to go.

"You have to. You told Gran you would."

"I won't know a soul there," Patty complained. "I don't care what any of them have to say."

"It's not about that, Patty. It's about respect. We are Pops's family and we have to stand by Gran."

Mavis sighed. "Let's just get it over with, Patty. Then we never have to go there again."

The United church was just as full as the one in Sydney. Gran was quite emotional. Whereas she'd known no one at the first memorial, she knew everyone here. I put my arm around her as I led her up the aisle. She seemed to get smaller with each passing day.

She had asked me if I would say a few words about Pops, if I felt able to. The thought frightened me, but I didn't want to let her down. We didn't tell Mavis or Patty.

This service was vastly different in that the minister actually knew Pops. You could hear the affection for him in his voice. When he talked about Pops's career in medicine and how he'd carried on the legacy of his father, who was revered in this neck of the woods, all of the congregation nodded and murmured, while some actually wept.

It made me proud.

And then the minister looked at me and motioned me up to the pulpit. Mavis and Patty and Uncle Donny looked confused. Just ignore them and breathe.

I walked up to the front and nodded to the choir, who looked sad, sympathetic, and encouraging at the same time. Then I faced the congregation. It seemed as though the entire town of St. Peter's was there. All I wanted to do was run out the back door, but I glanced at Gran. She was waiting with a smile on her face. This was for her.

"Pops always took me fishing. He told me there was no finer water than river water. That it was always moving, breathing life and carrying momentum along its journey to the ocean. That sometimes it would slow and calmly gather in soft pools, where tranquil fish would hide under the rocks away from prying eyes. At other times, the gush and force created by strong winds and rain would create white foam as it gurgled and roared past.

"He told me life was like that, always changing, always fluid. Not to worry if bad weather comes, because the sun will emerge from behind the clouds before too long.

"A river was the only place Pops found peace. I know we wish he was here with us, but if he has to be somewhere else, I'm glad his final hours were spent on the water he so loved."

When I got back to my seat, Gran rested her head on my shoulder. Even Mavis and Patty seemed pleased. Uncle Donny didn't look at me.

Once again, lunch was served after the service and once again Gran, Mavis, and Patty were mobbed. So was I, with people saying how beautiful my words were, but I wasn't interested in what they thought. I spent most of the time flitting from one spot to the next, darting away if I saw someone come towards me. If you pick up dirty dishes people think you're with the women's auxiliary, so I managed to avoid quite a few people that way.

At one point, Gran caught my eye and I went over to her.

"I forgot to take my pills. They're in the glove compartment of the car. Could you go get them for me?"

"Sure."

I put on my coat but didn't button it and headed out to the parking lot. Cars were parked every which way, even on the church lawn. Someone would be annoyed about that. As I headed back, there was a woman standing by the hall door watching me approach. She must have followed me outside. She looked vaguely familiar, but I couldn't remember from where. I gave her a quick nod and reached for the door handle.

"Excuse me."

I stopped. She unnerved me somehow. Her face looked haunted. "Yes?"

"You're George's daughter."

"Yes."

"How old are you?"

Who was this person? "I'm sixteen."

She swallowed and looked frightened. "What's your name?"

"Bridie."

The woman clasped the front of her coat and then pointed at my necklace. "Where did you get that?"

"It was my mother's. Who are you?"

She went as white as a sheet and backed away from me.

"What's wrong?"

"No. No. No. No. No."

She turned around and ran.

What was that all about?

☙

IT BOTHERED ME TO LEAVE GRAN IN HER HOUSE ALL ALONE. SHE told me she'd be fine and I wasn't to worry. The others were waiting for me in the car, so I wrapped my arms around my grandmother. "I wish I didn't have to go."

"Oh, honey, take care of yourself. I'll come down to see you very soon. I think we both need time alone to figure all this out." She hugged me again and we parted.

Ray drove us back to Sydney with unseemly haste. Even Patty noticed it. "What's the rush?"

"I've taken too much time off work as it is, with these memorial services every few days. I hope that's the last of them."

"What a rotten thing to say!" Patty shouted. "What if it was your dad?"

"Sorry. I didn't mean it."

Oh yes, he did. My like-meter went down a few notches for good old Sting Ray.

Mavis and I went home to a very quiet house. It was so quiet that Mavis started following me around like a puppy dog. I couldn't get away from her.

The lawyer called a few days later and asked to see us about Pops's will. I noticed Ray accompanied Patty to *that* meeting without complaint.

We sat in front of the man.

"The will is straightforward, and George named me executor."

Ray raised his hand like a kid in school. "I thought a family member was supposed to be the executor?"

"In some cases. Others prefer to hand the task over to someone who has more experience with these things."

In other words, Pops didn't trust Mavis to get this right.

The lawyer continued. "Mavis gets the house, and all assets are divided three ways."

Mavis frowned. "But Bridie is his ward. Not his real heir. Is she entitled to a share?" She looked at me. "No offense."

"None taken."

The lawyer smiled. "An individual can leave his estate to whomever he wishes. It is very clear that you, as his wife, have the bulk of the estate, as your home is worth a goodly amount. Since Bridie was raised as George's daughter, he felt that despite never being adopted, she deserved a share of his assets along with Patty. Is there a problem?"

"But she's not his blood."

"That makes no difference, Mavis. We don't live in the twelfth century."

"Well, I don't think this is fair. Bridie was Eileen's daughter, as they were always so eager to point out. George has given this child more than enough over the course of his lifetime. We don't even know who she is, for God's sake. This is very upsetting. It's bad enough I have to struggle now that George is gone, and now I'm going to have to fight for what is rightfully Patty's?"

"You are free to contest the will, Mavis. Just to warn you, it will cost time and money, and there's no guarantee you will win."

"How much are the assets worth?" Patty asked.

"Approximately $150,000. It was worth more, but George told me he was withdrawing a goodly sum in September of this year."

Mavis and Patty exchanged glances before Patty spoke up. "So instead of getting $75,000 each, we're stuck with $50,000 each?"

The lawyer nodded.

"I hope you're satisfied." Patty's eyes watered as she looked at me. "If you have any decency at all, you'll bow out gracefully."

"I think it's pretty clear what Pops wanted."

Mavis blew her nose into a hanky. "You ungrateful child. All these years, I've raised you and let you live in my house. And this is how you repay me."

The lawyer clearly found this scene distasteful. I should've warned him it was coming.

No one spoke to me on the way home. They dropped me off and continued on to Patty's, I assume. No doubt to talk about me.

The phone rang. It was the lawyer.

"Are you alone?"

"Yes."

"Is there any way you can come back to the office? I'd like to speak to you privately."

"Okay."

I took a taxi. I really needed to learn how to drive. With Pops's money, I could buy my own car and ferry Gran around.

Once again, I found myself sitting in front of the lawyer.

"Your father set up a joint bank account for Eileen O'Gorman and yourself when he took over as your guardian. It's my duty as executor to collect all the assets of the estate, but this joint back account is not in the estate. Your father wanted it left that way, perhaps because he suspected what his wife's reaction would be if she knew about it. I am under no obligation to tell her."

"So you're saying there's even more money coming to me? And Mavis never has to know?"

He nodded.

"Pops was one clever fellow."

"It's thirty thousand dollars."

"That will be enough to look after my grandmother. It's what Pops would want."

He stood up and held out his hand. "I can see why he thought you were so special."

Since no one was talking to me, I got kind of lonely in the days that followed the lawyer's visit. I ended up calling Eric. He started babbling when I said it was me.

"Can I come over?"

"Heck, ya! Just give me fifteen minutes to clean up my room."

"I don't care about that. Where do you live?"

It was quite a hike to get to Edgar Street. My cheeks were raw by the time I arrived. Fortunately, his parents were out and it was just the two of us. Eric had a forgettable face, but he exuded niceness and that's what I wanted.

"May I sit down?" I pointed at his mother's sofa.

"Of course."

"Come sit with me."

He rushed over and sat very close to me. "Like this?"

"Fine. Now kiss me."

He was all over me like slobbery dog. It took some time, but he eventually got the hang of it. Not that I was any expert, but I imagined your whole face didn't need to get wet. Of course he wanted more, and I obliged up to a point but pushed him away when he got too excited.

"What's wrong?" he panted.

"I want to be kissed without drowning and no touching below the waist."

"You really are the most peculiar girl. I've never had one tell me exactly what she wanted."

"You don't ask, you don't get. Also, slow down to fifteen miles an hour. You're going sixty in a school zone."

It was a pleasant way to spend the afternoon, but after a while I got bored. So I left.

"When can I see you again?" he shouted from his front door.

"You'll see me in school."

"No! Like this!"

"Probably never. Goodbye."

"Farewell, my one true love!"

On my way home, my limbs felt heavy. What was I doing? It seemed impossible that I had no one I could talk to. My inner circle had been erased over a couple of years. This must be what it's like to die in the desert. You keep trudging forward, but no one comes to your rescue, and there is just empty space on the horizon.

My anger burst out of the pocket I kept it in. Mama had had no choice but to leave me, but Pops had been planning it the whole time we were on our fishing trip. He took us all in with his parting gifts. Had that made it okay in his mind? To reassure us, after he was gone, about how much we were loved?

Sorry, Pops. If you loved us, you'd be here, and I'd be able to slap your face.

The rage kept building the closer I got to the house. But it wasn't my house, according to Mavis. I was the little intruder who'd made her life miserable, the ungrateful bitch who was stealing their money.

In the bathroom, I was staring at myself in the mirror. Here was the girl no one wanted. Maybe I didn't want her either. Maybe she should become someone else. I went out into the kitchen, pulled open the cutlery drawer, and grabbed the scissors.

I was still in the bathroom when I heard Mavis come through the door with Patty. It was the first time she'd come over since the lawyer's visit.

Mavis yelled, "Is there anything for supper?"

I walked out into the kitchen. They both shrieked at the sight of me.

"What did you do to your hair?!" Mavis cried.

"I cut it, obviously."

"All that beautiful hair!" Patty shouted. "Are you crazy?"

"I think so. I have news."

"Well, spit it out," Mavis said.

"You can have your money. I don't want it. I don't want anything from either of you. At times I've thought I loved you both, but I can't live here anymore. As you so eloquently put it, you don't even know who I am. I don't know either, but I have a hunch I'll be better off without you. I'm taking my belongings and Mama's. And Pops's fishing gear."

"Where will you go?" Patty asked.

"To Gran's. She likes me."

"But what about school?" Mavis said.

"I imagine they have one in St. Peter's."

"But what about looking after the house? Cooking?"

"This house belongs to you, Mavis. And I'm pretty sure you'll learn to cook when you start getting hungry."

For some reason, Mavis seemed agitated. "Look, I don't see why it has to come to this. I appreciate you bowing out of the financial picture, because Patty is the rightful heir, but that doesn't mean you have to leave the house or change schools. I don't mind you here for now. I'll even pay you to be a house-keeper, if you want. I don't want people saying I kicked you out of the house."

"You're not kicking me out, Mavis. I'm leaving because I have to. Kind of the same way Pops left, only my method isn't quite as drastic."

She glared at me. "Don't you dare insinuate my husband's death was anything but an accident."

I looked at Patty. "Was it? Was it an accident, do you think?"

Patty sputtered, "Of course it was an accident. Why would he leave us?"

"Peace of mind? But at least we got our goodbye presents. That was so nice of him. And now that I'm letting you off the hook, you can celebrate with your monetary winnings. You can pretend I never existed. And I can pretend you both love me."

I don't know what they did after that. I was busy cleaning up my hair from the bathroom floor and sink. After that I called Gran.

"I'm coming to live with you, Gran, whether you like it or not."

"You know I'd love it, but what about school?"

"I believe you're allowed to transfer."

"What does Mavis say?"

"Who cares?"

"How will you get your things here? Do you want me to ask Donny to help you?"

I flinched. "No, no. He's a busy man. I'll ask a friend."

Eric, who was in the depths of despair at the thought of me moving, manage to convince his father to help me take my things to St. Peter's in his truck.

Mavis stayed out of the way that morning. She was sniffling in her bedroom, not because I was going but because she was now left to handle things on her own. My prediction was she'd have the house sold within a month. She'd get an apartment and a maid. Maybe even a cook.

I was wrapping it up when I remembered Pops's pipes, so I went into his study and took three off his pipe rack. His favourite pipe and lighter were at the bottom of the ocean with him. An opened package of pipe tobacco was in his top drawer, so I took that too. Just as I was closing the drawer, I noticed a picture of him and Mama when they were kids, with their arms wrapped around each other, in their bathing suits. Donny was sticking his tongue out at them, naturally. I put it in my pocket for safekeeping.

Mavis didn't come downstairs when I left, but I glimpsed her peeking at me from behind her bedroom window. As I walked to the waiting truck, I realized that this was the last time I'd be in Pops's house. His big, lovely house. Despite the endless tension within its walls, I loved it and was suddenly bereft at the thought of leaving it. That's when I noticed Patty drive up. She must have been on her lunch hour. She got out of her car and met me at the end of the driveway. It was a blustery and frigid November day. Not exactly conducive for packing up one's life.

"I wanted to say goodbye. It didn't feel right not to acknowledge your leaving. You've been a big part of my life, even if you were mostly a pain."

"Good luck, Cake. I imagine we'll run into each other from time to time."

"Bridie. Do you really think Daddy killed himself?"

Why did I always have to be the adult? "Of course he didn't. He'd never have left us willingly."

She gave a big sigh. "That's what I think." She reached out and hugged me. "See ya around, squirt."

CHAPTER FIFTEEN

Eric had his arm around my shoulder the entire way up to St.
Peter's, and because he was doing me a favour, I let it happen.
Stuck in the middle of the front seat, I tried to keep my knees
from touching his father's. It was like being stuck in a jam jar.
At least if I had been with Uncle Donny, I would've been justi-
fied carrying a letter opener or an actual knife and threatening him with it. This way, I was surrounded by male energy
without any escape.

Eric and his dad were perfectly nice; it was just that I was
frantic about leaving and wanted to escape the heat blaring from
the air vents. Eric talked nonstop about how disappointed he
was that I wouldn't be in school anymore.

"You'll get over it."

"I don't think I will."

"I don't think he will either," said Eric's dad. "You're all he
talks about."

"Eric, you have to get out more," I said.

Then he turned the conversation to my hair. "Why did you
cut it? Not that it doesn't look very nice short, but it was so
beautiful."

"It's hair. It'll grow."

The sight of Gran's house was a huge relief. I introduced her
to Eric and his dad and they kindly trooped all my belongings
upstairs for me. Gran had tea and a sliced pumpkin loaf on the
dining room table and insisted they sit and have some nourish-
ment before heading back to Sydney. We had a nice chat, but
the whole time I was dying for them to go.

Finally, they got up from the table and after they said thank you and goodbye to Gran, I walked them to the truck. I thanked Eric's dad very much and he said it was no problem at all. No wonder Eric was so nice.

I kissed Eric goodbye—a short one; we were being watched. He hugged me and seemed genuinely distressed.

"I'll tell you what," I said. "I'll come back and be your date for prom next year. You can win the pool."

"Seriously? Thank you!"

"Now go."

"Farewell—"

"Farewell, Eric."

I turned and walked into my new home. Gran opened her arms and I headed straight for her.

"I'm so tired," I said.

She rubbed my head. "Why did you cut your hair, honey?"

"I don't know. I was angry."

"My poor sweetheart. It must have been awful, leaving the house. What did Mavis say?"

"Nothing. I didn't see her."

"I could throttle that woman."

Stepping out of Gran's hug, I sat wearily on the nearest kitchen chair. "I was glad she stayed away. Talking to Mavis is always a burden. Patty came to say goodbye."

"I suppose that's something, but she's not much better when it comes to empathy. Sometimes I find it hard to believe she's George's child."

"Well, they're happy now. I gave them my share of Pops's money."

Gran looked shocked. "No! Why would you do that? You're going to need that money."

"I didn't want to deal with them anymore, Gran. I have some money in another account that Pops put aside for me. They don't know about it. They've always considered me a parasite, and this is the only way I can break free of them."

That first night, I couldn't sleep. I missed my room badly. It was almost too quiet here. As my mind whirled, I wondered if I had done the right thing. Maybe I should have fought for my share. But whenever that thought took hold, I immediately felt suffocated. It was better to let it go, no matter what the consequences.

∽◇

BY THE TIME MY TRANSCRIPTS WERE DELIVERED TO THE HIGH school in St. Peter's, it was mid-December. I told the school I would start in January, since the loss of my father had hit me hard. They were fine with that; my grades were excellent. It gave me a few weeks' breathing room to come to terms with my situation. Leaving the house in Sydney was a lot more emotional than I had bargained for.

Living in the country with a barn and a dog was my dream— when my parents were alive. Being alone except for my elderly grandmother made me shiver at night. I wanted to be in my own bed, listening to Pops hum along with the kitchen radio as he prepared a midnight snack. How was it possible that I missed the arguments between Mavis and Patty as they stomped from room to room upstairs? That kitchen was alive with memories of Mama, and now I'd never see it again. The large, airy house was the only home I'd known and, in my haste to make a point, I'd left it too soon. A house was more than a building. It had its own energy, its own smell. I'd bet it missed me too. Hopefully Mavis wouldn't burn it to the ground.

Both Gran and I were sad, so it was tiring to try and be cheerful for one another. We finally agreed we could be silent if we wanted to, and that helped us in the long run.

It also helped that I took driving lessons. I'd forgotten that Gran had a car, since she never drove farther than around town to do her shopping. Driving to Sydney was too much for her. It was a 1958 Ford two-door ranch wagon, much like the one Pops had. He probably picked it out for her, although why he thought she needed something so big was a mystery.

Mr. Tremblay was my driving instructor. He was obsessed with country music and blared it from the car radio, which was a terrible distraction. I was in love with the Beatles, especially Paul McCartney, and listening to Buck Owens and His Buckaroos made my lessons just that much more excruciating.

The first time he saw me he asked if I was a boy, which didn't endear him to me. He talked my ear off, which I think was a strategy to see if I kept my attention on the road. The first time he let me loose on the highway it was exhilarating, like I was leaving behind all my troubles, but then I remembered my mother died in a car accident and that took the joy out of it. I couldn't think about anything without it turning dark.

That first Christmas without Pops was a pretty lonely affair. Gran didn't want to leave the house, and I was relieved that we wouldn't be seeing Uncle Donny and his family, since they decided to lie low too. Patty called me on Christmas Day, and I was happy to hear her voice.

"What are you up too?" she asked.

"I'm learning to drive, and I start school soon. Nothing exciting. You?"

"Ray and I are going to have a baby."

"Hey! Congratulations! What does your mom think about that?"

"She says she's too young to be a grandmother. Typical."

"Well, I'm not too young to be an auntie. If you ever need a babysitter, I'd be happy to oblige."

"Thanks, Bridie. I knew I could count on you."

A week later I got a letter from Patty. Inside was a cheque for twenty-five thousand dollars. "If I was a better person, this would be for the full amount we owe you. Mom doesn't know about this, so don't say anything. I think I'm getting mushy, what with maternal hormones rampaging through my body."

I read it over and over again. Then I took it downstairs and held it in front of Gran. She put on her reading glasses and her mouth dropped open. "Land sakes. I never would've believed it. Well, she's redeemed herself in my eyes."

"Should I keep it?"

"Of course you should keep it. It's yours and she knows it. Cash that before her mother finds out. How nice. I'm going to be a great-grandmother. Not that I'll ever see the child, but still. A part of George lives on, and that makes me happy."

"I'm furious that he's not going to see the baby. How could he be so selfish?"

Gran smiled sadly. "You're always going to feel that way, I'm afraid. It's inevitable for the family left behind."

"So...you know what Pops did? That it wasn't an accident."

"Oh yes, but I keep it to myself. Your children often disappoint you, but you love them anyway. You're allowed to be angry at your Pops, Bridie. He doesn't mind."

I deposited the cheque into my account the next day, and truthfully, I was very grateful for it. I picked up a card and wrote Patty and Ray a heartfelt note to express my appreciation. Patty was as close to a sister as I had, and I didn't want to lose our connection. Pops would have been proud of her, and I told her that.

AFTER TWO AND A HALF WEEKS OF KEEPING TO MYSELF, IT TOOK everything I had to get up and walk to school. There was a bus I could've taken, and maybe I would during bad weather in the winter, but it was only a mile or more, so I much preferred to walk.

Kids who've been together since primary at the same school can pick out someone new in two seconds flat. I was a curiosity, a firefly in a bottle, and all eyes followed me wherever I went. One thing I did notice was that I had the shortest hair of anyone in the school, including the boys.

I presented myself to the principal. He shook my hand.

"It's nice to meet you, Bridie. I knew your dad when we were in school together. I'm very sorry for your loss."

I nodded. "Thank you."

He told me where my homeroom was and said if I had any concerns to come and see him.

My classmates weren't quite as fashionable as the ones in Sydney, but other than that, they looked exactly the same. You had your king and queen bee sitting together, the minions who followed them everywhere, the smart kids, the shy kids, and the criminals. The comedian spoke to me first.

"Are you related to Twiggy?"

The class snickered.

"She's my second cousin."

That seemed to satisfy them. The teacher walked in and I thought that would be the end of the spotlight. Unfortunately, this lady knew Pops as well.

"Everyone, this is Dr. George Mackenzie's daughter, Bridie. God rest his soul. I'm sure your parents and grandparents will remember him and his father, Dr. Joe Mackenzie. I hope you will give Bridie a nice welcome to our community."

If any of them had a nice welcome for me, I made it difficult for them to deliver it, since I found myself scurrying away like hermit crab, eating my sandwich in the toilet stall and spending the rest of the lunch hour pretending to read a book. I had a devil of a time trying to figure out why I was so skittish.

After school, I set off before anyone could join me. The school bus lumbered by as I walked along the road with my head down. If I didn't watch out, I'd be labelled the queer one, which is what the old people called anyone who was different.

Gran was waiting to hear about my day. I flopped into the armchair in the living room. "I basically ran away from everyone. I didn't give anyone a chance to talk to me."

"Why's that, do you think?"

"I'm afraid they'll ask me about Pops."

"I doubt they will. They didn't know him."

"I can't believe he's gone, Gran. It's like I don't want to make a new friend, because Pops was my best friend, and no one will ever replace him."

She nodded and wiped her eyes with a tissue she had shoved up her sleeve.

"Sorry, I didn't mean to make you cry."

"You didn't. Tears come easily now. It's what happens when you get old. Life makes you weary sometimes."

That night, Patty called me to tell me Mavis was selling the house.

I cried all night.

By mid-February, I had my driver's license and two gal pals I liked to hang around with. Barbara and Linda were best friends, and you'd think they were twins, the way they finished each other's sentences. They were crackerjacks in the gossip department but not completely boy-crazy, which was a relief. They were smart and silly and I found myself coming out of my funk a little at a time. They also helped me forget that my last two letters to Judith had come back Return to Sender. Her family must have moved away and she never let me know. My old life felt well and truly over.

It also helped that Gran let me get a dog. A kid had a box full of puppies outside the grocery store one day. He said his mother told him to get rid of them, so they were free. I gave him two dollars, to ease the pain of watching the puppies disappear one by one. Hobbs turned out to be an Airedale terrier. His curly fur always looked like he'd just come out of the dryer. He was the friendliest soul, and he wormed his way right into Gran's affections, not to mention mine.

Aunt Betty came over one day for a visit, and Hobbs wiggled his way over and sat between her feet. "What's this? If I knew you wanted a dog, you could've had those two mutts Mom had. They drive me crazy."

"You couldn't do that," Gran said. "Your boys love them."

"They might love them, but it's *moi* who feeds the darn things."

As she patted the dog, she gave me a look. "Tell me again why you cut that fabulous hair of yours?"

"I needed a change."

"Did you save it? I could've made a wig."

"Sorry. It all went in the garbage."

"Oh, God."

I made tea for my relatives and put the scones I made earlier in the day on the table. Aunt Betty took two and wolfed them down. "These are just like Mom's. I have the same recipe, but I can't for the life of me make them taste the same. What's your secret?"

"I like baking."

Aunt Betty nodded. "That must be it. I hate baking, and the flour and butter know it."

When I sat in the rocking chair, Hobbs jumped up and curled into a ball on my lap. Just running my hands through his curls gave me a sense of peace. I couldn't believe I'd spent sixteen years without a dog.

"So, what's new with the family?" Aunt Betty asked Gran.

"Donny's kids are fine, apparently. Not that I see them, but Loretta calls from time to time to keep me updated. Donny's been made some mucky-muck at the hospital."

What a good term for Uncle Donny.

Aunt Betty looked at me. "Do you hear from Mavis?"

"No. But Patty stays in touch. She's pregnant, due in late June."

"Yes, your Gran told me. She didn't waste any time, did she? This is a first baby so you watch, the kid will be late and arrive on their first wedding anniversary in July."

"Maybe so."

"And I hear Mavis sold the house?"

I nodded.

"And where's her nibs now?"

"She's living in an apartment somewhere. I really don't care. I know Patty and Ray are getting the baby's room ready. Ray's been painting the entire house, from what she tells me."

Aunt Betty sipped her tea. "First-time parents are insane."

There was nothing new in Aunt Betty's world. "Men are so damned boring. Fraser works all day, and so do the boys."

"They're not boys anymore, Betty," Gran said. "They're twenty-six, thirty, and thirty-four."

"True. And not one of them says boo to me unless it's to ask what's for supper. I could stand on my head in the middle of the kitchen and they wouldn't notice me. Only those two crazy dogs show me any affection. If I'd known what marriage was before I got married, I would've head for the hills. Don't do it, Bridie. It's a gateway to drudgeville."

Gran laughed. "Oh, come on, Betty. It's not that bad."

"Your husband was interesting. And your sons actually left home. The only way my hulks will leave is if I plant a bomb under the dining room table."

"Why don't you get a job, Aunt Betty? That might occupy your time."

She squirmed in her seat. "No, thanks. Then I'd have to work."

When she left, Gran and I took to laughing.

"She's a case, that one." Gran said.

"I like her. She reminds me of Mama."

☙

BARBARA AND LINDA CONFRONTED ME AT MY LOCKER IN MARCH. "So, rumour has it that Jack Morris really likes you."

"Who's Jack Morris?"

"Only the cutest guy in grade twelve."

"If he likes me so much, you'd think he'd talk to me."

"He's not allowed to talk to lowly grade elevens. Everyone knows that."

"That's the dumbest thing I ever heard."

Barbara nudged me. "Just keep your eyes open. He's so dreamy!"

"I don't know what he looks like."

"As soon as you see him, you'll know." The two of them walked away.

Obviously, I wasn't immune to boys, but very few, if any, ever caught my attention—and now, thanks to my two silly friends, I found myself searching the hallways for cute guys. I knew all the grade elevens, but hadn't paid much attention to the grade twelves, who lorded it over everyone, seeing as how they were the top dogs in the school.

Since Barbara and Linda decided it was a game not to tell me who Jack Morris was, I played along, but decided to have some fun myself. I met Barb at the water fountain one afternoon.

"It's got to be that guy walking down the hall with green pants."

She looked and made a face. "Are you serious? He's terrible."

"I don't know. He's got great cheekbones."

"Ugh."

Two days later, I made Linda peek out of the girls' bathroom. "Is that him? The one with the checkered shirt?"

"That's Ronnie! He looks like a goat!"

They eventually caught on and wouldn't play with me anymore. It didn't matter, because the great Jack Morris decided to come down from the mountaintop and seek me out. I knew it was him the minute he strode towards me as I was leaving school. He had that cool swagger of someone who knew he was all that and a slice of cheese.

He stood in front of me and grinned.

"Hi."

"Hello."

"I'm Jack."

"Bridie."

"I know."

"You know? Isn't it against the law to fraternize with a younger grade?"

"I make my own rules."

Oh, spare me. I hated him. "See ya, Jack." I walked away quickly.

"Where are you going?" he called out.

"Home."

"Let me walk you."

"No, thanks."

When I told the girls about the encounter they nearly chewed my head off.

"Are you crazy? That's Jack Morris. Do you know how many girls would give their right arm to go to the prom with him?"

We stood around the melting snowy puddles by the swing set in the schoolyard during recess. "What is this obsession with prom? The kids in Sydney are just as bad. Now I'm sorry I promised Eric I'd go to prom with him next year. It seems so ludicrous."

Barb slapped Linda on the arm. "What if he wants to take Bridie to prom?! She'll be the most hated girl alive!"

"Something I've always aspired to. You two have spring fever. It's not like you to talk about boys constantly."

Linda sighed. "We've never been objects of desire. At least not to someone as gorgeous as Jack. We are living vicariously through you."

Barbara held out her little finger. "Pinky-swear you'll tell us everything if you kiss him."

Fortunately, the bell rang.

❧

ONE DAY IN APRIL, I TOOK GRAN TO THE GROCERY STORE. THIS was a two-hour ordeal, as she was always so pleased to run into friends who were still alive. They would stand in the middle of the aisle ignoring the cross looks of young moms in a hurry while they regaled each other with childhood memories. Once they moved on, Gran took great pleasure in telling me their life stories while we shopped.

"She had an uncle and aunt who were a brother and sister," she told me that day. "They lived alone, way out in the country. He took ill and called the doctor. The doctor asked where the sister was and the old fella said he didn't know. She hadn't been downstairs for three days. The doctor found the poor soul in her bed, as dead as a doorknob."

"Pops's father must have had stories like that."

"Oh, you wouldn't believe some of the things he told me in confidence. He wasn't supposed to tell me, but some cases weighed on his mind. He needed to share it, to lessen the load. I never said a word to anyone."

I took her arm. "He was so lucky to have you."

"We were lucky to have each other. It's always a blessing when you find someone you truly love."

"I wish Pops had had someone like that. I don't believe for a minute that Mavis was his true love."

Gran looked sad.

As we were leaving the grocery store, Gran tripped on the sidewalk, and I dropped my bags of groceries to catch her before she fell to her knees. As I steadied her, I was aware of someone running up to us.

"Can I help?" It was Jack Morris.

Gran was a little shaken, but otherwise okay. "Thank you, young man. We could use some assistance."

While I got Gran in the car, Jack picked up my groceries and put them back in the paper bags. "I don't think anything's broken," he said. "I'll put them in the car for you."

I opened the back door and he bent down and arranged them on the seat.

"I hope you're okay, Mrs. Mackenzie."

"I'm fine, dear. Thank you."

He closed the back door for me. "Are you all right?"

"Yes. Thank you."

"You're welcome," he said, smiling.

He watched me as I got in the car, and now I was flustered. The engine revved, which rattled me even more, and I lurched the car forward in my haste to drive away. Honestly, how embarrassing.

"Isn't he a nice young man?" Gran smiled at me.

"You know him?"

"I believe that was Jack Morris. He's the mayor's son. All those boys are handsome devils."

What bothered me was that I agreed with her. Jack was a handsome devil.

Drat and darn.

CHAPTER SIXTEEN

*Now I couldn't get the silly fool out of my mind. And I saw him every-*where at school. He stayed away from me but always gave me a big smile when he saw me. Obviously he was changing his tactics, and it appeared to be working.

Annoying.

Barbara and Linda kept me up to speed on what he said about me to others. How they gleaned this information was a mystery.

"He told Roy Dupuis that your hair was the coolest thing he'd ever seen."

"Linda, I don't know a lot about boys, but I highly doubt they spend their time talking about a girl's haircut. You're making this up."

"Okay," she sniffed. "I'm not going to tell you anything else, since you don't believe me."

One day, as I walked to school in the May sunshine and heard the trill of songbirds all around me, I caved. Barb was getting off the school bus. "Anything new on the Jack front?"

Barbara looked around to make sure no one was listening. "He's broken up with his girlfriend."

"He had a girlfriend? What a louse!"

"He's got several girlfriends, but this one was with him the longest."

"Several? He sounds like an idiot."

"Oh, Bridie. Who cares if he's an idiot? It's not like he's going to be your husband. Fooling around with someone is allowed when you're in high school. It'll be something to dream about when you get old and fat."

What if Barbara was right? Why was I always running away from something that might bring me a small pinch of happiness? Maybe it was time to shake things up.

By this time I knew where Jack's locker was, so I marched over to it and stood there. Lots of girls threw me hateful glances. How did they know I was waiting for him? This locker might belong to anyone. Was there a rule that said you must stay fifty feet away from his precious locker?

"Bridie?"

I didn't see him standing next to me, so I jumped. "Oh! Don't scare me like that."

"Sorry. I said your name a few times."

"I was daydreaming."

"About me, I hope." He gave me that lazy grin.

"Oh, seriously. Why do you ruin things by saying dreary stuff like that?"

He instantly looked hurt.

"I'm just telling you, Jack, that cheesy lines don't work."

"They've worked for me."

"If you plan on taking me out on a date, I suggest you drop what you've been doing and act like a normal person."

He gave me a genuine smile this time. "Am I planning on asking you out on a date?"

"According to my sources, you want to ask me to the prom. Is this true?"

"You are the strangest girl."

"I've been told that before. So, are we going or not?"

"I would love to take you to the prom. But I hope we don't have to wait until the end of June to see each other. Why don't we go on a normal date this Friday?"

"What do you propose we do?"

"Go to Big D's for a milkshake and fries?"

"I suppose so."

"Don't sound so excited."

I sighed. "I'm not very good at this dating thing, unlike you, who are an overachiever, from what I understand."

He laughed. "I'm not sure who your sources are, but it sounds like they know more about me than I do. Why don't you form your own opinions?"

"I will."

"I'll pick you up at seven."

"In a car?"

"No. On a donkey."

"Big D's is a mile down the road. I think we can walk."

"I live a little farther out of town. Would it be all right if I drove to your house and escorted you on foot to Big D's?"

"Do you know where I live?"

"Everyone knows where Dr. Joe Mackenzie lived."

"Okay then. That sounds fine. I'll see you."

"See you, Bridie."

My heart was pounding a little faster as I walked away, fighting to keep a normal pace when all I wanted to do was run.

I told my posse after school and they screamed.

Barb grabbed my jumper. "You're going on a date this Friday?! What are you going to wear?"

"Clothes."

Linda looked me up and down. "Don't wear that."

"I wasn't planning on it."

Barbara wanted to know where he was taking me.

"To Big D's for fries."

"You can't eat them," she said.

"Why not?"

"You can't be seen stuffing your face. He might think you eat too much."

"Barbara, you need your head examined. I'm sorry I told you now. I have to go."

"We'll be there!" they shouted together.

"Please do me a favour and forget I said anything." They pretended not to hear me.

Despite myself, I was bubbling with excitement after school on Friday. Gran noticed it. "If I didn't know any better, I'd say you were going on a date."

"I am. I can only have crackers and cheese for supper. I want to save room for fries and a milkshake at Big D's later, despite Barb's warning about eating too much in front of him."

Gran went to the sink to fill the kettle. "Who are you going with?"

"Jack Morris."

"Oh my. You snagged the biggest fish in the pond. He's the mayor's son, you know."

"Yes, you told me." I was rooting around the fridge for a piece of cheese.

She put the kettle on the stove and sat at the kitchen table. "Sit down, honey." She seemed a bit nervous.

I sat opposite her and waited. "What's wrong, Gran?"

"I feel it's my duty, now that your mother and father are gone, to give you advice about the opposite sex. A birds-and-bees kind of talk, although I imagine you know the basics."

Oh, she was sweet. "I do know how it works, Gran."

"Well, I'm going to tell you what I know about men."

"Fire away."

She clasped her hands in front of her. "They don't like bossy women. That doesn't mean you can't be bossy, but you have to hide it from them. Make them think everything's their idea."

"Good. I'll remember that."

"You know the expression, 'Don't give the milk away for free?'"

"Yes."

"That's a big one. They like to do the chasing. Make them wait."

I couldn't resist. "Make them wait for what?"

She shot me a look like she knew I was baiting her, but answered anyway. "Canoodling."

"Gotcha."

"Be kind. I raised two boys and I know how deeply they can be hurt by a woman. They have to put on a brave face so the world doesn't know their hearts are broken. It can kill them in the end."

There wasn't anything to say to that.

We had tea and crackers and cheese, and then I went upstairs for a bath. Thinking about Pops was the last thing I wanted to do tonight, so I put him to bed in my heart and told him I'd bring him out tomorrow. Sometimes that was the only way I could cope. And I often soothed myself with the notion that Pops and Mama were at least together, somewhere out there.

Trying to pick an outfit was daunting. I wished Patty were here. She always had good ideas about what to wear. In the end, I put on a plaid miniskirt and a white blouse with a Peter Pan collar, with red flats. My hair had grown out into a pixie cut, and was pretty cute. Short hair suited me. I felt grown up and liked the sensation of power it gave me. When my hair was long, I had felt vulnerable to the Uncle Donnys of the world.

Not anymore.

Jack arrived at the door on the dot of seven. He smelled divine and had on a new shirt. His blond hair was freshly washed. He held a bouquet, which he gave to my gran. She was delighted.

Oh, he was good.

Hobbs assumed he was going with us when we left for our walk to Big D's. Poor Gran had to grab his collar and tempt him with treats to get him away from the door. My guilt lasted until we couldn't see the house anymore.

It was a lovely spring evening, and the peepers were out in full force.

"This makes me so incredibly happy!" I laughed. "I never heard peepers on the street where I grew up. They're the best thing about spring, don't you think?"

He grinned. "I never thought about it. I've grown up with them and hardly notice the sound anymore."

"But you must notice things like that. It's the world welcoming you to another season. Like seeing robins, and hearing the creeks bubble and sing. You've been so fortunate to live in the country your whole life. Never take it for granted. Do you fish?"

"No. Too boring."

I was wildly disappointed in that moment. "Too bad. It's something else you could benefit from."

He looked away. "I have a feeling I'm not answering the way you want me to. That makes me nervous. I've never been nervous on a date before."

Gran's voice popped into my head. "Be kind."

"Don't be nervous. I'm just rambling. What do you like to do?"

As we walked, he told me about riding horses. His parents owned a big farm and ranch, and he grew up surrounded by them. "Best animal in the world."

"All animals are the best. Dogs in particular."

"You're going to have to meet my horse, Napoleon. You'll fall in love instantly. Kind of like I did when I first laid eyes on you."

My hand went up. "I told you. Stop with the cheesy one-liners."

"I'm serious."

When I looked at him, he seemed perfectly sincere, which made me blush. How horrifying.

We eventually made it to Big D's, and the place was hopping with kids our age. All the booths were taken, and the Beach Boys hit "Good Vibrations" blared from the jukebox. We sat on two stools at the counter and were swarmed by Jack's friends, most of whom I didn't know, but when I looked around I saw Linda and Barbara at a booth with four empty milkshake glasses between them. They must have arrived early. They waved and made swoony faces and I had to turn my back on them before I laughed out loud.

My fries were gone pronto, and I knocked back a strawberry milkshake rather hastily. The trouble was, I couldn't hear the conversations over the music so I did a lot of smiling and nodding. Jack would lean forward and repeat what was said, but when he did my mind would go blank and I'd concentrate on how wonderful his warm breath felt as he whispered in my ear.

Get a hold of yourself, Bridie.

After a while I began to notice the dirty looks from some of the girls. Soon I'd be the most hated girl in school. But did I care? Not in the least. That's something that happens when you lose people in your life. Very quickly, you learn what's important and what's nonsense.

Eventually, I couldn't stand the noise and asked Jack if we could go. He put down some money on the counter and took my hand. We made our way through the crowd and I looked back to wave at Barbara and Linda. They were still making kissy faces. If they paid attention to the other boys in the room they might have a better time.

It was such a nice night out, but it had turned chilly and I'd forgotten to take a sweater. Jack made me wear his jacket and took my hand again once I had it on. The silence was refreshing, and we didn't talk a whole lot on the way home. Just as we came around the corner of our driveway, before we would see the house, Jack stopped and put his arms around me and kissed me.

He was a pro compared to poor Eric and I was literally shaking by the time he let me go.

"I knew it was going to be like that," he said.

"You did? How did you know?"

"I can't answer; it would cross into cheesy territory."

I grinned. "I'll give you immunity for ten seconds."

"Your lips were made for kissing."

"Okay, that's pretty terrible."

"It's the truth." He kissed me again and I never wanted him to stop. This is what came from having a multitude of girlfriends to practise on.

When I came up for air I whispered, "I don't think I'm a good kisser. I haven't had a lot of practise."

"You're a natural."

How did he know just what to say?

Eventually I knew he'd be taking home a couple of quarts of milk if I didn't put a stop to it, so I unceremoniously broke away, panting, "My gran will be worried. I have to go."

He laughed. "You're not Cinderella and it's not midnight."

"I'm not wearing glass slippers, either, but I'm still saying good night."

I gave him back his jacket and ran into the house before he could say anything else.

Gran was dozing in the kitchen rocking chair, with a sleeping Hobbs at her feet. They looked so cute together, but it wasn't great that neither of them woke up with someone standing in front of them.

"I'm home," I said loudly.

They blinked, and Hobbs was the first to greet me. He forgave me for not taking him on my walk, in the way that dogs do.

"Did you have a nice time, honey?"

"Yes, but that jukebox at Big D's is much too loud."

"You sound like an old woman," Gran chuckled. "I think I'll go to bed." She kissed me as she went by. "Lock up."

I took Hobbs outside for his nightly pee and watched the stars as he rooted around in the grass for the perfect spot. Whenever I looked to the heavens at night, I felt like a grain of sand amidst all that splendour. What was it like for my parents to be a part of that vast blackness? Could they see me? Would Mama and Pops like Jack? Did they miss me?

All I know is that being in Jack's arms made the world a little less lonely. Wasn't that a good thing?

BEFORE I KNEW IT, I WAS JACK MORRIS'S GIRLFRIEND, AND everyone at school was aware of the fact. The death stares from girls decreased as the inevitable sank in, and they didn't want to seem pathetic so they pretended it didn't bother them in the least.

Barbara and Linda were suddenly promoted to cool girls, as they hung around with me and Jack from time to time. They both started going out with a couple of Jack's friends and now we had a little gang—but most of the time, Jack and I were alone. He took me out to his ranch to meet his mom and dad.

"This is my mother, Diane, and my father, Yardley. This is Bridie."

His mother approached me first. "So nice to meet you, Bridie. Jack has never brought a girl home, so this is a treat for me."

We shook hands. Then his father took my hand. He was a large version of Jack. "A pleasure, I'm sure."

Jack wanted me to meet his younger brothers, but they were scattered to the wind. Instead I met the famous Napoleon and I had to say, he was a magnificent beast. He was too intimidating to ride alone, so I got in the saddle with Jack and he put his arms around me to hold the reins. We walked through his parents' fields, enjoying the sunshine, and as I leaned against Jack's chest, I found myself relaxing for the first time in years.

AUNT BETTY ASKED ME IF I HAD A DRESS FOR THE PROM.

"Of course not."

"Do you want me to take you to Sydney to look for one? I don't mind."

The thought of anyone other than Mama going with me made me sad.

"No, that's okay."

It did occur to me that a lot of eyes would be on Jack and me at the prom, so I wasn't completely against the idea of looking great. It just seemed so petty. I said as much to Gran.

"Where did you get the idea that you're letting yourself down if you want to be pretty? It's perfectly normal to want to look nice. Your trouble is, you think too much. Drink a glass of warm milk every night before bed."

Sometimes Gran's advice made no sense.

But she did suggest I go see Nell Sampson down the road. She made very pretty dresses. "But she's an odd duck, so don't be alarmed if she bites your head off."

As soon as I drove the car up the laneway, I remembered coming here when I was thirteen. There was the cabin with its horrible history, and then the gingerbread house came into view. It made even more of an impression on me this time. It was an outstanding building, so imposing, perched as it was with the woods surrounding it like a secret. It was right out of a book. I loved it.

A dog announced my arrival and Nell came out of the house. It was her! The woman who'd made no sense at the church hall when Pops died. I knew I'd seen her somewhere before. When I stepped out of the car, her face was puzzled, and then she seemed to recognize me. Again, she looked frightened.

"Are you Nell?" I said.

She nodded.

"My gran told me to come here. She said you made beautiful dresses."

"You mean Jean Mackenzie?"

"Yes. I need a dress for the prom."

"You don't graduate until next year."

That was the last thing I expected her to say. How did she know? "I'm going with someone who's graduating this year."

"Well, I'm very busy. You should've come sooner."

"Oh. Okay then. Sorry I bothered you."

I got back in the car, but before I could turn the engine on she waved me back, so I got out again. I was starting to feel like a jack-in-the-box.

"I can fit you in. Follow me."

Nell and her dog went into the house, so I trotted behind them. The kitchen was a dream, everything I'd want in a kitchen if I had my own. It was so lived in. Two cats stared at me, one on the windowsill over the sink and the other near the wood pile by the stove.

"Hello?" I whispered.

"In here," Nell barked.

In my haste, I tripped over the dog in the doorway. "Sorry."

"Dog! Make way."

Dog lumbered over to the fireplace and flopped on the mat.

"It was my fault entirely," I told Nell.

"Do you want a short dress or a long dress?"

"Umm. I don't know."

"I think it's ridiculous for young girls to have long gowns. The only time you should have a long dress is at your wedding, and even then, it's an option and not a necessity."

"That settles it then. I'll have a short one."

She picked up her measuring tape and put it around her neck. "What colour?"

"Umm. I don't know."

"Pink, I think. It would go well with your skin tone."

"But isn't pink a silly colour?"

She looked exasperated. "What does that even mean? Pink is everywhere. It's the colour of a rose, a sunset, a rainbow, a kitten's toes. It's delicate and soft. It looks like you."

Why did I feel simultaneously complimented and reprimanded?

"That sounds fine, then. Thank you."

"What style do you want?"

I paused.

"Let me guess. You don't know."

I nodded and then shook my head too, just in case.

"Why don't you just leave it to me?"

"Okay."

"Lift up your arms so I can take your measurements."

She was very brisk and efficient, though she seemed to have a hard time touching me, almost as if she was afraid to let her fingertips linger on my skin. Her face was stony and yet vulnerable. I was aware of her glancing at me when she thought I wasn't looking, almost as if I were a sculpture in a museum or a curiosity of some kind.

It felt awkward.

"That's all I need. When do you want the dress?"

"For the last week of June."

"It will be ready."

"Thank you very much. How much do I owe you?"

"We'll discuss that when I've finished the dress."

"Of course. Thank you again."

She didn't follow me out into the kitchen so I left, taking one last look around. Gran was right. She was an odd duck.

The next time Jack and I were riding Napoleon, he asked me what colour my dress was, because he wanted to buy a corsage.

"Pink."

"That's a surprise."

"How so?"

"I've never seen you wear pink."

"Pink is the colour of a rose, a sunset, a rainbow, and a kitten's toes. It's delicate and soft, like me."

"I stand corrected." He kissed the back of my neck. "You're right. Delicate and soft."

The day came when I had to collect the dress from Nell. Gran insisted on giving me the money to pay her.

"It's my gift to you, sweetheart. Now take it."

When I rapped on the door, the dog barked and Nell said, "Come in. I'm in the studio."

I waved at the cats as I went through into the workroom. My dress was on a dressmaker's dummy.

"Here it is," Nell said.

It was the most beautiful dress I'd ever seen. The perfect shade of pink, like the inside curve of a seashell. It was sleeveless, with a straight neckline across the shoulder blades. It had an empire waist, and the bodice was made with tiny white and pink flowers, but the rest of the dress was chiffon. There was a satin bow right underneath the bodice, with the ends as long as the hem itself, which came above my knees.

All I could do was gape.

"Do you like it?"

"I love it! It's breathtaking! You're a genius!"

"Would you like to try it on, in case I have to do any last-minute adjustments? You can get undressed behind the screen."

She passed me the dress and I threw off my shorts and top and shimmied into it. "You'll have to help me with the zipper." I came out and turned around for her to zip me up. I faced the mirror and couldn't stop looking at myself. "This is perfect."

"It is perfect," I heard her say. "Do you mind if I take a picture of you in it? I like to keep an album of my dresses."

"Not at all."

I turned around and she had a camera ready. My hair was every which way, and I had old sandals on, but I supposed the point wasn't what I looked like, but the dress.

She took a couple of pictures and then put the camera down. "I don't need to do anything else to it. The measurements were bang on."

"I can't thank you enough." I managed to get the dress off myself and put my clothes back on. With it draped over my arm, I emerged from behind the screen. Nell had a plastic dress bag ready for me to place my outfit in.

"My gran will be so excited to see this. She gave me the money. How much do we owe you?"

"Nothing."

"But it's gorgeous! You can't take nothing for it."

"Your grandmother has been very kind to me over the years. It's my way of thanking her. I hope you have a wonderful time at the prom."

"Gee, I don't know what to say. Thank you very much. I'll always treasure it. I just wish Mama and Pops could see it."

Before I knew what I was doing, I reached over and gave Nell a peck on the cheek. She didn't seem to mind.

When I showed Gran the dress, she got misty. "Oh my. Oh my."

"She wouldn't take any money for it. She said it was her way of thanking you for being so kind to her over the years."

Gran shook her head and dabbed her eyes.

"She took a picture of me. Said it was for her album of dresses."

"An album of dresses?"

☜☞

AUNT BETTY MADE SURE SHE WAS WITH GRAN WHEN I GOT READY for the big night. "I've never had the pleasure of seeing a girl get ready for the prom. My neanderthals didn't even go. No wonder they don't have wives."

A rap on the door. Jack was here. Gran ushered him in. Taking one last look in the mirror, I pulled on short white gloves, which Barbara told me were the height of fashion. On my feet were a pair of pink strappy slingback shoes that were actually called "Twiggy" in the catalogue. They were obviously meant to be.

At this point I was so excited, I fairly bounced down the stairs and into the kitchen. Gran, Aunt Betty, and Jack stared at me.

I held out my arms. "What do you think?"

I heard a babbling of voices and Aunt Betty started sobbing right away. She couldn't see to take the pictures, so Gran had to do it. If Jack had smiled any wider his face would have split in half. I was over the moon with how he looked. I was sure his mother was very happy tonight. Oh, why weren't Mama and Pops here too? Don't think of that. Don't think of that. Be happy.

Gran and Aunt Betty kissed us both goodbye and then we ran out and got in Jack's car. He turned to me before he started the engine. "If I don't kiss you this minute, I think I'll explode."

"You can't mess up my Yardley London Luv Pink lipstick. Barbara found it for me."

"Do you have more?"

"Yes."

"Then I'm kissing you."

I finally made him drive away; Aunt Betty was trying to peer out the kitchen window, no doubt wondering why we hadn't left yet.

Now I know why proms are so special. You can forget who you are for a night. I had the best time. I was the only girl with a short dress on, which was odd. Didn't Nell tell her other clients about short dresses? But she was right. I looked young and carefree, while some girls looked like they were playing dress-up in their mother's closets.

Jack spent the whole night looking at me, which was terribly sweet. He was proud to have me on his arm.

It was nice to feel I belonged with someone.

CHAPTER SEVENTEEN

Patty had her baby the first week of July.

"You have to come and see him!" she cooed over the phone. "He's perfect. He looks just like Daddy, but Ray thinks he looks like his father. I'm sure you'll agree with me."

"What's his name?"

"Raymond George Albert. Ray Jr. for short."

How original.

Gran was excited to go and said we could stay with Uncle Donny. Not a pleasing prospect, but what could he do with his mother sleeping beside me?

Then Aunt Betty wanted to go too. Gran and I were realizing that she was a very lonely woman who would go anywhere just to get out of the house. So I asked Patty if I could bunk on her sofa.

"The baby might keep you awake. Mom has a couch too, if you'd rather."

Mavis or Uncle Donny. Tough choice.

We arrived in Sydney before noon on a Saturday, all of us with a gift in hand. Ray opened the door, still flushed with excitement over having a son. We hugged him and he led us into the baby's room. Patty was in a padded rocking chair, holding the little bundle. She'd put on a huge amount of weight since the last time I saw her.

"Come look," she whispered.

We tiptoed over and peered down. A tiny, wrinkled old man looked back at us. He even had a comb-over.

"How darling!" Gran exclaimed. "He does look like George, when he was a baby."

There was hope for this kid after all.

"He's pretty small," Aunt Betty noticed. "With the amount of weight you put on, he should be a bruiser."

Patty gave her a dirty look. "Thanks, Betty. Like you should talk."

"He's lovely, Patty," I said. "Does he cry much?"

"I don't know who cries more, him or me." And she promptly burst into tears. Ray came running and took the baby from his mother and scurried out with him. Patty searched in her bathrobe pockets for tissues. "I don't know what's wrong with me! I love him to bits, but if I'm left alone with him for too long, I start blubbering. Mom said she had the baby blues when I was born, so maybe this is genetic. I feel so stupid! Mothers are supposed to love their babies, not be afraid to hold them. I'm a failure!"

Gran put her arm around Patty's shoulders and gave her a squeeze. "This happens all the time. I remember Joe telling me about new moms who had a terrible time in the beginning, but it's just hormones and it will ease after a while. Go to the doctor if it gets worse."

Patty blew her nose. "My doctor is an idiot! When I told him I felt crummy, he said I should be happy that the baby was born alive because some women don't get that lucky. How was that supposed to make me feel better?"

"Where's your mother?" asked Aunt Betty. "She should be here to help you."

Patty sobbed. "She's only been here once! She says she's too afraid of the baby. They make her nervous and she can't handle it."

"What about Ray's mother?" Aunt Betty said. "Surely she can help."

"She works. She's the only mother I know who works, and I was lucky enough to get hitched to her son. I have no one!"

Poor Patty-Cake.

"I'll help you," I said.

She stopped mopping her eyes. "You will?"

"Of course. Aunt Betty can drive Gran home and I'll stay here for a couple of weeks. You don't mind, do you, Gran?"

"Not at all."

Ray gave me a huge squeeze before he left for work, as if he couldn't believe his luck. Gran decided they should leave, because Patty didn't need people hovering over her when she felt so exposed. Gran gave me a big hug goodbye. I assured her I'd be fine. Patty had enough clothes for me to wear and I could buy a new toothbrush.

I didn't know anything about babies but I knew something of loneliness, and I knew that was Patty's real problem. She had no one to fuss over her or make her a meal or hold the baby when she had to go to the bathroom. Simple things become gigantic when you're facing them by yourself.

Patty showed me the baby bottle paraphernalia and the regimen required to feed the little tyke, and when I felt I understood, I sent her to bed. She cried about that.

I gave little Sting Ray his bottle, then I burped him and changed his diaper, which was a disaster from my point of view. How did people not stab babies with these so-called "safety-pins"? It's a miracle I didn't poke him multiple times. Once he was in his bassinet, I pulled it around with me. I cleaned the kitchen, which really needed it. Then I tiptoed into Patty and Ray's room and removed the overflowing laundry basket. Patty was snoring like a sailor and wouldn't have heard a live orchestra rehearsal being conducted in that room.

Since the washer and dryer were downstairs and I didn't want to leave the baby upstairs unattended, I picked him up from the bassinette and placed him in the full laundry basket for the trip downstairs. That's how I did the wash. He loved the warmth and the shaking of the dryer too. I packed all the clean clothes around him for the trip upstairs.

He went back in the bassinet while I put the folded clean clothes in Patty's room, and then little Sting and I cleaned the bathroom. After that, he came with me back out to the kitchen and I looked in the fridge for something I could make for supper.

"We need to send Daddy shopping," I told him, so I made a list.

There were enough ingredients to make macaroni and cheese with tea biscuits and an apple crisp for dessert.

By then, Sting was informing me by silent messages through the air that he needed changing. I got the message loud and clear. Back to poking him with pins and then another feed.

Ray found me asleep in the rocking chair with Ray Jr. on my chest. Patty was still comatose.

When I finally opened my eyes, Ray bleated, "Thank you so much. You have no idea how much this means to us."

"It's no trouble. But before you come in for the night, I've left a grocery list on the kitchen table. Go to the store now, so the things are bought and put away before Patty wakes up."

Out he went, and baby and I rocked.

When Patty did finally emerge, it was to see her husband and me at the kitchen table, eating supper with baby in the bassinet beside us.

"What time is it?" She yawned and blearily looked around.

"It's almost seven. Come eat something."

"Seven! At night?" She quickly charged over to the bassinette. "And baby is fine?"

"Yes. He's been fed three times, changed four times, and slept all day."

"But how come he's not crying?"

"Because I wasn't crying, is my first guess."

She slid into a kitchen chair and looked around. "You did the dishes?"

"She did the laundry and cleaned the bathroom too, plus made this delicious supper," Ray told her. "I went for groceries."

Patty laid her head on my arm and patted Ray's hand. "You guys are the best."

It felt nice to be able to do something for her.

My bed was the living room couch. It was perfectly comfortable, but I didn't sleep soundly, being in someone else's house. I heard Ray cry before Patty did, and I sent her back to bed when she found me rocking him with a bottle.

"Bridie, I don't expect you to do everything."

"I know. But while I'm here, you might as well get caught up on your sleep."

We found a nice little rhythm as the days went by. Patty was able to take a hot shower instead of just rinsing her face under the tap with cold water. She sat under her portable hair dryer one day and put on a dab of lipstick.

"Now I don't feel like such a freak," she said.

The phone rang when I was up to my elbows in a boiling pot of water sterilizing baby bottles, so Patty answered it with Ray on her shoulder.

"Hello? Yes, one moment please."

She held out the phone. "For you. A nice-sounding boy."

I smiled and wiped my hands. Patty held the phone receiver to her belly. "You better tell me everything!"

"Hello?"

"Hi. It's me."

"Hi, Jack."

"I got concerned when I didn't hear from you for three days. I finally called your grandmother. I was afraid she'd tell me you'd skipped town."

"Well, I have, but only for a little while. I'm helping my sister with her new baby."

"You never told me you had a sister."

"I do. It's a weird arrangement. We're not biological sisters, but I've pestered her endlessly and read her diary, so that qualifies me as a pain-in-the-ass little sister."

"Gotcha. So, it's going to be a while until I see you. Napoleon is getting lonely."

"Napoleon is just fine."

"I'm getting lonely."

"You're going to be fine too."

"I'm not sure about that. Let me know when you get home."

"I will."

"I miss you."

"Goodbye, Jack."

There was no way I was going to tell Jack I missed him with Patty breathing down my neck. I hung up the phone and went back to my pot of boiling water.

"Spill the beans," she said. "Who's Jack?"

"He's a guy I go out with on occasion."

"What's he look like?"

"He's cute. Blond, blue eyes."

"What's he do?"

"He's basically running his father's ranch, now that his dad is in politics."

"Do you like him?"

"Of course."

"Aha! You better bring him for a visit sometime so I can see for myself."

That afternoon, Patty and baby were sleeping and I was copying out recipes from one of Patty's cookbooks. There was a loud banging on the front door and I ran to get it before the baby woke up.

It was Mavis. She'd put weight on as well.

She looked at me in shock. "What are you doing here?"

"I'm helping Patty. What are you doing here?"

"Visiting my grandson, since God forbid anyone bring him to see me." She pushed by me through the doorway and tossed her purse on the nearest armchair. "Where is he?"

"He's either in his cot or in his cot."

"Nothing's changed, I see. Always the joker."

"Why don't you wait here until the baby wakes up? I'll make you a cup of tea."

"No, thank you." She blew past me and headed straight for the baby's room. A moment later, Ray was crying. I could've belted her. Both Patty and I reached the door to his room at the same time.

"Mom! What do you think you're doing?"

Mavis was trying to hold the squirming child, and looked none too pleased about it. "What is wrong with him?"

"Put your hand under his head, for one thing," Patty cried. "Give him to me."

Patty practically ripped the baby out of her mother's hands. Motherhood makes you brave.

"How dare you come in here and wake him up? Do you know how hard it is to get him to sleep?"

"And that's the thanks I get for coming to visit. You were whining just the other day that I don't come over enough. If this is the type of reception I get, I don't think I'll bother."

My childhood came roaring back to me in that instant. "Why don't I make us all a cup of tea? Let's go in the living room. I'll get Ray's bottle."

I watched Mama do this a thousand times. Put everyone in a corner and calm them down with a hot drink and a cookie.

Things were much better once everyone was fed. Patty put Ray on a blanket on the sofa and mother and grandmother sat at either end, smiling at his antics.

It gave me an opportunity to collect the dishes and take them into the kitchen, where I washed them immediately. Then I headed downstairs with another load of laundry. It was quite a process to wash cloth diapers. I took a fresh batch out of the washing machine and took them outside to hang on the line.

When I came back in, Mavis and Patty were already at each other's throats. Poor little baby was squalling too. I picked him up and bounced him as I walked around the room.

"You both need to calm down if you want this child to be calm."

Mavis looked down her nose at me. "What do you know about rearing a child?"

"Nothing. But I know that I get upset when you two get upset, so I imagine it's the same for a little baby."

Patty pointed at me. "She's got more sense than you ever will, Mother. You can't come here bellyaching about your poor lonely life. I'm too busy to listen to it."

Mavis rooted in her purse and took out a tissue. "This is the thanks I get for raising you girls."

"You didn't raise us, you silly woman! Eileen raised us. You spent your time in bed, in the tub, at a luncheon, or drinking your way through another putrid cocktail party. Believe me when I say I'll be taking a page out of Eileen's book, not yours, as I raise my son."

It was the first time I'd ever heard Patty give Eileen the credit she deserved. I was in danger of crying, so I took off with Ray and shut the door of his room. He needed changing anyway. His little chest heaved up and down from his wails, but he quickly calmed himself as I washed his body and stroked his tiny head.

How could I have called him an old man with a comb-over? He was precious, with his pouty mouth and little button nose. So sweet and innocent and trusting. This must have been how Pops felt about me when he saved me, as my mother lay dying next to him.

Oh, my God. The love. The love was overwhelming.

Ray and I rocked away, listening to Mavis yell her way out of the house before slamming the front door. Patty peeked in and leaned on the door frame.

"Why did I think I wanted my mother to come over? It'll be a blessing if she leaves us alone for the foreseeable future."

"Your mother is not suited to infants. I believe that's why Pops had Mama come to stay with you when you were first born."

"I shudder to think what life would have been like without Eileen. I wish I'd told her how much I loved her."

"She knew."

Patty frowned. "Thanks, but you and I both know the truth. I was a brat."

Two weeks turned into three, but I didn't mind. I loved Patty's baby with all my heart. Being an auntie was an amazing thing, and I knew I would be close to my little puppy for the rest of his life.

The poor kid. He'd gone from Ray to Sting Ray to Puppy, and Puppy stuck. Even Patty called him Pup. I'm not sure Ray was too happy with it, but he was so thrilled to get his wife back that he would have called the kid Frankenstein if it meant peace was restored to his kingdom.

Patty herself told me to go home, that she was fine and could handle it from here. When I called Gran to tell her, she said Jack had asked if he could pick me up when I was ready to come home. I told her to call him.

Patty was pleased. "I'll have to get out my binoculars and spy on you two in the car before you leave."

"I apologize for all that, by the way."

"You've more than made it up to me. I'll never be able to repay you."

Jack was at the door at eight in the morning, which meant he'd had an early start. Patty thought that was adorable. She peeked through the curtains as he came up the walk. Ray held Pup in his arms. "Get away from the window, woman."

"Oh my God! He's a dreamboat! Are you mad, spending three weeks with me and a mountain of dirty diapers when you could've been with him?"

I opened the front door before Jack even knocked and jumped into his arms before he said hello, whereupon I kissed him with everything I had, and he kissed me back. Who knows what Patty and Ray were thinking.

When we finally realized we were standing in a doorway in view of all the neighbours, I quickly pulled Jack inside.

"This is Jack. Jack, this is my sister, Patty, her husband, Ray, and my nephew, Pup. Isn't he the sweetest thing you've ever seen?" I took Pup out of his father's arms as Jack shook their hands.

"Nice to meet you."

Patty was almost swooning at Jack's feet. "Hello! Now I understand why Bridie keeps you hidden in the country."

Ray looked at her like she was mad. "Patty! You're embarrassing the kid."

Jack did look like he was ready to go through the floor. "We should probably get going."

Instantly, I put my face against Pup's neck and breathed him in. "I'll miss you so much."

Patty had to eventually take him from me, because I couldn't make the move to pass him over.

The three of them walked out onto the step and waved goodbye. Patty blew kisses and pretended Pup was blowing them too. That just about killed me.

"For God's sake, drive before I get out of the car and kidnap him."

Jack drove away but I was still hanging out the window, waving at my baby. It was only when I couldn't see him anymore that I fell back into my seat with a huge sigh. Jack took my hand and kissed it.

"The next time you go away for three weeks, would you be kind enough to tell me beforehand? I nearly went out of my mind."

"Funny. I never gave you a single thought."

He laughed. "It's a good thing you kissed me before you said that."

We didn't go right home. We stopped at an out-of-the-way spot and walked together through the fields, towards the blue, shining water. We lay in the hot sand under the midday sun, while Jack traced my face with a blade of grass.

"What did you miss most?" I asked.

"This. Looking at your beautiful face."

"I missed Napoleon."

He grinned. "Did you, now?"

"His large, expressive eyes and long eyelashes. His soft mouth and strong back. The way he feels between my thighs."

Jack put his hand behind my neck and pulled my face close to his. "I've never said this to anyone in my whole life. I love you, Bridie. Being away from you was just what I needed to realize that my life is only complete if you're by my side. I don't care what we do, or where we go, but we need to do it together."

"Darn it, Jack. That wasn't cheesy at all. What am I supposed to say?"

"You know what I want you to say."

"I love you, Napoleon."

He sure loved me back.

CHAPTER EIGHTEEN

Almost a year later, Eric was on the phone.

"The prom is this Saturday. Did you forget?"

Unfortunately, I hadn't forgotten. "My prom is on Friday. Don't you have a girlfriend by now, Eric?"

"No. I told you. You are my one true love."

"But I have a boyfriend, and I'm not sure what he'll think about me going to the prom with you."

"Just tell him you're keeping a promise to an old friend."

That was true enough. Just do it and get it over with.

"All right. Pick me up at my sister's." I gave him Patty's address.

Jack wasn't too pleased when I told him. "You have to leave for Sydney the very next day? So much for staying out late and partying at your own prom. The guy sounds like a jackass."

"He's not. He's very sweet and he helped me move and I feel like I owe him."

"You can do what you want, obviously, but I think it stinks."

I put my head on his shoulder. "Don't be mad. I just want it over with. We'll have a great time on Friday night."

And we did. Once more my fabulous dress came out of the closet and once more Gran and Aunt Betty took pictures of us. Because I knew many more kids at the dance this year, we all had so much fun. Jack jumped up on stage with a microphone and sang along with the Monkees hit "I'm a Believer," pointing at me the entire time. Even I was swooning.

One of the happiest moments of my life was leaving that dance linking arms with Jack, waving and hollering good night to our friends as we walked to our cars. The future just stretched out before us like a red carpet.

We held each other for a long time before we said good night.

Jack kissed my nose. "I wish you weren't going tomorrow, or that you'd at least let me drive you. I can sit in the car and wait until the dance is over."

"And stay with me at Patty's? I don't think so. Besides, I'm going to take a few days and visit Pup. I can't believe it's almost his first birthday."

"Promise me you won't stay there for three weeks again."

"I am a grown woman, Jack Morris. How I spend my time is my decision. Don't get all possessive on me."

"I love you, that's all. I want to protect you."

"From what?"

"The world."

"Now you're being silly. I better get some shuteye. I'll be back by Monday."

I kissed him again and then slipped away.

Gran had baked a cake for Pup, an early birthday gift, and we wrapped it carefully and put it in the back of the car the next morning. In went my prom dress for the third wearing. Packed a few clothes and some stuffed animals and baby books. A big kiss for Gran and I was on my way.

I loved driving by myself. It made me feel grown-up and responsible. And the view along the way just lifted my spirits, although today it was grey and foggy, so I was careful going around the twists and turns. I had the radio blaring, which made me think of last night and the public declaration Jack had made. If your heart can burst from happiness, that's how it felt as I drove to my sister's.

Pup was the most adorable baby boy on the planet. And I could see for the first time that he did bear a resemblance to Pops.

It was the shape of his head, or the way he smiled, but Pops was definitely in the mix somewhere. He would have been so proud of him. They say men want sons, but Pops never mentioned it. It was seeing Ray carry Pup around like he was a trophy that convinced me it must be true.

Since we were having an early birthday party, Patty had invited her mother over to share the cake Gran had made. Things were clearly improving between mother and daughter now that Pup was a more enjoyable age. Mavis beamed with pride as we took pictures of Ray Jr. clutching a handful of cake.

I was weary from all the excitement the night before, the long drive, and spending the day with an energetic baby, but I dressed myself for this third and final prom anyway. I had called Eric back to tell him I'd meet him at the dance, instead of him picking me up. That way I could leave early if I was dying of boredom, not that I told him so.

He'd sounded disappointed.

"Sorry, my sister's baby is fussy, and people coming to the door are an unwanted distraction."

He agreed he'd meet me at the dance.

It was the first time Patty, Ray, and Mavis had seen my dress, and they were mightily impressed—even Mavis.

"Where did you get that gorgeous thing?" Patty wanted to know.

"A local dressmaker, Nell Sampson."

"Oh yes," said Mavis. "I remember her at George's father's funeral. Jean said she used her. Well, she certainly is talented."

"I know. And she wouldn't take any money for it either. She said Gran was always nice to her, and it was a gift."

"Speaking from a male point of view," Ray said, "your date is going to be over the moon."

"I can't believe I have to go through with this. I will never make a rash statement again."

"How does Jack feel about it?" Patty asked.

"He wasn't pleased, but Eric was nice to me once and I feel

I should be nice to him. I won't be too late. Leave the door open and I'll crash on the couch."

I kissed Pup several times before I left. He giggled and put his hands on my face.

Going back into the gym at Sydney Academy was like looking through a View-Master. Images from the past kept popping up in front of my eyes, yet it all felt like a hundred years ago. Had I gone to this school? Did I belong here?

Eric must have been looking out for me, because in a matter of seconds he was by my side, hugging me. "Thank you for coming! You look amazing."

"Thanks, Eric. You look very nice too."

Then he looked around at the crowd and pointed down at my head. "I told you," he yelled. "I told you I'd win the pool!"

Once everyone realized who I was I was swamped, which made no sense; I hadn't been popular when I went to that school, and I hadn't even been there for almost two years. A lot of guys came around, looking put-out as they handed Eric his money.

I was the star attraction at the fair.

I touched Eric's arm. "If you continue to behave like this, I'm going."

He seemed shocked. "I'm sorry. I didn't realize. I'm just so happy that this is finally happening."

"That you're collecting money or that I'm here?"

"I apologize. You're right. Let me start over."

In my head I kept telling myself to go, and then I'd argue with myself that I'd come all this way and should stick it out. Eric got me some punch, and we sat and chatted with some of the other kids. He wanted our picture taken at the picture wall. He said he needed proof that I was his date. We danced, and I spent the entire time wishing I was in Jack's arms instead. Poor old Eric was sweating right though his suit, and he stepped on my feet a number of times. But he looked like such a puppy dog, I couldn't stay mad at him.

By eleven I'd exhausted all conversational avenues and made a point of yawning. "I'm sorry, Eric, but I'm pretty tired. I went to my own prom last night and it was a long drive to get here today. I think I'll call it a night."

He looked panicked. "Already? I thought you'd at least stay until midnight."

"Why? What happens at midnight?"

"Cinderella leaves and the prince chases after her."

I couldn't tell if he was kidding. "Well, this scullery maid is saying good night. Thank you for the lovely time. I wish you all kinds of luck with your future endeavours. Please say hello to your dad for me."

"Don't I get a kiss goodbye?"

"Fine." I kissed his cheek. "Good night."

The dance floor was still rocking as I retrieved my clutch and took out my car keys. I hurried out into the street and walked briskly up the sidewalk to where I parked the car. It was quite far, as I'd arrived at the dance a little late. It was different now that it was pitch black, the streetlights covered with tree branches and leaves for the most part. I couldn't remember which side of the street I'd parked on, which irritated me. Jack always told me to pay attention to things like that, and I never did.

Finally I spied my car, and relief spread through me like a wave. I put the keys in the lock and opened the door. Someone pushed me from behind and fell on top of me across the front seat. A warm, sweaty hand covered my mouth.

"Don't scream. You're not allowed to scream."

It was that fool Eric, scaring the life out of me. I relaxed so he would take his hand away, which he did.

"Eric, I'm not going to scream, but I want you to get off of me. I'm uncomfortable like this, and I'm sure you are too."

"Yeah, I guess so." We settled ourselves as best we could, only now he was in the driver's seat and I was on the passenger side.

"May I drive you home?" he said. "You left so abruptly, and it's like our date wasn't over. It's supposed to end at midnight."

"Eric, this is not a fairy tale. I brought my own car so I could leave when I was tired, and I'm tired. I'm sorry that you thought I'd be here until midnight, but I have to go."

"You're a liar, then. You lied when you said you'd be my prom date. Prom dates go to parties afterward that can last all night. I was being respectful by only asking you to be with me until midnight."

I wanted to shake him until his teeth rattled. Why was I talking to this idiot? I looked at my watch, which was a mistake. The car keys dangled from my hand and he reached out and snatched them from me. Instantly, I knew that Eric was more than an idiot.

He cheered up. "Now I'll drive you home." He started the car. "Where to again?"

My mouth was so dry I had a hard time speaking. I gave him Patty's address.

"Oh yes, I remember now. But first we'll go for a drive."

Before he had the last word out of his mouth, I opened the passenger door and jumped out of the car. It was barely moving, so I managed to stay on my feet. I started yelling for help and ran as fast as I could, but I tripped on my shoes and fell with a hard bang on the pavement. My knees were bleeding as I scrambled upright, but Eric was right there. He picked me up over his head and carried me back to the car like a sack of potatoes. All the time, I was scratching and trying to bite him, but it was like he didn't feel anything. At first, I thought he was going to put me back in the front seat, but he reached in and lifted the trunk opener. He was going to throw me in the trunk. I was dead if I didn't do something.

"Eric. Calm down. I don't want to go in the trunk. It will mess my dress. Why don't we go back to the dance? I'll stay until midnight."

He hesitated. "Go back to the dance?"

"Yes. You've waited for it all year and silly me wanted to go home early. But I'm not tired anymore and I think we should dance again. Let all the guys see who your date is. You won the pool, remember?"

He put me down. "Okay, that sounds like a good idea."

He put my keys in his pocket and grabbed my hand and walked me back to the dance. I was going to be saved by the people and the lights. All I had to do was scream.

"If you scream, I know where your sister lives. She has a baby, doesn't she? I'd like to meet the baby sometime."

The fear that ran though me was like a living thing. Protect Pup at all costs. I would do whatever this maniac said.

We danced for another half an hour. By this point, I had to pee from all the punch I'd had earlier, so I told Eric.

"You can't go. You'll run away."

"I promise you I won't. I mean it."

"I don't believe you."

"Please, Eric. I have to go."

He pulled my arm and we left the gym but we walked right past the women's washroom and he pushed the door of the men's open. "This way I can watch you."

Just my luck, the place was empty, so I quickly disappeared into a stall and peed. The thought of leaving this perfect little box made me so sad. It was like my rational mind was shutting down, and it was harder and harder for me to think of the best course of action. What would Jack do? If Eric could lift me, I doubt I was strong enough to beat him up. But maybe I could, now that he'd threatened Pup. Bashing his brains in sounded remarkably easy.

"Hurry up."

I had to open the cubicle door. I needed help, but no one would hear my screams from here. Not over the music and merriment. So, I rushed by Eric and reached for the door handle, but he grabbed my hair. Just that alone woke the beast in me. There was no way I was going to let him have any of my power. I clutched my shoe and stabbed him in the eye with my kitten heel. He fell backwards and landed on the floor. In a flash, I remembered Laurel Beth, my angel at Pops's funeral, and gave Eric a kick between his legs. He howled and pulled himself into a fetal position. I had to stand over him to get my car keys out of his pocket.

"You complete bastard! Only a coward would force himself on someone!"

I wrenched the keys from his pocket and threw open the bathroom door. I ran like hell down the corridor and out the front door, sprinting up the street to my car, which was now unlocked. It took four tries before I could get the key in the starter, but once the engine roared to life, I put my foot on the gas and did a U-turn so I wouldn't have to drive past the school.

Should I drive to Patty's or drive straight home? The gas tank was only a quarter full. I couldn't take the chance on driving all the way to St. Peter's in the middle of the night. Pops always told me to fill the car when it was down to half. Why didn't I listen to him? I pounded my fist on the steering wheel.

"It's such a simple thing, Bridie, but no. You never listen to anyone! You think you know everything, and look what happened! This is your fault. Jack told you not to go, but you ignored him and now this. You're a stupid fool. A stupid, stupid fool! I hate you right now!"

I couldn't go into Patty's. I felt too dirty with my bleeding knees and ripped nylons and the sweat from Eric's hands all over my face. I didn't want to talk to anyone.

At some point I fell asleep behind the wheel. It was morning when Patty opened the car door and shook me awake.

"What on earth happened to you? You scared me to death when I didn't see you on the sofa this morning."

"Sorry."

"Were you drinking?"

"No. Just exhausted from two proms. It was a stupid idea."

"Let me help you up." She took my arm and pulled me out of the car. "Bridie! What happened to your dress? And your knees?"

"I fell in the parking lot."

"That Eric kid should've driven you home."

"I wanted to get away. He was starting to bug me."

"Go have a shower and I'll fix you some breakfast. Then you can have a nap."

So that's what I did. My whole brain was sideways and pounded like a drum. My limbs were heavy, like I'd been beaten, and my insides felt empty and lost. I kept reliving the moment I knew Eric was going to put me in the trunk of the car. He could've killed me and no one would have known where to find me.

Playing with Pup kept my mind off things. He helped me feel more normal. Patty wanted me to spend another night, but I told her I felt like I was coming down with something and I didn't want Pup exposed to it.

She held me close when I said goodbye. "Come back anytime. I miss you when you're gone. Can you believe I'm saying that?"

I laughed. "No, imagine what Pops would say!"

The Texaco man filled my car and wiped my windshield until it sparkled. He had such a nice smile. There were still gentlemen out there. But as I was leaving, his arm shot through the window and his hand touched my shoulder. I screeched and jumped back.

"I'm terribly sorry, miss. You forgot your receipt."

I nodded and whispered my thanks, throwing the receipt onto the seat next to me. I had to get my act together before I got home.

It was the longest drive of my life. There was no way I wanted to be in Sydney, and yet there was no way I wanted to sit with Gran and chat about the baby. Talking to Jack would be unbearable. He'd asked me not to go and I'd dismissed him. I know it wasn't the worst that could've happened, but I felt defeated and vulnerable just the same.

My only thought was to spend time with Pops. Go find a river and sit beside it. I chose Grand River, because it was close to home, but still far enough away that I wouldn't run into anyone I knew. There was a spot that Pops had taken me to. Eventually I found it and got out of the car and walked for a while.

There was a sandy clearing near the water with three large boulders that pressed against each other as if for comfort. You could settle yourself between them like an armchair and no one could see you if they were walking by from the road.

I told Mama and Pops what had happened, and I cried. Then I cried because I was making this a huge issue. It was a stupid episode and I'd gotten away.

But only just.

Pops always said that sometimes a moment can change your life. That every moment was a big deal, if we only paid attention.

The sun was going down by the time I got back into the car. When I pulled into the yard, Hobbs jumped and ran around with excitement. My chest started to pound. Here was a being made of pure joy. If Hobbs had been with me, this wouldn't have happened. If I'd stayed at home on Saturday, Jack and I could've taken Hobbs for a walk.

Naturally, Gran wanted to hear all about the trip, and I said it wasn't anything special, that I'd been too tired from the night before to really enjoy myself, that I should've stayed home. Then she asked about Pup and I told her he loved the cake and that Mavis and Patty had a good time together while eating it. That seemed to please her.

Once again, I faked a yawn and said I really had to hit the hay. As I gathered my belongings, she spied my dress.

"What happened to your beautiful dress?"

"Oh, I fell in the parking lot and it got ripped. There's dirt on it too. I don't think I'll be wearing it to any more proms."

"Oh, that's too bad. Give it to me. I'll try and get the dirt out of it."

I couldn't tell her I never wanted to see it again.

The next morning, I heard the phone ring. Gran shouted up the stairs: "It's Jack!"

"I think I have the flu. Tell him I'm sick and I'll call him when I feel better."

My "flu" lasted for two days. Jack got impatient and came over anyway.

Gran dithered by my bedroom door. "What should I tell him? He brought chicken soup."

That was so sweet. I missed him. "Tell him I'll be right down."

It really wasn't a stretch to make myself look pathetic. My face in the mirror was horrific, with pale blotchy skin and dark circles under my eyes. Very flu-like. I'd be able to fool him.

The minute I walked into the kitchen and saw him standing there, I put my hands over my face and started to cry. Jack immediately took me in his arms. Hobbs jumped up on me and Gran wrung her hands. "What's the matter with her?"

He hushed me like a baby. "You're okay. Tell us what happened. We'll listen."

I told them every miserable moment.

My Gran rushed out of the kitchen at one point. I looked at Jack. "I've upset her."

"I'll see if she's okay. Here, sit in the rocking chair." He put an old quilt around me. I didn't tell him it was Hobbs's blanket; Hobbs didn't mind me using it, anyway.

When Jack returned, he put on the kettle and made a pot of tea. He even rooted around and found a tin of chocolate-covered biscuits, which he put on a plate. Suddenly I was ravenous. And very calm.

He called up the stairs. "Mrs. Mackenzie, come and have some tea. Bridie and I are having a cup." Gran did come back and sat at the kitchen table. We sipped our tea together.

"What should we do?" Gran said.

"I don't want you to do anything," I told them. "I'm not going to the police. I can't prove that he did anything. As a matter of fact, I travelled a long way to go to the prom with him, which makes me look desperate. There were no witnesses. I didn't call for help when I could have, which is suspicious, now that I think about it. Why didn't I yell for help in the gym?"

Jack looked at me. "You said he knew where Pup lived, and that frightened you."

"Oh, right. But what a stupid thing to think."

Jack reached over and rubbed my shoulder. "No one would think clearly in that situation. It was just a thought."

The tension went out of my body when Jack talked like that. "Why are you so smart?"

"I'm not that smart. I shouldn't have let you go."

Gran shook her head. "You didn't know any more than she did that this would happen. It's no one's fault. Only Eric's. And here I was, giving him and his father tea and pumpkin loaf! What was I thinking?"

That made me laugh. "Yes, Gran. It's your pumpkin loaf that did it. You should be ashamed of yourself."

She wiped her eyes with Kleenex. "This isn't a laughing matter."

"Would you mind if I spoke to Bridie alone, Mrs. Mackenzie?"

"Of course, dear. You've been wonderful. I don't know what we'd do without you. I'll be upstairs, Bridie, if you need me."

"Thanks, Gran."

Jack sat in the rocker and I curled up in his lap, with my head under his chin. He had one arm around me and his other hand rubbed the ends of my toes. How did he know they were cold?

We sat for a long time and rocked together, Hobbs with his nose on Jack's leg, which made him look like he was nodding yes very slowly. That made me happy.

"I'm sorry. I dismissed your concerns and went anyway."

"You are stubborn but don't forget, you kicked his ass. You did that all by yourself."

When I snuggled into him, he tightened his grip on me. Right here I was safe, and that's all that mattered.

I kept nodding off, so Jack told me I needed to get a good night's sleep and he'd see me in the morning. We kissed each other and I was reassured.

But Jack banged the back door when he left and slammed the door to his father's truck before ripping skid marks in the gravel driveway as he tore out on the highway, his squealing tires burning.

I ran into Gran's room. She pulled down the covers and I crawled in beside her, curling up to her warmth.

"He's going to get hurt. I shouldn't have said anything."

"Let him handle this in his own way. Men have their own sense of justice. Let him be."

"But if he kills Eric, he'll go to jail."

"I very much doubt he'll kill him, but I sure wouldn't want to be Eric right about now."

"I don't know where he thinks he's going. He doesn't even know where Eric lives."

"Oh yes, he does. I told him."

CHAPTER NINETEEN

SEPTEMBER 1968

A little more than a year later, on my eighteenth birthday, I realized there were major decisions that needed to be made. Like what I was going to do with the rest of my life.

The year after I graduated from high school, I spent most of my time with Gran. She had developed a few health issues— nothing drastic, but they impeded her energy enough to change her lifestyle somewhat—so I told Aunt Betty that I was going to stay close to home until things sorted themselves out. My future could wait.

Whenever someone asked me what I'd like to do next I didn't have an answer, which made me terribly guilty because I knew that Pops assumed I'd be heading for university. But the thought of living away from home and leaving Jack didn't make sense to me at this point in my life. I'd already made my big "starting over" move when I left Sydney. Now I understood how Patty felt at the idea of leaving Ray. We were like every other dumb girl who loved a boy: hopeless.

The one thing I still enjoyed above anything else was baking. But how do you parlay that into a job? Especially in a small town where every second housewife was a crackerjack baker.

Aunt Betty to the rescue.

She came in one day to get the latest gossip, although why she thought she'd get it from Gran and me, I'll never know. We never went anywhere.

"I hate to bake. I'd pay you to do it for me. I have a few friends who are always grumbling about it too. I could give them a call and see if they want some loaves or buns every so often."

"Thanks, Aunt Betty! That would be great." I ran out to the secretary desk in the living room and rushed back with a pen and paper. "What would you like?"

I'd caught her off guard. "Well, I'm not sure right this minute."

"Bread? How many? Three loaves? Four dozen cookies to start. I could bake you a lemon pie. I've been practising Gran's recipe on Jack and I'm not sure he can eat any more."

"Can I get back to you? I'll have to see what's in my pantry."

She never did get back to me.

Gran rolled her eyes when I complained about it. "Did you honestly expect Betty to go home and try and figure out what she needed? That would require brainpower. Why don't you go down to the general store and see if they'd like some fresh baked goods? That's something the supermarket doesn't have."

That morning, I baked tea biscuits, bread rolls, cinnamon rolls, two zucchini loaves (since Aunt Betty kept trying to get rid of all the zucchini from Uncle Fraser's garden), a batch each of chocolate chip, oatmeal raisin, and peanut butter cookies. Everything was done by eleven.

Then Hobbs and I set off for a brisk walk down to Burke's store, carrying a big wicker basket of goodies covered with a red checkered tea towel. I thought if I looked like Dorothy from the Wizard of Oz, people would be more receptive.

"Don't bark, Hobbs. I'm trying to make a good impression."

Hobbs promised he'd be a good boy.

I sauntered in as if it were a last-minute decision to peruse the joint. There was a young man behind the counter I'd never seen before. Well, maybe he wasn't young, but he wasn't old either. I couldn't tell. He had a baby face, with the blackest hair and the bluest eyes. I wondered where Mr. and Mrs. Burke were.

He spied me and flashed a lovely smile. "Good day, miss. And isn't it a fine morning?"

"Hello. You sound Irish."

"Why, yes indeed, fiddle-dee-dee. Is it that noticeable?"

He made me laugh. "Just a bit. What do you think, Hobbs?"

Hobbs sat at my feet and grinned. He'd promised to be a good boy.

"And where are my manners?" He removed his cap. "I'm Danny Flynn from Dublin, and you are?"

"Bridie Mackenzie, and this is Hobbs."

"Pleased as punch to meet the two of you. May I interest you in anything from this shop? I told my uncle that I'd do my best to make sure the place didn't fall into insolvency while he's being operated on at the hospital."

"Oh dear. Nothing serious, I hope?"

"Well, we won't know that until they cut into him, I'm afraid. All we can do is hope for the best."

"I'll keep him in my prayers."

He smiled and put his cap back on. "I'm sure he'll have a speedy recovery, then."

I looked down at my basket. "Now I'm not sure what to do. I came to discuss some business with Mr. Burke."

"As I am the one Uncle Tim put in charge, I'm sure he'd be delighted if we discussed business."

There was no backing out now. I unfurled my tea towel. "How does this look to you?"

His eyes grew big. "That, sweet lady, is the prettiest sight this side of Galway."

"Would you like to try a sample or two?"

"Is the Pope Catholic?" He reached out and took a cinnamon roll and an oatmeal raisin cookie. He ate both with deliberate relish and even saved the last piece for Hobbs.

"That was delightful, Bridie. Did you know that Bridie is an Irish name?"

"No, I didn't."

"It's a nickname for Bridget, which happens to be my mother's name. So, whatever you are selling, Bridget, I am determined to buy it."

"Really? The whole basket?"

"The whole basket."

"I'm not sure what I should sell it for. I didn't think I'd get this far."

"How does fifteen dollars sound?"

"Are you joking? Okay!"

He went to the cash register and retrieved the money. "There you are, miss, with my everlasting gratitude."

I took all the baked goods out of the basket and placed them on the counter. "Thank you very much, Mr. Flynn! Have a good day!"

Hobbs and I fairly flew out the door and ran back home. I was flushed by the time I made it to the kitchen, whereupon I waved my money in Gran's face. "I made a sale! I have to bake more!"

The next morning I was ready to go with more delectable goodies. This time I took the car, since I had a lemon pie sitting on the top of the pile, and I didn't want it smooshed. Once again, I traipsed in and was greeted by the fabulous Mr. Flynn.

"Bridie! To what do I owe the pleasure?"

"I've come with more baking!" I looked around. "You must have sold everything you bought yesterday. Look what I have for you today." Once again, I threw the towel off as if I were a magician. "Who doesn't love a lemon meringue pie?!"

He opened his mouth and then closed it again.

"Is there something wrong?"

"No, not at all. I just didn't realize you wanted me to sell your wares."

"You didn't sell them?"

"Well, no."

"What did you do with them?"

"I ate them."

"You ate them?"

He nodded.

"*All* of them?"

He nodded again.

"But you need to sell them in the store. I can make a batch of baking like this every morning, and you sell it for me and give me the money."

"I see. And what does the store get out of it?"

"People come into the store to pick up my baking and remember that they need lighter fluid, or steel wool, or bacon."

"Or because I'm providing the premises for you to reach a greater audience for your cookies, you would give me a percentage of your take. That way everyone's happy. Well, not me, because I can't eat your cookies."

"That sounds reasonable. But now I have to figure out how much I should sell my baking for. If it's too low, I won't break even. If it's too high, it won't sell."

The bell rang over the door and two women walked in. Danny shooed me away and took the goodies out of the basket.

"Good morning, ladies. And a fine morning it is, is it not?"

They twittered at him. No wonder. What a pleasure it was to hear that lovely lilt instead of grumpy old Mr. Burke.

"Can I interest you in some marvellous baking this morning? Perhaps your dear husbands would like a special dessert tonight, or a member of the clergy will happen to drop by. Wouldn't it be thrilling to have a treat just waiting for his holiness in the pantry?"

One of the ladies took home the pie and the other took home a zucchini loaf and a dozen peanut butter cookies. When they left, Danny and I did a jig.

A week later, I was sure I'd found my calling. Hobbs and I made our morning delivery, as usual, but Danny looked a bit distracted. He was dealing with a few customers, so I ambled along the back aisle, just waiting for the men to leave. I lost sight of Hobbs. I didn't want to interrupt Danny, so I crept along the aisles, trying not to be seen. Finally, I spied Hobbs's tail wagging by the end of the front counter.

"Hobbs!" I whispered. "Here, boy."

He ignored me, which was unusual, so I quickly crouched down and held him by the collar. Hobbs had half a banana loaf in his mouth. Most of yesterday's baking was under the counter as well. Looking at it, it was more like three days' worth.

I knelt there feeling sick while Hobbs ate the last of the loaf. I heard Danny say goodbye to the gentlemen, and then he knelt by my side.

"It's a tragedy, for sure. I've eaten as much as I could, but I'm afraid my pants are getting too tight."

"I thought this was a good idea."

"And so it was! But the market is a fickle thing. There's supply and demand. In this case, we have too much supply and not enough demand. Now if we were in a mining camp with no women for miles, your baked goods would be worth a fortune."

I stood up and sighed.

"I hope this won't discourage you from coming to the store. You've been a bright spot in my day, so you have."

"I'll be around. Come on, greedy guts."

Hobbs slunk out of the store ahead of me. "Bye, Danny."

"Bye, Bridie. May your troubles be as few and as far apart as my grandmother's teeth."

❧

I MOPED AROUND THE HOUSE FOR A WHILE. JACK TRIED TO MAKE me feel better, but I was determined to sulk. He was busy on his dad's farm and there was no one around. Barbara was studying to be nurse and Linda was at teacher's college. Being left behind didn't feel very nice.

One day out of the blue I called Patty. "What's it like being a secretary?"

"I wasn't a secretary for very long, but I enjoyed it. When are you coming to visit? Pup is asking for you."

"I'll be down in a couple of weeks maybe, but right now I need a job."

"Try the bank. They're always looking for people."

That one off-the-cuff remark landed me employment. I walked into the Royal Bank and they happened to be looking for someone. Talk about luck. What was even more amazing was how much I enjoyed being a teller. Mrs. Beliveau was my superior, and she was a tough taskmaster, but I soon became confident thanks to her exacting standards.

The job of a bank teller is to handle money, but there's more to it than that. As Mrs. Beliveau explained, "You need to make the person feel important, like it's their money alone that's holding up the economy. People are proud of their hard work."

"But what do you do when someone comes in and they have very little money?"

"I hasten to add that this in not in the company manual, but make sad eyes like a beagle and shake your head in a sympathetic manner. Like it's not their fault that they're spending their money like water. That it's the goddamn government that's to blame."

"Gotcha."

By the time Remembrance Day rolled around, I knew everyone in the village. There were definitely regulars, and most of them were business owners. I enjoyed chatting to Nell Sampson. She often changed her position in line so she'd end up at my wicket.

She'd pass me her bank book and an envelope of money.

"Good morning, Bridie. How's your grandmother these days?" she asked one day.

"She's fine, Miss Sampson."

"Please call me Nell."

"Nell. That's such a pretty name. Is it short for something?"

"Eleanor."

"Danny Flynn told me that Bridie was an Irish name and it's short for Bridget."

"It's a special name."

"Is it? How so?"

"It's yours."

I blushed and counted out her money.

Mrs. Beliveau was impressed with the rapport Nell and I had.

"She's usually a sour old thing when she comes in here. What on earth have you done to her?"

"She's always been lovely to me."

The other customer I loved was Danny Flynn. He'd rush in with dead leaves flying behind him, in a panic because he had to put the Closed sign up at the store to bring in the cash for deposit. His hair was usually every which way and he always had stubble on his face, like he didn't have time to shave.

"Jesus, Mary, and Joseph," he panted. "Wasn't I wishin' I had one of your cinnamon rolls for breakfast this morning, because didn't I end up burning my porridge, and that's the third pot of my Aunt Janet's I'm apt to ruinin'. She's gonna kill me dead, I swear. I'm after trying to buy some new pots, but I never have the time. Running a general store is as time consuming as being a leprechaun on St. Paddy's Day!"

I made Danny a batch of cinnamon rolls and dropped them off at the store before work, along with a couple of Gran's old pots. She loved him, but then so did everyone in St. Peter's. Everyone was kind of hoping his Uncle Tim didn't recover enough to be back behind the counter. His Aunt Janet hoped not either. She said she needed to retire and put her feet up.

Danny put his hands up to his cheeks when he saw me coming. "Can it be? Oh, you're Saoirse, so you are!"

"Saoirse?"

"A lovely and beautiful girl, among other things. And not only goodies, but pots!"

"The pots are from my gran."

He came around the counter and held my shoulders. "You're a wonderful girl." And suddenly he reached out and grabbed my hair. I screamed and shoved him away. "Don't ever do that again!"

He looked distressed. "Please accept my apologies. I just—"

"I have to go."

I dropped the cinnamon rolls and pots and left quickly, my heart racing. Danny meant no harm, but it was my body. And anyone grabbing my hair brought me right back to the high school bathroom.

My hatred for Eric would last my whole life. Look what he'd left me to deal with. And he'd probably forgotten all about me by now. I fervently hoped that he'd always remember Jack.

Jack never told me what happened, but he seemed satisfied with the results.

☙❧

A BOUQUET OF FLOWERS AND A HEARTFELT NOTE APPEARED ON our back porch the next morning. Gran wanted to know who they were from. I told her about the Danny incident and she nodded.

"There will always be scum-of-the-earth men roaming around, but thank the Lord that there's also the dearest men too. Danny is obviously a genuine soul. You need to forgive him, or he'll eat himself alive. Just explain it to him."

So I did. It was after work and bitterly cold. The sky looked like it was about to blast us with our first snowfall. When I walked into the store, it was almost too warm, and yet there was Danny with a scarf wrapped around his neck. He looked up and froze.

"I'd like to talk."

He pointed at the door. "Turn over the sign and come in the kitchen. The place won't go bankrupt in fifteen minutes."

It wasn't the least bit odd, telling Danny about Eric. I already felt like I'd known Danny forever. He was a wonderful listener; he must've taken lessons from Mrs. Beliveau, because he looked proud and sympathetic at all the right moments.

"Well, you'll be happy to know that I've learned my lesson and will not be putting my hands anywhere near a woman without a written invitation that's been signed and notarized. Even a woman with a spider in her hair."

"I had a spider in my hair?!"

Danny nodded. "You were truly a Little Miss Muffet."

"I just love you," I smiled.

"I only like you, slightly."

We parted friends.

ॐ

EVERY TIME I THOUGHT NOTHING EVER HAPPENED, ANOTHER Christmas arrived on the scene. The years were passing by. Time to count again how many Christmases Mama and Pops weren't with us. Five and three years respectively. But at least Pup made Christmas fun again.

Gran and I were going to spend Christmas Day with Uncle Donny and Aunt Loretta. Mavis, Patty, Ray, and Pup were going to be there for dinner too.

Patty informed me how it worked. "Once you're married, you have to split it even-steven between the in-laws and the outlaws. Last year we were at Ray's parents; this year, it's Uncle Donny, only because they have a big enough table. Mom has nothing but card tables for her bridge club."

"But when will it be your turn?"

"Probably when number-two baby comes along, which will be happening before next Christmas, but don't say anything. I'm going to tell everyone at Christmas dinner."

I squealed. "Another puppy! I can't wait!"

Jack was disappointed that I wouldn't be in town. He wanted me to come to Christmas dinner with his family.

On Christmas Eve day, I made mincemeat pies. Two for our family, one for Danny, and one for Jack. I told him to come by and pick it up to take to his aunt's potluck. Then I helped Gran put up the decorations on the tree that Jack cut down for us earlier that week. I also made a chicken and dumpling stew to have before I took Gran to midnight service.

I had Gran's full-length apron on, and I was covered with flour and dumplings when Jack arrived for the pie. I wiped my hands on the apron.

"Good timing. I was just about to put tinfoil over the pie. Tell your mom she can heat it up in the oven beforehand if she likes."

"Right. Let's go for a walk."

"Now?"

"Just throw on a coat. We can take Hobbs."

Hobbs overheard and immediately ran to the door, ready to go. I peeked around the corner of the living room to tell Gran, but she was immersed in her detective show, *Mannix*, so I left a note instead.

There was a light snowfall as we walked down the driveway towards the highway.

"How far are we going?"

"Right...here."

We stopped by the curve of the driveway, where you couldn't see the house.

"What so special about here?"

He took my hands. "This is where I first kissed you."

I leaned against his chest. "Silly boy."

He got down on one knee and took a box out of his jacket pocket. It was like watching a movie. It didn't feel real. Then he took my hand again and opened the box with a nifty manoeuvre he must have practised.

"Bridie, I love you more than Napoleon. Will you please marry me, so the three of us can ride off into the sunset together?"

"What about Hobbs?"

"He's a given."

My hand was now over my mouth. "But I always said I was never getting married. That I planned on being a spinster for life."

"That was before you met me."

"So true. Yes, I'll marry you."

He took the ring and put it on my finger. I couldn't tell what it looked like because it was too dark, but that didn't matter. We kissed each other until Hobbs got tired of standing in one spot and started whining, wondering when the walk was happening.

We strolled arm in arm for a good mile, just so Hobbs would be happy. Then we went back in the house, and *Mannix* was over so I showed Gran the ring. She clapped her hands and hugged us both. It was a great moment.

Jack left with his pie, and Gran and I ate the chicken and dumplings while staring at the ring. Then we got ready for church, and on the way, I dropped the mince pie for Danny by his back door, since he didn't seem to be home.

The church was packed, as always, as there are no heathens on Christmas Eve. We greeted our neighbours, and Gran told everyone and their dog that I was engaged. You'd think she'd gotten the ring. A lot of little old ladies I didn't know kissed me and wished me luck. It was very sweet, actually, how happy people were for me.

I wondered what my family would think.

৩৬

THE FIRST PERSON I TOLD WAS PATTY. "I DON'T WANT TO TAKE away from your announcement about the baby."

"I've grown up, Bridie. Two people can have announcements. One doesn't take away from the other."

Wow. Still, I took my ring off so she could tell everyone first.

I spent the afternoon helping Loretta with the turkey dinner, because the last place I wanted to be was sitting in the living room with Uncle Donny and Mavis. At intervals I would run out so I could see what Pup was up to, running around with his new blocks in his mouth. My cousins Cheryl and Ellen were put to good use by their mother, setting the table, while the boys played with their new hockey tabletop game.

Uncle Donny seemed to be more smashed every time we came out with a serving dish. Poor Ray looked hopelessly weary. If there's anything worse than sitting with boring relatives on Christmas Day, it's sitting with boring relatives who aren't technically your own.

"Dinner is served!" shouted Aunt Loretta.

The twelve of us jockeyed for our seats, Aunt Loretta pointing and shaking her arms to try and get her kids' attention. Uncle Donny sat at the head of the table, almost nodding off at this point, still with a tumbler of rum and Coke in his hand. Loretta told Gran to sit beside him, probably to discourage him from belting them down quite so quickly.

Fortunately, I was seated by Patty, who had Pup perched on her lap, since she forgot to bring his high chair. But passing him back and forth between us wasn't a problem.

Aunt Loretta had the foresight to bring the turkey in already carved. The thought of Uncle Donny with a knife was terrifying. It took about fifteen minutes for everyone to get at least something on their plates, and then Gran spoke up, because she knew Donny wouldn't.

"May we say grace?"

Uncle Donny cried, "Pease porridge hot, pease porridge cold, pease porridge in the pot, nine days old!" And then he laughed.

We looked at him with varying degrees of disgust. And then Gran bowed her head. "Thank you, Oh Lord, for this, thy bounty. We praise you, in Jesus's name, Amen."

"Amen," we parroted.

Everyone talked at once to get rid of Uncle Donny's words, still floating around in the air. It's funny how the older you get, the more you see. At Christmas dinners before, I hadn't been aware of the undertones around the table—I was too busy thinking of my gifts under the tree.

We all zeroed in on Pup, because there's nothing like a toddler to put everyone back in a good mood. Patty must have felt it too. She dinged her water glass with a fork. "Next year, our darling Pup will be a big brother!'

Mavis looked as proud as a peacock, and so she should have. Gran beamed at everyone. The rest of us around the table clapped and Uncle Donny whistled like he was at a hockey game. Patty held out her hand to me, which I assumed was her sign for me to go ahead.

"And I'm getting married!" I took my ring out of my sweater pocket and put it on my finger.

Cheryl and Ellen were at the age where this was very exciting. They both left their seats to come and take a look at it. Mavis had a pained smile on her face. She hadn't grown up the way Patty had. But everyone else shouted congratulations and I was pleased being the centre of attention. I looked at my ring and wished Jack could have come with me.

Uncle Donny tossed back the rest of his drink. "Well, well, well. I guess I better get into shape now that I'll be walking you down the aisle."

My blood froze. "You're not walking me down the aisle."

Uncle Donny looked at Gran, confused. "What's she talking about? Her father is dead. I'm her father's brother. It's my duty to walk her down the aisle. There's no one else."

Gran looked at me. "I suppose he's right, Bridie. There is no one else."

I stood up. "He will walk me down the aisle over my dead body."

Everyone's eyes were on me now. Gran looked heartbroken, and I instantly regretted making a scene, but it was one of those moments you can't take back.

"What do you mean?" Aunt Loretta said. "Why can't he walk you down the aisle? George would have wanted him to."

Mavis agreed. "Yes, George would definitely have wanted him to."

I looked at Patty. She was trying to figure out what was going on. Then Ray reached over and took my hand. "I think what Bridie is trying to say, with an unfortunate manner of speaking, is that she already asked me to walk her down the aisle, seeing as how I'm her brother-in-law and am closer to her age, and we've grown up together through the years. I'll always be her Sting Ray and she'll always be my Squirt. I was thrilled and honoured when she asked me before dinner. It's no reflection on you, Donny. It's just that we'd like to keep it within our own family."

I reached down and hugged Ray with all my might.

Gran patted Uncle Donny's hand. "Your day will come, Donny, with two beautiful daughters of your own."

I could tell that Aunt Loretta and Uncle Donny were annoyed with me for the rest of the night, but I wouldn't see them until next Christmas so hopefully the whole incident would be forgotten by then. I just had to get through sleeping in their guest bedroom tonight.

When Patty, Ray, and Pup left, I walked them to their car. I hugged Ray all over again. "You really saved my bacon in there."

"What was that all about, anyway?" Patty asked.

Ray leaned close to her ear. "Remember, you told me about that incident with your Uncle Donny, how he kissed you in your bedroom at one of your mother's cocktail parties? I assumed he probably did something like that to Bridie, in which case, no wonder she doesn't want the old goat touching her on her wedding day."

Patty gave my shoulder a shove. "Did that jerk try it out with you too?"

I nodded. "He kissed me on the lips when I was nine. It was revolting."

Patty gave Ray a big hug. "You're a hero. And if this baby is a girl, that asshole is never getting anywhere near her."

"Oh, don't worry," said Ray. "I'd kill him with my bare hands."

When I went down to the guest room, Gran was already on her side of the bed. She looked at me sadly. "That wasn't very nice, dear."

"I know. I'm sorry."

"He is your father's brother. Donny was only trying to help. He thought he'd be doing you a favour."

"True."

She sighed. I quickly got undressed and didn't even bother brushing my teeth. I didn't want to meet my helpful uncle in the hallway. I got in the bed and turned out the lamp on my side.

"Merry Christmas, Gran."

"Merry Christmas, sweetheart."

The next morning, we went upstairs and Loretta made us a cup of coffee and a piece of toast for breakfast. Donny wasn't even up. No doubt he couldn't get his head off the pillow.

She saw us to the door.

"Goodbye, Loretta," Gran said. "Thank you for the lovely meal."

"You're welcome, Jean."

"Goodbye, Loretta," I said. "Everything was delicious."

"Oh, I forgot," She quickly ran down the hall and came back with my mince pies. "We don't like mince pies in this house."

I took them back. "I'll remember that."

Gran and I looked at each other in the car as I pulled out of the driveway.

"Well, you were told," Gran said.

"Wasn't I just?"

We were almost home when we saw Danny Flynn, wearing pajamas, an overcoat, and unbuckled boots at his garbage can. I stopped the car and rolled down the window. "Merry Christmas, Danny!"

He rushed over to the car window. "And a very Merry Christmas to you fine ladies."

"What are you doing out on this cold morning?" Gran asked him.

"Oh, it's a complete disaster. I came home last night to find some kind soul had left me a mince pie. I wonder who?" He smiled at me.

"I have no idea," I smiled back. "But why is it a disaster?"

"I had to wrestle three raccoons for it, and didn't the little buggers win. I'm disposing of the tinfoil pie plate, but not before licking it with my fingers."

"Well, do I have a treat for you." I picked up the two mince pies that were between Gran and me and passed them out the window. "Enjoy."

"Oh! Blessings upon you! May you escape the gallows, avoid distress, and be as healthy as a trout!"

CHAPTER TWENTY

Working as a teller was a great occupation if you wanted everyone to notice your engagement ring. Barbara's and Linda's mothers were in the bank in the same week, and both commented on how pretty it was and how they'd tell the girls when they spoke to them next.

How quickly you go from being best friends to acquaintances when you head in different directions after high school. I'd no more think of calling them than they'd call me now. It might be different if we saw each other on the street, but we'd never call each other long distance. Still, I planned on inviting them to the wedding, if they wanted to come. They were the only girlfriends I had.

It was the end of January when Nell came into the bank. She was her usual self until she saw the engagement ring on my finger.

"Is that what I think it is?"

I held out my fingers to look at my ring. "Yes, isn't it lovely?"

"What's your grandmother thinking, allowing you to marry at such a young age?"

It was the last thing I expected her to say. "Pardon me?"

"You're much too young to embark on such a journey. You need to grow up and see the world. You need to get an education and not waste your life in this suffocating small town."

That made me mad. "Like you, you mean?"

She slammed her hand down on the counter and withdrew her bank book. "Exactly. That's exactly what I mean."

She strode out of the bank. Mrs. Beliveau came running over.

"What did you say to her?"

"She asked me about my engagement ring and I showed it to her."

Mrs. Beliveau grunted. "It's jealousy. The spinster on the hill can't stand to see anyone else happy."

It was my habit now to stop at Burke's on my way home from work. I always bought something, even if it was just a package of Juicy Fruit. Danny was my sounding board—when he wasn't busy charming every old woman in Richmond County.

"Can you believe the gall of that one?!" he cried. "She's always got a face like a mackerel. Someone told me her parents owned this store a long time ago, and she hates the sight of it. Well, the feeling's mutual, I'm sure. Don't pay her no never mind. You're free to do what you want but I do confess, my heart is broken now that you've been spoken for."

"If I didn't know Jack you'd definitely be my next choice."

"I'm going to spend my long lonely winter nights thinking about ways to knock him off."

The very next night, I was invited over to Jack's parents' house for supper. It was a bit nerve-racking; I hadn't seen them since the engagement. Jack told me his mother was dying to see the ring, since he hadn't shown it to her before he gave it to me.

A big no-no, apparently.

You could definitely tell this was a house full of boys. Everything smelled like a barn. His mother obviously made an effort to keep things relatively neat but with five boys, Jack being the eldest, she had her hands full.

There wasn't a lot of conversation at supper. His dad scooped up his stew and then excused himself. "No time for girl talk, I'm afraid. I have a council meeting tonight. Boys, muck out the stalls. I'll say good night, Bridie."

"Good night, Mr. Morris."

The boys followed, one by one, as soon as they scraped their plates until it was just Jack, his mother, and me.

"I wanted to see you, to ask if it would be all right if I hosted an engagement party for you and Jack on Valentine's Day. We're related to half the town, and this place isn't fancy enough, so I thought we could rent the legion and have a dance."

"That's too much work, Mrs. Morris."

"Please, call me Diane. Or Mom. What I wouldn't give for a girl to call me that!"

Jack grinned at his mother. "I was supposed to be her girl."

"And so were your brothers. Oh well, at least I have one in the family now, so I want to celebrate it."

"What can I do to help? I could bake."

She put her hands out to ward off that idea. "I have seven sisters and they're all ready to do battle. I want this to be fun for you and Jack. All you have to do is arrive looking pretty, which is obviously a very easy thing for you to do."

"Thank you. That's so sweet. What do you think, Jack?"

"I think I'm going to enjoy it just fine, with my two best girls."

On the drive home, I brought up something that was on my mind. "Now that everyone is going to know about this, what are we going to tell them about when we're to be married? And where we'll live? We've never talked about it."

"I have to save some money first, so as much as I want to marry you tomorrow, I think it will be another year at least before we can think about it. Dad said he'd pay me a higher wage, but I still might need another part-time job to make ends meet. There's a small house on the edge of our property that needs to be fixed up. We could look at it and see what we think."

"Or we could always ask Gran if we could live with her. She's already told me that the house will be mine someday. She's giving me the house and leaving money to Patty."

"Do you really want to live with your grandmother? As sweet as she is, we'll want our privacy, won't we?"

Laughing, I said, "Now what on earth would we be doing that we couldn't do in front of her?"

He pulled the car over to the side of the road. "I'm going to show you ten things right now. Come here."

❧

FOR SOME REASON, AUNT BETTY GOT ALL TWITTERY ABOUT THE mayor's wife hosting a party for us.

"And she's renting the legion? God, Aunt Jean, we'll be counted among the higher-ups now! Marrying into the mayor's family is like marrying into royalty around here. There's no higher official in these parts."

"They're just Jack's parents. I really don't think they see themselves as royalty. Diane is so down-to-earth."

"Diane! Did you hear that, Aunt Jean? Diane! Oh, lordy, I'm going to have to get a new dress for the occasion. You will too, Bridie. Ask Nell to do it for you."

"No. She told me I had no business being married."

Gran looked at me. "She said that to you?"

"She wanted to know what you were thinking, letting me get married so young."

"I see. Well, she's entitled to her opinion."

But it did leave me in the lurch. I did want a new dress for the occasion, and I only had two weekends to find it. Hopefully the weather would cooperate and I could drive to Sydney and look for something there with Patty.

The weather held, and I drove down to Sydney on Saturday morning. As I was leaving the driveway, a car was coming up. I didn't recognize it. I pulled over to the side and the car stopped and the window rolled down. I nearly died. It was Nell.

"What are you doing here?"

"I need to speak with you."

"Sorry, you've already said everything you need to say to me."

"Please, Bridie. It's important."

"I'm late for an appointment. Excuse me."

"Bridie, I need to tell you—"

I drove off, more than annoyed. I didn't need a big lecture on how I was a silly girl for marrying so young. Who did Nell think she was?

Patty had arranged for her mother-in-law to take Pup for the day. We got in the car and she put her hand on my arm. "I know you're going to kill me, but I asked Mom to come along."

"Patty!"

"Look, suddenly she's all gaga that you're marrying a politician's son and she insists that she's going to the party with Ray and me. When she found out you were coming to look for a dress, she wanted to go with us. When you do something right, you're her daughter. When you do something wrong, you're a leech. It will be ever thus."

"She's going to be disappointed. Jack's dad looks and smells like a farmer."

Mavis was waiting in the lobby of her high-rise apartment building, for which I was grateful. I'd never been inside her apartment, and I wanted it to stay that way. She was still a traitor in my eyes for selling our house.

We walked down Charlotte Street, looking in the shops that sold dresses. All three of us had vastly different opinions on what I should look for. Despite being annoyed with Nell, I still believed her that a short dress was young and fresh. I was eighteen, not thirty. Mavis wanted me to look like a bridesmaid, and even Patty thought I should be more dressed up.

"It's just a family dance. It's not a ball."

Now I was stuck in a dressing room, with Patty throwing dresses over the top of the door. "There's young and fresh, but you don't want people thinking you should be sucking on a lollipop either. You need to be a little more sophisticated."

"I need to have Jack recognize me."

Mavis kept dragging over dresses shrouded with lace. "Look at the detail."

"Mavis, I'm hitting the legion, not a Paris runway."

In the end, I stuck to my guns and bought what I liked: an A-line minidress. It had a flowered print in yellow and orange, an inverted pleat down the front, and cap sleeves. I planned on wearing a headband in my hair and large, white, circular earrings. I saw Twiggy wearing a pair in a magazine, and I knew they would look great with my short hair. To top it off, I'd wear white vinyl boots. I didn't care if it was winter. I'd look like a bright flower and I knew that Jack would love it.

Mavis mumbled about why she'd even bothered coming before I gladly dropped her off. Patty and I went to pick up Pup, and I played with him for a couple of hours before I left for home.

☙☙

AT WORK, I STARTED TO GET WORRIED. EVERYONE WHO DROPPED into the bank said they were going to the party. How was it possible the Morrises knew so many people? Maybe my outfit would be too casual. This was supposed to be a fun night, but I started to break out in a cold sweat at the thought of it.

Jack told me to forget about it, so he was basically no help. "What are you stressing for? It's just a bunch of people dancing and eating. Then they go home."

Oh, to have a man's mind.

Even Danny didn't know what the fuss was about. "Wind yer neck in and take a wee dram."

"I have no idea what you just said."

It was Nell's regular deposit day at the bank and I dreaded seeing her again. She headed straight for my wicket. Why couldn't she leave me alone?

"I must speak with you," she said.

"Look, I already know you don't want me to get married, but it's none of your business."

She pounded her fist on the desk. "Yes, it is. It's very much my business."

My eyes filled with tears, and I saw the other customers looking at us. Mrs. Beliveau saw the situation and hurried over. "What's the matter?"

"Nothing is the matter," Nell said. "I need to speak with Bridie privately."

"Well, you've come to the wrong place for that," Mrs. Beliveau snapped. "This is a place of business, and you have no right coming in here and upsetting my staff. Please leave."

Nell looked at me. "I'll wait outside."

"You'll do no such thing," my boss said. "If I see you loitering out there, I'll call the police."

Nell looked pained as she left the building. Mrs. Beliveau put her hand on my shoulder. "Don't let her upset you. She's a crackpot. Don't give it another thought."

That was impossible. What on earth did Nell want? I called Jack and told him about it.

"She's off her rocker," he said. "Forget about her. No one is going to ruin our night."

I tried to forget about it, but it can't be a good thing when you want something to be over with before it's even begun. Aunt Betty drove to the house that night so she could come with us.

Uncle Fraser had begged off.

"Oh, who wants him there anyway? Yawnin' to beat the band before the clock strikes nine. I'll have a better time without him. What do you think of my new dress? I picked it up at Nell's today."

In spite of my annoyance with Nell, I had to admit it was a very pretty suit. She certainly knew how to hide a woman's pounds. Gran wore a silk dress with a navy-blue jacket, and of course her lovely mink coat and hat. Now she did look like royalty.

Patty, Ray, and Mavis arrived, and the three of us crawled in on top of them to drive down the road. When we got to the Legion, it looked like every car in town was parked beside it.

"I'll never find a parking spot here. Why don't I let you girls off, and I'll find something down the road?" said Ray.

We agreed and the five of us scrambled out and hurried up to the door. Already the music was blaring and the roar of conversation was loud. The place was very warm, thanks to all the bodies milling about. Jack and his parents were by the inner door and I introduced my family one by one. Jack took off my coat and whistled when he saw my outfit. I could relax. He was the only one I wanted to please. He took my hand and whispered in my ear. "You're the most beautiful girl here."

There was no reason for me to be worried. We had a fantastic time. Diane and her sisters decorated the hall with balloons and streamers, and they had a corsage for me and a boutonniere for Jack, who thought it was silly. He managed to accidently lose it quite quickly.

I didn't realize how much fun it was to go to a dance with so many different ages. A bunch of Jack's uncles took to the floor every time the twist came on. I saw one of them nab Mavis and take her for a twirl around the dance floor. Even Aunt Betty was whisked away, much to her delight.

Diane made sure that Gran had the best seat, and she knelt down by her chair, the two of them in deep conversation, no doubt talking about Jack and me.

Jack and I made our way around the room, everyone congratulating us. It almost felt like a wedding. We danced together for most of the night and then, when we'd worked up an appetite, we ate ourselves silly on sliced ham and turkey, meatballs, rice, potato and macaroni salads, rolls, cheese, cold cuts, and a whole table of desserts.

Towards the end of the evening, Jack's father signalled for the local band to stop the music and he whistled for quiet.

Everyone turned and gave him their full attention.

"I'd like to thank everyone for coming tonight. Diane and I are very happy that our son Jack has found the girl he wants to spend his life with. Bridie seems to be an exceptional young lady, and we look forward to welcoming her into our family. As Diane keeps harping on, we finally have a girl!"

Everyone clapped and hooted. Jack and I stood beside his parents with our arms around each other, and Jack gave me a big squeeze. Our families crowded around us.

Jack's dad pointed at the band and the music resumed.

As I basked in the glow of this wonderful moment, I suddenly saw Nell approaching us. Her eyes were red and puffy like she'd been crying, but from the set of her jaw, I knew she was going to lay into me yet again and my heart sank. She was going to ruin this for me. Why?

I stepped forward and held out my hand. "Don't. Whatever you're going to say, don't do it."

"I'm very sorry, Bridie. I'm so very, very sorry. But you can't marry Jack. He's your half brother." She pointed at Mr. Morris. "This man is your father."

There was a roaring in my ears. I looked up at Jack, who was looking at his dad.

"I don't want to hurt you, but it's time you knew the truth about who you really are."

One of Yardley's brothers started towards her, but Jack stopped him. "Let her talk."

Most of the party continued around us as Nell wrung her hands.

"Gervais and Maggie Landry lived in the cottage at the end of my road. The one the kids say is haunted today. Well, it *was* haunted, with the misery of alcoholism." She pointed to the man on her left. "You know that, Angus! I told you Gervais pushed his wife down the stairs and killed her, but you said there was no proof and made their daughter, Jane, live with a man who couldn't take care of a dog, let alone a child. I did my best to watch over her, but one day I saw her walk across the field with a young man who had blond hair. I knew he was up to no good. I ran as fast as I could, but I didn't get to Jane in time. By the time I arrived, he was already running away."

I couldn't bring myself to interrupt Nell, couldn't tear myself away from her. There was something compelling in her voice; she spoke with so much force and precision, as though she'd been holding something terrible inside.

"Jane had been raped. She was fourteen years old. I knew who the young man was. I went to his father's garage and told him what his son had done. He's sitting right over there." She pointed to an older man in the crowd. "Bernard Morris. He said if I said anything to anyone, he'd burn down my house. And so I was helpless, but I did have proof. I brought it with me tonight."

She held up a jackknife. "It's been in a safety-deposit box all this time. Here are the initials on the knife: YM. Yardley Morris. You know damn well it's yours. I found it beside her torn dress."

No one said a word, but Jack reached out and took the knife.

"Jane got pregnant, and I knew her life would be hell if her father found out. I wanted to protect her! But I did a foolish thing, and I've regretted it every day since. I asked George Mackenzie to help me. George and I were lovers. I bullied him into taking Jane away, to try and get her settled in a new place, with a new family, and hopefully have the baby adopted, so Jane could have a chance at a better life.

"But they had a car accident, and Jane went into labour. George was able to deliver the baby before Jane died in the car. He took Bridie home and raised her as his own."

For a moment, the sound of the party—the band, the laughter, the dancing, the clatter of dishes—receded. Nell's voice spread out and around me; it was the well I was tumbling down into, the only sound in the world.

"But he never told me! He said Jane had died and I assumed the baby had died with her. I can never forgive him for that. Why didn't he tell me? This child of the child I loved never knew about me. Never knew who she was. And that's George's fault. But I think the guilt killed him in the end.

"When George told me Jane died, I swore at him and told him that I hated him and I never wanted to see him again. Then I ran down to Gervais's house and told him he'd killed his daughter. That she'd killed herself. That I'd found her sweater on the beach and she'd drowned rather than be with him. I needed a story to explain her absence. He never cared about that child for one second of his life. Alcohol was his only love, and he killed that girl with his blatant neglect.

"I know Bridie is Jane's daughter. Tonight, she's wearing a necklace that George gave me when we were young and in love. I gave it to Jane the day she died. It's exactly like the one I'm wearing now. The one George sent to me before he died."

My fingers went to my necklace. It was the only thing that felt real in this moment. My body was numb.

"I know I'm to blame for this mess, but there are also people here that should be ashamed. You might think you're a big man now, Yardley Morris, but you were a pathetic coward when you ran away after raping that innocent fourteen-year-old. And Bernard, protecting his son when he knew he was capable of such a thing. Threatening me instead of listening to me."

At this, Mr. Morris seemed to snap out of a trance. He looked down at Nell and hissed, "Bullshit. Bullshit, Nell, and you'll never prove otherwise." He stalked away through the revellers, an ashen Diane following him. We watched them go, saw Diane turn back and look helplessly at Jack as she hurried away.

Nell looked me square in the eye. "I know you will never forgive me, Bridie, but someday I hope you realize that the mistakes

I made were not done out of malice. They were out of love. Love for your little mother, whom I adored. Your dad wanted you so badly because he knew I loved your mother. He wanted to make it up to me. He always blamed himself for that car accident, but that wasn't his fault. And he did save you. I will always be grateful for that. But that's why he loved you so much. You were my child's child. He needed to make amends.

"I will always love George Mackenzie. And I will always love you, Bridie. And I'm deeply, deeply sorry that you had to learn the truth about your father, Jack. None of this is your fault. You are an innocent victim, as is your mother. I'm so sorry you had to get hurt."

She quickly disappeared, leaving us to look at each other.

The circle of our families erupted with indignation, crying, and shouts of disbelief. I heard only my own heartbeat. Jack looked at me. "Go home, Bridie. I'll come to you tomorrow."

Then he ran out of the building, his brothers after him. Most of the guests were still having a great time.

Ray had his hands full trying to herd my relatives through the crowd. They were all weeping but me. I got my coat and turned to him. "I need to walk."

"It's too cold out!" he shouted after me. "Wait!"

I couldn't wait. I needed air. Out the door I went, and the only relief I had was to run. But my vinyl boots were slippery and I kept falling. There was no feeling in my body, so I had to keep moving to know I was alive.

I ran down a side street and tried to get lost among the buildings so Ray wouldn't find me, but I knew if I didn't get inside soon I'd freeze. Maybe that would be a good thing. Just fall into the snow and turn into ice, so no one could touch me. But I kept going until I instinctively ran to the one door that would save me. I banged on it. "Help me! Help me!"

Danny opened the back door and didn't ask me anything. He just reached out and bundled me inside. He took off my coat and frozen boots, wrapped me in a quilt, and made me sit by the fire. He handed me a hot drink, which I cupped in my hands, and then boiled the kettle, filled a water bottle, and put it behind my back. He even put thick socks on my feet. And the man who was always nattering stayed silent.

We sat together as tears leaked out of my eyes and fell onto the quilt. The only time he left me was to reach for the phone.

"Hello, Mrs. Mackenzie? I want you to know that Bridie is with me. I'll keep her safe until she's ready to go home." There was a pause. "It's no trouble at all. She needs to be alone right now." Another pause. "No, she didn't tell me what happened and I don't want to know. Right. Right. Okay. Goodbye."

At some point I fell asleep, too exhausted in mind and spirit to keep my eyes open, but I knew I was safe so I let the darkness overtake me.

When I finally opened my eyes, I could see daylight behind the blind in the kitchen. Danny was curled up on a rug in front of the fire, a crocheted throw over him. What was I doing in Danny's kitchen?

And then the wall crumbled, burying me alive. I couldn't help it. Great sobs burst forth and I had no idea how to make them stop. Danny leapt up and knelt before me, putting his arms around me as I sat in the chair. I put my head on his shoulder.

"I don't know what to do, Danny. I don't know what to do."

"Hush now, lamb. You don't have to do anything right this minute."

"I can't marry Jack. He's my brother."

"Your brother?"

"My half brother. His father is my father. He raped my mother. My poor little mother, who never had a chance to have a life."

"Oh, pet. That's terrible. Terrible."

"I love Jack. It's not Jack's fault. I love him so much. How am

I going to live without him? People will say we're sinners. That we're evil in the eyes of God. We only loved each other. Why is that a sin? We've only given each other happiness."

He had no answer for that.

I wanted to stay in that chair for the rest of my life, but I needed to pee so I slowly unwrapped myself and stiffly walked to Danny's bathroom. As I washed my hands, I looked in the mirror. I didn't recognize myself. My eyes were bloodshot, I had black under my eyes from my mascara, one earring was gone, and so was my headband. The pretty girl who'd gotten ready for her big night was nowhere to be seen. I knew she was never coming back.

☙

DANNY INSISTED ON FEEDING ME BEFORE I WENT HOME, BUT HIS cooking left a lot to be desired.

"The oatmeal isn't burnt, but it is lumpy. Just throw a bag of brown sugar and a pint of cream over it and you'll never know."

It was my first half-hearted smile. I took a bite and then put my spoon down. "I can't eat, Danny. It's not the porridge. I just can't stomach anything at the moment."

"Right, of course. What was I thinking."

"I better go. You'll have to open the store."

"The store can wait."

"As much as I'd like to live here for the rest of my life, I better go and see Gran. She'll be worried."

He nodded and collected my things and then drove me back to my house.

"Oh, God. Ray and Patty and Mavis are still here. And Aunt Betty. Goddammit. I just want to be alone!"

Danny took my hand. "I believe you heard this bad news together. They are trying to process it too. I imagine they think you'll want their support."

I looked at him. "But don't they know how hard this is for me?"

"Of course they do. But family has a way of ignoring that sort of thing. You'll be all right, love. If it gets to be too much, just come back to the store. The back shelves need dusting."

He still had my hand, so I pulled his gloved hand to my lips and kissed it. "Thank you."

He nodded and I got out of the car. I stood there as he drove away. And then the back door opened and Hobbs came running out. Now here was the one soul I wanted to see. He wiggled all around me as I patted and scratched his back end. Gran was standing outside on the porch. She was going to get cold. There was nothing I could do but go forward. I walked into her arms and she held me close.

"My poor love. My dear child. We'll get through this."

"How?"

"One day at a time."

That sounded like it would take way too long.

When we walked into the kitchen, the rest of them were there, all looking as horrific as I did. Mavis was leaning over on a chair like she was strapped to the mast of a ship with an all-hope-is-lost look. She definitely wanted me to know that she was the injured party in all this.

She pointed at me. "I knew there was something fishy about your story! I sensed it from the very beginning. And Eileen must have been in on it!"

Patty turned to her. "Mother! Shut your mouth. We've already listened to you whine through the night. But yours isn't the biggest tragedy, is it?" Patty strode forward and held me in her arms. "If you need to get out of here, Ray and I talked about it, and you're more than welcome to stay with us."

Ray nodded. "More than welcome."

"Thanks, guys."

"It's all my fault!" cried Aunt Betty. "The day I went to order my suit, she asked me who Bridie was marrying, and when I said the mayor's son, I thought she was going to faint right in front of me. I didn't know it was because of that. I thought she had taken a turn, that's all. Why didn't I keep my big mouth shut?!"

"It's okay, Aunt Betty. She would've found out soon enough. Someone was bound to tell her eventually. You can't keep a secret in this town."

We looked at each other.

"Okay, apparently you can keep a very big secret. But now it's out and my life is ruined. If Nell professes to love me so much, why didn't she stay quiet? What difference would it have made if we'd gone on with our lives?"

"It's illegal, for one thing," Mavis piped up. "Your kids would be ret—"

"Mom!" Patty shouted. "I don't want to hear another word from you."

Mavis stood up and pointed her finger at Patty. "Listen, girlie, you have no idea what it's like to find out your husband has been unfaithful to you in public. I will forevermore be a laughingstock in this town."

"You hate this town, Mom, so you don't ever need to come back here."

Mavis then turned on Gran. "You knew all about it, didn't you? If they were sweethearts before we were married, you knew he loved her and didn't love me, and yet you let me marry him and have a miserable life, trying to figure out why George was my husband but not my husband. There was something I couldn't put my finger on. He always denied it, but I knew I didn't have his heart."

Mavis held her head in her hands as she paced in front of the stove, trying to keep herself together, trying to make sense of things.

"Then he brings Eileen into the mix for some unknown reason and I was supposed to be okay with that. Once that was established, this one drops into our lives and turns everything upside down. A whole tangle of lies I've been trying to break through my entire life. And now that goddamn Nell woman insinuates that George killed himself because of this. He was so unhappy with me that he wanted to end his life instead of live with me. Well, maybe I sound like I'm feeling sorry for myself, but right now I am. I'm feeling very sorry for myself. I've basically been alone my whole life."

"Mom…"

"Do you know how it feels to be unwanted? Yes, Bridie has to deal with a shock, and it's not fair to her or Jack, but at least they are young enough to make something of their lives, while I molder away in my goddamn one-bedroom apartment."

Gran went over and put her arms around Mavis. Mavis cried into her shoulder, and at that moment I did feel terrible for her. Even Patty went over and gave her mom a hug.

A great weariness came over me and all I wanted was to take a bath, but someone knocked at the door. Poor old Hobbs gave a tremendous bark, upset as he was with the atmosphere in the kitchen.

Oh, God. I couldn't see Jack in front of all these people. Ray saw my panicked look and went to the door. "I'll tell him to wait until we're gone."

But it wasn't Jack. It was Angus Turnbull, the police chief. He took off his hat as he stood in the doorway. "I was wondering if I could speak to you folks."

Gran stepped forward as the matriarch of the family. "Please sit down. Can I get you a cup of tea?"

"No thank you, Mrs. Mackenzie." He sat down and we sat around the table with him. "I thought you'd like to know that I've spoken to Nell Sampson and the Morris family."

My heart started racing. Keep it together.

"There were a lot of allegations thrown about last night, and it's my duty to address these accusations and try and find the truth, to see if any laws have been broken, and to bring the guilty to justice.

"One thing I do know is that Nell Sampson came to me years ago to accuse Gervais Landry of pushing his wife down the stairs, resulting in her death. She said that the little girl, Jane, had told her about it, but when I asked Jane, she denied it. I realize now that the father was in the room when I asked her, and in hindsight, I'd do that differently. Nell was very upset when I told her there wasn't anything I could do. There was no proof.

"Unfortunately, in those days, there weren't enough social agencies to try and help a family in need, and most had to cope on their own. Nell never did file a complaint about Yardley Morris, because his father, Bernard, frightened her. She absolutely did the wrong thing, letting George take that child away. I could charge her with kidnapping. She says that Jane went willingly."

"She was a child!" I shouted. "Children do whatever adults say."

"You're right. And Jane was a minor, so even if she did agree, it's irrelevant. I haven't had a chance to go over the file of Jane's case, but I will. Obviously people were lied to, including the authorities and George's wife."

"That's the understatement of the year," Mavis muttered.

"Nell is prepared to face whatever the legal consequences are. She says she's entirely to blame and she's relieved it's out in the open."

"Well, bully for her!" I shouted. "I'm glad she got that off her chest. It doesn't matter that she snuffed out the life Jack and I had planned!"

Angus Turnbull nodded sadly.

Patty spoke up. "You said you talked to the Morrises?"

"Yes."

"And?"

"Yardley Morris is denying the allegation."

I threw my hands in the air. "How can he deny it? I'm here!"

"He says Nell Sampson has always had it in for him. That he spurned her advances when he was a young lad and now she's trying to get back at him. That he did some work for her once, and that's when he lost his knife. He says he doesn't know who had sex with Jane, but it wasn't him. And he plans on suing for defamation of character."

My head was whirling. "Wait. Are you saying that he's not my father? If that's the case, then I can marry Jack! All of this has been a huge mistake!"

I looked around at my loved ones for confirmation that last night was a huge drama that had nothing to do with Jack and me, but I slowly realized they didn't look convinced.

"So...which story is true? Tell me what I'm supposed to believe."

"I can't tell you, Bridie," said the police chief. "Yardley could be lying to save his own skin, or he could be right and Nell is off her head—which many people will tell you is quite possible. She's always been a loner and has a temper. Maybe being a spinster has addled her brain."

"Don't be ridiculous, Angus!" Gran shouted.

The police chief instantly looked twelve.

Gran looked exasperated. "Whether the woman is married or not has nothing to do with it. Yes, she's an intense soul, but she's never done anything to warrant that kind of talk."

"Other than steal my husband!" Mavis cried.

"George had no business marrying you, Mavis. You're right. I knew he was in love with Nell, but your children don't always do the right thing and you're helpless in the face of it. I always hoped that it would sort itself out. But I certainly never dreamed that this terrible thing was playing itself out. All my questions about why George was always so reluctant to bring Bridie home when she was young have suddenly been answered. Everything is falling into place."

"Do you believe that Jack's dad is my father, Gran?"

"If I had to pick who was telling the truth, I'd pick Nell. That grandfather, Bernard, always thought he was above the law. I can see him passing that along to his boys. But never to Jack, my love. He's a wonderful young man. And a credit to his mother, Diane, who really was so excited about having you in her family."

Aunt Betty's chins were trembling. "Yardley Morris is a no-good rat. All politicians are slimy bastards."

I knew that Gran was telling the truth, but I didn't want to believe it. The police chief had given me a glimmer of hope and I didn't want to lose it.

Angus Turnbull stood up. "That's where it stands, and it goes without saying that I will be contacting you as further developments arise. If you need anything, you know where I am."

We muttered our thanks and he left.

I stood up as well. "I can't deal with this anymore. Thank you for staying and being here to support me, but I need to be alone."

Everyone hugged me goodbye, even Mavis. I'm sure they were feeling relieved to be going home.

"Gran, I'm taking a bath. And I need Hobbs to come with me."

"In the tub?"

"I haven't gone nuts. I just want to look at his sweet face while I soak."

"Okay honey. Take all the time you need."

Lying in hot water up to my chin helped enormously. Looking down at Hobbs was also a blessing. He lay with his head between his paws, but whenever I peeked over, his eyes found mine and I was reassured.

The idea of crying didn't soothe me. The idea of never being bothered again did. The world needed to let me be. Even Jack. The thought of seeing him gave me the shakes, and then I thought about what last night must have been like for him. To hear his father denounced. To know that it was his father's fault we couldn't be together. His sorrow beat mine by a country mile.

Eventually, I wandered back downstairs and saw Gran had fallen asleep in front of the television. She was worn out, so I covered her in a blanket and left her alone. No sense in waking her up to send her to bed. Then Hobbs whined at the door and I opened it to let him out to pee.

That's when I saw Jack's truck. It was idling.

Slowly, I put on my coat and boots and walked to the truck. There was nothing to prepare me for when I opened the door, so that took a few moments. Jack wasn't even looking at me. He was staring into space.

I was sitting in the passenger side before he acknowledged me.

"Hi."

"Hi."

There was nothing to say.

"How long have you been here?"

"An hour, maybe."

"Why didn't you come in?"

"I didn't want to see your grandmother."

"She thinks you're wonderful."

He made a face. "I guess I take after my mom."

"The police chief came to see us."

"Yeah, he was at our house last night."

"So maybe Nell Sampson is deranged and your dad isn't my dad. We can get married and forget all about this."

He gave me a pitying look. "Is that what you think, Bridie? That this spinster made it all up and now she's going to ruin my dad by telling this crazy story and making our lives miserable just for the hell of it? That he conveniently lost his knife at her house, but instead of giving it back to him, she kept it all these years so she could use it as a prop for her accusations?"

My heart started to race and my cheeks went hot. "What are you saying?"

His face twisted. "He did it. I know the bastard did it. He's always taken what he wants. I've seen him in action countless times. People do what he says, or there's consequences. I've lived with it my whole life. And I had to listen to my mother cry all night long because she knows he did it too. He's making up bullshit to cover his tracks. He doesn't care who he hurts or who he lies to as long as he gets off the hook. He'll never admit to it. It would ruin his career. That woman on the hill has no reason to hurt us. Did you see her face last night? Did you hear the agony in her voice? She loved your mother. She loved her. And when she bravely went to tell my grandfather what she'd seen, he told her to keep her mouth shut or he'd burn down her house. And there's another person who is perfectly capable of saying something like that, because I've seen him in action too."

My head kept shaking no.

He grabbed my shoulders. "It's true, Bridie. The whole thing is true. I know it in my bones. I don't want to believe it. Don't you think I want to say that the spinster is lying and that we can get married? Nothing would make me happier, but I'm not about to be covered in lies ever again. You and I are related by blood. And according to the laws of this country, we can't get married. That's the horrible truth."

"Let's run away. Take me away right now and we'll drive until we can't drive anymore and we won't tell anyone where we are. We can live our whole life and people will never know."

"We'll know."

"I don't bloody care. We can promise to never have children, if that's what they're so worried about. It will just be the two of us. I'm good with that. Please, Jack. Let's go."

He let me go instead.

"I'm leaving, Bridie. Not you. Me."

I hit him. "Don't say that. What are you talking about?"

He looked out the windshield again. "I'm going and I'm never coming back. My mother knows. She told me to take the truck, and she's given me money to make a new start."

"No! I have money. I can take my father's money and we can have a new life."

"I can't live in that house anymore. I can't look at my father or I'll kill him. Mom's right. I need to get away from here. She's stuck. She can't go because of my brothers, but one day I'll make enough money and I'll send for her."

"Are you going to send for me too?"

He turned to me. "No, Bridie. I will love you forever, but I want you to be free. Free to love someone else, because I know there will be a man who will one day win your heart, and he'll be the luckiest guy alive."

I wiped my nose with my sleeve. "Why don't you say something cheesy? That's what I want."

He gave me a small smile.

"How can you leave me alone?"

"I'm not. I want you to look after Napoleon for me. Mom will arrange for you to take him when you're ready."

I held my face in my hands. "Jack, please don't leave me."

"Get out of the truck."

"Please don't leave me."

"Get out of the goddamn truck, Bridie!"

I screamed at him. "I hate you! I hate you so much!" I jumped out of the truck and slammed the door and instantly he put his foot on the gas and made a big turn, the tires sliding in the snow. I ran after him.

"Don't go, Jack! Don't go!"

His tail lights disappeared through the trees. I kept running until I slipped on the ice and fell, sprawled on the hard gravel. I rolled over and saw the grey clouds skitter away as I watched them. Hobbs ran to me, thinking this was great fun, and licked my face. I held him and wept into his curly coat.

CHAPTER TWENTY-ONE

My grandmother called the bank and asked if I could have a leave of absence. Mrs. Beliveau asked Gran when she thought I could return to the bank. Gran hesitated and said she didn't know. Mrs. Beliveau sympathized greatly but said they needed the position filled. It wasn't anything personal. And if at some point I did want to return and they happened to have an opening, they'd be delighted to have me back. Gran thanked her for her time.

She told me this as she was spooning soup into my mouth. I never got out of bed; the only time I ate anything was if she brought it up to me. She tried being sympathetic, amenable, and worried, but nothing worked.

After a couple of weeks, it became our routine. She even tried to make me feel guilty by saying that Hobbs was getting depressed not going for his walks. But he didn't look depressed to me. He was very happy curled up next to me on the bed.

One day I heard the phone ring downstairs, and a couple of minutes later Gran yelled up, "It's Patty. She wants to talk to you."

"Tell her I love her and thanks for calling, but goodbye."

"Bridie Jane Mackenzie! You get off your ass and come down here and speak to your sister!"

This was a new tactic. I gave a dramatic sigh and pulled the covers off the bed. Then I stomped downstairs with my terrible bedhead and sighed again. Gran held out the receiver, looking annoyed.

I took it from her. "Hung Foo's Oriental Palace. May I take your order, please?"

"I'll have two egg rolls, a bucket of wonton soup, and a dill pickle. This baby is a maniac. How are you?"

"Shitty."

Gran tsked. "Don't swear."

"Don't listen in on private conversations, Gran."

Patty chuckled. "Getting on each other's nerves?"

"You could say that, but it's all my fault. The poor woman doesn't know what to do with me, do ya, Gran?"

"My shows are on." She disappeared into the living room.

"I was thinking of coming up tomorrow. Ray doesn't need the car. Pup is missing you."

"He's going to have to go on missing me, because I refuse to let you drive all the way up here on icy roads with one and a half children in the car. I absolutely forbid it."

"I'll be fine."

"Patty, listen to me. I can't deal with the thought of losing anyone else. I know it's stupid and neurotic, but if something happened to you on the way up here, I'm afraid Gran will be left with a note that says I've gone fishing."

"It's that bad, is it?"

"Yep."

"Okay. I wanted to cheer you up, not have your suicidal tendencies go hog-wild."

"I appreciate that. What's new with you?"

"I eat for two—no, make that three—and I'm always tired and I have sore feet and a hemorrhoid. Other than that, great."

"Should I ask how your mother is?"

"She's been pretty quiet lately. I think she's licking her wounds."

"She has enough of them."

"Funny how you start seeing your mother as a person when you get older. I keep thinking of how it would be if I knew Ray didn't love me but pretended he did. It must be like chasing a ghost your whole life."

"The whole thing has been a nightmare for a lot of people."

"Chin up. I'm not coming. I'll sit on the floor with Pup and we'll play the new xylophone Daddy was kind enough to bring home yesterday."

"Kisses all around." I hung up and stomped back to bed.

Another week rolled by. We were now into March, but the landscape outside looked the same. Snow on the fir trees, snow covering the ground, icicles hanging from the roof. The same as the night of the party. It was like reliving the same day over and over again. Maybe I'd feel better in the spring.

Unlikely.

Someone knocked on the door one morning and Hobbs bolted off the bed and ran down the stairs to protect Gran in case it was a burglar. There was a deep rumbly voice, obviously a man, and since Gran and I didn't have any gentlemen callers, I was curious enough to sit at the top of the stairs and listen in.

Then I recognized the voice. It was Angus Turnbull, the police chief.

"I'm back to fill you in on the investigation."

"Please sit, Angus. Is it a criminal investigation?"

"Maybe. We've learned that George lied to the police about where he picked up Jane Landry, and he let them think she was a hitchhiker. Now Nell says that he only knew her name was Jane, that she didn't tell him Jane's full name or where she lived, which in my mind makes things worse. He was complicit in a conspiracy to take the child away from her parent."

"I see."

"There are records that say where Jane Landry is buried. Apparently, George paid for her burial. He and his cousin Eileen attended it."

"And then he and Eileen raised the child, giving her a loving home."

"Well, yes—"

"Now tell me about Mr. Morris. Are you charging him with sexual assault?"

"Not at this time. There is no evidence or eyewitness—"

"Excuse me? There's a knife, and Nell Sampson said she saw Yardley run away. Isn't that all the evidence you need?"

"Nell didn't report it to the police when it happened—a huge mistake, which she admits—so it's a he said, she said scenario. There's no record of an assault ever happening. Yardley maintains that Nell's trying to frame him. We don't know if she took the knife from the scene, or how she got hold of it. He still maintains that Jane must have had sex with someone else. Which we can't prove. We also can't prove that he *is* Bridie's father."

"It doesn't sound like you have a lot to go on in any aspect of this so-called investigation."

"It's a bit of a mess."

"Then can I give you some insight from the families directly involved?"

"Sure."

"My granddaughter is upstairs, afraid to go out into the world, because she has lost everyone she has ever loved. She has lost her biological mother, the woman who raised her like a mother, a grandmother, her father, who killed himself over this mess, and the young man she loved and wanted to marry. Nell Sampson has lived her life alone, in agony, because of one foolish, misguided mistake that she's been paying for for nearly twenty years. My daughter-in-law was humiliated in public over her husband's infidelities. Diane Morris has had her own family ripped to shreds by this revelation, and her eldest son has been forced to go live elsewhere and lose the love of his life because of his father's actions. By now, the entire town must know that Yardley Morris is a monster and his reputation is in tatters, despite his efforts to deny and deflect blame. If you can't prove anything, if three of the principles in the story are in their graves, why don't you let it go? Just let us be. My son is gone. He made a mistake, and he paid for it. Nell made a mistake, and she's paid for it. Jane had her life taken from her. My granddaughter and her young man never did anything wrong, and yet they are paying too. I want you to leave us alone. I don't want to hear about what Yardley Morris is doing or not doing. He's going to face his judge and jury someday, but perhaps you should concern yourself with the possibility that Mr. Morris could rape again. That's where your duty lies."

There was a long silence, and then Angus Turnbull cleared his throat.

"I think you're right, Mrs. Mackenzie. I think this is a story that needs to come to a close."

"Thank you, Angus. If you'd see yourself out."

The back door shut and I heard my grandmother crying. I ran down the stairs and saw her at the table with her head resting on her arms, looking helpless and small. But she was a giant in my eyes at that moment.

I knelt by her side. "I'm sorry, Gran. I'm sorry I've made this so much worse for you."

She embraced me and kissed my head. "You've done nothing wrong, Bridie. We're both doing the best we can."

"We'll be okay. We have each other."

❧

APRIL WAS A CRUEL MONTH THAT YEAR. WINTER DIDN'T SEEM TO want to loosen its icy grip, so there was no relief, no sunshine. Most of my time was spent in my room, reading or looking out the window. The questions I had about my little mother, as I now thought of her, were mounting, and I confessed that to Gran one day.

"There's only one person you can ask about Jane. I'm sure she'd be happy to tell you."

"I don't want to speak to Nell."

"I understand your bitterness towards her, but she's not the villain in the story. If it weren't for her, you'd never have known Pops, or Mama, or me, for that matter. Who knows where you'd be, with a fourteen-year-old mother and an alcoholic grandfather who neglected her. Your best hope might have been an orphanage."

I stewed on that for a while.

It was a nice morning in early May when I felt my blood stir. My room started to feel like a cage, so I told Gran I was going to Burke's to see Danny.

"Thank the Lord!" she cried. "That poor man has rung our doorbell countless times trying to see you and I kept sending him away, as per your instructions."

"What? I said I didn't want to see anyone, but that didn't include Danny!"

"Well, you should've made that clearer. I need baking powder, by the way."

Hobbs and I headed out and breathed in the spring air. The ground was still soft with melting frost, and tiny buds were appearing on tree branches. The wind carried fresh gusts from over the water, and I realized that it was blowing my hair in my face. My hair was getting long again and I hadn't paid attention. Most of the time I avoided the mirror; sadness was etched on my face and I didn't need to be reminded of it.

Hobbs pushed his way in front of me into the store. Danny's face lit up when he saw him. "Hobbs, me old son! Where on earth have you been? I've got two months' worth of dog biscuits taking up space under here."

Hobbs ran around the counter and gratefully accepted a handful of treats. I leaned on the counter and smiled. "We've missed you. Gran and I got our wires crossed. When I said I didn't want to see other humans, I didn't mean you."

"Since you've been gone, I've been as useless as a chocolate teapot."

"Me too."

He patted my hand. "How are you feeling?"

"Empty."

"What doesn't kill us makes us stronger. Who was the fool who said that?"

The bell rang and in walked Diane Morris. We looked at each other in shock. Neither one of us said anything.

"'Tis a grand day for it," Danny said loudly, trying to help. It didn't work.

"May I speak to you outside, Bridie?"

My feet followed her outside, but my brain was still in the store.

"How are you, dear?"

"Fine."

"You've been on my mind since...."

"Right."

"I thought you might come by and take Napoleon. Jack's been asking."

"Has he? He just expected me to take a horse and look after it?"

"I'm sorry. I thought you loved Napoleon and wanted him."

"This was Jack's idea. Not mine."

"Oh. Well, don't feel you have to."

"I don't feel anything at all, Mrs. Morris."

She put her hand over her mouth and her face crumpled. "I'm so sorry, Bridie. I feel responsible. If I hadn't had that party, none of this would've happened."

"None of this would've happened if your husband hadn't raped my mother. Are you still married to him?"

"Life is not easy, Bridie. I have four sons who depend on me now, and I'm only a housewife. I gave all my savings to Jack so he could get away from here. It's a bad situation."

"Yet another reason to be a spinster. They don't depend on men to look after them. You've just confirmed that my original plan to never marry is the right one. I feel sorry for you, Mrs. Morris."

"You have every right to be angry, Bridie. If it helps, know that my husband is no longer the mayor. It serves him right."

"I don't care about him. How is Jack, anyway?"

"He's living—"

"I don't want to know where he lives."

"He's working."

"Which is more than I've been doing. Guys seem to cope so much better than us gals when it comes to romantic breakups."

"I wouldn't say that. He's—"

"I don't want to know. Sorry, I have to go."

I turned on my heel and walked back into the store. Danny and Hobbs had worried looks on their faces.

"Was it terrible?" Danny asked.

"Pretty much."

Danny looked around frantically, seized a candy necklace, and put it in my hand. "Here."

"I need baking powder too."

಄

I TOLD GRAN ABOUT RUNNING INTO DIANE MORRIS.

"Poor Diane."

"She wondered when I was coming for Napoleon."

"How did Jack think you were going to manage a horse? We don't even have a barn."

"I know, right? It's a ridiculous idea."

She kept stirring her pot of stewed prunes. "You know who does have a barn?"

"Who?"

"Nell."

"Nice try, Gran."

At night I'd dream about Jack and I riding Napoleon. Sometimes I woke up thinking it had actually happened, only to be bitterly disappointed. Jack was lost to me, but a part of him was living and breathing down the road. The idea took hold that maybe I would feel better with Napoleon to look after. I was doing nothing with my life. This would fill the empty hours.

But that meant approaching Nell.

One morning I woke up, got dressed, and told Gran was going to see Nell about a horse.

"Good luck."

Although it was only half a mile to her house, I didn't think I was ready to walk past the cabin alone so I took the car.

The cottage looked exactly the same. Still boarded up, empty and staring. My mother had lived there. My grandfather and grandmother had lived there. It belonged to me, by rights. But maybe it was haunted. Everyone associated with the cabin had met a terrible end. It was probably in my genes to live a miserable life.

Too late, I realized I was getting upset. This was not the way to approach someone for a favour. Especially someone I was iffy about in the first place.

When I pulled into Nell's yard I immediately looked at the barn. It seemed to be in sturdy shape. Everything about the place was up-to-date and cared for. And she wasn't relying on a man to help her. So, it could be done.

Two dogs came from behind the barn and wagged their tails over to the car. I got out and reached over to let them sniff my hand. When I looked up Nell was on her back porch, holding a swatch of fabric.

"I knew you'd come one day," she said. "When you were ready."

"Can we just get it straight that I will never forgive you?"

"Understood."

"Good. I'm looking for a barn to board my horse."

"I didn't know you had one."

"I don't. It's Jack's. He asked me to take care of it, which was a really stupid idea since I know nothing about horses and don't have a barn."

"I have two horses. One is a mare and the other a pony. They're older now. Your horse must be a gelding if they are to get along."

"A gelding?"

"Has he been castrated?"

"I think so. I'll have to check."

"Mine are in the field, if you'd like to see them. Let me get my coat."

While waiting for her, I looked down at her dogs. Mutts. The smaller one's eyes were two different colours, one green and one brown.

Nell walked across the yard with a jacket and gloves on.

"What are the dog's names?"

"Dog and Dog."

"Isn't that confusing?"

"They're always together, so it's easier."

She walked me over to the fence. "This back field is very spacious. There's more than enough room for another horse."

The horse and pony ambled over to the fence. Nell took two apples out of her pocket and handed me one. We held out our hands and the animals gobbled up the apples.

"What are their names?"

"Mare and Pony."

"Wow. You don't put much thought into this, do you? That mare is definitely a Lucy and the pony is Shortbread. My horse is Napoleon. No calling him Horse if he ends up here."

"Right."

"May I see the barn?"

"Surely."

We walked over to the barn, and she opened the door. A flood of memories came roaring back of Mama and Pops and playing with the collies at Nana's house that summer. The stalls and the hay reminded me of a time when I'd had my whole family with me. I had to cover my face so Nell wouldn't see.

She pretended not to notice. "I can give you the space, but you will be responsible for your horse's upkeep. His feed, hay, accessories, et cetera. I don't ride. My horses are my pets. They help keep the grass down, along with my sheep, who are grazing behind the barn."

I gathered myself. "I suppose their names are Sheep, Sheep, and Sheep."

"How did you know?" Nell said.

"How much to board Napoleon?"

"No charge. Just make sure I never have to take care of him. I'm at capacity looking after my own animals. You can come and go as you please. You don't have to check with me first, although it might be a good idea to give you a key to the house, just in case."

"What do I need before Napoleon gets here?"

"Come into the kitchen and I'll prepare a list."

Sitting in the kitchen being stared at by Cat and Cat was disconcerting. I realized now that my mother, Jane, must have spent time in this very room.

Nell was prattling on about what I needed to buy, but I figured if she was writing it down too, I didn't have to listen. It annoyed me that I still loved this space. Had my little mother loved it too?

She passed me the paper. "That should do it." She got up and reached for a key hanging by the door. "And here's a spare key."

"Thanks."

Nell sat down again. "Is there anything else?"

"What was my mother like?"

Nell smiled. "Jane was a sweet girl, but very innocent and unworldly. She lived alone most of the time, so she didn't blend well with other children. She was sickly, too, because she wasn't cared for properly. She missed a lot of school, and half the time I don't think the teachers even noticed. It seems she was a forgettable child to everyone but me. I did my best for her, but it wasn't enough. I'll regret the day I sent her away until I die. It was all my fault."

I grabbed the paper and key off the table. "You can say that again."

Out the door I went.

When I stormed into our kitchen, Gran looked concerned. "Did she reject the idea?"

"No. I can board the horse for no charge. It's a great place."

"Well, then. You should be happy about that."

"Right."

The rest of the night, I soaked in the tub with Hobbs keeping me company.

෯෭

BEING ANGRY WITH THE WHOLE WORLD WAS TIRING. I RESENTED having to call Diane Morris to ask if she could somehow bring Napoleon over to Nell Sampson's barn for me. She said it wasn't a problem, which annoyed me. Why was she helping me? She was getting rid of her son's horse. Didn't that bother her?

It irritated me that I had to use Nell's barn and that she was letting me do it for free. I wasn't a charity case. If she was trying to be my friend, she could forget it.

Danny agreed with me. "She's an evil one. What has this store ever done to her? I can't imagine why she's being so generous. She's trying to trick ya, so she is. That sort always does."

"What sort?"

"Spinsters. They're always spinning."

GRAN TOOK A MESSAGE ONE DAY THAT DIANE'S NEIGHBOUR would drop the horse off at one o'clock the next day, so I had to call Nell and ask if that would be convenient, even though she'd said to come anytime. I wasn't planning on being her buddy, so I made sure to keep it formal.

Nell said that would be fine.

Sleep eluded me that night. What was I doing? Napoleon was a big horse, and I couldn't ride him alone. Would I need lessons? What did he eat? This was a foolish idea, and yet the thought of seeing him quickened my breath, even though in my heart I knew there was no part of me that was prepared to see Napoleon again.

One o'clock came and went and still I sat with Nell at her kitchen table. She kept herself busy snipping the threads of a hem. She had a basket of fabric in front of her. She nodded her head at it. "You'd be doing me a favour if you took that seam ripper and took out these hems."

Did I want to do her a favour? She was taking my horse, so I picked up the thingy and a piece of cloth.

"You pull the seam apart a little and then take the hook and rip the stitch. Just go along and you'll find it starts to rip easily."

It was actually kind of soothing. One thing I noticed about Nell was that she wasn't afraid of silence. She didn't fill up the air with empty words. I suppose since all her time was spent alone she was used to the quiet.

The clock in the kitchen sounded off the seconds as we sat quietly. After a while it drove me crazy that she didn't talk.

"What's this material for?"

"I take the remnants of garments and use them to make dolls for children who need them."

"Oh."

"I made a doll for your mother once. It had a red velvet coat."

I looked at her.

"She called it Bridie."

The seam ripper fell out of my hand and clattered to the floor. Neither of us said anything until, once again, I couldn't take it.

"How...why...?"

Nell looked stricken. "Your mother must have lived long enough to tell George your name."

My head dropped and I stared at the piece of cloth in my hand. Nell got up from the table and fetched me a glass of water. Then she retrieved the seam ripper and placed it beside me before falling back into the chair. I drank the whole glass and started ripping. She did the same.

The clock eventually struck three.

"Where are these people?"

"They might be having trouble getting the horse into the trailer. Sometimes horses can be brats about it. Especially if they're high strung."

The words were no sooner out of her mouth than we heard the rumble of a truck and trailer slowly approach the barn. We went outside to greet Diane's neighbour.

The man who was driving the truck got out and approached us first. His helper looked about sixteen. He stayed seated in the cab.

Diane's neighbour was quite striking—if you liked a dark, broody look. And he sure was throwing daggers our way.

"Look, I'm sorry we're late but that horse did not want to come here, and I can't say I blame him."

"And you are?" said Nell.

"Mitch Curry." He looked at me for the first time. "Bridie?"

"Yes."

"I don't have a whole lot of time for gossip, but I gather my neighbour Jack wanted you to have his horse. A little thing like you isn't gonna be able to handle this beast. What the heck was he thinking?"

"He clearly wasn't thinking, but that's the situation we're in."

"I'll tell you what. I own a farm not far from here. Why don't I take the horse for you? I actually know how to ride. I've ridden Napoleon before and he's a stubborn beast."

"Well, so am I, and I want him."

"You're a fool."

"And you are a rude, insensitive jerk."

He shook his head. "Women."

He signalled for his helper and the kid got out of the truck. They both went to the back of the trailer and opened the doors. Mitch went inside and we heard Napoleon whinny his displeasure. The mare and pony in the field had wandered over by the fence to watch the fun. Dog and Dog were patiently waiting too.

It sounded like a battle of wills was going on inside the trailer. Mitch shouted at the kid to get out of the way as Napoleon stomped his hooves. Eventually, ever so slowly, Napoleon backed out of the doors and stood in the yard, shaking his head in disgust.

Nell stood enthralled. "Oh, Bridie, he's beautiful. I can see why Jack loved him."

I fell to my knees. It was like seeing Jack standing there.

Mitch held on to Napoleon's reins and watched me. The kid got some equipment out of the back and put it in the barn. Nell went over to Mitch and said something to him. Then the two of them walked the horse into the barn and stayed there for quite a while.

Eventually the boy went back in the truck and Mitch reappeared. He approached me and knelt beside me.

"You need to pull yourself together if you're going to be responsible for these twelve hundred pounds of horse flesh. This isn't a pussycat."

"I don't like you."

"I don't like you either. But the lady in there said that she'd pay me to teach you how to ride and look after this horse. And I'm not stupid enough to turn down what she's offering."

"She had no business telling you that."

"The first lesson starts tomorrow morning at six. I'm a busy man and that's the only time I can fit you in."

He straightened up and walked back to his truck. I had to get up to move out of his way as he circled around the yard and disappeared down the laneway.

When I got to the barn, Nell had already given Napoleon a feed of hay and fresh water. She was brushing his coat softly and speaking quietly to him. When I approached, Napoleon stretched out his neck and put his mouth near my cheek. I breathed him in.

"Do you remember me?"

The horse lifted his head as if to say yes.

CHAPTER TWENTY-TWO

My very first lesson in horseback riding was spent in the barn, shovelling manure.

"This is the most important job there is," Mitch said. "You keep your horse's stall clean at all times. It's a never-ending task."

He was being paid to watch me break into a sweat.

"Now do the mare's and the pony's stalls, while you're at it. That lady has enough to do."

My determination to call his bluff made me shovel with the best of them. But when I went to pick up the handles of the wheelbarrow, I could hardly lift it.

"Lesson number two. Never fill the wheelbarrow so full that you can't manoeuvre it. Take some of that out."

"Why don't you do it for me and I'll remember next time?"

"What are you, a baby?"

I scowled at him, picked up a shovel of manure, and dumped it at his feet.

"Keep going."

When that odious task was completed, he looked at his watch. "I have to go."

"But—"

"See you at six tomorrow."

And he drove away.

That first week I never got out of the barn. There were lessons on food, brushing, and learning the names of things.

"This is a bridle. It's part of the tack or harness of a horse. It consists of a headstall, bit, and reins."

"I know what a bit and reins are."

"Excellent. Now this is a saddle."

"I know that."

"But did you know that a saddle is made up of different parts? This is the fork, the horn, the seat, the cantle, and Cheyenne roll. We have the seat jockey, the back jockey, and the skirt. There's the rear rigging dee, the flank billet, the flank cinch, the cinch connecting strap, the front cinch, and the stirrup. This here is the hobble strap, the fender, front rigging dee, the latigo, the front jockey, latigo holder, and the tee gullet. Now, are you going to remember that?"

"I'll remember the skirt."

He rolled his eyes. "Spoken like a true—"

"Woman. Yes."

"You're a baby. How old are you?"

"Eighteen. How old are you?"

"I'm twenty-five."

"Married?"

"Never."

"Well, at least we have one thing in common."

When he left, Nell came outside and asked me how things were going.

"The guy is obnoxious. He thinks he knows everything."

"I believe he does. He has his own horses. Everything you're doing, he's doing too."

"When is he going to let me get on the actual horse? You're paying him to stand around and pontificate."

"He'll let you on the horse when he feels you're ready, and not before."

Two weeks went by and I still wasn't on Napoleon's back. The next step was to lead him by the reins around the yard and in the field. Mitch said that Napoleon had to get comfortable with his new surroundings. That horses didn't like change and it was useless to rush them into anything.

Gran made me pancakes and bacon or eggs and sausages in the morning to fill me up. My appetite had returned with a vengeance from working all day with the three horses. My clothes felt a bit tight, and Gran was pleased to see it.

"You have roses in your cheeks again."

"Only because that maniac has me standing outside all day."

"Hobbs is getting very sad, you know."

My heart dropped. I'd been so busy listening to that irritating man, I hadn't realized how my schedule had changed. "Sorry, Hobbs! You're coming to the barn with me today. I don't care if Nell or Dog or Dog don't like it."

Nell didn't care and neither did Dogs.

And wouldn't you know it, Hobbs fell in love with Mitch. He followed him everywhere, and I noticed Mitch smiled a lot more with Hobbs around.

"This is an Airedale," he said. "My grandfather had one. They're great dogs."

It got to the point that Mitch spent most of his time focussed on my dog. I'd had enough.

"You are supposed to be teaching me how to ride, not flirting with my pet."

"You're—"

"Do *not* say I'm a silly baby."

"You're right."

That stopped me in my tracks. "I am?"

"Let's get on this horse."

Mitch had to put his hands on me to get me up into the saddle. It felt like Jack the first time he'd helped me sit on Napoleon.

"I'd forgotten how high it feels up here."

"We'll go slow." He took the reins and led me around the field while the other animals frolicked around us.

"I'm not used to sitting up here by myself. Jack always sat with me."

"He didn't do you any favours, then. Riding a horse is one of the best things in life, and you need to do it by yourself if you're going to get anything out of it."

As he walked ahead of me, I had a chance to look at Mitch. He was taller than Jack and had a different build, strong and wiry, the muscles and sinews in his arms well defined. His thick, chestnut-coloured hair was long, the ends curling from underneath his ball cap. He must spend his life outdoors, I thought, because his skin was tanned even this early in the year. And he was always chewing on a blade of grass or a toothpick.

The gait of the horse lulled me as I sat. When I closed my eyes, I felt Jack behind me, and that was a comfort. God, I missed him.

"You're not bawling, are you?" Mitch shouted at me.

My eyes opened and I wiped them with my shirt sleeve. "So what if I am? What difference does it make to you?"

"Do you see Napoleon here crying about his new lot in life? No, he's getting on with it. Stop wallowing about something that isn't going to change."

"How do you know?"

"Everyone in this village knows what happened to you. Even me, and that's saying something because I never listen to gossip. But for some reason your story has fascinated the people around here, and I've had to hear the sad tale numerous times whether I wanted to or not."

"And what do you suggest I do, since you're such an expert in everyone and everything?"

"Let him go. He's your half brother. Love him like a brother, care about him, but let him get on with his life so you can get on with yours."

"What do you know about my life?"

"You're eighteen, you're not in school, and you're not working. You're living off your grandmother and this spinster on the hill is paying for these lessons. Why do these people owe you a living? You think you're the only person who's lost someone? Or even several people? That's what life is, and brooding about it isn't going to bring them back. If you're not careful, you're going to be known as the harpy on the hill."

He let go of the reins and walked away.

"How am I supposed to get off this horse?"

"With difficulty."

He got in his truck and roared off. I let out a yell that startled Napoleon and I quickly realized I needed to stay calm, hold the reins, and get control of him.

Nell came out about an hour later and leaned on the fence. Napoleon and I were still walking. Hobbs sat under a bush, getting some shade.

"I made a lemon meringue pie. It's your Gran's recipe. She gave it to me once. Would you like a piece?"

"Sure. Would you mind staying here while I try to get off this animal? I don't want to break anything."

"Just slowly slide off him. He'll wait for you."

She was right. I left him grazing with Lucy and Shortbread, but Hobbs followed me into the house, much to the dismay of Dogs.

Nell's pie was pretty good, but not as good as Gran's or mine. We sat and ate and didn't talk. I got used to sitting with her. Up to a point.

"I've decided I'm going to pay for my own horse lessons. Thank you anyway."

"Okay," she said.

That was it. No questions. She really was the easiest woman to be with. The complete opposite of Aunt Betty.

"What was Pops like as a kid?"

"He stuttered."

That surprised me. "He did?"

"Not terribly, and not all the time, and he did outgrow it, but the kids would make fun of him, like horrible Angus Turnbull."

"The police chief?"

"Yes. He and his wife, Myrtle, were the class bullies. But you know, Myrtle was the first person who asked me to make her a dress, and that's how I started my whole dressmaking business. You take the good with the bad."

"When did you know you loved Pops?"

"When I was seventeen, I lost my parents in a car crash."

"You've lost three people you loved in car crashes?"

She nodded. "I thought I didn't love my parents and that they didn't love me. I had a lonely childhood. George told me that my parents did love me, but that sometimes people have a hard time expressing it. It made me feel better during that terrible time."

I took a sip of tea. "If you loved each other, why didn't you get married?"

"Your father asked me several times, but I always said no. Because of my childhood, I was afraid to be a mother and I didn't think it was fair to George because he'd always wanted a family. I was wrong. Jane was like a daughter to me, and I adored her. I've been wrong about a lot of things over the course of my life."

❧

ON THE MORNING OF JULY 13, PATTY CALLED ME. "I'M LOOKING at your niece right now."

I screamed and scared Gran.

"What's wrong?!" she shouted from the bathroom.

"Patty had a little girl!"

"You didn't need to give me a heart attack! Congratulate them for me."

"Gran sends congratulations. What's her name?"

"Kimberly Bridget."

I howled.

"What's wrong?!" Gran shouted from the bathroom.

"The baby's name is Kimberly Bridget!"

"I hope the baby isn't as loud as you are!"

"What did Mavis say about that?" I asked Patty.

"She wanted to know why she wasn't named Kimberly Mavis."

"And you said?"

"'That's for the next girl.' She doesn't know that this is the last kid. I'm only doing this twice."

"When can I come down?"

"You? Whenever you want, and the sooner the better."

By this time, I knew Mitch's number and where he lived. I called him. A woman answered.

"Hello. Is Mitch there?"

"He's out in the fields. Can I give him a message?"

"Yes, please. I'm Bridie Mackenzie—"

"Oh, Bridie. I've heard a lot about you."

Because I was still so excited over Patty's news, I stupidly said, "From who?"

"Why, Mitch, of course."

"Oh. And you are?"

"His mother, dear."

Mr. Independent lived with his mother. Hmm. Who'd have thought?

"I can't see him for a couple of weeks. I know he's only coming over once a week now, but my sister just had a baby and I'm going down to Sydney for a while to help her."

"Aren't you a dear? I'll be sure to tell him, Bridie."

"Thank you, Mrs....Curry."

"Goodbye, dear."

Thinking about it, I'd probably live with Mrs. Curry too. She sounded nice.

I called Nell and told her the same thing, but I had to ask

nicely. "I know you said you didn't want to take care of Napoleon but it's only for a couple of weeks, and I'll try and make it up to you when I get back."

"You will. You can do some painting around the house."

"It's a deal."

After kissing Gran and Hobbs goodbye, I set off in the car. The weather was hot and sunny. I had my windows down the whole way, and I had to put my hair in a ponytail to get it off my face. As I drove down the road, glancing at the stunning scenery of the Bras d'Or Lakes glistening in the sun, I found myself whistling. Whistling!

Sometimes you have no idea how far you've come until you take yourself out of your own routine.

The baby was adorable, naturally. I couldn't get enough of her, but Pup wanted my attention too, and it made Patty's life easier if I kept him occupied while Patty spent time with her new daughter.

"I can't believe the difference it makes, having a girl instead of a boy."

"What do you mean?"

"With Pup, I never gave a thought to him turning sixteen or going to his prom or his wedding. I've already got Kimberly's outfits planned. It's like playing with a little doll. When I think back to Mom always putting me in cute outfits and never wanting me to get dirty I can kind of get it, but I'm not going to be that dipsy-doodle about it."

Patty didn't suffer from the baby blues this time, and what a difference it made for the whole family. She even enjoyed having Mavis over because Mavis, too, was enraptured by Kimberly. Ray was over the moon with his new little one. It was a pleasure seeing these parents together with their kiddies.

Patty couldn't get over the difference in me.

"You look fantastic. Like you've been hiking every day."

"The very best thing I could have done was take Napoleon. He forces me to get outside in the fresh air."

"The horse does, or the guy, what's-his-name?"

"Mitch. Yeah, he's pretty bossy too."

She gave me a sly smile as she rocked Kimberley and I put on Pup's socks. "Tell me about him. Is he cute?"

"No! He's too intense to be cute. He'd bite your head off if you suggested such a thing."

"A definite creep, then?"

"Not a creep, just someone who thinks he's right all the time."

"Like you, ya mean?"

I threw a teddy bear at her feet.

About a week into my visit, Mavis called and asked me to come over to her apartment. That was the last thing I wanted to do.

"Bring Pup too. That way Patty will get some rest."

My nerves got to me, driving with Pup in the car. I made him sit right beside me so I could use my arm as a shield when I slowed down. He was as good as gold. I told him so.

"Good, Dee?"

"Yes, sweetheart. Very good."

Pup loved going in the elevator. He wanted to push all the buttons but boy, was I going to scrub his hands when he got home. He knew which one was his grandmother's door and banged on it. "Mave!"

She actually had her grandson call her by her first name. Why was I not surprised?

When I stepped into the room, my heart gave a lurch. Our dining room set was the first thing I saw, followed by some pieces of our living room furniture. But it made me feel nostalgic rather than sad. These were Mavis's things, not mine. I didn't have to be afraid of this anymore.

The entire time I was there, she had me stop Pup from getting up on the furniture and run around collecting the Royal Doulton figurines on the cabinet shelves. This was not a safe zone for children. I was almost more exhausted from this than shovelling horse manure.

She finally produced some store-bought cookies, which kept Pup occupied for more than two minutes.

"You're looking much better, Bridie," she said.

"I feel better."

"Amazing what time will do."

"Yes."

"In that vein, I feel I owe you an apology for the way I behaved towards you when you were a little girl."

If she had lit me on fire, I would have been less shocked.

"I've had time to reflect, since the night of...the disaster... and now that the truth has been laid out for all of us, it gives me a perspective: the bigger picture."

All I could do was nod.

"You were an infant, like Kimberly. You had no say in who you belonged to. It was ridiculous of me to be jealous of you, to think that your father loved you more than Patty. I know he loved you both, but he expressed his love for you in a more protective way, knowing you had no one else. I was angry, because I knew something about the situation felt off. I really did feel like he was lying to me, and it turns out I was right. I wasn't crazy after all. But again, that wasn't your fault and I'm sorry."

"I could be a brat."

"You could. But all kids are brats sometimes. And I was immature enough to let it get to me."

"I'm not sure what to say."

She clasped her hands on her lap. "'I forgive you' might be nice."

"I do forgive you, Mavis. I grew up in a lovely home, with all my needs met. I have a sister and these two wonderful babies in my life. I've learned a bit about my mother Jane's life, and I realize that *she* was the one who had nothing. I had everything. And that's because Pops, Mama, and you let me thrive. I don't think of my childhood without thinking of all five of us together."

She let out a deep sigh. I reached over and hugged her. It still felt a bit awkward, only because she never was a great hugger. Not like Mama, who enfolded you in her big arms and comfy tummy.

We turned our attention to our boy and chatted about how handsome and clever he was. It was...nice. Not complicated or fraught or fractious, maybe for the first time in my life. Just nice.

When I got back to Patty's, the magnitude of what had happened hit me like a bolt. Mavis and I were friends. I was beginning to realize you can never have too many of those.

Patty's mouth hung open like an unhinged door. "Say that again?"

I said it again.

"I've never in my life heard my mother apologize to anyone. Not even me, more's the pity. Wait until I tell Ray. Do you think she's had a mini-stroke or something?"

"She looked perfectly normal."

"Wow. Nothing's impossible. Oh, by the way, will you be Kimberley's godmother?"

This was just the best day.

CHAPTER TWENTY-THREE

All summer and into the fall, I painted Nell's house. She hired some-
one to paint the outside shingles, but I picked away at the inside
whenever I wasn't riding Napoleon. She said she didn't care
how long it took me. And because she wanted all her rooms
done, she insisted on paying me.

"But I owe you for looking after Napoleon."

"I have a confession. Mitch came up here after you left
and rode Napoleon down to his farm and looked after him. He
doesn't want you to know."

"Great! Now I owe him!"

"Don't you dare. He'd be furious. You know how he gets."

That man. But it did make me grin.

Sometimes Gran would drive up and join us for lunch. She
said she was getting too lonely by herself all day long. Once Aunt
Betty heard we were having regular chin-wags, she wanted to
come too. Gran was sure that Nell would put the kibosh on that,
but she said Aunt Betty was welcome.

That's how we heard that Fraser needed a new hip but was
too stubborn to get one.

"He'd rather hobble around than fix the dang thing."

"Just as well, Betty," Gran said. "You'd have to pick up the
slack."

She looked like that thought hadn't occurred to her. "I suppose he shouldn't be too hasty."

It's also how we heard about Mitch's family. Aunt Betty filled
us in between bites of carrot cake.

"If he's as stubborn as his father, that's saying something.
Frank Curry was a farmer, cabinetmaker, and, in his spare time,
an amateur boxer. That's what killed him."

"He died in the ring?" I said.

"No. The next day. His doctor told him not to fight. He'd had some kind of a bleed behind his eye during his last bout and the doctor said he should quit altogether. But he was making good money in those days. The trouble is, once you're dead you don't get a paycheque, and his wife, Maud, had to go to work cleaning houses."

"Does Mitch have a brother? There was a younger kid with him when they delivered Napoleon."

"Yes, Will. He was born a couple of months after his father died."

"How does Mitch make his money now?" I asked, pretending not to notice Gran and Nell exchange glances.

"He farms. They have a nice piece of land. You can't beat his vegetables. He boards horses. He goes out with his cousin lobster fishing sometimes, and he's a crackerjack machinist. He can fix anyone's farming equipment; most guys take their tractors and such to him rather than the dealership. He's a jack of all trades."

"I'm surprised he found time to come and teach me how to ride."

"It is a mystery," Nell said.

❧

NELL HAD GORGEOUS TASTE IN FABRICS, BUT SHE WANTED HER walls white.

"They look fresh that way," she said.

Today I was starting her bedroom. "Why don't you go with something different? Like a pretty robin's egg blue? It's only paint. If you don't like it, I'll paint over it."

She thought about it. "No, white will do. I'll make a bedspread in robin's egg blue. And colourful pillows. You can improve anything when the backdrop is white. Not so easy when you start with a difficult colour."

"It's your room."

When I was moving furniture about to get things away from the walls, the drawer to her vanity opened. Inside was a pipe. It had to belong to Pops. I lifted it out and sat on her bed, putting my nose up to the bowl and smelling the familiar scent of his favourite tobacco. A deep longing filled me, an ache.

"I've missed you so much," I whispered. "Why aren't you here?"

Nell appeared in the doorway with a drop cloth. She saw me on the bed holding the pipe and put the cloth up to her mouth. We looked at each other for a long moment and then she came and sat beside me.

"Whenever I need him," she said, "I take that out and he comes to me."

"Do you ever get over a lost love?"

"No."

That hurt.

"But that doesn't mean that you can't find love again, I suppose. The trouble is, you have to want it. And I never did."

"Why?"

"If I were eighteen again, maybe, but I was too set in my ways, and too angry at men in general."

"Oh?"

"I was raped."

My stomach turned over. I stared at her. "That's awful."

She nodded.

"What are the chances of you and my mother sharing the same fate?"

She looked out the window. "Unfortunately, not unheard of. There are always men who will take advantage of a situation."

"I had an...incident once."

"Then you know that it's better to dwell on the men who instill our lives with love. Like your father."

"Like my Jack."

Her head turned towards me. "There are lots of them out there. You're young enough to find one."

"Oh, I already have."

"Who?" she sputtered.

"Danny Flynn. He's my best friend. He works at Burke's store."

"The Irishman? He's quite a character. I can see why you like him."

"He saved me the night of...you know. I ran to his door and stayed there all night. He never asked a thing. Just kept me warm and safe."

"Then he's a hero in my eyes."

"He thinks you don't like him."

She smiled. "I don't like the store. It's got nothing to do with him."

"You need to get past that. It's just a building, for heaven's sake."

"You're probably right."

❧

THE DAY I FINISHED THE LAST OF THE PAINTING IT WAS THE middle of September, my nineteenth birthday, and I celebrated by taking Napoleon for a ride. It was a glorious day, almost hotter than any summer afternoon, and I put my hair up under my cowboy hat, something Gran had surprised me with a few weeks before.

I trotted through the village and waved to people I knew. They were getting used to seeing me on my horse. When I went by Burke's, Danny came out with a big carrot for Napoleon and a lollipop for me.

"You look like Annie Oakley," he shouted with laughter. "You're not in Alberta, girlie."

"And might I remind you, you're from Ireland so you don't belong here either."

"Go 'way with ya! There's more Irish and Scottish in these here parts than anywhere else in the world."

A customer stuck their head out the door of the shop. "Are you planning on yakking all day, Danny Flynn?"

"Must fly!" He blew me a kiss and ran back into the store.

Did I know where I was going when I turned down Mitch Curry's laneway? I couldn't decide, but now that I was here, there was no sense in stopping. Napoleon's ears perked up. He recognized this place.

The laneway was lined with trees, the branches reaching out to one another, creating a canopied tunnel. It was a long way in. They'd have to get a plow to get rid of the snow in the winter. But when the trees cleared, there was a vast expanse of fields leading right down to the water. I could see a small but comfortable house, a nicer-looking barn, and a garage with farming equipment strewn by the open doors. There were also a couple of sheds and what looked like a small greenhouse near the kitchen of the main house.

Mrs. Curry had a line of washing out on her clothesline; it was a perfect day for drying sheets and towels.

To the left was a fenced-in field where at least six horses were grazing. There were a couple of goats, too, and a slew of chickens hanging around a coop by the barn.

This belonged in a storybook. My heartrate went down just looking at it.

Napoleon and I sauntered up near the house, hoping that Mitch would see me and come out to greet us, but he was nowhere to be found. Before I got down to knock at the door, a woman I assumed was Mitch's mother came out on the deck.

"Good afternoon," she said. "You must be Bridie. I recognize Napoleon."

"Hello, Mrs. Curry."

"Please, call me Maud. I'm assuming you're looking for Mitch?"

"Yes. Is he about?"

"He was, but then he said it was too nice a day to waste and he went fishing."

I laughed. "He never struck me as the fishing sort."

She grinned. "He rarely relaxes, so I'm always happy when he heads to the brook." She pointed towards the back of the field. "When you get down near the water, there's a clearing on the left that leads to a deep brook. It doesn't look like much, but it's got a few trout in it. I imagine that's where he'll be."

"Thank you."

"Enjoy your day. Bye, Napoleon."

We took our time crossing the field. Every now and then, Napoleon put his head down to graze, and I let him. The day needed savouring.

Mitch and I saw each other at the same time. He had his back against a tree, his pole in the water almost an afterthought. He scowled when I got close.

"What are you doing here?"

"What a pleasant greeting."

"Did my mother tell you where I was?"

"Yes, after saying a big hello to Napoleon. It was almost as if she'd met him before."

"She's just nice to animals. She's nice to everyone."

I hopped down with minimum fuss, hoping to impress him with my dismount, but he didn't comment on it. Napoleon walked a few feet away to nibble on some lush-looking grass.

"Do you mind if I sit down?"

"No."

"You don't happen to have another pole, do you? I'm an avid fisherman when I get the chance. My father taught me. But it's been a while since I've had the opportunity."

"Sorry. I didn't think I'd have company."

"That's all right. Did you catch anything yet?"

"No. That's not the point of fishing."

"What is the point?"

"To get away from people."

That made me laugh. "You sound just like my Pops."

"Napoleon looks good. If you rode all this way, you must be getting more comfortable on him. Someone taught you well."

"Yes, I had an excellent teacher. A bit grouchy, but I learned to ignore him. Our lessons are over now, so I don't have any stress in my life."

He made a face.

We sat and stared at the brook. Sitting quietly was coming easier to me, thanks to Nell.

Mitch eventually spoke. "Have you finished the painting?"

"Yes. Everything looks marvellous."

"I wonder why she's fixing the joint up? Maybe she's planning to move."

The thought instantly upset me. "What do you mean? Do you know something?"

"Whoa. It was just a comment. I know nothing about her plans."

"What would I do? That's where Napoleon lives."

"You can always board him here. I could use the money."

"You're too far away."

"Obviously not. You're here, aren't you?"

I stared into the water, my mind racing. Why *was* she fixing up the place? She couldn't leave. There were still a thousand questions I wanted to ask her. I was so busy trying to keep her at bay that I might have lost an opportunity for her to give me information that only she had. She was the only person who remembered Jane. That connection couldn't be severed.

"Stop worrying," Mitch said. "She obviously adores you. She's not going anywhere."

"Do you think so?"

"Look, she's not a warm and bubbly person like my mom, but when she looks at you, I see it. When she talks about you, I hear it. You would not believe how much she paid me to give you lessons."

"I'm assuming as much as I was."

"Not by a long shot. I wasn't pleased when you took over."

"So why did you keep coming?"

"She paid me the difference. But more importantly, I owed it to Napoleon. He needed someone who knew what they were doing."

"Have I passed your rigorous standards?"

"Not bad for a baby."

I gave him a death glare.

"I'm only joking."

His pole leapt forward and out of his hand. I grabbed it and held on. "You've got something."

"Bring it in."

It certainly wasn't the salmon Pops and I had wrestled with, but he'd caught a nice little trout. Big enough for a helping or two. An hour later he caught another one, and then we walked back to the house, Napoleon trailing behind us.

His mother insisted on cooking them for us for lunch, with some boiled new potatoes and butter. She had a wild blueberry pie just out of the oven, with vanilla ice cream she'd churned herself.

"Maud, I haven't had a meal this tasty since my mama died. Thank you."

Maud gave me a big grin. "Why thank you, Bridie. I never get compliments like that from my boys."

"Hey!" Mitch frowned. "That's not true."

I waved goodbye and took my time going home. I still wasn't sure why I'd gone, but I was very glad I had. And if I didn't know better, I'd say Mitch was glad too.

IN NOVEMBER, WHEN THE AIR HAD THE FIRST HINT OF WINTER blowing through it, I went up to Nell's in the car. Since it looked like it was going to rain or hail or snow, I decided to be safe. Napoleon's stall needed mucking out and so, it turned out, did Lucy's and Shortbread's. By this time, I was basically looking after all the critters on the property, and again Nell was paying me.

"Honest pay for honest work."

The way she was so free and easy with her money, I wondered if she had a lot of it. I was still trying to figure out what I was going to do long-term to keep the wolves from the door. Having the nest egg helped lessen my worry, but that wouldn't last forever if I spent it on my day-to-day life. For the first time, I wondered if I should go away to school—but the thought of leaving Gran and my pets made me sad.

Nell was finishing up a doll when I arrived. It had a big pink bow on its head and a pretty blue dress and sweater.

"That's awfully cute." By now I was comfortable enough to put on the kettle when I arrived. The tea bags were in a small tin she kept on the counter. "Who's this one going to?"

"A woman called and said her neighbour's child was sick. She wanted something to bring to the hospital when she visited."

"Remember when you said you'd made my mother a doll?"

"Yes."

"Do you think it's still around?"

Nell put the doll on the table and instantly looked anxious. "It is."

"May I see it?"

Nell looked away for a few moments and then sighed. "Of course." She got up and left the room, coming back a few minutes later. She handed me the old and worn-in little doll. The face had been rubbed off from hugging, and the red velvet coat was patched in a few spots.

"She loved this doll. I wish she'd taken it with her."

I touched the face. "She left it behind for me."

"Jane would be happy about that."

"Do you mind if I keep it?"

"It was your mother's. It belongs to you."

"So does the cabin. Do you think we could go see it?"

She suddenly looked wary. "Are you sure that's a good idea?"

"No, but I'm curious. And technically, that cabin belongs to me."

"I had a handyman board it up years ago when the front door blew in during a storm. No one else was going to do it."

"So, there you go. No one cares. There's nothing to steal, from the way you've described it."

"All right."

We walked down the lane with a crowbar and stood in front of it. Getting closer, I realized that it was bigger than it appeared. And more forlorn.

Nell took the crowbar and pried the piece of wood nailed to each side of the door frame until it let go. Then she took out a key and opened the door.

The building was sturdy, from the look of the floor, stairs, and roof. There was precious little furniture in it and only a few pots by the stove. Everything was drab, dirty, and dusty.

"This is where she lived?" I said. "No colour, no comfort, no happiness? My poor little mother."

"It was a disgrace. I shouldn't have been so afraid of Gervais. I should've done more to protect Jane, despite what he threatened."

"He obviously didn't care about anything. If he killed his wife, he could easily have killed you too."

"Then I should've shot him and claimed it as self-defence and just taken Jane with me."

"They would've sent her to an orphanage. A spinster isn't allowed to adopt children."

Nell looked around, her face anguished. "Why does the world make things so difficult? You have a child in need and a woman who wants to help, and yet that's not enough. It's all about the rules."

As hard as I tried not to, my focus became fixated on the stairs. They were narrow and crooked. They looked unforgiving.

"These are the stairs my grandmother fell down?"

"Yes."

I decided to meet them head on and went up to the two bedrooms and bathroom. They were pokey and colourless. The largest room, I presumed, was the parents'. It was horrifying. The sheets on the bed were black with mold. It was so disturbing that I walked straight out. When I walked into Jane's room, I almost cried. There was nothing in it to provide any kind of comfort. How was it possible that she lived here without losing her mind? A wave of gratitude swept over me that at least Nell had been in her life.

When I went back downstairs, Nell had some documents on the table. "I found these in the wardrobe. It's the deed to this property, and your grandparents' birth certificates. You'll need this to prove that you are the heir, and this place belongs to you. We'll go to a lawyer I know and ask what the process is to transfer the deed to your name."

"Does it really matter?"

"It's property. And property has value. You might want to fix this place up for yourself, despite the sad story of the people who lived here."

"They were my family."

"Your grandmother was a sweet woman. She would have adored you."

Now that I'd been inside the space, my fear had lessened. This was a forgotten part of my past, but it didn't have to remain that way.

We went back to Nell's house and I poured us some tea, while we looked at the doll on the table.

"When you think about it," I said, "Bridie is a funny name for a little girl to make up by herself."

"Her mother and I were surprised when she blurted it out. But she was very clear."

"Did Jane want to leave with my father that day?"

Nell's face fell. "When I told her the night before, she cried. She didn't want to leave me, but I assured her that she could come back to me someday. That George would make everything better. I truly believed he would, Bridie. If I'd known...."

We sat for a few moments in silence, and then she abruptly got up and left the room. I finished my tea and rinsed out my cup before going outside to the barn. As I brushed Napoleon, I realized that Nell had lost not just the child she loved that day, but also my father, the love of her life. No wonder her grief was still palpable nineteen years later.

Was I going to be like that? Wandering around like a lost soul, mourning Jack forever? I'd always thought of Nell as a tough old bird, but now she seemed a fragile woman, hiding from the world. Was I setting myself up for the same fate?

When I took the doll home, Gran held it. "My, my. What a precious thing to have."

❧

CHRISTMAS ROLLED AROUND AGAIN. THANK THE GOOD LORD that we didn't have to spend it with Uncle Donny and his crowd. Aunt Loretta's family was descending on them. Patty and Ray told us they'd bought a Hide-A-Bed and we were welcome to bunk with them for the night. Just as Patty had predicted, now that baby number two had arrived, they were going to have Christmas in their own house.

Gran and I had a great time playing with the kids. Kimberly was now six months old and as chubby as a Buddha. At two and a half, Pup was surprisingly sweet with her, but he was also quite determined to open her gifts as well as his own. A quiet talk in the corner with Dad settled him down.

Mavis looked rather good, and she shocked us when she said she was going to New York with a couple of girlfriends in the new year.

"Just a shopping trip, and we'll take in a few Broadway shows."

Gran was pleased for her. "That's just the sort of thing you should be doing. I wish I'd done it when I was younger."

Mavis was hesitant. "You're...you're not suggesting you want to go with us?"

Gran frowned. "No, Mavis. Don't worry. I wouldn't dream of cramping your style."

She was still fuming the next day on the drive home. "As if I'd want to go with that one to the big city. Honestly, she's the most annoying woman."

I delivered my Christmas gifts back home a couple of days late. All baked goods, of course.

Danny clapped his hands when he saw a pumpkin pie, an apple pie, and a wedge of fruitcake. "You're my angel, Bridie Mackenzie. You're the only reason I'm not a bag of bones, which is such a comfort to me Mam, who is constantly whining about the state of my health when I send her the odd picture."

"Your mother should come over for a visit."

"My fourteen siblings would take a turn if Mam left them. She's the only thing between them and eternal damnation."

"Fifteen children? Is she crazy?"

"She's crazy in love with the Pope, don't ya know."

Nell got a lemon loaf, mince tarts, and shortbreads. Then I took my oatmeal carrot muffins out to the barn and gave my three horse buddies their treats, which they gobbled down in a jiffy. I saved two for Dogs.

There was still a large chunk of fruitcake left, along with a date loaf, cranberry pudding, and more shortbread. Perhaps Mrs. Curry would like them.

Perhaps Mitch would like them.

It was a very cold afternoon when I drove to the Curry house and knocked on the door. Maud answered and looked very pleased to see me. "Come in, Bridie. What a delightful surprise. How are you, dear?"

"I'm great." I passed her my wicker basket. "This is for you, Mitch, and Will."

She peeked inside. "The best gift ever. No one thinks of giving a homemaker baked treats, but what a relief it is to put your feet up and know that dessert has been made." She took the goodies out of the basket and laid them out on the table. "Pretty as a picture."

We chatted for a while, but then I blurted, "Is Mitch here?"

"He'll be around the buildings out back. Will is off with a school chum. If you want to wander about and try to find Mitch, be my guest. He'll have his nose immersed in some engine and won't know what time of day it is."

I took my basket and waved goodbye. Then I headed to the barn.

"Mitch?"

A few horses looked out of their stalls at the sound of my voice. Horses are nosy creatures.

"Mitch?"

I peeked around one corner, and there was Mitch and a woman with their arms around each other, kissing. It was like having my face slapped. I must have cried out, although I didn't notice because Mitch and the woman parted quickly and looked in my direction.

Mitch looked shocked. "Bridie?"

My first thought was to get out of there as fast as I could, so I took off running. I heard Mitch call after me but I kept going. I threw open the car door, revved the motor, and took off as fast as I could, watching Mitch get smaller and smaller in my rear-view mirror.

When I got home, I slammed the back door. Hobbs came running over to see if I needed help. Gran peeked her head around the corner.

"Something the matter?"

"Men!"

I ran up the stairs, and before I slammed my door I heard Gran say, "Get used to it, sweetheart."

She and I sat in front of the television on New Year's Eve, watching the crystal ball drop in New York City. At midnight, we toasted ourselves with warm milk.

"1970. Who can believe it? You'll turn twenty this year," Gran said. "It's a new decade. Full of promise and opportunity. What will it bring, do you think?"

"A life of spinsterhood, like I predicted when I was thirteen. It's my mission in life to live alone."

"Oh, Bridie. Sometimes I think you're as foolish as Mavis."

"Gee, thanks, Gran. You're a peach."

๑๒

BEFORE JANUARY WAS OVER, I HAD MY OLD JOB BACK AT THE bank. The girl who'd replaced me was having a baby and her husband didn't want her working anymore.

I'd get up very early and go to Nell's to look after the critters then return after work to bed them down for the night, so instantly my days became very full.

We also got news that the cabin was officially mine. Nell's lawyer contacted Pops's lawyer, who happened to have a copy of a letter signed by Pops, stating that I was the granddaughter of Gervais and Maggie Landry and that my mother, Jane, was buried in Hardwood Hill Cemetery. Once I signed the paperwork, I was a landowner—of a dreary cottage, but also of five acres of trees. That pleased me no end.

On Valentine's Day, I was in a black mood. I kept my head down at work, certain that everyone there remembered my awful day the year before. It might have been my imagination, but a few old dolls stared at me longer than necessary. It happened from time to time in the village as I went about my day. People would recognize me and whisper behind my back. I always ignored it, but it never failed to make me feel sick.

As I shuffled the paperwork of my latest customer, I felt the presence of another person. It was so irritating when people showed up at my wicket before I waved them forward.

When I looked up, there was Mitch. Of all the fantastic luck.

"What are you doing here?"

"I need money."

"Oh, of course. It's Valentine's Day and your girlfriend needs flowers."

"She's not my girlfriend."

"Oh, sorry, do you always neck with women who walk into your barn?"

Mitch looked around, annoyed. "What is your problem? Who I kiss is no business of yours."

"You are so right. Your bank book, please."

He passed it over and shuffled in front of me, hands in pockets.

"How much money do you want to withdraw?"

"How much do you think a dozen roses would be?"

I made a face. "I wouldn't know. I'm a spinster, remember?"

"Give me fifty."

"Fifty? That's a tad overboard. But let me guess, you'll want to buy a box of chocolates as well."

"And while I'm at it, an engagement ring."

"Who knew you were so cheap?"

He put his face closer to me when he noticed a lady leaning over at the next wicket to hear what we were saying. "Did I ever give you the impression that I wanted you to be my girlfriend?"

"I never noticed."

"Don't you remember I told you I'm never getting married?"

"You're not the only one. I've been saying since I was thirteen that I wanted to be single and run...a boarding house...."

I forgot he was in front of me.

A boarding house. I could fix up the cabin and make it into a fishing retreat, like the one Pops and I went to. That would generate income. If I used my nest egg to renovate the place, I could advertise and rent it out weekly to avid fishermen. And offer to make sandwiches and sweets for their lunches. That would be a huge selling point.

"Bridie!"

Back to earth. "What?"

"Are you planning on giving me my money?"

"Oh, sure." I counted out his bills and passed them to him.

"Do you want to go on a date or what?"

"No, thank you. I'm going to be busy."

He stalked off. It was only after he left that I realized what he'd said. Well, anyway, I was going to be a businesswoman. No time for romance.

Before I hurried to Nell's after work, I stopped in to see Danny to tell him about my fantastic idea.

"Surely, it's a grand thought. I've often had fisherfolk come in and ask if there were places to rent. We could make a big sign and post it in the store window."

"I'll advertise in the newspaper, too."

"But do you have the money for such a project? I'm skint meself, or I'd gladly give you some."

"Thanks, Danny, but I think I'm going to be okay."

After I finished in the barn, I ran into Nell's kitchen, but she was at her sewing machine in the other room. It was the first time I noticed her wearing small glasses, for close-up work. She quickly took them off when she saw me.

"You look excited."

I told her my grand scheme.

"That sounds like a very good idea. You could start fixing the place up in the spring."

"I could do the inside now, cleaning and painting every day."

"You're working, remember?"

"Well, I'll do what I can. What should I call it?"

"Not the Haunted Cabin."

"Pops's Paradise."

When I got home, I burst into the kitchen. Sitting on the table were a dozen red roses, a box of chocolates, and a box of Cracker Jack.

Gran came in from the living room, grinning. "Mitch came by and asked me to give you these. He said to tell you that he had enough money left over to buy his mother a dozen roses."

Men. Just when you want to strangle them, they do this kind of thing.

CHAPTER TWENTY-FOUR

Our first date was a disaster. I'd brought Mitch over to the cabin to show him my grand idea. He wasn't impressed.

"It looks like a dump."

"Of course it's a dump right now, but once I clean and paint it will look so much better."

"I can see you're going to have to replace those beams."

"Beams?"

"The big pieces of timber holding up your roof."

"Are they bad?"

"They're warped from having no heat on all these years." He looked under the sink. "Just as I thought. All your pipes have frozen and they burst. That's a big job to replace. You've probably got mold where the water seeped into the floorboards and plaster. That's going to cost you. I think you'd be better off tearing this place down and building something new, but that's going to—"

"Let me guess, cost me?!"

"There's no use shouting at me. I'm pointing out the obvious."

"Stop raining on my parade. I can't tear this place down."

"Why not?"

"It's where my mother grew up and as nasty as it is, it's the only connection I have to her."

He gave a big sigh. "All right. But be prepared for a lot of things you won't see right off the bat. You're going to need a contractor."

"I was hoping you could do the work."

Mitch turned around and stared at me. "This is our first date, and already you expect me to build a house for you?"

"I'll help."

"I'm so relieved. We'll get it done in no time."

"Really?"

"Of course not! This is going to take a long time. Years, even, if we're doing it by ourselves."

"Oh. I was hoping to have it up and running this summer."

"You are delusional."

My feminine wiles suddenly popped out of nowhere. I walked over to him and put my arms around his neck. "The great news is, you said you'd help me do it. I'm so grateful."

He put his hands on my waist. "How grateful?"

I kissed him, which I couldn't believe I was doing. I was expecting it to feel like kissing Jack, but this was a total otherworldly experience.

He finally let me come up for air, and I blinked a bunch of times and stared at his lips. "What are you thinking about, Miss Bridie?"

"How I want you to do that again."

He did. And again. The date ended on a high note.

Gran knew it the moment I walked in. "Did you have a nice time?"

I slid into the armchair by the television and held up my chin with my hand. "It was amazing."

"You deserve to be happy, Bridie."

The minute she said that, I thought of Jack. "I told Jack I'd love him forever."

"And you will. But that doesn't mean you can't love someone else too. Jack wanted you to be happy, remember?"

I slid to the floor and joined Hobbs on the rug. "He's such a good kisser, Hobbs. Almost better than you."

Hobbs kissed my face all over, as if to refute this fact.

☜☞

Summer came and went and we were woefully behind on our self-imposed schedule. Mitch was right. We kept running into things we hadn't thought of and just as we got one problem fixed, another would pop up almost immediately.

After two months of this, Nell found me one evening crying into Napoleon's haunches as I rubbed him down.

"What's wrong?"

"I thought it was going to be so easy to convert the cabin into something nice, but at this rate I'll be old and grey before my first customer comes through the door."

"Dearest, did you *honestly* think the two of you could get this done yourselves? Mitch has a large farm to take care of, and you're working full-time and taking care of the animals. You're putting unrealistic expectations on yourselves, which can't be good for your relationship."

"What relationship? We're too busy to canoodle."

"You need some hot chocolate. Come inside."

Following her like a big baby, I plunked myself on a kitchen chair and rested my head on my arms. "I'm so tired all the time. And Maud told me that Mitch fell asleep at the supper table the other night."

She mixed up her secret hot chocolate recipe, which I believe was just milk, sugar, and cocoa, but it always tasted better than anything I made. She said it was my father's favourite drink. I didn't know that. He never drank it at home.

When I was nearly finished the mug, she had that look that I was beginning to understand was her don't-argue-with-me face.

"I want you to hear me out. From the time Jane was a tiny girl, I put money away for her education. When I heard she'd died, I continued to put money away, because I couldn't bear not to. I know you're using your father's nest-egg money for these renovations, but I'd really rather you didn't. You never know when you might need it. I would dearly love to use the money I saved for Jane to fix up her home. It would give me so much pleasure to see it become a cozy spot for everyone to enjoy. I feel in my heart that Jane's mother, Maggie, would love to see the cabin the way she wanted it. A bright, colourful place that she never got to enjoy. And for me to be able to, in some small way, bring that about would make me feel so much better about everything. When I say you'd be doing me a favour, I mean it."

"Oh, I don't know...it's my dream. As Mitch said to me once, 'Why do these people owe you a living?'"

"He said that?"

I nodded.

"Well, he can keep his nose out of my affairs. I'm not suggesting you two don't work at it at all, but if I hire a contractor to do the big work, that will free you both up to do the cosmetic work. You'll probably have it done by next spring."

"I suppose I should talk to him."

She looked exasperated. "Spinsters do not talk to men about their decisions. That is your house, not his. Remember that. You are capable of making up your own mind about what should be done. Don't ever get in the habit of deferring to a man. And that applies even if you're not a spinster."

"You've convinced me. Thank you, Nell. I will quite happily take all the money you have."

"You're not getting all of it, missy."

CONTRARY TO MY WORRIES, MITCH WAS OVER THE MOON ABOUT the contractor. He actually went up to Nell's place and kissed her on the forehead. "You have saved my life, not to mention my back. Could you not have suggested this a couple of months ago?"

"I wanted to see if you two were serious about it. It's easy to say you're going to do something; it's another thing to do it."

He was also cheered up by the fact that there was now more time for canoodling. We would ride our horses to out-of-the-way spots on weekends and spend the afternoon lying in fields or on a rocky beach, looking at clouds rolling by; or we'd sit by a river and fish, but forget that we were fishing as we lay in each other's arms, talking about nothing.

Mitch was too over-protective of me. "You're just twenty. I'm twenty-six. I'm robbing the cradle, according to Will. He likes to point out he's only three years younger than you."

"I've weathered a lot in these last twenty years. I'm not an innocent. And despite your condescending talk about being a baby, I am a grown woman. And if I love something, I love it. And I might just love you."

It was the first time I'd even thought it, and here I was saying it out loud—when everyone knows the guy has to say it first.

He looked a little shaken up.

"Too soon?"

"You have the ability to astonish me almost every single day, ya know that?"

"Is that a good thing?"

"It could be." He lowered his head and I was lost in the smell of his cheek against mine. He certainly knew how to love me that day, but he didn't say the words out loud.

I took note of this.

༄

IT TOOK THE CONTRACTOR ALL FALL TO DO THE BIG WORK. THE beams did end up having to be replaced, and quite a few of the floor joists. The chimney needed replacing and the plumbing turned out to be a major headache. We decided to take some space from the bigger room and add more room to the bathroom. It made sense to make it more comfortable for renters. Mitch and I did the bathroom renovations ourselves, and built the kitchen cabinets and put in the new windows.

After cleaning and scrubbing the entire place, we decided to do the inside painting during the winter. The outside wouldn't be done until the spring.

The cost of new appliances was something else I had to consider. We needed new furniture, a dining room table, new beds, mattresses, and pillows. Nell said she wanted to make the quilts, sheets, and curtains.

Once I had it in my mind what I wanted to do with the cabin, I drew a plan for a garden around it and made a list of seeds to order. Gran saw what I was doing and grunted.

"You don't do that here. That cabin is going to be better than this place."

"This place is marvellous, Gran. We could rent out two bedrooms now if we wanted to. You could do the cooking."

"You're becoming a real-estate mogul."

I even talked the ear off the loans officer at the bank, asking him how I could get a loan if I wanted to buy more property. He laughed at me. Told me to come back with a husband and then we could talk.

It seemed incredible that yet another Christmas was here. Though 1970 had flown by, I did need a few days to relax, and Gran and I were looking forward to seeing Patty and her family. Kimberly was a year and a half old, and Pup, three and a half. It didn't seem possible.

In the weeks before Christmas, Gran developed a cough. It didn't seem like anything to worry about. She'd wave me off when I suggested she go to the doctor. I could see she was tired, but she said that it was old age. "I am eighty-one, after all."

On December 23, the day we were supposed to go to Patty's, I put my foot down. "I don't think we should go. You need to stay home and rest. We'll have a quiet Christmas."

She surprised me by agreeing. I called Patty and told her.

"Oh dear, we'll miss you, but you're right to keep her home if she's feeling poorly. I'm just not sure what I'm going to do with this mother of all lasagnas I made for dinner."

"Freeze half of it. We'll eat it next time we're down."

On Christmas Eve, Gran finally admitted she wasn't feeling so hot. I was in an instant panic; her doctor's office was closed. She told me she didn't think she could go to church, which made me even more anxious. I called Mitch, and his mother insisted on talking to me.

"Has she got a fever?"

"A slight one, I think, and she must be cold. Her lips are a bit blueish."

"I'll send Mitch. You two take her to the hospital."

"What do you think it is?"

"I'm no expert, but it could be pneumonia. Anything at her age could be serious."

When I told Gran that Mitch and I were taking her to the hospital, she was annoyed. "It's Christmas Eve. I have a rotten cold. Stop worrying."

I looked out the window while I waited for Mitch. It was snowing heavily, just our luck.

When Mitch arrived, we bundled the protesting Gran into the truck and left for Port Hawkesbury. The snow was coming straight at us. Mitch had to use the low beams only, because the falling snow was too mesmerizing with the high beams on.

I had my arm around Gran the whole time, wrapped up in a quilt. Now that she had resigned herself to going, she'd stopped pretending everything was fine and was slumped against me. None of us talked, although Mitch and I exchanged glances over her head. All I could think about was how grateful I was that he was here.

When we arrived, the triage nurse sent Gran right through and she was seen by a doctor in no time. He ordered x-rays and, sure enough, she had pneumonia. They admitted her and I stayed by her side.

I sent Mitch home, even though he didn't want to go.

"There's no sense in you sitting with me on Christmas Eve. You go home and I'll call you if I need anything. I might get you to bring in some clothes for me if I have to stay here for a few days. I also need you to look after Napoleon if I'm away for any length of time. That will be a huge help."

He nodded and looked at Gran. "I hope you feel better soon, Gran."

"Thank you, dear. You're the best."

We walked out into the hall and I hugged him goodbye. "Thank you."

He held my face in his big hands. "I love you, Bridie."

I took note of this.

❧

GRAN WAS VERY SICK. I NEVER LEFT HER SIDE. MITCH CAME BACK several times to bring me things. Nell showed up with a crocheted throw in Gran's favourite colours of yellow and blue. Even Patty, Ray, and Mavis came to visit a few times. Uncle Donny roared in like the superior being he thought he was and started barking orders at the nurses.

Nell had called the bank to tell them my grandmother was ill, and I'm not sure how she wrangled it, but they said they could give me a little time off while this crisis was going on. That meant the world to me.

Gran was slipping away. No one had to tell me. I would hold her hand, and she'd try and give it a squeeze back. I was drifting off one afternoon when I heard her say, "I don't want you to be sad."

It instantly made me beyond sad.

"I've had a good life, so much more than I thought I would after George's death, and that's thanks to you."

I kissed her bony knuckles. Her wedding rings were so loose they were falling off her finger.

"I'm tired. I want to be with my husband and son."

"Say hi to them for me."

She nodded and closed her eyes.

In the end, Uncle Donny, Aunt Betty, and I were the only ones in the room, standing on either side of Gran. The minute Uncle Donny realized she'd gone, he put his head on her chest and cried his heart out. He was even louder than Aunt Betty. For the first time I saw him as a little boy who loved his mother, and I felt sorry for him. You can be the biggest jerk alive but still become a little lost soul when your mom dies.

Losing Gran was not like losing the other loved ones in my life. They'd been ripped out of my arms, whereas I'd had a chance to say goodbye to Gran. She and I had spent these last ten days together, and we'd acknowledged what we meant to each other. It was a proper farewell, an easing out of this life and onward, a far more natural process than the other deaths I'd experienced. And so I knew I would survive this loss.

The church was filled to capacity. All her loved ones were there. Seeing Uncle Donny's family was a nice treat because they were growing into adults and were no longer just a gang of bratty cousins. Aunt Loretta had forgiven me by now, and it was good to see her too. I introduced Mitch, Maud, and Will to everyone.

Poor Uncle Fraser limped badly as he walked down the aisle with Aunt Betty and their three gigantic sons. I wondered where they came from, since Uncle Fraser was a normal size.

Patty got me alone at one point and said, "How is it you have the most gorgeous men?" Then she sighed and looked at her balding husband. "But Ray beats them all. He's the best daddy in the world."

Ray knew we were talking about him and smirked.

"You can say that again," I smiled.

We were able to bury Gran, as the ground wasn't as frozen as we thought it might be. As we laid her to rest beside Joe and the plaque with my father's name on it, I was comforted that she was between them. It felt right.

Nell stayed away, of course, but she did say she'd run down to my house and get the tea and sandwiches ready for afterwards. It turned out I'd told her the wrong time, and her car was still at the house when we showed up. I saw her peek out the window with a look of horror and quickly disappear.

"Oh crap," I said to Mitch.

We trooped in and Nell was nowhere to be seen. I was relieved, thinking she must have slipped out the front door, but Hobbs kept sniffing around the downstairs closet and I knew she hadn't quite made it.

"Are you in there?" I whispered.

"Just open the front door and I'll run," she whispered back.

So I did. I opened the front door and then the closet door, and she darted out, one boot on, the other in her hand. I quickly closed the door behind her and went back to my guests, relieved. Then Uncle Donny's son Bill said, "There's some lady out front trying to steal a car."

Naturally, everyone looked out the window. There was Nell, standing by her car, but she had obviously forgotten her keys in her haste. I quickly took the keys off the peg by the kitchen door. "Oh, that's just my neighbour who came to help me. She forgot these."

I ran out the door and over to the car. "I'm so sorry. I thought we'd be longer than this."

"Just give them to me. I think she's coming."

As Nell struggled to put the key in the car door, I turned around to see Mavis charging towards us through patches of snow.

"That's her, isn't it?! You're that Nell creature who ruined my marriage!"

She hit Nell's back with her open hands. "How dare you come near us! This is for family only and you're not a member of this one, as much as you've tried to be!"

Trying to stop Mavis from thrashing Nell was tougher than I imagined. Thank goodness Mitch came out to help me. He held Mavis with her arms down by her sides.

Nell had opened the car door by then, but she turned around and said sincerely, "Please forgive me, Mavis. I take total responsibility for hurting you. It was never my intention to ruin your life."

"But you did, you stupid bitch! Women like you are despicable! I hope you rot in hell!"

Nell looked like she was going to cry. She got in the car and drove off as fast as she could.

"Let go of me, Mike—Marvin—Malcolm—whatever your name is!"

Mitch let her go and she pointed at me. "You had no right to ask her here today."

"I know. You're right, Mavis. It was stupid. I wasn't thinking. Please forgive me."

She adjusted her pantsuit. "I need a drink."

As she marched back into the house, Mitch looked at me. "That's the woman you grew up with?"

I nodded.

"No wonder you're crazy."

Poor old Mavis didn't calm down because we had no alcohol. "Who doesn't have at least of drop of medicinal sherry in their house?"

"Drink this warm milk, Mavis," I offered. "Gran always said it cures what ails you."

"I'd have to drink it straight out of a cow for it to work on me. I can't believe you were so thoughtless."

Mitch cleared his throat. "Bridie has just lost her grandmother. I think we can forgive her a lapse in judgement. It's been a long couple of weeks."

"Quite right." Patty threw daggers at her mom.

"I see. So once again, Bridie's feelings are to be considered first. Why am I not surprised?"

Patty picked up her coat. "Forgive us, Bridie, but I think we need to go home. It's been a rough day for everyone. Come on, Mom."

"Fine, fine. I know when I'm not wanted." She picked up her coat and put it on.

I kissed Patty and Ray goodbye. I tried to kiss Mavis, but she held out her hand. "Not yet. I'll need several martinis before I can kiss you again."

It was the best I could hope for.

In the end, the teenagers went outside and had a snowball fight while Uncle Donny, Aunt Loretta, Aunt Betty, Uncle Fraser, and I sat around the table with our teacups and squares and told Mitch stories about Gran.

Aunt Betty looked at Uncle Donny. "Do you remember how cross she was at George for telling Eileen to jump off that cliff? She didn't speak to him for a week."

"It was the only time I heard her tell him off. I was the one who always got it in the neck."

Aunt Betty snorted. "With good reason. You were a jerk."

"He may be a jerk, but he's a harmless jerk." Aunt Loretta's smile was bright with the ignorance of a wife who will not see.

They finally left and Uncle Donny gave me a normal hug. "Thanks for taking care of Mom. I never worried when she was with you."

"Thanks, Uncle Donny."

Mitch helped me clean up, and then we sat in the living room in front of Gran's beloved television.

"Do you want me to stay?"

"No, thanks. I need to be alone."

"I wonder how Nell is doing."

"Don't go inside the house if you see to the horses. She'll need time to lick her wounds after that encounter."

"I often wonder why people make the choices they do in life."

My head leaned on his shoulder. "Their lives are more complicated than they appear on the surface. And often we lie to ourselves or make up our own truth. That's when we get in trouble."

He squeezed me. "Are you sure you're only twenty?"

"I feel like I'm a hundred and five at the moment."

Mitch told me he loved me again, which I noted, and then kissed me good night. It was only after he was gone that I realized how quiet it was. Hobbs looked forlorn on the rug, so I patted the sofa and he snuggled next to me. This was a big treat.

"Gran's not here to tell you to get down. I wish she were."

I turned on her television and Hobbs and I watched her favourite shows.

CHAPTER TWENTY-FIVE

When I got back to work I was told I'd used up all my sick days and vacation days, which I understood. No more days off for me. But I didn't want any; being off work only reminded me how lonely it was when I wandered through the house.

On the first Saturday I had off, which wasn't until the first of February, I went to the cabin to paint. When I walked in, I found Nell up on a ladder, whitewashing the trim.

"What's going on?"

"My eyes needed a rest, so I came here. Didn't figure you'd mind."

Nell must have worked on the painting through the week, because each night I arrived after work to find more of it done. Mitch was happy about that; he was swamped with machinery repairs.

With Nell so often at the cabin, I finally asked her about her own work. "Have dresses suddenly become unpopular or something? You're never on your machine."

"I'm taking a break. I'm actually thinking of retiring."

"You're only sixty-one."

"Thank you for reminding me."

❦

THE CABIN WAS FINALLY READY FOR RENTERS ON THE FIRST DAY of August, 1971. Only a year late, but it looked great. We had the shingles painted red and the door a bright green. Nell said red and green were the opposite on the colour wheel and it made sense. Mitch wasn't convinced.

The inside was spare but cozy. It wasn't for people who were going to lounge there all day. They'd be out fishing, so we stuck to necessities like big armchairs and a nice dining space. We did have comfortable beds, pillows, nice towels, and big claw-foot tub. The kitchen was outfitted with the essentials, so people could cook their own food—I'd realized I couldn't do everything myself.

Danny called me after the sign went up in the window and in the newspapers. "They're comin' out of the woodwork! I've had five people asking about it already. You're going to be a millionaire, child!"

"Simmer down. That's not very likely."

"Get this. They're also asking if there are places around here to rent for the whole summer. Some bigwig came in the other day from Chicago, if you don't mind. He was looking for a place for his family to stay. Little old St. Peter's! What's the world coming to?!"

Naturally, my mind went a hundred miles an hour. I ended up at Nell's, the place I always went for advice or support.

"What do you think about me renting Gran's place for the summer? Danny says there are people asking when they come in the store."

"Well, they couldn't find a sweeter spot. I've always loved that house. But I think you're missing the bigger picture."

"What's that?"

"Where are you and Hobbs going to live if you rent it out?"

I forgot about that. "Umm...here?"

"Here? With me?"

"Unless you're planning on leaving the country."

Nell looked down at her lap and I saw her hiding a small grin.

"That would be nice," she said.

When I told Mitch, he looked annoyed. "You're going to live with Nell? When are you and I going to get time alone?"

"That's the first thing out of your mouth? Not, 'Gee, Bridie, what a great idea, having two properties bringing in money'?"

"How do you know people will even want it?"

They wanted it, all right. Both the cabin and Gran's were booked straightaway. It wasn't as easy as I imagined it would be at the cabin, since some people are slobs and I kept having to scrub the place down to get it ready for the next lot. Most fishermen came for a week, so there was a quick turnover. Gran's was booked for a couple of weeks at a time, even a month, but there again if something went wrong I was called up day or night to come and fix whatever it was.

One night it was a dripping tap. I tried to fix it but ended up calling Mitch at ten at night.

"Oh, yes. This was a great idea, wasn't it?"

"Just fix it, and I'll make sure there's something in it for you."

He chuckled. "I'll come over and drive you home the long way around."

Much to my delight, the cabin also attracted hunters in the fall. Not that I liked hunters very much, but if they were willing to pay, I was willing to take their money. It's a sad fact that I ignored what they were doing by day. I'm obviously not a very nice person. And then, holy cow, ice fishermen wanted it. We even had people asking if they could Ski-Doo in the winter. I didn't know anything about Ski-Doos, but I assured them that if they wanted winter fun, St. Peter's was a great place to come.

Danny had the great idea to advertise Gran's place as a writer's retreat. "They'll come in droves all year. The next W. B. Yeats, James Joyce, or Oscar Wilde could be writing their epic at your dining room table!"

And didn't three of them show up a month at a time through the winter. I was absolutely gobsmacked by the success of these ventures. And I had to say, it was so much easier to just run out the door at Nell's and feed the critters. I did it in my pajamas sometimes.

Nell and I never got in each other's way, because I was gone all day at the bank and she went to bed early. I was making a habit of living with wonderful women.

☙

IT WAS NOW THE SPRING OF 1972, AND I WOULD BE TWENTY-TWO this year, living the life of Riley as the owner of two so-called boarding houses, and as another spinster on the hill. My childhood dreams had come true. My savings account was healthy, so I was my own woman financially, and I was paying for half of Nell's expenses even though she said that wasn't necessary.

"That's what independent women do. They pay their own way."

"You're right—where's my rent? It was due a week ago."

It was a glorious day in May when I left work, looking forward to taking Napoleon out for a ride. There was no better way to celebrate spring than to walk through a meadow on horseback. It was hard to believe that once I'd been afraid of this horse. He was my best friend in the whole world—after Mitch, and Nell and Hobbs, and Danny and Maud, and Patty and Ray, and Pup and Kimberly. Okay, and Mavis sometimes.

I went out into the parking lot and looked up.

There was Jack.

My heart turned over and I actually wiped my eyes to make sure I wasn't hallucinating. Then I stood there, numb. What was I supposed to do? Pretend I hadn't seen him?

"Hello, Bridie."

I didn't say anything. I couldn't.

"You have long hair. It's beautiful."

"What are you doing here?"

"My maternal grandfather died. I came for his funeral, to pay my respects."

"I'm sorry to hear that."

He'd filled out and was even more good-looking than I remembered. What bothered me was that my heart starting beating rapidly just looking at him. What would those hands feel like on me now?

"I should've gone home after the funeral, but I couldn't be here and not see you. My mother thinks I've gone. I'm leaving right after this. Will you come with me for a drive? I'll bring you back here."

"No."

He looked at his feet. I turned around to see if anyone could see us out here in the parking lot.

He raised his eyes. "Please?"

NO! I heard myself shout in my own head. "Okay," I said out loud.

What the hell was I doing in this truck? The truck that had nearly run me over in its escape. Every nerve in my body knew I wasn't supposed to be here; I even crouched down so no one would see me as we drove out of town.

I'm not sure how we ended up at Point Michaud beach, but suddenly we were staring at the water through the truck windshield as the waves rolled up onto the sand.

He kept looking at me, and I wanted him to stop. "What do you want, Jack?"

"I needed to be sure you were all right."

"You could've written a letter."

"Don't be mad at me. I try not to be angry, but now that I'm back here, I realize how much I miss this place. How much I lost the night I left. You have obviously continued to make a life for yourself here, and it makes me wonder if I could do it too."

I sighed; I didn't know how else to respond.

"Would it bother you if I came home?"

"Yes."

"Why?"

I glared at him. "Are you serious? And have everyone stare at us like we're circus freaks? 'There go the incestuous brother and sister.' The old biddies would have a field day."

"I don't care what they think."

"People never forget in small towns. No matter what happens in our lives from now on, we'll always be *that* couple. Quite frankly, it's been easier without you here."

He looked away.

"We were in love, Jack. I loved you more than anything, and now you're sitting here and it's taking everything I have not to jump into your arms. The feelings we had for each other, have they completely disappeared? Are you telling me that you don't want to kiss me right now?"

"I do, very much. But I can't." He kept his face turned away from me. "I'm married."

My head collapsed against the seat as I gasped for air. I found the door handle and fell out of the truck, running up the beach to get away from him.

"Bridie! Come back!"

"Stay away from me!"

He caught me around the waist, twirling me around as I kicked out at him.

"Stop! Stop it, Bridie!"

Then I twisted around until we were facing each other, and I slapped him so hard that his head snapped back. "You came all the way back here to tell me you were married? Why?"

We were both out of breath, and he released me, putting his hand up to his cheek. "My mother told me you were with someone. That you were happy with him. I wanted to make sure that was true, so that I'd stop feeling guilty about loving someone else. I wanted to know that you'd gone on without me. And I wanted to find out if maybe I could come back here.

I miss my family. You know my father was voted out of office, and he's left town. But my brothers miss me, and I miss them."

I sank to my knees in the sand and then sat, having no energy to stand anymore. He did the same. We didn't say anything as we fought to catch our breath. The wind whipped my hair around, and I had to push it out of the way.

"I feel like a fool," I eventually said. "I keep forgetting that this happened to you too. Is it awful of me to still have feelings for you? Am I a bad person?"

"Neither of us is bad. Love isn't bad. I think we'll always love each other. But that can't stop us from moving forward."

"Did your mother tell you who the man is?"

"No."

"Do you want to know?"

"Okay."

"Mitch Curry."

Jack smiled. "Oh, he's a great guy. I always admired the way he looked after his mother and brother. He was never in town, drinking or carrying on. He was mature for his years."

"He had to grow up fast. Like me. And your wife?"

"Her name is Sandy. She's very sweet and has four sisters. My mother came out to visit us and she loved her."

"I'm glad. Your mother always wanted a girl."

"Now she's got five of them."

"But won't Sandy be sad to leave her home, if you move here?"

"We live in PEI."

"PEI! You only went as far as PEI?!"

"My mother wasn't made of money. That's as far as I got."

We started to laugh and laugh and laugh. I had never laughed like that in my life. We ended up rolling around in the sand, breathless with the absurdity of it.

Tears streamed down my face. "Here I was, picturing you as cowboy, herding cattle and eating beans by a campfire."

"I work at a car dealership."

That set us off again.

It felt so good to sit and laugh together. Turns out, that's what I'd missed the most: his friendship. Maybe there was room for him in my life after all.

The sun was starting to set when he stood up and reached down to take my hand. We held onto each other for a long time. There was no need for words. We'd manage to figure this out.

He drove me back to my car. "One thing I wanted to know. How's Napoleon?"

"He's perfect. He was my greatest gift. Thank you."

When we got to the parking lot, I leaned over and kissed his cheek before I got out of his truck.

"See ya, kiddo."

"See ya, Bridie."

꙾

I HADN'T EVEN REALIZED WHAT A BURDEN I HAD BEEN CARRYING until the weight lifted on that beach. A part of me wished I could go home to an empty house and leap in the air, dance around naked for the hell of it, and make myself a banana split at midnight if I wanted to.

Maybe I'd made a mistake not getting a place of my own. Gran's house was currently occupied by a bunch of birders from New England who were chasing some poor feathered thing that had been seen around the area. They told me it was most likely because of a bad storm. I thought maybe the poor bird needed some peace and quiet and came to Cape Breton to get away from this manic bunch.

Instead I went to sleep at Nell's, and the next day, because it was a Saturday morning and Nell had already gone to town, I drove right to Patty's house in Sydney.

She was in the middle of making lunch for two screaming kids and a husband who was hammering at something
downstairs.

"Welcome to the madhouse," she said. "Turn that grilled
cheese over for me, will you?"

While I turned the bread, the phone rang. Patty reached
over her ironing board and answered it. "Hello, Mother. What
is it this time?"

Patty rolled her eyes at me while taking Kimberly's hand
out of her glass of milk.

"Look, Aunt Loretta is allowed to have a party without inviting you."

I made a face while I watched the frying pan and tried to
ignore Pup shimmying up my leg.

"It doesn't matter if all the hospital people are going. Look,
if it bothers you that much, confront her with it. It's not like you
to keep your mouth shut. All right. Call me back."

Patty hung up the receiver. "It's like having three kids to
deal with. Pup, get off your Auntie Dee."

We sat around the table, Kimberly deciding she wanted to
be in my lap, which annoyed her brother. Patty told them if they
didn't knock it off they could go to their rooms. Ray arrived on
the scene, covered in sawdust.

"Hi, Bridie." He looked at Patty. "When's lunch?"

"Oops," I said. "Sorry, Ray, I ate your sandwich. I'll make
you another one."

Patty waved her hand at me. "He can make his own lunch."

"Do you see the way she treats me?" Ray said.

The phone rang again.

"Oh, God, it's Mavis. I'll be downstairs." And he disappeared.

Once again, Patty rolled her eyes. She didn't even say hello.
"What happened? Uh-huh. Uh-huh. Uh-huh. She said that?
And what did you say? Uh-huh. Well, we can cross her off the

Christmas list this year. I'm not going to call her! This has nothing to do with me! Mother! All right. I'll call her later. I have to
go."

Patty hung up the receiver once more. "Someday I'm going
to get on the Newfoundland ferry and never come back."

"Poor you."

"This happens constantly. I'll call Aunt Loretta and remind
her that Mom invited her to all of her cocktail parties, even if she
never went, and now that Dad is gone it would be a nice gesture
to include her with the hospital crowd. I know Mom can be a
handful, but surely it's no skin off Loretta's nose if Mom sits in
a corner and feels like one of the gang again. The woman spends
most of her life twiddling her thumbs. Now, why are you here?
Not that I'm not happy to see you."

I told her all about my meeting with Jack. She sat holding up her chin with her hand. "It's straight out of a Harlequin
romance."

"The thing is, I think that maybe I can love him without
guilt. Everything isn't blown out of proportion. It's like anyone's
first love. You always remember, but you don't feel bad about it
anymore. It feels good to know that he's not crying into his beer,
blaming me for ruining his life. We want each other to be happy."

"Are you going to tell Mitch?"

"I'm happy, not stupid."

❧

WHEN I GOT HOME THAT EVENING, I DID SPILL THE BEANS TO
Nell. She listened intently but didn't say much, just that she
was glad I felt better about the whole thing. Then she went to
bed. To be frank, I was a little disappointed. She was supposed
to love everything about me, but she seemed almost annoyed.
It was weird.

The next day was Sunday, so I rode out to Mitch's place
and found him sick in bed. Well, I didn't find him. I heard his

voice yelling from the bedroom, "I'm a grown man! You can't keep me in bed!"

"I can so!" Maud shouted back from the kitchen.

"What's wrong with him?" If someone else was about to die on me, I was going to hold my breath until I turned blue.

"He's got a rotten cold and he's miserable. I told him to stay put and you'd think I threw him in jail. He's free to get up and go if he wants, but if he pretends I'm the one who wants him in bed, he'll stay there. He can't seem to do it on his own."

"Men are babies."

"So true. Stay for lunch and keep me company."

"Okay. Where's Will? Are you sure he lives here? I never see him."

"He's a teenager. He's allergic to his mother and his home at the moment. They grow out of it."

"He doesn't know how lucky he is. I lost Mama when I was thirteen. I would give away everything I have to spend another afternoon with her."

"That's the way I still feel about losing my mom. It's the one thing that never goes away. A longing for your mother. When I think of the stories I heard about young men crying for their mothers while they died in battle, it breaks my heart."

We looked at each other bleakly. Then she said, "How did we get on this topic? Want to help me hang out some clothes?"

Hanging out clothes in the spring sunshine is almost as good as riding horseback through a meadow.

While Maud warmed up some corn chowder for our lunch, I popped in to see the invalid. He was lying sprawled on his back with only his pajama bottoms on, his arm thrown over his eyes to keep out the sun.

"Hello," I said.

He didn't move. "That better not be you."

"It's me."

"Go away. I refuse to let you see me like this."

"From where I'm standing, you're looking pretty good."

He couldn't completely hide his grin, but he didn't move. "I'm a sick boy and you'll get all germy and sweaty if you come near me."

"Mmm. Sounds fun."

Now he lifted his head. "Shh! My mother's in the kitchen."

"You're right. I better go before I have my way with you."

He threw his head back on the pillow and put his arm back over his face. "You better not be here to tell me that something needs doing at the cabin or at Gran's. It'll have to wait."

"No. The birders are out stalking Foghorn Leghorn, so they're too busy to complain about anything."

"It hurts to laugh. Go away."

"I love you."

"Okay."

"Say it back."

"It back."

"You're a dope."

"So you keep telling me. Strangely, you insist on hanging around."

"Lunch is ready," Maud yelled from the kitchen. "Would you like some corn chowder, Mitch?"

"Just kill me now!" he shouted.

I left him alone.

CHAPTER TWENTY-SIX

One morning in June, I awoke at six to thunder and lightning and sheets of rain falling against the window. Hobbs was under my blankets, shaking.

"It's okay, buddy. God is just bowling, or whatever people tell their kids." He wasn't convinced, and he stayed under the covers while I went out to the bathroom. The door to Nell's room was still closed. That was unusual. She was always up before me.

It was chilly enough for me to go back to my room for my bathrobe and slippers. Then down the stairs to put on the kettle for tea. I let Dog and Dog out because despite the rain, they looked like they needed to pee. Cat and Cat were lying together in front of the stove. That was unusual. They purred in unison, and I petted them until the kettle eventually boiled, and the Dogs scratched at the door to come in. I had to towel them off. They were soaked.

My toast popped, and I spread peanut butter and jam on it before I took my tea to the table, looking forward to finishing up my crossword puzzle from the night before.

That's when I saw a letter addressed to me in Nell's handwriting:

Gone fishing.

I grabbed it and was in hysterics before I read it more closely: *I haven't gone fishing.*

"Jesus Christ!" I screamed. "Are you kidding me?!" I ran to the window and saw that Nell's car was gone. She wasn't upstairs sleeping, which was just as well because I would have gone up there and killed her.

"What a rotten thing to do, Nell! You scared the life out of me."

And I scared the life out of the animals. Even Hobbs was in the doorway, fretting.

"Sorry. Sorry. False alarm." I chugged my tea down with my toast, because there was no way I was opening this letter on an empty stomach.

Then I delayed some more, putting my hands together in prayer. "Please, God. I cannot take one more thing. Do you hear me? I'm praying to you, Maggie, little mother, Mama, Pops, Nana, and Gran. If any of you care about me at all, put a good word in with the big guy and tell him I'm sick to the back teeth with drama. I want my life to be boring from here on in. Have you all got that?"

I opened the letter.

Dearest Bridie,

You know I love you, so I'm not going to go on about it. There's not a lot to say that hasn't already been said between you and I, and so I feel the time is right to escape my beautiful prison.

You will find that my lawyer has papers bequeathing you my estate—but don't worry, you're not getting all of it, Missy. I've left you the house, the land, the barn, and of course my critters. And money for their upkeep. Feel free to call Dog, Dog, Cat, Cat, Horse, Pony, and the Sheeps whatever you want.

I am leaving this dreary town at last, and it's all because of you. You have shown me that life goes on despite great heart-ache, and that you can love another. I never realized that. I was so busy being the spinster on the hill that I forgot I had free will.

Your loving spirit has been a joy to me, and I believe you were meant to come back into my life to teach me this great lesson.

I am off to see the wizard. I will forward a post office box when I settle in whatever part of the world strikes my fancy.

In the meantime, I know it will take you about three days to turn my house into a fabulous bed and breakfast or whatever else you have brewing in that beautiful head of yours. I know it will be in loving hands.

I owe you everything,
Nell

The phone rang at nine thirty.

"Hello?"

"Bridie, are you planning on coming to work today?"

"I'll be there in ten minutes."

৯৩

YOU CAN BE HAPPY FOR SOMEONE AND STILL BE ANNOYED. NELL had left without letting me say goodbye, left me alone with this giant house to look after. Even though I really loved the house, I didn't like being there by myself.

"Sell it," said Mitch.

"And live where? With you?"

"No."

I hit him on the arm. "What do you mean, no?!"

"Well, if you want to, but it's pretty cramped at our place. I was thinking you might like to buy something small, close to me."

"You want me close, but you don't want me on top of you, is that it?"

"You're putting words in my mouth."

"It's so refreshing to know exactly where I stand with you."

"I told you from the very beginning that I was never getting married."

"I'm not either! And certainly not to you."

"That's fine by me!" He left, but I noticed he only went to the barn.

"It's fine by me too!" I shouted after him. He shut the barn door, and I knew he was in there muttering to Napoleon about what a harpy I was.

There was no way I would sell this place. It would be perfect for a bed and breakfast, but I couldn't run it all by myself. I'd have to hire someone to help me. Someone friendly and engaging, used to dealing with the public.

Hobbs and I went for a walk.

"Hobbs!" Danny shouted as we walked into the store. "My darling boy. Your mother's been very naughty. She never comes to see me anymore."

"How would you like to live with me?"

Danny looked at me funny. "As much as I love you, Bridie, you're not exactly my cup of tea, if you know what I mean."

I laughed. "Thanks, I got that. I'm hiring you to look after my house, not sleep in my bed."

He gave me a sly look. "What are you up to?"

"Nell has skipped town and left me her house. I'm turning it into a bed and breakfast. I need you to manage it for me. I'll pay you whatever they're paying you here."

"Er, they don't pay me. I'm the lad who was kicked out of Ireland for being a ponce. Uncle Tim and Aunt Janet kindly offered me room and board, but not much else. They do love a bargain."

"If that's the case, there's no reason for you to stay. The only thing you need to do is learn how to cook."

"Shite! I knew there'd be a snag."

"Don't be foolish. Any idiot can learn how to cook."

"Not this idjit."

"I will teach you myself."

"Oh, feck!"

Danny gave his aunt and uncle one week to find a replacement, which I thought was generous, seeing as how they were basically using him as slave. He was so delighted when he saw the inside of Nell's house, he wept.

"I've come home at last!"

We decided to sleep in the small room off the living room so we could turn the three bedrooms upstairs into guest suites, but I often found myself on the living room couch. Danny snored like a trooper. Naturally, Hobbs slept with him.

Mitch shook his head over the whole thing. "You're sleeping on a couch in your own house. Sleep in your bed until a guest actually arrives. Are you sure you've thought this through? Bed and breakfasts require food. Your other two properties, people feed themselves. One wrong move and you could kill someone with botulism."

"Is there anything else you can think of to dampen my mood?"

It took all summer to get the place up to snuff. When we were done, you'd never have known there used to be a dressmaking studio in the house. Now it looked like a real living room, albeit with a quirky edge. Danny loved to drape old fabrics of Nell's on curtain rods and banisters. I was getting as neurotic as Mitch. "You can't leave that there, Danny. Someone will fall down the stairs and kill themselves."

"Like that would happen in a million years."

"It happened my grandmother not fifty feet from here."

"Oh, damn. You do have the worst backstory of anyone I've ever met."

Trying to teach Danny how to cook breakfast dishes every night after work just about killed me.

He was so remorseful. "I told you, I'm as useless as tits on a bull."

It took a week before he got the hang of cracking an egg without pieces of shell in it. He burnt every pat of butter he put in a frying pan. The dogs—Buddy, Josie, and Hobbs—stayed right by his side, because he was feeding them undercooked and overcooked bacon.

A fried egg seemed beyond him, so I had him whip up pancake batter. That was worse than the eggs.

"You told me to look for small bubbles before I turn the pancakes over, but when I do, they're still oozing on the other side and they splatter everywhere, or they're completely burnt. How is it possible?"

We tried toast. It didn't go well.

Danny wept. "I can't do anything. I'm ruining your dream."

"Nonsense. Just let me think."

"Can I make you a cup of tea while you think?"

"God, no."

It hit me later that day. Maud came into the bank. "Hi, sweetheart."

Maud.

"Maud, I have a proposition for you."

She looked puzzled. "Okay."

"But first I need your bank book so it looks like we're actually banking." She passed it to me and leaned in closer.

"When I open my bed and breakfast, would you be able to come to the house every morning we have guests and cook them breakfast? You wouldn't have to clean up or anything. Danny will take care of the housekeeping duties and the dishes. You can be in and out in a couple of hours, depending how many guests we have. I will pay you well."

She looked surprised. "Me?"

"Yes, you! You're a fantastic cook, and I'm assuming your boys are old enough now to get their own breakfasts, if you haven't completely spoiled them already. It would give you some pin money."

"I suppose I should talk to the boys."

I opened her bank book. "A widow does not need to ask her children for advice. She can make her own decisions. And if you don't mind me saying, it looks like you could use a few extra dollars."

She instantly blushed, and I was mortified. "Forgive me! That was a terrible thing to say, and certainly none of my business."

"Don't worry. I know you didn't mean it to sound harsh. There's truth to what you're saying. I could use the extra money. I'll do it. Gladly. It will be a nice change."

I ran around the counter and kissed her. Mrs. Beliveau gave me a shocked look.

So did Mitch when he found out.

"You've got my mother running around like a chicken with her head cut off, experimenting with soufflés and omelets. She had six different types of muffins on the counter this morning.

"What a terrible thing to endure, your mother's delightful cooking."

We were riding out to our favourite fishing spot, without the fishing gear. I'd packed a picnic.

"Your mother is really excited about this. She could use some flavour in her life, and spending a couple of hours with Danny in the morning would cheer anyone up."

He still looked like a small boy who'd had his favourite lollipop taken away. "I don't want her getting tired out."

"Is your mother eighty?"

"No."

"Seventy?"

"No."

"Sixty?"

"No! Okay, I get your point."

"How old is she, anyway?"

"Fifty-one."

"Then the woman needs a new adventure. Be happy for her, instead of thinking of yourself. She's not just your mother."

He didn't say anything about it after that. He was too busy making me feel like a woman.

❧

When I told Danny, he kissed my feet. Literally.

"I've died and gone to heaven! This is the most beautiful house, and I've been cleaning it every day just for fun."

"I noticed that manure pile out back has a swirl on it."

Danny might not have been able to boil an egg, but he loved housework, and the place was immaculate. All the painting I'd done for Nell paid off in spades. The inside of the house was very impressive, and all of Nell's bedspreads, crocheted throws, and pillows made the rooms look inviting.

Pops's nest egg was being put to good use, and that was before I decided a selling point for this place would be a petting zoo.

I told Mitch over the phone.

"I'm painting the barn red and the fences white, and I'm getting some chickens and a few goats to go with the sheep and the horses. I think a cow would be a nice touch."

"Are you crazy, woman?! You hardly have time to breathe as it is."

"Once this gets off the ground, I might be able to stop working at the bank."

"Oh, good. Less money is just what you need."

Mitch was a worrywart.

But even Patty and Ray wondered if I was biting off more than I could chew. I was spending Thanksgiving with them. Pup and Kimberly gave me their handprints shaped like turkeys and I planned on framing them.

"Is this bed and breakfast going to be lucrative in the winter?" Ray asked. "I imagine you have to have steady customers throughout the whole year to make it successful. So that would mean having the yard and driveway plowed out every day in the winter. It's a big responsibility."

"I'm not afraid to see what happens. If it's a disaster, I still have the cabin and Gran's, which have been very lucrative so far."

Patty held a sleepy Kim. "Please don't burn the candle at both ends for too long. Something's going to give."

Before I went home I stopped in to see Mavis and told her about my plans.

"Your father would be very proud of you."

I burst into tears, which was mortifying. Mavis jumped up and dithered. "Stop that. You're making a scene. Do you need some money?"

What was she talking about?

"No, I don't need any money," I sniffed. "That was such a nice thing to say."

"I'm not a complete cold fish."

My new adventure started the first of November. With a little advertising, I'd have the place humming in no time. The guests would roll right in.

They didn't.

November was apparently not a great month to start. Neither was December, nor January 1973.

I was shaken. So were Danny and Maud. Here we thought we had this brilliant idea and nothing was coming of it.

It wasn't my fault, but it felt like it was. Danny was nursing a cold one morning and looked at me forlornly. "I'm Freddie the Freeloader. I should go back to the shop. I'm living off you like a parasite."

"You're family, Danny. That's what families do. I'll hear no more talk about you going back to the shop."

Then one day we got a booking for all three rooms, for two nights starting on Valentine's Day, under the name Smith.

"If this is a joke," I fretted, "I'll kill someone."

They turned out to be Jack's wife's family, down to celebrate an engagement party for Jack's younger brother. Diane was a sucker for punishment in my opinion.

Jack stayed with his mom, but Sandy, her mother, and her sisters stayed with us. All of them were delightful, and they absolutely loved Maud's cooking and Danny being Danny.

When they left, I happened to be home. Sandy sought me out.

"I do know what happened between you and Jack."

My eyes lowered to the floor. "I wondered."

"Jack always talks about you with such affection. I can see why."

"And you are a lovely girl, Sandy. Thank you. I'm glad Jack is so happy. He deserves it. I'll always remember that you and your wonderful family were our first guests."

"I'll tell everyone about this place. It's amazing."

Slowly but surely, the reservations kept coming. We weren't bustling, but we were busy enough to know that we were offering something unique. Our guestbook was filling up with nice compliments, and the best part of it for me was seeing Maud and Danny getting along like a house on fire. I was almost jealous of their relationship. They were speaking in code after a while. I was missing all the good stuff when I went to work at the bank. Maud looked and acted like a different person—still as sweet as ever, but with more confidence. Even Mitch noticed a difference.

"You see? I was right."

"Yes, dear," he said.

❧

IN APRIL, A POSTCARD ARRIVED IN THE MAIL WITH A PICTURE OF the northern lights. When I turned it over, there was a post office address on it. It was from Norway. Nell had drawn a small heart in the corner, but that was it.

"Details, woman!"

I spent the rest of the day taking pictures of the house, Danny, Maud, the animals, and the new sign at the end of the road: *The Spinster on the Hill Bed & Breakfast.* Once the pictures were developed, I wrote a newsy letter, ordering Nell to write back with more than just a heart, and sent it off to her.

The very next day I got sick. Really sick. Patty's warning about burning the candle at both ends had come to fruition. I was suddenly more tired than I'd ever been and spent most of the day in bed with a bucket.

Danny was the world's best nurse. Almost too good. He hovered like a bat and it got on my nerves after a while. "I don't like an audience while I'm puking."

"I'll be behind the door."

After three straight days of this, Maud came to see me, even though we had no clients. She sat on the end of the bed and seemed nervous.

"You look dreadful, honey."

"You shouldn't be here. I have the stomach flu, and I don't want you to get it. It's a nightmare. I can't keep anything down."

She opened her mouth and then closed it.

"What?" I said.

"Have you considered it might not be the stomach flu?"

"What else would it be?"

"Could you be pregnant?"

I felt the blood drain from my face. Bad enough that I hadn't even considered it, but it was Mitch's mother asking. That meant she knew that Mitch and I...canoodled.

"I'm sorry, Bridie. It's none of my business, but if you think it could be the case, you need to see a doctor."

"Oh my God. What have I done? I'm so stupid."

"You're not stupid, dear. Millions of other girls have had the same thing happen to them and the world is still turning."

"But I always said I was never getting married. I'm the spinster on the hill."

"As much as I would love it if you and Mitch did get married, there's nothing to say you have to. People will gossip, but you've certainly lived through that before."

I reached out and took her hand. "Thank you for always being so nice to me. I've fallen into this nest of wonderful women and can't imagine why I've been so lucky."

She brushed my hair out of my face. "You're very easy to love, Bridie."

"Don't tell Mitch."

"Of course not. It's your news to tell. But can I just hug you?"

She squeezed the life out of me and squealed in my ear. Someone was excited.

But not as excited as Danny. "I'm going to be an uncle! How marvellous!"

"You can't say anything, Danny. I don't even know if it's true. I need to see the doctor."

"Oh, you're pregnant, girlie. I've watched me mam go through this a hundred times."

"I'm surprised she's still alive."

"So is she."

It turned out I was pregnant, and I had something horrible called hyperemesis gravidarum, which was a very scary term for really miserable morning sickness, except it lasted all day and night. I called Mitch to come and get me from the doctor's office. He assumed I still had the stomach flu.

He took one look at me standing outside the office and I saw his face register shock. I was a mess, babbling away as he ran around the truck and held my arms to look me straight in the face. "What is it? My God, you look so thin. Are you dying?"

"I wish! I'm so sick."

"Why aren't you in the hospital? Where's that asshole doctor?"

"I don't need to go right now, but I might. It depends on how bad this gets."

"What is it?

"A baby!"

"You're not making sense."

"I'm having a baby. Your baby. This is your fault."

He looked how I must have looked when Maud had told me. Like the thought had never occurred to him.

"What do you think happens when two people canoodle? They have a baby noodle!"

"Holy shit. Are you serious?"

"No. I always call you to come pick me up even though my car is right over there. What am I going to do? He said this could last for sixteen weeks or more."

"Let's get you home. I'll make you some tea."

"No! I hate tea. I hate water at this point."

He held my hand on the drive home and stayed with me while I crawled back into bed. He pleaded with me to sip some water, and I did. But it didn't stay down long.

Danny was hovering by the door. "She keeps doing that. It's not good."

Mitch wiped the damp hair off my forehead. "You know, you're going to have to change the sign to *Spinster and Baby Bed & Breakfast*."

"Oh, I know. Because you're never getting married."

"This puts a different slant on things. I might like a sign that says *Curry & Son* at the end of the driveway."

"How do you know it will be a boy?"

"*Curry & Daughter* would be fine too."

We kissed and stared into each other's eyes, seeing only the future.

I had to go to the hospital two days later. They wanted to be sure I was getting enough fluid, so I was hooked up to an IV pole. I dragged it with me to make a phone call.

"Mrs. Beliveau. I'm dreadfully sorry, but I quit."

"Is something wrong?"

"I'm having a baby out of wedlock."

"Oh, my."

"You can say that again."

I took another dime and called Patty. "I'm having a baby."

"You are not."

"I'm having such a baby that I'm in the hospital over it."

"What?! I'll be right there!"

And she hung up on me. The stupid woman was coming.

Boy, was I glad to see her two and a half hours later. She got through the door and I wailed, holding my arms out for a hug.

She patted my back. "You poor darling. Is this morning sickness?"

"This is sickness sickness. You can't even pronounce the name of it, that's how horrible it is."

"Are you sure you're pregnant? You look like a bean pole."

"I've lost seven pounds. This bean is going to be the runt of the litter."

"What does Mitch think about this?"

For the first time that day I smiled. "He said noodles are his favourite thing."

"Okay, that's a private joke, and I won't ask what it means."

Patty sat with me for the whole day while I upchucked and then fell asleep from exhaustion. She was still with me when it got dark. Danny was by the bed too. They were chatting quietly.

"You need to go home," I whispered.

"I'm going to stay at a fabulous bed and breakfast, and then run over to see you in the morning before returning to the zoo."

"Okay." I fell back to sleep smiling.

I stayed in the hospital for nine days but Danny, Maud, Mitch, and even Will came to keep me company. Danny filled me in on my business empire.

"There's a bunch of old hags renting Gran's for a week," Danny said. "They say they're a book club celebrating twenty years together. But I think they're making plans to kill their husbands."

"That can be our next advertising strategy. Come to our Murder Mystery Weekend."

"After that, there's a troupe of Buddhist monks expected. They're on holiday for ten days."

"You're joking."

"Yes. I didn't want you to know that more birders are showing up."

"Oh, God. One of them will leave behind their very expensive binoculars again and expect us to ship it back to them. They really are more trouble than they're worth."

"We've got the cabin booked solid for fishing season. There's not a safe fish anywhere in Richmond County, poor little buggers."

"What about the B&B?"

"A steady stream of illicit lovemaking is going on. I think it's got something to do with the name Spinster on the Hill. People are perverted."

When I got home, it didn't feel like home. It felt like Danny's B&B in some weird way. I tried to help now that I wasn't working, but either Danny or Maud would shoo me away and I'd end up in the field complaining to Napoleon, Lucy, and Shortbread.

"All this has become a well-oiled machine without me. What am I supposed to do? Other than be someone's mother." Napoleon bunted my head and then my tummy very softly. "You know it's in there, don't you?"

My sickness was still there, but it was easing up enough for me to sit out on the porch swing and while away the afternoon.

When was the last time I'd sat and watched the birds? They were lovely. Maybe those birders were on to something.

The thought of my own baby was thrilling but worrying at the same time. My mother had died having me. It wasn't something I could get out of my head easily, even though it was the car accident that had killed her. I knew that me being born, me just existing, had meant traumatic experiences for so many people. I was wanted but not wanted.

This baby needed to feel completely secure, even though it was doing everything in its power to be a giant misery guts at the moment.

Maud shouted from the kitchen. "Buttermilk pancakes are ready, if you feel up to eating."

For the first time in weeks, I did.

Later that day I was in the barn giving Napoleon a brushing, or more like a patting, since my energy hadn't fully returned. But I loved being with him and felt much better being by his side.

"Did you miss me while I was in the hospital?" He snorted and flung his head up and down. "Why, thank you, kind sir. I missed you too."

The barn door opened and Mitch came in, Hobbs at his heel.

"Yay! My three favourite men are here."

Mitch came over and kissed the top of my head. "How are you feeling?"

"Better."

"Want to feel great?"

"Sure."

He took Napoleon's brush from me and tossed it to the ground. He also took of his ball cap and tossed that away too.

"What's going on?"

He reached into his shirt pocket and got down on one

knee, taking my left hand in his. "Miss Bridie Jane Mackenzie. This never-getting-married business is starting to bug me. You and I are bringing a noodle into the world and I have a feeling our noodle wants to belong to just you and me and Napoleon and Hobbs. So please do me the honour of becoming my wife. I can't imagine anyone else I'd rather argue with for the next seventy years."

Then he placed a pearl ring on my finger.

"How did you know I love pearls?"

"You're always wearing that necklace, so I figured you must. And by the way, would you please stop asking questions until you've answered mine?"

I jumped on him and we ended up rolling around in the hay with Hobbs. "Yes, yes, yes, I'll be your wife!"

Napoleon whinnied his approval.

CHAPTER TWENTY-SEVEN

Mitch and I were married on a bright September morning. I was six months pregnant, but if I'd been trying to hide this pregnancy I would've done a great job. You couldn't tell.

Maud patted my belly. "It looks like you're going to have a bunny."

We only had Maud, Will, Danny, Ray and Patty, Mavis, and Aunt Betty at the church. Uncle Fraser begged off. His hip was acting up.

A crown of daisies encircled my long hair, and I had a bouquet of daisies and baby's breath in my hands, which I secretly thought was quite funny. My dress was short, fresh, and youthful as per Nell's instructions, and covered with little white flowers, which I think gave the minister indigestion as he'd heard the rumours about the baby. He didn't come straight out and ask us, which Mitch was hoping he'd do.

"So you can say what to him?"

"It's 1973. Get over it already."

Ray walked me down the aisle, but he was so nervous he was damp. I kissed his cheek anyway.

Mitch gave me a gold band with little diamonds all the way around. They looked like stars.

When the minister said, "You may kiss your bride," Mitch made sure he kissed me like he meant it. Something else for the minister to chew over.

We went back to the B&B, and Maud had everything prepared ahead of time. We had a lovely brunch of ham and cheese quiche, waffles with cream and fresh fruit, croissants, bacon, muffins, coffee, tea, and orange juice with champagne. It felt so good to want to eat again, but I was still leery of taking too much at once.

And then Maud unveiled the wedding cake she'd made for us. It was white, a traditional three-layered cake, and as we cut into, we were expecting fruitcake. She surprised us with chocolate, Mitch's favourite. He gave her a big hug. I loved how much he loved his mother. It made me feel safe.

We kicked back our shoes and everyone wandered into the living room. Everyone except Will, who went out to visit the horses.

Mavis had a glass of champagne with no orange juice. She waved off Maud, who had the juice bottle in her hand. "No need to ruin it with that. So, where are you two going to live?"

"We don't know yet."

"You don't know yet? Isn't that a little strange?"

"I technically have three properties I can live in, but I'm too greedy making money off them at the moment."

"But this house is big enough for you, isn't it? All your bedrooms don't need to be made into guest suites. Or you can kick this guy out of here and take his room." She held up her glass towards Danny.

"Mother!"

Danny pointed at himself. "Me? This place would go to seed inside a week if I weren't here with my magic broom and duster."

Mitch was trying not to laugh at Mavis's gall. Mavis noticed it.

"What's your solution then, sonny boy? I know one thing. If George was here, he'd want to know where his baby was going to live when she has her own baby. A woman needs to be in her nest before her child comes into the world, so this is no small matter. It's up to the man of the house to make these arrangements. Bridie has enough to worry about carrying this child of yours and feeling mighty ill while doing it."

That sucked the gaiety out of the room quickly. But I realized she was right. And from the look on Danny, Patty, Aunt Betty, and Maud's faces, they knew she was right too.

"Where *are* we going to live?" I asked.

Mitch realized the crowd was now against him. "I don't know. Can't we discuss this another time?"

"No."

"Okay. You're my wife, so you'll live with me."

"In your childhood bedroom, or are you planning a major renovation of your house? Excuse me, Maud's house."

"I don't have the money to do that right now and like you said, it's Mom's house. I can't just start tearing down walls."

Maud put her hand up. "Yes, you can. I don't mind."

Danny hopped into the air. "I've got it! Maud can come live here with me, and Mitch and Bridie can live at Maud's."

Now Patty put her hand up. "Aren't you forgetting about Will?"

"That's right," I said, even though was I always forgetting about Will because he was never around.

"He can flit between the two houses," Maud said. "He usually sleeps in the barn anyway."

Mitch nodded. "That's true."

"Your brother sleeps in a barn?" Mavis downed her champagne. "What's wrong with you people?"

"Are you sure this is all right with you, Maud?" I asked. "It's your home we're talking about."

Maud smiled. "Our barn is nicer than my house. Living here would not be a hardship. I love every minute of it. I'd be quite happy to stay here until you've added on to the house, or whatever your plans will eventually be. But Mavis is right. We need to get Bridie settled and prepare a nursery. I'd much rather she did it away from the public."

Patty laughed. "Can you imagine the gossips when they find out Maud and Danny are living together?"

Danny clapped. "Oh, my sainted mother will be chuffed at the news!"

Mavis put down her glass and rooted in her purse, taking out a small piece of paper. She stood and walked straight to me. "This seems very appropriate, now that we've had this discussion. I'd like you to have this."

I reached out and opened it. It was a cheque for twenty-five thousand dollars. My hand covered my mouth. "Mavis!"

"This is the money I owe you. Your sister gave you half years ago, and she thinks I don't know, but I figured it out. It was the right thing to do. In my heart, I know your Pops would want to be part of this happy occasion, and this money can go a long way to helping you build your nest for our grandchild."

I was so overcome I couldn't speak. I stood up and hugged her, this other mother of mine. Then Patty ran over and we embraced. Pops would be so happy.

❧

WE DECIDED NOT TO DO ANYTHING WITH THE HOUSE UNTIL THE next spring. We needed time to go over plans, not just for the near future, but for when Maud eventually returned. She liked the idea of a separate space for herself so we could be close but not on top of each other. The idea of having a grandmother at my beck and call was reassuring. And this grandmother in particular.

When I mentioned this to Danny, he got very upset. "When Maud leaves, I'll be the only spinster on the hill!"

"Maybe we could advertise for a cook who's...more your cup of tea."

He instantly cheered up. "Why, that's a grand idea. Why didn't I think of that? Although how would I advertise for something so specific? Neat-freak pansy looking for a baking poof?"

"We'll definitely avoid the want ads in the *Cape Breton Post*. Perhaps a little farther afield would be best."

We cleaned out Maud's room, with her blessing, and scrubbed and painted it white. I was mindful of Nell's advice. You can bring colour in if you have the right background. This was also not a nursery per se. It was our room, with a bassinette in it. I took my favourite quilt from Nell's for our bed after washing it and leaving it out on the line for three days. But I bought everything new for the baby.

Patty, Mavis, and I went shopping together in Sydney, and they were very helpful.

"Only buy a few items that are three to six months. They grow right out of those." Patty handed me some six-to-nine-month pajamas, which looked gigantic.

Mavis thought so too. "She's having a hummingbird, not an ostrich. Just because your babies were huge doesn't mean they're all like that."

Patty grit her teeth. "You have an uncanny ability to be rude no matter what the topic."

I'd missed this.

After we finished our purchases, we went for a quick lunch at a local coffee shop. We'd just sat down when Mavis hit my arm.

"Isn't that Loretta over there with another man? Don't look!"

"Mother, we have to."

"Don't be obvious."

My head swivelled slightly and, sure enough, there was Loretta looking bright eyed and bushy tailed. Patty bent down to pick up an imaginary napkin and her face confirmed it.

"It *is* her!" she whispered. "I wonder who that is."

"He's a fine-looking specimen," Mavis said.

"Eww. Don't be gross, Mother."

"What? I can't admire a man's good looks? You think we're made of stone after sixty? Wait until you girls get to be my age. You're in for a big surprise."

"Do you think she's cheating on Uncle Donny?" I said.

Patty took a sip of water from the glass the waitress put in front of her. "I hope so. He's been feeling up every broad from here to Yarmouth for years."

Mavis fiddled with her collar. "Don't be vulgar."

In that instant, Loretta looked over and gave us all a big wave. She and the man got up from their table and hurried over.

"What a marvellous coincidence," she said. "This is my cousin Harvey Healy, from the Valley. Harvey, this is my family. My sister-in-law, Mavis Mackenzie, who I told you about, and her girls, Patty and Bridie."

Harvey shook our hands. "So nice to meet you all."

"I was planning a dinner party for tomorrow night, Mavis, and I told Harvey here that I knew someone who would love to go on a date."

"I would?"

"Yes! That way the table will be even."

"Please, Mavis. I don't want to be third wheel," said Harvey.

Mavis got flushed and began babbling a little. Patty put her hand over her mother's and said, "Mom would love to go, wouldn't you, Mom?"

"Yes, yes. Thank you."

"Loretta told me where you live, so how about I pick you up at seven?"

"Fine, fine."

Loretta clapped her hands. "It's all settled. Until tomorrow! Bye, girls."

We said goodbye, and then Patty and I turned to Mavis.

"Did that just happen?" she said.

Patty shoved her mother's shoulder. "You've got a date! With a fine-looking specimen!"

"What's his name? Harvey Valley? Healy Harvey?

Patty and I laughed and laughed. She was so giddy.

☙

IN NOVEMBER, THE GREAT ANIMAL SWAP TOOK PLACE. OUR LIVES were so busy that it became impossible to keep running up to Nell's to look after the critters. I'd taken Hobbs, Buddy, and Josie with me when I moved in with Mitch. Cat and Cat stayed with Maud and Danny. I never got around to naming them, and Danny thought they should keep their Christian names.

My petting zoo wasn't working out so great. One of the goats chased Danny around the yard, and a couple of sheep escaped one morning, which made him a very angry Little Bo Peep. Maud's wrist was a bit sore, so she didn't want the responsibility of milking the cow. Daisy was coming home with us.

Will was a huge help with the animals. They knew him well, and all three horses went into the trailer quite willingly when it was their turn. He even collected the chickens with no problems. The boy needed to be a vet.

Having all the animals in one place was a giant worry off my mind. When I looked at our very pretty empty red barn before I left, my mind started whirling. Danny knew that look and came out with a piece of fudge.

"Here. What are ya thinkin'?"

I took a bite. "We're going to turn this into an antique store. It will be a great way to introduce people to the B&B."

"We don't have any extra antiques, unless you count Mavis."

"We'll gather some up. On the days you're not busy, you and Maud will scour the countryside."

"Aren't you supposed to know about antiques before you sell them?"

"Did I know anything about fishing cabins or rentals or bed and breakfasts? No. I learned on the go. This will be the same thing. Antiques are just old things. We have enough stuff floating around this county to keep us going for years. We won't be Sotheby's. People who come from away are looking for butter churns to put on their front porch at home. They're not interested in pedigree. A lobster trap and some fishing rope will do."

He nodded slowly. "Did you ever notice that whenever you have an idea, it always involves other people?"

I hugged him. "I won't be fat and pregnant for long."

"Pregnant, no. Fat, never."

My due date was December 11. In the week leading up to it, Mitch found me outside, cleaning up the woodpile. He marched me into the house and lay beside me on the bed, with my head snuggled into his shoulder.

"I forbid you to leave this room. Everything is done. Everything is spic and span. The baby's clothes are ready to go. The diapers are bought. Mom has filled the freezer with suppers. Will even washed the dogs for you. Your three enterprises are filled with a variety of oddballs, and the money is rolling in. All you and I have to do is basically nothing until baby arrives, so I order you to go to sleep. Do you hear me?"

I was asleep.

Thankfully, God let me have this one boring moment. Everything went like clockwork. On December 11, I woke up to contractions. I sat around all morning because they weren't amounting to much, until Mitch called his mother and she and Danny roared over in a panic. Then they watched me most of the afternoon until they couldn't stand it and called Patty and Mavis, who showed up around five.

I asked if we should call Aunt Betty, and they all shouted, "No!"

"But she's Mama's sister."

She showed up at five thirty.

At seven, they staged a mutiny and insisted Mitch take me to the hospital. Will waved goodbye from the barn. Our five mother hens had their set of car headlights about six inches behind us the whole way.

"They're going to cause an accident," Mitch grumbled.

"Ignore them."

"Ignore Danny, Patty, Aunt Betty, and Mavis? That's like ignoring a bowl of porridge overflowing on the stove."

"At least we have your mom."

"Thank God for small mercies."

We were a three-ring circus running into the hospital, and then thankfully, Mitch and I were escorted away from the madding crowd and it was just us for the rest of it. Mitch was so calm that I was calm. He'd kiss my forehead and tell me what a wonderful woman I was, and I'd focus on the life that was insisting on arriving to meet us.

She arrived with no fuss at all. All the funny business she put me through, and in the end it was like a soft breath escaping. She looked at us both with big eyes. She didn't cry, but her father and I cried enough for three.

Mitch kissed me over and over. "I love you, Bridie. And I love our baby girl."

I took note of this.

CHAPTER TWENTY-EIGHT

NELL

My bed-sit is so cozy. When I look out the windows the snow-capped mountains are there to greet me, with the small town nestled in and around the lake. Everything in Norway reminds me of a Santa's village, the kind toy railroad tracks wind around, with lights in every window pane, street lamps, and the stars twinkling in the night sky. The northern lights are what drew me to this place, and even now there are green and bluish streaks in the sky, as if someone is doing a paint-by-number. The sky on Spinster's Hill was mostly velvety black. Very beautiful, but black.

I want colour.

In the morning, I get dressed, make my bed, and put the kettle on. It feels odd not to have animals to feed, but it's also so freeing to not have to think of such things. I put down my toast and wait for it to pop up so I can smear it with peanut butter and jam. I'm looking forward to doing my crossword puzzle now that Bridie isn't here to fill it in on me. I'm sipping my tea when I hear the mail drop though the door.

It's no doubt an advertisement of some kind. Bridie's too busy to send many letters. The last one she sent I keep on the small refrigerator, with the pictures of the new Spinster on the Hill Bed & Breakfast and their staff. What a clever girl she is. Everyone knows where the spinster on the hill is in that part of town, and to use my reputation for advertising is pure genius.

Reaching down, my heart leaps. Bridie's handwriting. Just in time for New Year's Eve. She has scotch tape on the envelope seam, which annoys me, but I realize it feels like there are pictures inside, so I forgive her. Now to find a sharp knife. I slide the envelope open, and out comes pictures of a family. Whose family? I look closer and catch my breath.

Tears keep getting in the way, so I have to compose myself to look at the pictures properly. It's definitely Bridie and Mitch looking down at a small bundle. Bridie has a baby. She never even told me she was pregnant. Because she didn't want to worry me, probably. That's the kind of girl she is.

A closer picture shows the baby with blond hair and the most perfect little nose and mouth. It has to be a girl. She's too pretty to be a boy, even at this age. I quickly unfold the letter.

Dearest Nell,

Meet our new daughter, Jane Eleanor. She's the sweetest little thing and she's so good. She never cries, just looks at the world with a curiosity that would make Pops proud. She's ever so dainty, the complete opposite of me, and Mavis is beyond in love with her, buying her poufy dresses, which should annoy the crap out of me but doesn't.

Mitch is so smitten. He carried her out to the barn the other day, even though I thought that was a bit much. He introduced her to all the animals, and he said she smiled. I think it's a bit too soon for her to be smiling, but if he says so, who am I to argue?

The businesses are doing well. You wouldn't believe the crazy people we get, but Danny puts them in their place if they get too weird. He says he can out-weird anyone, and I believe that's true.

I am so happy, Nell. I miss you, but I know you are finally free to live the life you want. We'll see each other again. We'll come to you, most likely. I'd love to visit Norway! We can take Jane skiing and drink hot chocolate.

I owe you everything.
Bridie

There's a soft knock on the door. I wipe my eyes and open it. It's Arne, the man who lives down the hall.

"Good morning, Nell."

"Good morning, Arne."

"I'm just checking to make sure you don't forget the party we're having in the lounge area tonight."

"I'm not likely to forget that, Arne."

"Because it's New Year's Eve. Of course."

"No. Because you'll be there."

His eyes crinkle. "Oh, Nell." He shakes his finger at me. "No wonder you're so popular with the men."

I smile. "I'll see you tonight. I have a few errands to run."

Quickly, I put on my coat, boots, hat, and mitts, and I grab my purse. I step outside and take a deep breath of clean, crisp, cold mountain air.

It's a brand new year tomorrow. A time for new beginnings.

But right now I'm off to the shops to buy red velvet for the coat of a doll that belongs to a little girl named Jane.

Complete your collection with the new **Lesley Crewe Classics** series, available at fine bookstores everywhere.

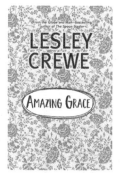

978-1-77471-085-2

978-1-77108-964-7

978-1-77471-032-6

978-1-77471-121-7

978-1-77471-030-2

978-1-77471-122-4

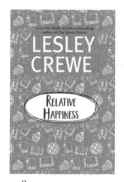

978-1-77471-123-1

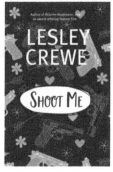

978-1-77108-963-0

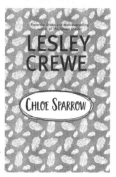

978-1-77471-190-3

Lesley Crewe is the author of twelve novels, including the *Globe & Mail* bestselling and 2022 Canada Reads longlisted *The Spoon Stealer*, *Beholden*, *Mary, Mary, Amazing Grace, Kin*, and *Relative Happiness*, which was adapted into a feature film. She has also published two collections of essays, the Leacock–longlisted *Are You Kidding Me?!* and *I Kid You Not!* Lesley lives in Homeville, Nova Scotia. Visit her at lesleycrewe.com.